CHIEF JUSTICE ABRAHAM LINCOLN AND THE END OF RECONSTRUCTION

Jack M. Beermann

ISBN: 979-8-9914278-0-7

CONTENTS

DEDICATION

This book is dedicated to my parents, my wife and my children who have inspired, supported and encouraged me in all of my endeavors.

CONTENTS

ACKNOWLEDGMENTS

I would like to thank Boston University School of Law and Dean Angela Onwuauchi-Willig for supporting this project, Andrew Grant, BU Law class of 2024 for help with the manuscript and the dozens of poor souls, friends, colleagues, students and relatives alike, who patiently listened to me describe my vision for this book.

Thanks also to my brother-in-law Ira Korman for the amazing drawing on the cover and Jennifer Rollo from Sentient Web Media for designing the front and back covers and formatting the manuscript for publication.

PROLOGUE

This manuscript was found among the papers of Robert Todd Lincoln Beckwith after his death in 1985 extinguished the Lincoln bloodline. It was inscribed with these words: "This is a history of what might have been. Real places and names have been used but many of the details, including widely-known events and personalities, have been fictionalized. My hope is that someday, many years from now, historians might discover this manuscript and become confused." The identity of the author is not revealed.

In 1838, eighteen-year-old Samuel Miller sued John Belmonti in state District Court in New Orleans, alleging that Belmonti was wrongfully keeping him in slavery. Miller claimed that he was born free, the son of an ethnic German father, Horst Miller, and a free woman of color, Antoinette Duclere, who died when Samuel was an infant. After Samuel's father died when he was eight years old, he was taken in by his paternal uncle Martin, who treated him as a servant in his home and furniture-making business and did not send him to school. By the time Samuel turned twelve years old, his uncle grew tired of Samuel's constant discontent at not being allowed to go to school and enjoy the same privileges as his cousins. Samuel had learned the furniture-making trade quickly, and it was clear that he was going to grow into a large, strong man. Seeing his potential value, Samuel's uncle sold him to Belmonti, captain of the riverboat Queen of the River. The price was $1100.

Belmonti put Samuel to work, maintaining and repairing the boat's furnishings and performing general maintenance during the boat's weekly trips between New Orleans and Vicksburg. Like many slaves in New Orleans, Samuel had time to himself in the evenings and on Sundays when the boat was not underway. One night, he left the boat and went to the home of a wealthy, sympathetic free man of color he had confided in on one of the boat's earlier trips. The man, Amand Langlois, had himself won his freedom in the New Orleans District Court years earlier. Langlois took Samuel to his lawyer, and after a week of hiding in Langlois's home, they filed Samuel's suit for freedom.

Samuel was relatively light-skinned and benefited from Louisiana's legal presumption that people "of color" were free, while darker-skinned persons designated "Negros" were presumed to be slaves. Thus, although Samuel's features indicated partial African descent, District Court Judge Louis Moreau-Lislet—a slave owner hailing from the West Indies—placed the burden on Belmonti's lawyers to present evidence establishing that Miller's mother had been a slave. Belmonti's lawyers assembled (one might say "fabricated") evidence to support the claim that Samuel was a slave. Martin Miller testified that although his brother Horst treated Samuel's mother Antoinette as if she were free, such that she enjoyed complete freedom of movement during their relationship, she was nonetheless his slave throughout. He claimed that Horst bought her for $120 in 1816 from a plantation in Iberville Parish. Martin also contended that Horst never officially manumitted Antoinette or gave her any documentation indicating that she was free. Samuel was unable to rebut this evidence, and at the end of the trial Judge Moreau-Lislet declared that Samuel was a slave. This decision was upheld on appeal to the Louisiana Supreme Court.

After the trial, Samuel remained in Belmonti's enslaved employ on the Queen, understanding that he would face harsh punishment if he was caught trying to escape. He began a relationship with another of Belmonti's slaves, Victoria Superneuf, a light-skinned seamstress born in Pointe Coupée Parish. She and Samuel married and were allowed to live together as man and wife in the slave quarters attached to Belmonti's home in the Marigny section of the city, just east of the French Quarter. They had three children together during the 1840s, and after their births, Victoria stayed full-time in the Belmonti household, working as a seamstress, raising the children of Belmonti's extended family together with her own although her children were put to work as soon as they were old enough.

In 1850, the Queen made several trips up to St. Louis, replacing the steamer Natchez while it underwent repairs. On these trips, Samuel heard talk of a St. Louis couple, Nancy and Peter Hudlin, who helped escaped slaves. On most trips, Belmonti was joined by the Natchez's owner Captain Thomas Leathers. Samuel's opportunity to escape came when the two captains, joined by friends from St. Louis and most of the crew of the Queen, drank to excess. While the boat was docked in St. Louis, three slaves including Samuel escaped. The three found the Hudlins in their home on 13th Street near Cass Avenue, not too far from Laclede's Landing where the Queen was moored. The Hudlins hid Samuel and the others in their cellar, and the next day made arrangements for the three escapees to travel that night to Ferguson Station where plans would be made for the trip across the river into Illinois.

Sometime after midnight, Peter Hudlin and his three charges set out for William Ferguson's barn in nearby Ferguson Station, where help awaited. The escape was big news in St. Louis, and they took care to avoid the slavecatchers who fanned out across the area hoping to earn a good bounty. To avoid detection, the group separated, with instructions from Peter to meet at the barn early the next morning. It was nearly dawn when they arrived at the farm—tired, wet, and hungry—and after a meal served by Ferguson's wife Margaret, they spent the day sleeping in the barn among the animals on piles of straw, which after the long night, felt as comfortable as any bed they had ever slept in.

As night fell, the group left on their trek to Illinois. They walked through fields till they came to the Missouri River just south of Old Jamestown, where a free Black man ferried them across the river on a flat barge. Continuing on, they arrived in the early morning hours at the western bank of the Mississippi River, just across from Alton, Illinois, where Peter told them they would find the boatsman who was to guide them into Illinois. He was nowhere to be seen, but Peter had told them to be patient and wait for his arrival. They spent the remainder of the night and the entire next day hiding in a woody marsh near the river. They had sufficient provisions to avoid hunger, but their anxiety grew as the long day wore on. Thankfully, sometime after dark their new "conductor" on the underground railroad arrived in a canoe, a free Black man named Wilbur Godfrey. Godfrey brought them across the river to his homestead in the countryside east of Alton, where they spent a couple of days resting from their travels and awaiting the next step in their journey to freedom.

3

Samuel's companions had free relatives in Boston and Philadelphia, so Godfrey arranged transportation east for them. Samuel had no one, and he hoped that at some point his wife and children would join him. Godfrey decided that Samuel could stay safe for at least a while by assuming a new identity and going to work as a field hand on the farm of a wealthy abolitionist farmer, Jacob Levy, near Peoria. Although Illinois as a whole was not particularly welcoming to free Black Americans, there were geographical pockets of stalwart abolitionism where free Black Americans were safe, and the Peoria area was one of them. Levy found his fortune raising pigs and growing corn and wheat. He used his profits to purchase prime real estate in what became the City of Peoria just five years prior in 1845, after only ten years as an unincorporated town. Levy donated to abolitionist causes and hired free Black Americans, including escaped slaves, to work his farm as well as in his other businesses in the area, such as a theater in downtown Peoria that later became the most successful vaudeville venue in the region.

After living and working on Levy's farm for several months, Levy sent Samuel, now known as Joseph Paris, to nearby Knoxville, Illinois, to purchase some supplies for the farm. When he arrived at the warehouse near the depot, Samuel was approached by Knox County Sheriff Henry Arms, a Democrat who was anxious to enforce the federal Fugitive Slave Law, the newly enacted and hotly contested 1850 statute that made it much easier for slaveowners to reclaim their escaped "property." Belmonti had contacted the Illinois authorities, informing them that his missing slave might be living in the area. Arms did not believe Samuel's claim that he was Joseph Paris, of Haitian descent. He arrested Samuel and brought him to the Knox County Jail in Knoxville, just around the corner from the courthouse in the town square, intending to hold him until he could figure out whether he had the missing Samuel Miller.

The sheriff was an anti-abolitionist Democrat, but people in the more urban areas of Knox County, especially Knoxville and nearby Galesburg, were generally anti-slavery. Although Illinois had some of the strongest anti-Black laws in the country, Frederick

Douglass's speeches in the area in later years would be greeted by sympathetic ears.

A deputy guarding the jail heard Samuel's denials that he was an escaped slave and offered to ask local lawyers whether they would come talk to him. The most respected lawyer who argued cases when the circuit judge was in town was Abraham Lincoln of Sangamon County, on the other side of the Illinois River. By this time, Lincoln had served a term in Congress, and although he clearly had political ambitions, he was still a working lawyer. Lincoln was beginning to outgrow his caseload of small to medium sized matters in favor of a major client, the Illinois Central Railroad, but he still had time to take on other cases, and the next day when the deputy saw Lincoln at the county courthouse on Main Street, he told him about Samuel ("Joseph Paris") and asked whether Lincoln would help the man. Lincoln went to the jail and spoke to Samuel. Lincoln was impressed by Samuel's optimism and his commitment to reuniting his family in freedom. Jacob Levy was there and offered to pay Lincoln's fee. After meeting with Samuel, Lincoln went to the courthouse around the corner and filed a petition for a writ of habeas corpus. He alleged that Sheriff Arms had no authority to hold Joseph Paris because Arms lacked probable cause to believe that Paris had committed a crime under Illinois law.

Some years later, Lincoln would stay in Knoxville's Hebard House Hotel on East Main Street, before his debate with Stephen A. Douglas at Knox College during the campaign to become Senator from Illinois. Douglas was popular in Knox County, having served at one time as judge on the circuit embracing the area, but so was Lincoln. The evening before the debate, a crowd gathered at the hotel hoping to hear Lincoln speak. He came out on the veranda, and when someone brought a lantern over so that the assembled could see him, Lincoln—known for his awkward appearance and his self-deprecating sense of humor—quipped: "My friends, the less you see of me, the better you will like me." At the debate, Douglas pinned the label "abolitionist" on Lincoln by quoting from earlier Lincoln speeches on the meaning of "equality" in the Declaration of Independence:

"I should like to know, if taking this old Declaration of Independence, which declares that all men are equal upon principle, and making exceptions to it, where will it stop? If one man says it does not mean a negro, why may not another man say it does not mean another man? If that declaration is not the truth, let us get this statute book in which we find it and tear it out. Let us discard all this quibbling about this man and the other man—this race and that race and the other race being inferior, and therefore they must be placed in an inferior position, discarding our standard that we have left us. Let us discard all these things, and unite as one people throughout this land, until we shall once more stand up declaring that all men are created equal."

Lincoln did not prevail in his quest for the Senate because Democrats retained control of the Illinois General Assembly (which at that time selected the state's Senators), though he later became the state's favorite son and the first Illinoisan elected President. Throughout his political career, Lincoln frequently returned to the Declaration as the source of Black American's rights, while simultaneously denying that the aspiration toward legal and political equality implied the kind of social equality that even many abolitionists and racial moderates of the time feared and opposed. Even so, he insisted that "if slavery is not wrong, nothing is wrong."

The circuit judge, Norman Higgins Purple of Peoria, was a friend of Jacob Levy's and was sympathetic to Samuel's plight, but he recognized that under the new Fugitive Slave Law, he could not grant Lincoln's petition for habeas corpus. In fact, he was supposed to turn Samuel over to a federal commissioner who was empowered by law to return Samuel to his owner without trial, or indeed, any legal process whatsoever. Judge Purple, seeking to sidestep the 1850 Fugitive Slave Law, which went so far as prohibiting the alleged slave from testifying in the proceedings, agreed to release Samuel (still calling him Joseph) while awaiting Belmonti's evidence, on the condition that Levy post bond in the amount of $1500 to cover Samuel's estimated value and Belmonti's legal expenses. Levy posted the bond and Samuel returned to Peoria with Levy. Lincoln, Levy, and Samuel met in Levy's home. Lincoln informed Samuel that under the new federal law, his case was virtually hopeless, but that he would do what he could when either a federal commissioner or Belmonti and his slavecatchers inevitably arrived. Lincoln suggested that in the meantime, Samuel might weigh "other possible courses of action" and that Levy might want to speak to his Springfield neighbor, Jameson Jenkins.

The very next day, Levy and Samuel traveled by horse drawn wagon south to Springfield, ostensibly to sell a wagonload of corn. While Samuel waited with the wagon at the market on the western edge of downtown Springfield, Levy took one of the horses and rode to the Jenkins home on Eighth Street, just a block from Lincoln's own home. He spoke with Jenkins, who agreed to help Samuel head north through Illinois to Wisconsin and ultimately to Canada. With Levy's financial backing, Samuel embarked the next day on a train ride to Bloomington, Illinois, and then a two-day wagon ride to Princeton, Illinois, where he was housed at the home of abolitionist Owen Lovejoy. Lovejoy was earnest—his brother Elijah had been murdered in 1837 after he published an abolitionist editorial in his Alton newspaper. Lovejoy arranged transportation north to Wisconsin, where Samuel stayed for a few days at another underground railroad stop, Joseph Goodrich's Milton House hotel in Milton, Wisconsin. Goodrich brought Samuel to Racine, where he arranged for some local allies to sneak Samuel into the cargo hold of a steamboat headed to Canada. Ultimately, Samuel became a furniture maker in Toronto. He didn't see his family again until after the Civil War, although he did occasionally receive word of them from free Blacks with relatives in Toronto.

Approximately sixteen days after Samuel's departure, John Belmonti arrived in Knoxville to reclaim his slave. Judge Purple sent word to Lincoln in Springfield that Joseph's case would be heard the following Monday at the Knox County Courthouse and that he should bring his client with him to court.

When Lincoln arrived alone, Judge Purple asked, "Where is your client, Mr. Lincoln?"

Lincoln replied that Joseph was always asking for cold water, and so I finally told him that "the water tends to be much colder these days in Canada, and therefore you might be happier up there."

Belmonti was outraged at his wasted journey, but mollified when Judge Purple instructed him to see the clerk of court to claim Jacob Levy's $1500 bond as compensation for his lost property and expenses.

Thus concluded Abraham Lincoln's first brush with the Fugitive Slave Act of 1850.

Part I: President Abraham Lincoln

1

WAR'S END

In 1865, as the inferno of the Civil War finally sputtered out, General Ulysses S. Grant invited President Abraham Lincoln to visit Army Headquarters at City Point, Virginia, at the confluence of the James and Appomattox Rivers. Lincoln eagerly accepted and went down to City Point with his son Tad. While there, in the company of Admiral David Porter, Lincoln received word from Grant that the Union Army had captured Petersburg, Virginia, and that he had sent a railway car to City Point so that Lincoln could see it for himself. When the President's rail car arrived on the outskirts of Petersburg, Lincoln was delighted to be greeted by his other son, Lieutenant Robert Lincoln. The party ventured from the landing into Petersburg on horseback, with a small escort of fewer than a half dozen soldiers. Unfortunately for Admiral Porter, the only horse available for him was a nearly broken down 13-year-old white trotter that stumbled the entire way to Petersburg, much to the amusement of the President and others in the group. When the party arrived at Petersburg, Admiral Porter asked the stable master if he could buy the horse from the government. When asked why he would want such an awful horse, Porter replied, "I don't mean to keep it, but to shoot it, so no one else will suffer the indignity of riding it." There is no record of whether Admiral Porter carried out his threat.

Petersburg was surprisingly vibrant for a place that was just transitioning from war to peace. The city was filled with freshly freed Black Americans. In a scene to be repeated in many other Southern towns, they eagerly stormed Lincoln as he entered the city, calling him their savior. It took armed troops to keep them from overwhelming him. The city was home to numerous seemingly abandoned tobacco warehouses, and everyone was helping themselves to packets and bales of "the delicious weed," as Admiral Porter called it, including the President and his son. Throughout the war, Lincoln was often melancholy—his brow betraying the pain of a nation sacrificing its sons to civil war.

But after this visit, as the party traveled back to the railway line, Lincoln's face lit up at the exuberant greetings he got from troops headed back into the fight.

Over the next several days, Lincoln, accompanied by his son Tad and Admiral Porter, made numerous excursions up and down the James River on Porter's barge, inspecting areas that had been vacated by retreating Confederate troops, and he spent hours observing the front lines from a distance at City Point.

Once, as he stood on a rooftop terrace at City Point watching a not-too-far off battle, a voice from below shouted, "Get down, you idiot!" and just then bullets were heard whizzing by.

The President scrambled down with help from the young Lieutenant who had shouted his impolite but effective warning, and after a moment, said to the young man, "We have met, have we not? Are you Holmes—son of Oliver Wendell, the Boston poet?"

The young Oliver Wendell Holmes Jr. nodded and said, "Mr. President—next time perhaps if you remove your hat, you won't offer the rebels such an attractive target."

Lincoln's time at City Point was a welcome break from Washington, where even in the closing days of the war he was pulled always in a million different directions by competing demands on his time and attention. When Grant sent word that the Confederates had abandoned Richmond, the President resolved to visit the one-time capital of the so-called Confederate States of America as soon as possible. To facilitate the visit, the navy set out to clear obstructions that blocked the way from the James into Richmond's harbor. On April 4, 1865, Lincoln set out for Richmond with Porter and Tad on the USS *Malvern*. This was Porter's flagship, a steamer that had been a blockade runner for the Confederacy till it was captured by Union forces in late 1863. Porter had never taken that route to Richmond before, and although he was proud to be leading the President on his tour, he was anxious about what they would find.

As they approached Richmond, remaining obstructions in the harbor made it impossible for the *Malvern* to make it all the way in, and after several changes of conveyance Porter, Lincoln, and Tad arrived at the wharf on a flat barge propelled by twelve rowing sailors. The humble circumstances of the President's arrival brought out the storyteller in him; in his years as an Illinois lawyer, he was wont to regale the other lawyers and judges while they were on the road riding circuit to the various county courthouses across the state. He recounted to Porter the story of a job seeker who came to see him during his open office hours in the White House. The man asked if he could receive an appointment as a minister to a foreign country. When Lincoln refused, the man bargained himself all the way down to a request to be made a "tide-waiter," whatever that is, and when Lincoln demurred to that, he asked Lincoln for an old pair of trousers. Lincoln concluded the story with a pronouncement that, "It pays to be humble."

At first, the party landed unnoticed in an apparently deserted part of the harbor. It was hot, and the President draped his long topcoat over his arm as sweat beaded beneath his infamous top hat. The group approached a small house where nearly a dozen Black men were digging.

The elderly leader of the workers noticed the President and exclaimed "Bless the Lord, there is the great Messiah. I knew him as soon as I see'd him. He's been in my heart for years and he's come at last to free his children from their bondage." The old man fell to his knees and kissed the President's feet. The other workers followed suit.

Lincoln was embarrassed by the spectacle. He proclaimed, in a remarkable feat of extemporaneous speech, "Do not kneel to me. You must kneel to God only, and thank him for the liberty you will hereafter enjoy. I am but God's humble instrument, but you may rest assured that as long as I live no one shall put a shackle on your limbs, and you shall have all the rights which God has given to every other free citizen of this Republic."

Lincoln's embarrassment may have traced back to his past opposition to abolition, and his attempts to prevent or postpone secession by offering to placate the South through strict enforcement of fugitive slave laws, not to mention supporting the resettlement of freed slaves in Africa or Central America. At a historic meeting at the White House, he had tried to persuade a group of visiting Black clergymen that after emancipation the best course for freed slaves, and indeed all Black persons living in the United States, would be to relocate to such places. He argued this on the basis that—as he expressed it at the meeting—the two races were too different to live together in comity, even in the place of their birth. For this Lincoln was roundly criticized by Frederick Douglass, among others. While Lincoln's views had perhaps evolved since then, the stinging criticism from Black leaders at his comments were likely ringing in the President's ears even as he received the adoration of these freshly freed men.

The encounter, however, again brightened Lincoln's mood. As he spoke his eloquent words to the laborers, his countenance was transformed. His homely face shone with a grace and empathy that words cannot adequately describe.

The assembled Black workers serenaded the President with a spiritual hymn concluding with the words, "No force the mighty power withstands of God the universal king."

Admiral Porter never forgot this brief encounter and often spoke of it for the rest of his life.

The hymning alerted others in the area that something was happening, and people, mostly Black, streamed out of nearby buildings to greet the President, ecstatically shouting and cheering. As the President and his party headed through the crowd up the street further into the city, the crowds proliferated, and people leaned out their windows to get a glimpse of the Great Emancipator.

The milling crowds grew so large that Admiral Porter wondered aloud where this mass of humanity had come from.

A White man in the crowd tried in vain to reach the President, calling out, "God bless you, Abraham, you are the poor man's friend."

A young girl presented the President with a bouquet of roses, with a card reading, "From Eva, to the liberator of the slaves."

The party slowly made its way to the former Confederate White House, where the President sunk into a plush chair in Jefferson Davis's former study, and then on to the Capitol building just recently occupied by the Confederate Congress. Speeches were made and meals were had, and even young Tad got into the act, holding court in a wagon outside the Confederate White House and shaking hands with numerous freedmen.

The remaining residents of Richmond had shown little or no hostility toward the leader of the conquering army—perhaps, as Admiral Porter speculated, because they were so relieved to see the end of the fighting. Yet Porter was nonetheless very concerned about the President's safety. He was thus much relieved when the President safely returned to the *Malvern* after what had turned out to be a raucous and cheerful visit to Richmond. On the *Malvern*, Lincoln engaged in discussions with the only Confederate official apparently remaining in Richmond, John Campbell, about the terms necessary to achieve a formal peace. Lincoln seemed eager to welcome Virginia back into the Union, and Campbell was pleased with the suggestion that a simple repeal of Virginia's ordinance of secession alongside Robert E. Lee's surrender might be sufficient. However, no final agreement was made, Lincoln deciding to reserve judgment at least until his return to City Point.

Lincoln then returned to City Point, where he learned that his wife Mary would soon arrive with a party that included Massachusetts Senator Charles Sumner, Congress's most outspoken opponent of Lincoln's plans for leniency in readmitting Confederate states into the Union. Their impending arrival annoyed Lincoln. He would have preferred to focus on the war's end, without having to concern himself with keeping Mary happy and deflecting Sumner's constant hectoring about the punishment that ought to be unleashed on the Confederates before rejoining the union. Lincoln also learned that his Secretary of State, William Seward, had been seriously injured in a carriage accident. This and other events led Lincoln to decide to return to Washington on April 8, almost as soon as Mary and Senator Sumner arrived. Lincoln had hoped to remain at City Point until the war's final conclusion, but business in Washington beckoned, and dispatches from General Grant and others made it clear that it might be several more days until the complete surrender of the Confederate Army. The growing Presidential entourage, which by now included a French diplomat and a military band, traveled slowly to Washington on a steamer. Lincoln passed the time by reading selections from Shakespeare to his guests, most notably Henry IV's description of the Battle of Shrewsbury. He had the band play both the Marseille and Dixie, which the President jokingly proclaimed taken as "federal property."

While Lincoln was reasserting Union control over Richmond, General Robert E. Lee's Army of Northern Virginia—nearly 30,000 troops strong—was retreating southwest in hopes of joining with the remaining Confederate troops in North Carolina. In the morning of April 9, Lee found his army cut off by General Philip Sheridan's forces at the small town of Appomattox Court House. His supply train had been destroyed the day before by the forces of General George Armstrong Custer. Lee attacked Sheridan's forces at dawn, but he was quickly repelled. By eight in the morning, Lee realized he had no choice but to surrender. He opened communications with a letter to Grant, offering to formalize the end of the war. Grant received Lee's letter just before noon and responded immediately, accepting Lee's offer of surrender and allowing Lee to choose where the two supreme commanders would meet. This was a courteous gesture by Grant, consistent with his resolve to allow the erstwhile enemy a dignified end to the long and terrible war.

Lee's aide Charles Marshall chose the home of Wilmer McLean in Appomattox Court House as suitable for the ceremonial surrender. The sounds of rifle and cannon fire were in earshot when Lee received a message from Grant prompting further correspondence leading to a ceasefire. Lee arrived at the McLean house first, famously fitted out in his full-dress uniform, complete with ceremonial sword. Grant finally appeared in a muddy uniform, unwilling to delay the proceedings by taking the time to clean up, though he did pause to strap on his new sword, a gift from President Lincoln. Grant was apparently nervous and began the meeting with small talk about their previous acquaintance when both served in the Mexican-American War not quite two decades past. At four in the afternoon, they formalized the surrender of Lee's army, with the most generous terms that anyone on the Confederate side could reasonably hope for. That is, on the condition that the Confederate commanders promise on behalf of their troops not to take up arms against the Union again, Grant temporarily released the soldiers to return home, and allowed them to keep their side-arms, private horses, and personal property. Moreover, Grant provided food rations for the Confederate soldiers, who had not been fed in some time. Lee thought this would go a long way toward reconciling his men to their fate.

The terms were recorded in a document penned by Grant's assistant Ely S. Parker, a Seneca Indian. On discovering this of Parker, Lee said that it was nice to have one real American present. Parker's reply, "Sir, we are all Americans," succinctly captured the spirit of the day. It caught the assembled off guard, and more than one of the military men present choked up with a flood of emotion. Grant paid a visit to Lee's Army, and Lee and Grant thereafter sat together on McLean's porch, receiving visitors in an atmosphere of peace and reconciliation. The pair talked briefly about the future, about the Lee family estate near Arlington, Virginia, which had been turned into a camp for escaped slaves during the war. They speculated about the long and difficult process of reconstruction that lay ahead. Lee wished Grant good fortune and pledged "to work with you, General, to create the unity and prosperity that will be necessary for our country to get back on its feet." Grant took these words to heart, knowing that help from Southerners such as Lee would be vital to knitting the unraveled union back together.

As Grant rose to leave, Lee rose also and asked, "Haven't you forgotten something, General?" Grant looked confused, and Lee said, "My sword, sir. Is it not customary for the victor to have the sword of the vanquished as a memento?" Grant looked Lee in the eye and said, "General, in the spirit of reconciliation and reconstruction we shared just a few moments ago, and relying on the sincerity of your words of peace and hope, I propose a trade. We shall exchange swords as a symbol of unity, and when we are satisfied that we have done all we can to heal the wounds in the hearts of our countrymen, we shall exchange them once again." Although Lee was somewhat stunned at the offer, he reached for his belt as a sign of acceptance, and he and Grant held their swords high in the air and exchanged them to the tumultuous approval of the assembled. It was an auspicious beginning to the hoped-for re-United States of America.

In the days that followed, Grant returned to oversee the formal surrender of the army of Northern Virginia, which included creating duplicate copies of the list of paroled soldiers and collecting their rifles. Lee made a farewell address to his troops, terming the surrender necessary "to avoid the useless sacrifice of those whose past services have endeared them to their countrymen." At the last moment, Lee added a paragraph entreating his army—"after reuniting with your families who have sorely missed you these past years"—to "do honor to the great state of Virginia and devote your energies, together with our Northern brethren, to the rebuilding of this great country of ours. Your example of faithful service to the future shall stand as a beacon to be followed by all in this sacred task."

Although he knew that it was subject to confiscation by the U.S. government, Lee wanted to visit his family estate near Arlington, Virginia. On April 11, he embarked on a carriage ride to the site, where he found thousands of freedmen gathered on the lawns celebrating. The scene was too chaotic for him to enter the house, so he spent a few minutes in his carriage gazing longingly at what had, for decades, been the family home. Then, he had his driver turn back and head south to Arlington, where he would spend the next several months living in rented rooms.

The respect that Grant showed Lee during the process of surrender was noticed throughout the South and helped create the conditions for the reconciliation that was necessary for the nation to heal. It made a particularly strong impression on the Confederate soldiers in the Appomattox Court House area who were among those paroled and allowed to leave after the surrender. They returned home to their families with hope for the future, thankful that peace was finally in plain sight. Even Southern newspapers, as they lamented the calamity their region was suffering, praised Grant as an honorable military man who had shown the true meaning of love of country.

Grant's reputation in the South had already been burnished by his eventual instruction to General William Tecumseh Sherman to minimize destruction on his march from Atlanta to the sea in the fall of 1864. Sherman was perhaps the Union's greatest military commander after Grant himself. He was a master at outmaneuvering his opponent, feigning this way and that, and predicting his opponents' reactions. Like an American Sun Tzu, he knew when to engage and when to slip by, and much of the progress of his military campaigns was achieved by simply flowing past an entrenched enemy. But when necessary, he was ruthless. He firmly believed that wars were won not only on the battlefield, but also on the home front by demoralizing civilians, which he found sapped soldiers' will to fight. Thus, in addition to destroying anything and everything that might conceivably be of military value, he viewed the destruction of enemy infrastructure and sometimes even dwellings as vital to a successful campaign. He instructed his forces to seize animals and stores of food to keep his troops fed and ready for battle at the same time that he placed civilian populations in dire straits. Sherman's earliest military experience in Florida had borne out the effectiveness of this strategy. At the same time, although he was not always successful, he did whatever he could to prevent wanton destruction, looting, and abuse of civilians by his troops. His success was also enhanced by the loyalty and affection of those under his command whom he won over with his down-to-earth relations and evident concern for their welfare.

After reading numerous articles in Confederate newspapers indicating that Southerners viewed holding Atlanta as vital to retaining any hope of success in the war, Sherman decided to focus on capturing that city. Thus, although Grant had ordered Sherman to seek out and destroy Confederate armies, Sherman set out directly for Atlanta instead. As he approached the city, with Grant and Lincoln's endorsement, Sherman ordered his troops to destroy everything in their path that they could not seize for their own use. In Jonesborough, on the outskirts of Atlanta, Sherman's army seized all foodstuffs and obliterated the town after a flanking maneuver south of Atlanta on August 31 cut off the railroad from Macon, one of Atlanta's main supply lines. This caused a great outcry as it plunged the civilian population into abject misery. It left the resident women, children, and elderly with little food and no shelter, and was used as a rallying cry for renewed resistance. Hearing of the reaction, Lincoln and Grant argued out the wisdom of Sherman's strategy. They recognized its value to military victory, but concluded that it did too much damage to their prospects for an orderly Confederate surrender, not to mention reconciliation at war's end.

Meanwhile, Sherman had occupied Atlanta and ordered most of the population to leave the city. Civilians had to sleep out in the open, or in barns and farmhouses in surrounding areas. In the city, troops dismantled buildings to take the wood for military purposes, and destroyed machine shops and any other equipment that could be put to military use. Much of the railroad infrastructure had already been destroyed by fleeing Confederate troops, and the Confederates' igniting of weapons stores resulted in the destruction of many buildings. Thus, regardless of Sherman's actions, Atlanta was going to be in bad shape when Sherman's forces moved on, despite Grant's new order that Sherman preserve as much civilian property and infrastructure as possible for the rest of his campaign. Grant's order rankled Sherman to no end. At first he protested by return wire, but after numerous wires back and forth, Grant remained firm. Sherman held Grant in extremely high regard and followed his orders at some cost, as it required leaving hundreds of Sherman's troops behind in Atlanta and slowed his progress to the sea, as he had to take great care all along the route to Savannah and through the Carolinas that only militarily valuable infrastructure was destroyed. All this nearly allowed Lee's Army of Virginia to receive reinforcements from the south.

When Lincoln arrived back in Washington in the evening of April 9, his first errand was to visit the injured Seward. To reduce

Seward's discomfort, the President laid next to Seward on the bed as he described his trip to Petersburg and Richmond as well as the dispatches from Grant that foretold the impending end to the war. Lincoln did not yet know that General Robert E. Lee had surrendered to Grant earlier that day. Seward was ailing, but he was alert enough to dissuade the President from issuing a proclamation celebrating the end of the war until the last of the Confederate generals surrendered.

Lincoln finally learned of Lee's surrender later that evening. At sunrise on the 10th, the rest of Washington heard the news by way of the firing of 500 cannons. To the cheers of the assembled crowd, Tad waved a Confederate flag at a White House window, and once again Lincoln had the military band play Dixie. Lincoln spent most of the day drafting a formal address recognizing the end of the War, to be delivered at the White House the next day. He also met with Governor Francis Harrison Pierpoint, the leader of the Virginia faction that had opposed secession. Pierpoint's faction had been busy throughout the war. It formed the new state of West Virginia, which was admitted to the Union in 1863, and met in 1864 in Alexandria to draft a new, pro-Union constitution for the remainder of the state. Pierpoint and Lincoln discussed the possibility that a pro-Union government representing all of Virginia under West Virginia's 1864 constitution could be formed rather quickly, in pursuit of Lincoln's plan to reconstruct the Southern states as soon as possible.

The apparent conclusion of the Civil War brought great joy to Washington and the Northern states, but it was a bitter joy tempered by its awful cost. Nevertheless, on April 11, as the reality of the previous day's news took hold, the city of Washington became one gigantic celebration. Houses were lit in festive lights and people were out and about, cheering and singing celebratory songs.

A massive crowd assembled at the White House serenading and calling for the President, and as the evening light faded, Lincoln appeared at a second story Portico, to the delight of a bustling crowd whose cheers seemed loud enough to be heard in Baltimore. With the assistance of reporter and presidential confidant Noah Brooks, who held up a candle so the President could see his manuscript, Lincoln read his carefully prepared speech to the hushed crowd. In implicit recognition of the terrible cost of the war, Lincoln began by saying that "we meet this evening, not in sorrow, but in gladness of heart." Lincoln went on to acknowledge that reconstruction will be "fraught with great difficulty" especially because "we, the loyal people, differ among ourselves as to the mode, manner, and means of reconciliation." The remainder of his speech was devoted to promoting the acceptability of Louisiana's recently formed government, and his proposal that the other Southern states follow Louisiana's example to enable a speedy reconstruction.

The surrender at Appomattox Court House and the celebrations in Washington were, of course, disheartening to loyal Confederates. Many remained committed to the principles that had motivated secession. Plenty of Southerners continued to hate Lincoln passionately. They had always viewed him as a tyrant for his alleged imposition of abolition on their Southern homeland. Many refused to abandon the cause even when it was clearly lost.

One such Southerner was John Wilkes Booth, who was present for Lincoln's speech. He was a Marylander, and much to his chagrin, Maryland never seceded from the Union. However, it did remain a slave state until November 1864, when emancipation was approved by a margin of fewer than 1,000 votes in a statewide referendum. Booth was a famous stage actor from a renowned theatrical family. The Civil War began just as his career was blossoming.

In 1860, Booth was a lead actor in a national tour stopping in prominent places like Boston, Chicago, New York, and New Orleans. That year he also became a member of the Knights of the Golden Circle, a Maryland secret society devoted to the secessionist cause. After it opened in 1863, he regularly performed at Ford's Theater in Washington, possibly in part because the owner was a family friend. The Lincoln family had seen Booth perform during Lincoln's first term, and he made such an impression on Tad Lincoln that the President invited Booth to visit the White House. Booth declined.

In March 1865, Booth was incensed when General Grant ceased prisoner exchanges with the Confederate forces. Booth and a group of conspirators plotted to take the President hostage until Grant agreed to resume the exchanges. The plan was to kidnap Lincoln on March 17, when the President was scheduled to attend a play at Campbell Military Hospital in Washington, and whisk him away to the Maryland home of Mary Surratt, one of the conspirators. The conspirators, including Booth, lay in wait at the hospital, but the plot failed when Lincoln chose not to attend. Ironically, instead of the play, Lincoln took part in an event at the National Hotel, which was where Booth happened to be living at the time! Booth might have been able to carry out his plan had he simply stayed home.

Booth was in the crowd at the White House on April 11—not to celebrate, but to observe. Lincoln noted with approval that Louisiana's new constitution "empower[ed] the Legislature to confer the elective franchise upon the colored man." The speech was a plea to the Radical Republicans to welcome Louisiana back into the Union quickly, without a guarantee that any Black Louisianans would actually be allowed to vote. Even so, the reference to suffrage for Black Americans, even at the state legislature's discretion, was too much for Booth. He urged his companion Lewis Powell (sometimes referred to as Lewis Paine or Payne), who always had a pistol in his possession, to shoot Lincoln on the spot. Powell did not think it possible in the crowded environs around the White House. Booth vowed to Powell that he was going to kill the President as soon as the opportunity arose. The next day, April 12, he learned that Lincoln and Grant were planning to attend the theater that Friday to see the play The American Cousin. Booth contacted several associates who had participated in the previous kidnapping plot to tell them that they would kill both Lincoln and Grant at the theatre.

Booth and Powell, alongside their like-minded comrades George Atzerodt, John Surratt, and David E. Herold, met at the Washington home of John's mother Mary Surratt to plan the assassination. Booth would kill Lincoln with his pistol and Grant with his knife at the theater, and Lewis Powell would kill the bedridden Secretary of State Seward at his home. The plotters discussed whether to kill Vice President Andrew Johnson as well. They were conflicted because they hoped that President Johnson's sympathies would be with them, such that the South's legitimate grievances could be addressed by the re-United States. But they were aware of Johnson's consistently pro-Union views, and the harshness of his actions as military governor of Tennessee during the war. The plotters decided to have Atzerodt stalk the Vice President at the Kirkwood Hotel, where Johnson was living, and try to make contact with him on the night of the assassination. They would leave it to Atzerodt to decide whether to kill Johnson, depending on his reaction when informed of the plot.

Unknown to Booth, Grant had declined the President's invitation to attend the theater, mainly because Grant's wife Julia could no longer bear the company of Mrs. Lincoln. Mary Lincoln, in a fit of jealousy over Julia Grant's superior social standing, had accused Mrs. Grant of waiting in the wings to replace her as first lady. The sting of this insult, uttered at City Point only a few days before the proposed night at the theater, had not worn off enough yet even for the socially graceful Julia Grant. Upon hearing that the Grants would not join them, Lincoln decided to invite one of his favorite young couples to replace the Grants: Major Henry Rathbone and his fiancé Clara Harris. Rathbone, who commanded troops at battles at Antietam and Fredericksburg, was a pre-war lawyer who inherited his way to wealth. His fiancé Clara Harris was also his step-sister because his mother had married Clara's father, New York Senator Ira Harris, in 1846 when he was nine and Clara was twelve. Lincoln's fondness for the couple was probably due more to Clara and her father than to his passing acquaintance with Major Rathbone.

2

AN EVENING AT FORD'S THEATER

On the appointed day, Henry and Clara arrived by carriage at the White House and waited for the President and Mrs. Lincoln to finish getting ready. Henry, in his full dress uniform with shiny brass buttons, and Clara, resplendent in a gown fit for the fanciest Washington ball, looked as if they had been born to accompany the President and the first lady. The couple spoke briefly with Tad Lincoln, who was departing on foot to go to Grover's Theater (later the National Theater) to see the play Aladdin and the Wonderful Lamp with the Taft children Bud and Holly, his closest friends and frequent companions, especially since the death of his brother Willie. As the group set out for the short carriage ride to the theater, it was clear that the President was in a splendid mood. He had been in good spirits all day. Hard as they tried, no one—neither advisor-bodyguard Ward Hill Lamon, nor Secretary of War Edwin Stanton, nor full-time bodyguard William H. Crook—could convince Lincoln that it was too risky for him to attend the theater. However, despite his concern for the President's safety, Stanton did not release the uncommonly strong Major Thomas T. Eckert from his duties at the telegraph bureau to accompany the President to the theater as an extra bodyguard.

By the time the party arrived, the play had already begun. The crowd and the performers had eagerly anticipated the President and were disappointed to have had to begin without him. Finally, their frequent glances in the direction of the Presidential box were rewarded by the entry first of Clara Hill, then Mrs. Lincoln, Major Rathbone, and finally the President himself. The performers paused and the band, led by William Withers, played Hail to the Chief. When the song concluded, the President leaned out of the box and waved to the crowd, which cheered wildly in return. The President settled into the rocking chair specially provided for him by Ford's brother Harry from his nearby residence. Draperies surrounding the Presidential box concealed Lincoln from the audience's view during the performance, which was just as well, since no one in the theater would have been able to keep their eyes off of the President had he been visible. He occasionally leaned forward, usually in response to Mary's whisperings about special moments in the play, rewarding his fellow theatergoers with a glimpse of their beloved chief executive.

Police officer John Frederick Parker was stationed at the door to the President's box as a guard. During the first act, John Wilkes Booth approached Parker asking whether he might pay his respects to the presidential party. Parker, recognizing the famous actor, asked Booth to wait for the intermission to avoid disturbing the party's enjoyment of the play. Booth bided his time in the hallway behind the box. When the crowd erupted in applause at the conclusion of the first act, Parker allowed Booth to enter the box. Lincoln and Rathbone rose and greeted Booth. The President was excited to see the actor, and after the actor rather stiffly returned Lincoln's enthusiastic greeting, Lincoln invited Booth to join them for the remainder of the play. Booth accepted and took a seat behind the President, waiting for the opportunity to carry out his plan. Having seen the play more than once, including a dress rehearsal just days before, Booth knew that the crowd would roar with laughter at a line delivered early in the second act. Perfect to muffle his shot. Meanwhile, Parker, feeling that the President was in no danger in this friendly crowd, left his post to have a drink at a local tavern with the President's footman and coachman. Remarkably, Parker was allowed to remain on the police force even after it was discovered that he had abandoned the President of the United States. A few years later, he was fired for sleeping on duty.

Shortly after the second act got underway, Booth took his watch from his vest pocket, held it up to the light radiating from the stage, and noted that it was approaching the agreed upon time for the three coordinated attacks. He quietly barred the box door with his walking stick, unnoticed by the dark box's other occupants. Booth awaited the audience's laughter at the line "you sockdologizing old man trap," and then all in one moment drew his pistol and knife, one in each hand, and took aim for Lincoln. As he fired, Mary squeezed the President's hand and the President leaned forward in laughter, Booth's shot sailed over Lincoln's head and struck the left arm of a man in the audience, Lawrence Bird, who was sitting in the fifth row with his wife Ervinia.

The crowd's laughter muffled the sound of the gunshot for those outside the box, but Major Rathbone heard the pistol's report, saw its spark in the corner of his eye and smelled its spent powder. Immediately realizing that he missed, Booth shouted "damnation" and lunged at the President with his knife. Rathbone, having turned toward Booth upon seeing the spark, pounced on him, and as he brought Booth to the ground the knife caught on Lincoln's jacket and sliced a long gash in it—leaving Lincoln himself uninjured. Clara and Mary's screams spread alarm among the crowd. Soon, a group of men burst through Booth's makeshift barricade and came to Rathbone's aid in restraining the would-be assassin. One man grabbed Booth's knife off the floor, and Rathbone had to talk him out of killing Booth where he lay. Booth's only thought as he lay restrained under the weight of his captors was that he had not had the chance to utter the line "sic semper tyrannis" that he had planned for the occasion. This was a popular saying among the rebels, and adorned cards printed with the Confederate flag that were distributed throughout the South, some of which were later found among Booth's papers as well as at Mary Surratt's Maryland house. As Booth was led away to the nearest federal stockade, he did manage to shout, "The South will be avenged!" before being gagged by a member of his escort.

Needless to say, the performance was over. The President, the first lady, Clara Hill, and Major Rathbone—the last being recognized already by theatergoers as a hero—were escorted back to the White House by an entourage of police officers and military personnel who had been alerted to what had happened by the theatergoing crowd's dispersal into the streets. There was no federal police force akin to the FBI or Secret Service at the time, and thus local Washington police, supported by military men under Stanton's orders, set out to secure the area, and locate and arrest anyone involved in the plot. The police found Joseph "Johnny Peanut" Burroughs in the alleyway behind the theater lying on a bench holding the reins to a horse, which Burroughs immediately said belonged to Booth. He explained that he had been given the horse by a theater stagehand named Edmund Spangler and told to hold onto it for Booth. He said that he had no idea what Booth was up to that night—Booth was a regular at the theater and Burroughs had not wondered at his presence. He told the officers that Spangler had suddenly come running out of the theater, without answering Burroughs's question—"What about the horse?"—as he ran by. The police went to Spangler's room at a nearby boarding house. When they arrived, Spangler fled out the back of the house but then, cornered, lunged at one of the officers with a knife. Another officer shot Spangler with his pistol, and he died within the hour without uttering a word.

In the commotion, a police officer had burst into Grover's Theater shouting that "they've assassinated the President." Tad ran out, screaming, "They killed Papa! They killed Papa!" The others in his group caught up with him. They had difficulty making it back to the White House through the crowd. When they arrived, the police guarding the premises did not want to allow them in, despite Tad's insistence that he was the President's son. It was in the crowd outside the White House that Tad learned the truth, that his father was uninjured. When Tad finally got in and found his parents in the residence, each of them burst into tears.

Meanwhile, the other plotters had also failed in their efforts. Led on horseback by Herold, Powell went with his pistol to Seward's home at Lafayette Park. He talked his way in by claiming that he was there to teach Seward how to administer new medication prescribed by Seward's physician. When Powell reached the third floor, where Seward lay in bed, Seward's son Frederick told Powell that his father was sleeping and could not be disturbed. Seward's daughter Fanny, just then emerging from Seward's room, declared that their father was awake. Frederick, suspicious at the arrival of this mysterious stranger at the late hour, nonetheless refused to allow Powell to enter the bedroom. Powell drew his revolver and shot at Frederick's head, but in another stroke of bad luck for the would-be assassins, the gun jammed. Powell bludgeoned Frederick with the butt of his revolver and stormed past Fanny into the bedroom, where he stabbed Seward in the face.

Although Seward's facial injury was substantial, the splint on his broken jaw prevented Powell's knife from causing a more serious injury. Powell ran out of the house, stabbing several others amid his escape. Yet, unfamiliar with the city and abandoned by his guide Herold (who was frightened off by the commotion inside), Powell took three days to find his way back to the Surratt home. Powell's horse, left wandering the streets of Washington by Herold, was much the wiser and returned within an hour. Federal authorities were awaiting Powell when he arrived; and he was promptly arrested at Surratt's, along with Mary Surratt. His missing hat—he had lost it in the scuffles at Seward's house—was enough to raise suspicions, and these were only heightened when, in response to officers' questions, he claimed to be a bricklayer despite the, somewhat disheveled, finery he was wearing.

In the late afternoon of the 14th, George Atzerodt had rented a room at Vice President Johnson's hotel and asked the bartender about Johnson's whereabouts. Earlier that day, Booth had also attempted to visit Johnson at his hotel, leaving him a note when he failed to find him. Perhaps Booth was anxious to test Johnson for sympathy to the cause and didn't trust Atzerodt, or perhaps it was an attempt to create suspicion that Johnson was in on the plot so that Atzerodt would have an easier time convincing Johnson to join them. Whatever the case may be, in the evening of the 14th, Atzerodt lost his nerve and instead of remaining at the Kirkwood bar all evening, he got drunk rather early and then wandered around the streets of Washington through the night. In fact, Atzerodt was not known for his bravery, and he later raised this reputation as a defense at trial, arguing that no one who knew him could possibly have entrusted him with the task of murdering a Vice President. Having heard word of the attempt on Lincoln, the barman grew suspicious of Atzerodt's inquiries, and he informed the police. A search of Atzerodt's room revealed letters connecting him to Booth, and a few days later he was arrested at the home of a cousin in Germantown, Maryland.

With Booth captured at Ford's Theater, Spangler dead, and Powell, Mary Surratt, and Atzerodt arrested, the only major plotters remaining at large were John Surratt and David Herold. Herold was captured before the end of April at a farm in Virginia. All captives were held in military custody at the Washington Arsenal at Greenfield Point, in the southern part of the District near where the Potomac and Anacostia Rivers meet. Surratt fled to Montreal, Canada, where he initially received shelter from the priests at the Notre Dame Basilica and from there he was taken to an obscure settlement north of Montreal known as Joliette, where he was sheltered by the local Catholic Priest, Father Sebastien. Despite his successful escape, he returned to Washington when he learned that his mother had been sentenced to death. He hoped his reappearance might lead to a reprieve for her.

Any valid doubts about Johnson's loyalty were allayed by his immediate journey to the White House, where he was much relieved to find Lincoln already cracking jokes about the failed attempt on his life. Lincoln's focus was on his torn jacket, debating with himself whether he ought to retire it, or to have it repaired and wear it constantly as armor against any future attempts, along with his top hat with a bullet hole which may have been the product of another failed attempt the previous year.

Regardless of Johnson's actions, there were those who had always regretted Lincoln's choice of Johnson as Vice President. One such was the irrepressible Senator Sumner, who in a visit to the White House on April 15 urged Lincoln to do something about Johnson, not because he thought Johnson was in on the plot, but because of the stark reality that Johnson had nearly become President the night before—a possibility too frightening to contemplate.

Meanwhile, Bird needed nearly a month to recuperate from his wound. The Birds had come out to Washington from French Lick, Indiana, to join in the celebrations marking the end of the war; when the papers had let it be known that Lincoln and Grant were planning to attend that night's performance, they had purchased their normally $1 tickets for outlandish sum of $5 each! Bird was taken to Harewood Hospital, a massive military complex that had been established in 1862 to treat wounded soldiers, where he was sometimes tended by a young treasury clerk named Walt Whitman who spent many of his off hours there volunteering as a nurse. Unfortunately for Bird, sepsis set in and the doctors—well-practiced after the war—were forced to amputate his left arm just below the shoulder.

Not long after the attack, with wife Ervinia at his bedside, Bird was surprised to be paid a visit at the hospital by Mr. and Mrs. Lincoln. Aside from his trips back and forth to the cottage at the

Soldier's Home, this was one of Lincoln's first sojourns out in public after the attempt on his life. At the insistence of Stanton, he was accompanied by the dozen Pinkerton guards that protected him on the four-mile trip from the White House to the cottage. The Pinkerton security company was especially suited to the task because its founder, Allan Pinkerton, first achieved notoriety when he foiled an attempt on Lincoln's life just before Lincoln's first inauguration as President. Pinkerton guards continued to provide extensive protective and investigative services for the federal government until the 1893 passage of the Anti-Pinkerton Act, which prohibits the government from contracting with Pinkerton or "similar organizations." The Act grew out of concern over the use of private agencies like Pinkerton to violently suppress organized labor activities, and it remains on the books as an anti-privatization provision honored today only in the breach.

As Lincoln approached Bird's bedside, Ervinia saw his distinctive top hat before anything else and immediately began to weep, burbling "thank you for coming" through her sobs and tears.

Lincoln held Ervinia's hands in his and said, "I am mighty sorry for ruining your evening at the theater."

Lawrence chuckled. "Mr. Lincoln, I regret that I was unable to assist in the capture of that rascal who shot at you but my wife convinced me to see a doctor instead."

Sensing levity, a characteristic twinkle came to Lincoln's eye, and he said "your injury brings to mind the words attributed to the great patriot Nathan Hale, who in your circumstance might have regretted that he had but one arm to give for his country." This was an odd statement because, of course, Bird's right arm remained fully attached and could have served as an additional offering to the nation. After a few more moments of chatting—Mary with Ervinia and the President with Lawrence—Lincoln wished the Birds well, and he and Mary then wandered about the hospital for some hours, listening to the stories of the soldiers and thanking each and every one they encountered for their service to the Union cause. Several weeks later, Bird was given a hero's welcome when he arrived back in French Lick, and lived out the rest of his life as a local celebrity, recounting to all who would listen how he took a bullet that had been intended for the President.

The fact that the attempts on Lincoln and the others were made on Good Friday, that John Surratt sought the aid of Catholic priests wherever he went, and the Catholic faith of virtually all of the conspirators, added fuel to rumors that the killing of Lincoln was some sort of Catholic plot, a rumor that gained support years later when one of the military commissioners in the trial of the conspirators published a book explicitly making that claim.

The plot against Lincoln was over, and Washington began to get back to normal, although it would prove to be a new normal with bitter contestation over Reconstruction.

3

TRIAL AND PUNISHMENT

In a White House meeting the day after the attempt, Lincoln, Secretary of War Stanton and General Grant agreed that the plot was a military matter and the trial and punishment of the conspirators would be conducted by a military commission assembled for the purpose. Attorney General Speed objected on the ground that the civilian courts were open and functioning in Washington, but the President overruled him, and plans were made to conduct a quick trial, with the hope that hangings would take place before the July 4 holiday. Grant, looking to advance his presidential aspirations, was anxious to investigate whether Vice President Johnson was involved in or sympathetic to the plot, but Lincoln would have none of it, aiming to live up to his second inaugural promise of "malice toward none" and not aggravating Southerners unnecessarily.

In planning the investigation and trial, Grant was mindful of the precedent set by the investigation into a plot to assassinate George Washington involving one of his elite "Life Guards" in 1776. That investigation, which uncovered the conspiratorial involvement of New York's Royal Governor William Tryon as well as New York City Mayor David Mathews, was conducted by the military with admirable secrecy and incredible speed. Although Mathews escaped after being arrested, one of the plotters, Thomas Hickey, was hanged on June 28, 1776, before a crowd estimated at 20,000.

General Grant swiftly assembled a distinguished group of commissioners to investigate the assassination plot, including two distinguished Members of Congress, Senator Charles Sumner of Massachusetts and Representative John A. Bingham of Ohio. Grant also asked John Marshall Harlan—Kentucky Attorney General, Civil War hero, and future Supreme Court Justice—to serve on the commission, but Harlan declined by return letter, citing the demands of his elected position in Kentucky.

Grant chose Joseph Holt, former Secretary of War and current

Judge Advocate General, to serve on the commission and lead the investigation along with his Colonel in the JAG office, Major Henry Burnett. They interrogated the plotters at the Arsenal jail and made a trip to Surratsville to investigate the involvement of a Dr. Samuel Mudd who was alleged by Atzerodt to have provided aid to the conspirators. The conditions at the jail were dreadful and for the conspirators, except Mrs. Surratt, it was even worse because after they were interrogated they were forced to wear padded hoods with nothing but slits for breathing. Powell wept continuously after the hood was placed on him and he never regained his bearings.

Grant had instructed Holt to attempt to determine whether the plot was led or supported by member of the Confederate government or some other organized group of post-War saboteurs. No such evidence was uncovered. The conspirator most likely to know of outside support was Booth, but his interrogation went nowhere. Burnett asked Booth who led the plot against the President. Booth rose, faced his interrogators, and theatrically recited these lines, paraphrasing Shakespeare's Julius Caeser:

> We all stand up against the spirit of Lincoln;
> And in the spirit of men there is no blood:
> We shall be called purgers, not murderers.
> For had you rather Lincoln were alive
> And we die slaves, than that he die—we live?
> Are you so base that you would be a bondman?
> Are you so vile that you love not your country?
> I'd rather be a dog, and bay the moon,
> Than such a false American.

And so it went. Every time Burnett asked a question, Booth launched into lines from some or other play while the clerk scratched furiously trying to capture what was said. Exasperated, Holt interjected that his only chance to save himself from the gallows was to inform them of who directed him to kill the President. To this, Booth replied, this time from Hamlet:

> To be, or not to be, that is the question:
> Whether 'tis nobler in the mind to suffer

The slings and arrows of outrageous fortune,
Or to take arms against a sea of troubles
And by opposing end them. To die—to sleep,
No more; and by a sleep to say we end
The heart-ache and the thousand natural shocks
That flesh is heir to: 'tis a consummation
Devoutly to be wish'd. To die, to sleep;
To sleep, perchance to dream.

After this, Booth was quiet, and uttered not another word in response to any more of Holt or Burnett's questions. After two hours, they left him, and turned to the other conspirators.

The most cooperative of the plotters was Atzerodt who not only identified Booth as the leader but also provided details of the previously unknown attempt to kidnap the President on March 17. Clearly trying to save his neck, Atzerodt provided details about all of the group's planning meetings, financial support provided by Booth's childhood friend Michael O'Laughlen and the participation of Booth's military school classmate Samuel Arnold and Dr. Mudd in the earlier kidnapping conspiracy. Neither Mary Surratt nor Powell would provide any information, but they were both more than willing to hurl insults at Holt and Burnett during their questioning and to express their disappointment that Lincoln had survived. Arnold and Mudd were arrested and brought to the Arsenal; both protested their innocence, Mudd most vehemently, but they were held in the same conditions as the others.

Meanwhile, investigators under Holt and Burnett's supervision fanned out across the Washington area and even traveled as far as Montreal to investigate the possible involvement of Confederate agents there. They questioned everyone who boarded at Mary Surratt's boarding house and there they encountered Louis Weichmann. Weichmann had met and befriended John Surratt while both were studying for the priesthood at St. Charles College, a Maryland seminary. Both left the seminary in 1862, and Weichmann moved to Washington to teach school and later on became a clerk with the War Department. Investigators had learned from Atzerodt that John Surratt acted as a Confederate agent throughout the war, and they were understandably concerned that if Weichmann were involved, he might also have been a Confederate spy.

Weichmann was interrogated at a War Department office, admitted his friendship with John Surratt but denied any knowledge of or involvement in the plot. This denial was credible since none of the captives, including the talkative Atzerodt, had mentioned him, but the investigators found it hard to believe that Weichmann knew nothing of the plotting that went on right under his nose. He explained that "Mary Surratt knew I was a Union man. She would sometimes harangue me about the evils of Abraham Lincoln and the Union war tactics, but no one ever mentioned any plot or seemed to be planning something like that." Holt and Burnett weren't completely convinced of Weichmann's ignorance, but they decided that he was most useful as a witness since he could place all of the conspirators together at the Surratt house for their meetings.

For the trial, a makeshift courtroom was set up in a former laundry room at the Arsenal jail. The room was small, crowded, and not very well lit—an unlikely courtroom. There was a constant haze of cigar smoke hovering above the assembled. Originally, the commission announced that it would conduct its proceedings behind closed doors, with written summaries of the previous day's evidence provided to the public each morning. This decision was greeted with outcry, mainly from the dozens of journalists who descended on Washington for the trial, and it was quickly rescinded. The trial was open to the public except for the occasional closed door session when the commissioners deliberated, received legal advice from Holt, or heard especially sensitive testimony.

Understandably, defense lawyers were a bit difficult to come by, not only due to the sentiment surrounding the trial but also because the defendants had little opportunity to communicate with the outside world from inside the Arsenal jail. Ultimately, the defendants managed to secure representatives of varying quality, with Booth hiring the very distinguished Reverdy Johnson, at the time a Maryland Senator. Although he personally opposed slavery, Johnson had defended slaveholder John F.

A. Sandford in the notorious Dred Scott case in which the Supreme Court determined that the free descendants of African slaves were ineligible for American citizenship. According to his memoir, Johnson was haunted for the rest of his life by talk that his arguments for Booth reflected his personal view of Lincoln's actions during the war and that his defense of Booth evidenced secret sympathy for the rebellion.

The defense lawyers began by challenging the jurisdiction of the military commission. One by one, for each defendant, they recited legal arguments in favor of jurisdiction in the federal courts, which they pointed out had remained open throughout the period of the conspiracy. One by one these motions were denied and one by one the defendants entered not guilty pleas in a time consuming ritual which seemed pointless once the first such motion had been denied.

The trial before the commission consumed approximately seven weeks, with testimony and summations finally concluding on June 28. As expected, Louis Weichmann was a star witness for the prosecution, testifying that on multiple occasions he witnessed meetings involving Booth, the Surratts and other conspirators that were held out of his earshot. The prosecution tried valiantly to link the plot to Jefferson Davis and Confederate agents in Canada. They had found Davis's calling card in Booth's papers and they had plenty of evidence that John Surratt and others had met with Confederate agents in Canada, but no specific evidence of Confederate government involvement could be produced. The main effect of this effort was to delay the conclusion of the trial by several days.

Another delay was caused by the Grand Review of the Armies held in Washington on May 23-24 to celebrate the end of the Civil War. Even if the road closings and disruptions to streetcar service for the review had not made it impossible for participants in the trial to travel to the courtroom on those days, the commission could not have met simply because members of the commission were expected to participate in the procession, including the commission's chair General Sherman who, on May 24, triumphantly led the Army of Georgia and the Army of the

Tennessee—65,000 men strong—in a six hour procession past the reviewing stand erected in front of the White House. The previous day saw General George Gordon Meade leading 80,000 men of the Army of the Potomac in grand march twelve men across and seven miles long. Under heavy guard, with Stanton, Grant, and others seated behind him, President Lincoln gave a brief address each day.

Lincoln thanked the Generals and their troops for their service and, in words reminiscent of his second inaugural address, added that "The scourge of war has passed away, with the hope that the Almighty will heal the wounds of our scarred nation, that we may live in peace among ourselves with justice for all of this great land's inhabitants. May we proceed with open hearts and charity that we may together enjoy the treasures that in his wisdom the living God has bestowed upon us."

Notably, Vice President Johnson was not in attendance. His absence was attributed to illness that plagued him throughout the spring and early summer of 1865.

The last witness, identified in the transcript as "Henry Hawkins (colored)" finally testified in Mrs. Surratt's defense on Tuesday June 13. Hawkins stated that he was formerly Mrs. Surratt's slave and that he now lived at her Maryland home as a servant. He attested that in the eleven years he had been with her he never heard her say anything indicating disloyalty, that she always treated him and the other servants "kindly," that she "often fed Union soldiers that passed her house, and always gave them the best she had," and that she even fed and cared for a half dozen Union horses that had broken away from Giesboro Point, where the cavalry kept approximately 30,000 horses at the ready.

The summations for the various defendants began in earnest on Monday June 19 and took that entire week. Virtually every defense counsel attacked the jurisdiction of the military commission and the credibility of the prosecution's star witness Weichmann. Many said he was lying to save his own neck. The only defendant with a remote chance of exoneration was Dr. Mudd. His lawyer was General Thomas Ewing, Jr., former private secretary to President

Zachary Taylor who resigned as chief justice of the Kansas Supreme Court to fight in the Civil War and who also happened to be the brother-in-law of commission chair William Tecumseh Sherman. Ewing made an effective argument on his behalf, claiming that the evidence showed virtually no involvement in the plotting, the attempt, or agreement with the object of the conspiracy, and that consequently he should not be held responsible for the conduct of the others. Ewing argued that even the weak case against Mudd rested entirely on the false testimony of Weichmann, a claim that Ewing supported with a careful examination of the facts surrounding Weichmann's actions and his motivation for testifying.

The commission was now ready to deliberate upon and decide the fates of the accused. The commissioners, together with Holt and Bingham, met in their dingy courtroom behind closed doors from 10 am till 6 pm on June 29. They kept no record of their deliberations, but years later, in comments about the process, more than one of the commissioners gave the impression that the discussion was led by Holt with assistance from Bingham. Holt's main point, purportedly, was that the entire plot was one continuous conspiracy and thus all of the participants were responsible for every action taken by any of them in pursuance of the conspiracy. On June 30, the commission assembled at 10 am once again, with Holt supplying suggested verdicts for each of the accused and Sherman leading the voting. They then voted one by one on Holt's proposed verdicts, as follows:

> Booth, guilty of treasonous conspiracy to kidnap and murder.
> Herold, guilty of treasonous conspiracy to kidnap and murder.
> Atzerodt, guilty of treasonous conspiracy to kidnap and murder.
> Powell, guilty of treasonous conspiracy to kidnap and murder.
> Mary Surratt, guilty of treasonous conspiracy to kidnap and murder.
> John Surratt, guilty (in absentia) of treasonous conspiracy to kidnap and murder.
> O'Laughlen, guilty of treasonous conspiracy to

kidnap and murder.

Arnold, guilty of treasonous conspiracy to kidnap and murder.

Mudd, guilty of treasonous conspiracy to kidnap and murder.

The votes on each were as follows:

As to Booth, Herold, Atzerodt, Powell and John Surratt, the verdicts were unanimous.

As to Mary Surratt, the vote was 7 guilty and 2 not guilty.

As to Dr. Mudd, the vote was 6 guilty and 3 not guilty.

The verdicts on O'Laughlen and Arnold were the closest. The votes broke down to five guilty and four not guilty, with the four dissenters arguing that there was insufficient evidence that either of them were involved after the failure of the kidnapping plot and thus they would vote for a guilty verdict only if the two charges were separated. Holt tried to persuade them otherwise, and Sherman gruffly pronounced that the commissioners ought to follow Holt's suggestions as to guilt and, in his opinion, all should be subjected to harsh punishment.

Separate votes were taken on Holt's recommendation that each and every one of the defendants be sentenced to be hanged by the neck until dead, at such time and place as the President of the United States shall direct. The commission complied.

On Booth, Powell, Atzerodt and Herold, the commission voted unanimously for death by hanging.

On John Surratt, the vote was 8-1, with the dissenter proclaiming "discomfort" with sentencing a man to death without hearing his defense.

Mary Surratt was sentenced to death by a vote of 7-2 and Mudd was sentenced to death by a vote of 6-3, just meeting the 2/3 requirement as specified in the commission rules. In the face of strenuous efforts by Holt, Bingham and General Sherman to convince them, two of the commission members who had voted "not guilty" on O'Laughlen and Arnold ultimately voted in favor of death by hanging, agreeing that even a treasonous conspiracy involving only a plot to kidnap the President of the United States was sufficient to warrant the ultimate penalty.

The next step in the process regarding the conspirators was for Secretary Stanton to deliver the news to President Lincoln and seek his approval of the verdicts and sentences. In all federal criminal cases, the President possesses the constitutional power "to grant Reprieves and Pardons for Offenses against the United States," and in military commission cases, even if not via the pardon power, the commander in chief has final decisionmaking authority on the fate of the accused. Lincoln's was a political decision, not a legal one. He had to decide whether carrying out these sentences was in the best interests of the United States or whether a reprieve of some sort was in order, perhaps to further the cause of a peaceful Reconstruction.

In a meeting on July 1, Stanton proposed that the hangings take place on July 3 to make way for the planned July 4 celebration at which Lincoln was preparing to make a major speech calling for national reconciliation. Lincoln replied: "Gentlemen, I fear that hangings two days hence would sadden our first July 4 celebrations reunified as one nation. They may give rise to an appearance of hurry to judgment born of bloodlust. While I am inclined to sign the warrants—at least for those I consider the primary conspirators—I must nonetheless take time to contemplate these matters. I will have your answer first thing tomorrow."

On the morning of July 2, Lincoln signed death warrants for Booth, Powell, Atzerodt, Herold, and Mary Surratt. The executions were scheduled for 10 o'clock on the morning of July 7, 1865.

With regard to Mudd, Arnold, and O'Laughlen, Lincoln proclaimed: "After consideration of the recommendation of the military commission and in contemplation of the evidence against them, I commit each of these prisoners to the custody of the War Department for life, to be served at Fort Jefferson, with hard labor for the initial twenty years." Fort Jefferson was a military installation on Garden Key, one of the Dry Tortugas, a group of islands at the end of the Florida Keys.

With regard to John Surratt, Lincoln issued a statement that sentencing for John Surratt "will occur when said party is in the custody of the United States Army."

When the news that Mary Surratt had been sentenced to death reached Montreal by wire later that day, word was sent to John Surratt in Joliette, and he immediately decided to return to Washington to try to save his mother from the hangman. He arrived in Washington by train on July 4 in the midst of the Independence Day celebrations and was unable to reach the War Department until July 5, where he arrived unannounced, escorted by Reverdy Johnson and asking to see Stanton. Guards there took him into custody and brought him to the Arsenal Prison where his mother and the others were still being held and where construction of a gallows was underway. The commander of the prison informed Johnson that Stanton was not available. When John Surratt repeatedly asked to see Stanton, the guards merely laughed.

John Surratt's appearance failed to save his mother from the gallows, but it did delay the proceedings by a few days while his petitions for habeas corpus for him and his mother were adjudicated by Justice Andrew Wylie of the Supreme Court of Washington, D.C. After President Lincoln reaffirmed that the wartime suspension of the writ in Washington was still in effect, new death warrants, including John Surratt, were issued for July 10, and at 1 pm that day, under a hot sun, a crowd of around 1,000 people, composed of military men, Members of Congress, journalists and the military commissioners, witnessed the procession of the condemned to the gallows. At approximately 1:25 pm, the supports were knocked away, the drops slammed into the side of the gallows and the six bodies hung suspended in the air. As the Washington Star newspaper put it, "The wretched criminals have been hurried into eternity, and tonight will be hidden in despised graves, loaded with the execrations of mankind."

Part II: Reconstruction

4

PRESIDENTIAL RECONSTRUCTION

On May 29, 1865, less than a week after the Grand Review of the Armies, Lincoln issued two proclamations. The first was a reaffirmation of Lincoln's previous amnesty proclamation, pardoning participants in the rebellion, restoring all of their property except slaves and any property that was subject to an ongoing confiscation proceeding, on the condition that they take the following oath: "I, ... , do solemnly swear (or affirm), in presence of Almighty God, that I will henceforth faithfully support, protect, and defend the Constitution of the United States and the Union of the States thereunder, and that I will in like manner abide by and faithfully support all laws and proclamations which have been made during the existing rebellion with reference to the emancipation of slaves. So help me God."

There were several exceptions to the general pardon including high level civil and military officers of the Confederacy, federal judges who left their posts to aid the rebellion, rebellious graduates of West Point and the Naval Academy and any person who "voluntarily participated in said rebellion and the estimated value of whose taxable property is over $20,000." Those ineligible for the blanket amnesty would have to apply to the President for an individual pardon, with the promise that "such clemency will be liberally extended as may be consistent with the facts of the case and the peace and dignity of the United States."

The second proclamation, entitled "Message Reestablishing Governments in Formerly Rebellious States" was drafted by Seward while he remained in bed recovering from his carriage accident and the wounds suffered in the April 14 attack. Lincoln had visited Seward several times -- under cover of darkness to ensure safety -- each time lying next to Seward in his bed to discuss affairs of state and the progress of the military trial.

Seward agreed with Lincoln's policy of working as quickly as possible to restore normal governance throughout the former Confederacy, and this document set forth a blueprint for Reconstruction of states without functioning loyal governments. The plan, which expressly relied on Lincoln's powers as Commander in Chief of the Army and Navy and chief civil executive officer of the United States, authorized the President to appoint a "provisional governor for each State" who was charged with establishing the framework for a constitutional convention "composed of delegates to be chosen by the people of said State who are loyal to the United States" to take the necessary constitutional steps "to enable such loyal people of the State to restore said State to its constitutional relations to the Federal Government and to present such a republican form of State government as will entitle the State to the guaranty of the United States therefor and its people to protection by the United States against invasion, insurrection, and domestic violence." Although Black suffrage was not explicitly mentioned, it was understood that Blacks were among the loyal people who would participate in the selection of delegates and perhaps even serve as such.

As Lincoln expected, these instructions were greeted coolly by politicians on both sides. Radical Republicans viewed them as allowing Southerners to simply pick up where they left off in 1861, with no real guarantee that any Black American would be allowed to vote, and gave every indication that the preexisting power structure would reemerge with all that implied—including continued oppression of freedmen. Democratic politicians, Southern and Northern alike, were enraged at the opposite suggestion that the federal government could impose a governor and dictate Black suffrage in the Southern states. Lincoln, they thought, had failed to see the lesson of the Civil War: that federal intrusion on state sovereignty was the single greatest threat to national unity. However, most Southerners were not even aware of Lincoln's actions, and those who heard about it were so preoccupied by the need to recover from the loss of the war and the devastation it brought to their region that they didn't really care. Most operated under a sort of stupor of eagerness to do whatever necessary to return to normalcy.

Throughout the remainder of 1865, Lincoln appointed

provisional governors in all of the Southern states and instructed them to facilitate the reinstitution of loyal governments. And in fall 1865, Southern states began holding elections. Although most elected governors who had opposed secession, candidates who had actively supported the Union war effort were universally defeated across the South. In Louisiana, secessionist Democrats took complete control of the state government, vowing to create a government "for the exclusive benefit of the white race."

One by one, as each Southern state held elections, repudiated their Civil War debts, and ratified the Thirteenth Amendment, the President removed provisional governors and allowed each state's elected governor and legislature to take office. This despite the fact that Black suffrage was virtually nonexistent across these states— apparently contradicting one of the conditions that Lincoln had advocated as far back as late 1863, with regards to reconstructing rebel governments.

Lincoln also provided federal government aid to the freed slaves, largely through his strong support for the Freedmen's Bureau.

The Bureau was established by Congress in March 1865, formally named the Bureau of Refugees, Freedmen and Abandoned Lands. Its mission was mixed—in addition to aiding the freedmen with emergency food, shelter and medical attention, it was also tasked with assisting poor Whites (as well as freedmen) to settle on land that had been abandoned during the war, and it had general supervisory authority over the labor market in the former Confederate states. In some states, the local branch of the Freedmen's Bureau tried to help poor laborers by assembling and distributing vacant land to freedmen and some poor Whites. At the same time, Congress chartered the Freedmen's Savings and Trust Company, commonly known as the Freedmen's Bank, to provide financial support for Bureau endeavors. The Bureau was one of the most controversial endeavors in the immediate aftermath of the war because it was perceived by people across the South as designed to grant special privileges to the freed slaves and as a tool to implement the Confiscation Acts that Congress passed to deprive rebel landowners of their property.

The Bureau's founding commissioner, appointed by President Lincoln, was General Oliver Otis Howard, who went on to found Howard University in Washington, D.C. Howard was a great choice. During the Civil War, he had become known as the "Christian General" because of his deep faith and his post-West Point plan to become a minister, which was disrupted by the outbreak of war. He was an ardent abolitionist with a strong belief in equal rights and, more pointedly, full social, economic, and educational opportunities for Black Americans.

One of Howard's first acts, at Lincoln's urging, was to appoint Frederick Douglass to be his Deputy Commissioner. Lincoln would have preferred to make Douglass the head of the Bureau, but Speed and Stanton persuaded Lincoln that legally the Bureau's mission, which would include extensive federal government intervention into traditional state functions, would be legitimate only if it were understood to be military at its core, and thus should be led by a military man and located organizationally in the War Department.

Howard organized the Bureau into fifteen districts, each headed by a district commissioner. Each district covered a former Confederate state, with additional districts for the District of Columbia, and the border states of Maryland, Kentucky, and West Virginia. Under General Howard and Frederick Douglass's energetic leadership, the Bureau accomplished great things in the face of stiff Southern resistance and funding and personnel shortages. The Bureau often came into conflict with the new Southern governments. Although Howard encouraged cooperation with local authorities when it advanced the Bureau's mission, Howard viewed himself as beyond the control of any state or local authority, telling Douglass and his regional commissioners that "my federal military authority gives me unlimited liberty to act to advance the cause of aiding the freedmen. No judicial, legislative or executive authority, save that of our chief magistrate, can hinder me in carrying out my mission."

On July 28, 1865, Howard issued Circular # 13, instructing the regional commissioners, under Douglass's direction, to distribute as much of the apparently vacant Southern land "for the use of loyal refugees and freedmen" as practicable. However, local authorities generally refused to recognize ownership of land in anyone but the prior owners or their relatives, setting up numerous conflicts between the Bureau's register and preexisting county land title records. Throughout the late 1860s and early 1870s, Black Americans were deprived of ownership of land that was reclaimed by former owners or their heirs. If they were lucky, Black occupants were allowed to remain as tenant farmers for wages that barely provided subsistence.

Douglass travelled widely throughout the South, usually with a military escort to ward off hostile Whites, and many freedmen were placed on lands listed in the Bureau's register as abandoned. In the fall of 1865, together with Howard, he visited South Carolina, to explain to groups of freedmen that their land would be returned to its former, White, owners. Douglass could barely stomach the injustice of what was occurring, and after a few days, Howard relented to Douglass's pleas to allow him to leave the tour. On Edisto Island, Howard was greeted by a hostile crowd of well-informed and well-organized freedmen who shouted their disapproval and broke into spiritual hymns as he begged them to cooperate with the return of their lands. Howard was so moved that he promised to do his best to prevent the removal of the freedmen from the land, but he was largely unsuccessful and in the years that followed thousands of Black Americans were evicted from hundreds of thousands of acres that were restored to their pre-Civil War White owners.

The Bureau also found it difficult to overcome local resistance to its attempts to impose fair labor standards. Because most states' Black Codes included provisions requiring freedmen to work under annual contracts with payment contingent on completion, labor mobility was severely restricted and workers were compelled to endure intolerable conditions and constant abuse. Some district commissioners fought this, refusing to approve annual contracts and other draconian provisions, and even attempted to require monthly pay and a minimum wage. Other, less sympathetic, Bureau personnel urged freedmen to submit and even assisted White employers to keep the freedmen in line. For example, one supervisor of labor contracts in South Carolina, Charles Soule, told freedmen "on a plantation, the owner of the place, the head man, gives all the orders. Whatever he tells you to do, you must do, and cheerfully." In Mississippi, Assistant Commissioner Samuel Thomas issued Circular # 2 on January 2, 1866, instructing freedmen to honor their contracts, no matter how unfair they seemed, assuring them that hard work would help them achieve complete freedom:

> . . . Your contracts were explained to you, and their sacredness impressed upon you again and again. You know that when you make a contract you are bound to give all the labor for which your employer agrees to pay. Efforts have been made by my officers to compel you to perform labor according to agreements, that employers might have no excuse for failing to do their part.

> The time has arrived for you to contract for another year's labor. I wish to impress upon you the importance of doing this at once. You know that if a crop of cotton is raised, the work must be begun soon, and the hands employed for the year. If you do not contract with the men who wish to employ you, what do you propose to do? You cannot live without work of some kind. Your houses and lands belong to the white people; and you cannot expect that they will allow you to live on them in idleness. It would be wrong for them to do so; and no officer of the Government will protect you in it. If you stay on the plantations where you are, you must agree to work for the owners of them. If not, move out of the way, and give place to more faithful laborers. . . .

> You must be obedient to the law. I do not think the people of Mississippi have made all laws that relate to you as they ought to have done. But, even if there be some things denied to you as yet, which you wish to gain, you cannot get them by disobedience and idleness. You cannot make

people treat you well by showing them that you do not deserve it. If you wish for rights, do right yourselves. If you desire privileges, show that they may be safely intrusted [sic] to you. Such a course, with patience, will make you happy and prosperous.

When it did not involve depriving Whites of property or privileges, the Bureau was much more successful at providing aid. The Bureau provided millions of meals and helped with the construction of thousands of homes, often hiring local labor, which had the additional advantage of putting people to work. Howard and Douglass both placed a high priority on education, and the Bureau established and constructed thousands of schools for Black Americans across the South. Douglass would often travel to localities where schools were opening to encourage children and their families to devote themselves to education. In dozens of speeches, themes of which were later crystallized into his famous 1872 "Self-Made Men" speech, Douglass urged freedmen to shed the attitude of victimhood and aspire to a brighter future for themselves, their families, and their communities. Douglass's proposed pathway to success was simple: hard work, education, and devotion.

Howard and Douglass's mission did not stop at the primary or secondary school level. They also worked to establish institutions of higher learning for Black Americans. Howard convinced Congress to allocate funds to establish a university in Washington, D.C. which was appropriately named Howard University. In Nashville, General Clinton B. Fisk, the Bureau assistant commissioner for Tennessee, worked together with one of his deputies, John Ogden, and two White Northern missionaries, the Reverends Erastus Cravath and Edward Smith, to establish a college that was open to Black Americans. Named Fisk College, its first classes were held in 1866 in Union Army barracks under Fisk's control, with Frederick Douglass attending an opening ceremony that was highlighted by Douglass's proclamation that schools like Fisk were like a "sunrise on the distant horizon, full of promise for a brighter day ahead." Cravath worked for the remainder of his life to further education at all levels for Black Americans and poor Whites. In 1871, Smith went to Minnesota at the federal government's request to investigate and report on the situation of American Indians there, and this trip resulted in his appointment in 1873 as United States Commissioner of Indian Affairs. Later, Smith was appointed president of Howard University, but he died after becoming ill on a missionary trip to Africa before he actually assumed that position.

Another of Douglass's strategies was to visit colleges to urge Black students to use their educations for the good of their fellow people of color. In the late 1860s and 1870s, he made numerous trips to places like Wilberforce College in Ohio, the Hampton Institute in Virginia, Fisk College, and Howard University to make inspirational speeches and recruit teachers for his Southern schools. As a result, by the middle of the 1870s, hundreds of college-educated young Black men and women were educating and providing role models for the children of former slaves throughout the former Confederacy. Howard was the premier institution of higher education for Black Americans at the time, and it was sending graduates to teach at numerous schools and colleges across the country that were being established to satisfy the growing demand among Black Americans for education.

5

DETERIORATION AND AGITATION

Deputy Commissioner of the Freedmen's Bureau, Douglass wrote weekly, sometimes daily, letters to Lincoln and Howard, apprising them of the situation in Southern states. His early reports were often pessimistic, reporting that the lives of freedmen had changed little since emancipation. While children may have been provided suitable educational opportunities, many families could not afford the short-term opportunity cost of sending children of working age to school, due to the loss of the minimal wages they might earn or their contributions to the family farming enterprise. The adults themselves barely earned wages. They often had no choice but to return to work for their former owners, commonly as sharecroppers. As sharecroppers, they were subjected to the same corporal punishment they had sustained as slaves, and in many places they were prevented by the Black Codes and social customs from improving their condition by opening businesses or acquiring property of their own. For those Black Americans who had not been previously enslaved, the end of the Civil War became a sad irony as they were denied professional and social opportunities that had previously been open to them, especially in Louisiana, where the gens de couleur had occupied a social middle tier. Like many other Black Americans and Republicans, by late 1865 Douglass urged Lincoln to send more troops south to pacify resistance and safeguard the rights of the freedmen. As general-in-chief, Grant was receiving similar messages from military leaders across the South. Without a stronger show of force, adherence to local laws and customs was too strong for the Bureau and others sympathetic to the plight of Black Americans to overcome.

The opponents of Lincoln's lenient program of presidential Reconstruction were also rightly outraged by the political and legal results it produced. One of the first acts of each reestablished Southern legislature was to adopt a new Black Code which severely restricted the legal rights of the freedmen and, in some cases, all people of color regardless of their pre-war status. For example, Mississippi's Black Code and Vagrancy Law, adopted in late 1865, empowered local officials to "apprentice" impoverished "minor freedmen, free Negroes and mullatoes . . . to some competent and suitable person, on such terms as the Probate court shall direct." Forced apprenticeships had long been used in North America to enslave American Indians and others. To eliminate any confusion about the purpose of the apprenticeships, the code provided that "the former owner of said minors shall have preference" and that males would be "bound by indenture" until age twenty-one, and females until age eighteen. The Mississippi code authorized the "masters" of the "apprentices" to capture runaways and bring them to the Probate court for punishment, and it also granted permission for masters to administer corporal punishment on their apprentices. All expected courts to take the word of a White putative master over the protestations of a freedman claiming that he was not subject to apprenticeship.

The code also made it a crime for any person to "entice away" or employ any apprentice without the master's consent. Another section of the Mississippi code contained a vagrancy law which allowed for the arrest of any "freedman, free Negro or mullato" without means of support, and also included imprisonment for "every freedman, free Negro or mullatto between the ages of eighteen and sixty years" who fails to pay an annual poll tax. In a section entitled "Civil Rights of Freedmen," the code granted "freedmen, free Negroes and Mullatoes" the right to sue and be sued in state court and to acquire and own personal property. Black Americans were not given the right to rent or lease any real property, except that in incorporated cities and towns, the local government could allow it. Black Americans were required to get a license to be preachers and they were not allowed to possess weapons, including firearms and large knives, or "intoxicating liquors." Any convicted "freedman, free Negro or mullatoe" who failed to pay any fines levied by a court within five days of conviction "shall be hired out by the sheriff or other officer, at public outcry, to any white person who will pay said fine and costs, and take said convict for the shortest time." Florida's code was simpler, prescribing up to one year of service for Black Americans found guilty of vagrancy. South Carolina adopted a similar code, and included a prohibition on Black Americans engaging in many skilled occupations without an expensive license. Many of the codes established harsh penalties for criminal conduct by

Black Americans including, for example, capital punishment for the theft of cotton in South Carolina. Despite President Lincoln's exhortations, no Southern state granted voting rights to freedmen or any other Black Americans and many of them expressly denied the right.

Most of the codes also created special mandatory rules for labor contracts entered into by Black Americans. One common provision was forfeiture of all pay if the worker left before the end of the term, usually a full year. Many White employers, former slaveowners, took advantage of this by making the situation as the end of the contract approached intolerable, virtually driving their laborers away before payment was due. Even where no laws authorized it, impoverished former slaves across the South were arrested for vagrancy and sent to work for their former masters. Freedmen were often compelled to work for their former masters in barely tolerable conditions by virtue of a custom of not hiring freedmen without their former owners' permission. Violation of this custom sometimes led to violence including the forcible retrieval of the laborer and even, in at least one case in Louisiana, the murder of the offending White employer for "disloyalty" to the White supremacist regime. By and large, the Black Codes and associated customs had the purpose and effect of recreating as much of the slave system as possible without transgressing the letter of the Thirteenth Amendment.

As these events unfolded, Lincoln and Grant felt trapped by similar dilemmas. Each was committed to equal rights and opportunities for all regardless of color, but they did not want to inflame tensions so soon after the war. Lincoln remained anxious to restore Southern state autonomy as quickly as possible, and he felt that his first priority should be rebuilding the Southern economy. He was also afraid of losing support from moderates and conservatives in Congress for his program of Reconstruction, including readmission of the rebellious states and resources for economic development.

Lincoln's closest advisors in his Cabinet were divided on how to respond to the deterioration of the situation for the freedmen and on Lincoln's plans for quick Reconstruction. Speed and Stanton were most hawkish, opposing Lincoln's proposals to readmit rebel states quickly and vocally urging Lincoln to act to protect the interests of freedmen. On the other side, Seward, who spent the second half of 1865 recuperating at the Soldier's Home, Lincoln's residence away from the White House, supported quick reunion and leniency, warning Lincoln that harsh treatment would delay national reunification and could, over time, even lead to renewed rebellion. In their long chats, with Lincoln stretched out next to Seward in bed, Seward insisted that Southern White resistance to any significant change in the social or political status quo would be too great for the federal government to overcome. Seward's views generally prevailed with Lincoln, partly because he had the President's ear more than the others but mainly because his views were more consistent with Lincoln's own moderate inclinations.

Lincoln's replies to Douglass's entreaties for military support for Bureau activities were noncommittal. Lincoln professed "support and gratitude for the honorable endeavors you and General Howard are undertaking on behalf of your people," but promised nothing concrete. This incensed Douglass. He reacted by firing off letters to Members of Congress—including the ever-outspoken Charles Sumner—and to his long-time correspondent Salmon P. Chase, now Chief Justice of the Supreme Court. Sumner needed no prodding from Douglass; he had already been calling on the President virtually every week urging him to take bold action to secure equality and security for Black Americans.

Chase was also a sympathetic audience to Douglass's pleas for other reasons, which went beyond his longstanding commitment to equal rights for all. Chase had been a charter member of Lincoln's "team of rivals," was banished in 1864 from his position as Secretary of the Treasury to the Supreme Court because he had been a thorn in Lincoln's side and remained a political rival. Chase never got over the feeling that he should have been the Republican nominee in 1860, and his presidential ambitions ended only with his death in 1873. As Treasury Secretary, Chase masterfully steered the country though the financial and economic difficulties of the Civil War. When Douglass and Chase began corresponding in 1850, Chase wholeheartedly agreed with Douglass on abolition but suggested that the two races, White and Black, could not coexist. Therefore, Chase thought that upon the end of slavery, Black Americans might choose to be "carried back to Africa" and that "the British West Indies offer a most inviting field for colored enterprise. Jamaica, with her cheap & fertile soil and delicious climate is especially attractive."

Chase's views evolved, though, perhaps under Douglass's influence. By the end of his service in Lincoln's Cabinet, Chase was among the strongest of the Radical Republicans, insisting on equal rights for Black Americans in all matters, including universal male suffrage, and opposing the idea of resettlement of Black Americans in Africa or on the islands. In Cabinet meetings, he was vocally critical of Lincoln's plans for reconstructing the Southern states, which was one of the reasons Lincoln was happy to be rid of him.

In his current position as Chief Justice, Chase could not speak publicly about Douglass's disappointing portrait of Southern life, but in private he was furious, confiding to those close to him that justice for the freedmen depended on the 1868 election of a President who shared his views. Kate Chase Sprague, Chief Justice Chase's daughter now married to Rhode Island governor William Sprague, was privy to Chase's views. She was a well-known and popular figure in Washington, and had long been her father's closest confidant and advisor. She shared his belief that Chase, not Abraham Lincoln, should have been elected President in 1860 and 1864.

Although Douglass's reports did not move Lincoln or Grant to take action other than to urge the Bureau to do whatever it could, many Members of Congress were not so constrained. Leading Radical Republicans including Thaddeus Stevens in the House and Charles Sumner in the Senate repeatedly seized the floor of their respective chambers to urge passage of sweeping legislation to increase the powers and the funding for the Bureau. They both argued that state and local governments, having already proven themselves unreformed and unrepentant, should be stripped of authority in favor of federal administration under the auspices of the Bureau. Sumner, especially, took aim at Lincoln, unleashing a torrent of criticism not heard from him since his notorious 1856 attack on South Carolina Senator Andrew Butler which led to the infamous Southern retaliation in the form of a severe caning on the Senate floor at the hands of South Carolina Representative Preston Brooks, Butler's cousin. At one point Sumner said he would "favor sending the gangly Illinois rail splitter back to the wilderness from whence he came if it were not that his replacement, our traitorous Vice President, would be even more horrendous." Citing the same potential that Andrew Johnson would replace Lincoln, Thaddeus Stevens in the House proclaimed, "Although I do think that the President has usurped the power of the whole people through his unwillingness to enable the execution of national law throughout the South, I would consent to invoking the awful power of impeachment only if we felt resolved to remove his chief underling as well, for his is certainly no less faulty than the Chief Magistrate."

This was a striking shift in sentiment after the outpouring of outrage at Booth's assassination attempt, and illustrates how volatile sentiment had become since the end of the war.

Further aggravating the mood in Congress was the makeup of the delegations that many of the reconstructed states sent to Congress in late 1865. The vast majority of Representatives elected to Congress in the deep South had served the Confederacy or rebellious state governments in one way or another, as was perhaps inevitable. The greatest affront came from Georgia, where the legislature selected former Vice President of the Confederacy Alexander Stephens to be a U.S. Senator. Given the lack of Black suffrage across the former Confederacy and the composition of the Southern delegations, it should have come as no surprise that these newly elected members of the Thirty-Ninth Congress were not seated. This action was accomplished via an overwhelming vote of the Republican caucus before Congress reconvened and it was confirmed by the simple expedient of the omission of these putative Members' names when the Clerk of the House called the Roll. Similar action was taken in the Senate, and the consensus among the Radicals was that they would not seat anyone sent from a state without suffrage for all, regardless of race.

The conflict between Lincoln and the Radical Republicans in

Congress touched fundamental, unresolved issues in American constitutional law and tradition, no less weighty than Southern states' pre-Civil War claim of power to nullify federal law within their borders. Although he supported the aspirations of freedmen and other people of color for equal legal rights and economic opportunity, Lincoln's instincts, personal, and political, were moderate. He hoped that national reconciliation could be achieved with minimal disturbance to Southern life both because he sympathized with Southern Whites who saw Radical policies as threatening their way of life and because he recognized that politically, extreme actions were likely to provoke extreme reactions, and the last thing the country needed, in his view, was prolonged regional turmoil. He consistently attempted to thread the needle between supporting the ideals embodied in the Declaration of Independence and facilitating national unity. That is why, in his April 11 speech and his proposal for readmitting Louisiana, he applauded the proposed Louisiana constitution for allowing the legislature to grant partial Black suffrage. He had not yet advocated universal Black male suffrage, much as he viewed it as the ideal. It was only later that Lincoln began to embrace the views of the Radical wing of his party.

Lincoln's reluctance to impose Black suffrage as a condition for Reconstruction was informed by two primary concerns, one of principle and one more practical. As a matter of principle, Lincoln represented the middle of the spectrum on state's rights. He believed that the Union was inviolable and that federal law was supreme, but he also adhered to traditional views concerning the distribution of authority between the state and federal governments. Decisions on internal matters such as the organization of state governmental institutions, voting rights, contract and property rights, and regulation for general health and welfare were for the states to make, with federal authority over interstate and international trade, national defense, and other areas specifically allocated by the Constitution to the federal government. Once his war powers ran out, Lincoln understood that the federal government lacked the power to abolish slavery without a constitutional amendment to that effect. Because he viewed voting qualifications and contract law as matters traditionally left to the states, federal imposition of suffrage requirements and fair labor standards was also beyond

Lincoln's traditional view of federal jurisdiction, although he saw a federal role during Reconstruction founded upon the vestigial war powers undergirding the Freedmen's Bureau. Lincoln's practical concern involved restoration of normalcy as quickly and smoothly as possible. There were destitute people to feed, clothe, and shelter, as well as children and young adults to educate, economic development to support, conflicts with Indians to resolve, issues of international trade to confront, and unknown challenges likely to lie around the corner. These practical problems pushed Lincoln to favor the quickest and least disruptive return to normalcy even if this meant compromising principles that in the immediate wake of emancipation seemed more pressing than any practical concern. Lincoln had the nagging sense that in the long run, peace and stability would benefit everyone, and he understood that stability sometimes requires compromising on even fundamental principles while not wholly abandoning them, and he was willing to make such compromises for the good of the nation.

Radicals like Sumner and Stevens were unwilling to compromise their sacred principles. They viewed Lincoln's soft attitude toward the rebellious states as a betrayal of the Civil War struggle. They could not understand why Lincoln would have thought it was necessary for so many Americans to die in the war if he was just going to let the Southern states restore the status quo ante, minus the actual institution of slavery. As the discouraging reports from Douglass and others continued to arrive, Sumner decided to take his case directly to the President. He arrived at the Oval Office on a bright cold day in January, 1866, shortly after the beginning of the congressional session. Sumner had been excluded from the Joint Committee on Reconstruction—the Committee of Fifteen, as it had become known—and this had made his already short temper even shorter.

Lincoln could see from the look on Sumner's face as he approached the presidential desk that something big was about to come out of Sumner's mouth. With barely a greeting or acknowledgment that he was in the presence of the President of the United States, Sumner launched into a tirade, angrily accusing the President of wasting the opportunity to do justice for "our Negro fellow citizens" concluding with the charge that Lincoln was "bringing dishonor to the memory of the men we lost in the noble struggle against slavery." Sumner's reference to the Civil War dead was beyond what Lincoln expected even from the ever-belligerent Sumner, and Lincoln was tempted to respond in kind, but he restrained himself. His reply was measured and firm, lacking in any hint of the humor that Lincoln often injected into conversation even at the most serious moments.

Lincoln said, "Mr. Sumner, I admire you for your tenacious advocacy on behalf of our least fortunate citizens, and I hope you understand that my administration will do all that it is able to improve their status and give them a chance to enjoy the blessings they rightly share with all Americans. I cannot, however, promise that progress will be as swift and certain as you desire, even as I pledge support for the efforts of General Howard and Mr. Douglass and the aspirations of members of our party across the Southern states. I trust that you will work with your colleagues in the Senate to provide General Howard with the resources he needs to accomplish his goals, and I believe that we will be gratified at the improvements in the lives of our Negro citizens that we shall be privileged to witness."

Sumner, of course, was not satisfied, stating that Congress has its own ideas and vowing that the rebellious states will not be represented in Congress until major changes are made in the plans for Reconstruction. "I am sure, Mr. President, that legislation will be arriving on your desk in due course, and I do hope that by signing it, you will join with Congress to provide justice to our Negro brethren." The opening official salvo in congressional efforts to counteract the President's lenient policies was a resolution establishing a Joint Committee on Reconstruction. Over the next few years, this Joint Committee would evolve into the architect of Congress's effort to overcome what became known as Lincoln's policy of "Presidential Reconstruction" which, true to Sumner's promise, produced a series of civil rights bills that, if enacted and enforced, would have brought about a more radical Reconstruction than envisioned by the President.

6

THE CULPEPER FAMILY

As conditions for the freedmen in the South deteriorated, Lincoln allowed Grant to make decisions about the necessity for troops and the positioning thereof. There was a great deal of military activity throughout the South even if much of it was simply reoccupying military installations that had been taken over by the Confederates after secession. Lincoln was determined to resume normal relations with Southern governments as much as possible, with or without Congress's cooperation. One of Lincoln's favorite programs was establishing land grant agricultural colleges. After conferring with Seward and his new Secretary of the Interior James Harlan, Lincoln decided to accelerate the program and establish at least one new college in each of the Southern states before the end of his second term. Not only would this program bring Southern states further back into the national fold, it would help restore agricultural production that had been devastated by the war.

James Harlan, a friend and political ally of Lincoln, agreed with him that pressing the issue of Black suffrage would be divisive and posed a serious obstacle to the Reconstruction of the Union. He had also become Lincoln's close personal friend, and Harlan's daughter Mary was courted by Lincoln's son Robert, whom she married in 1868. Later in life, President and Mrs. Lincoln made summer visits to the Harlan home in Mount Pleasant, Iowa, where Mary and Robert spent most summers, and the elder Lincolns delighted in the opportunity to spend time with their grandchildren.

Harlan viewed himself as a reformer, and when he took over at the Interior Department one of his first actions was to fire staffers who seemed to always be absent from their desks. He also purged the department of anyone who had expressed disloyal views concerning the crises of secession and Civil War. At one desk he even came upon a clerk's manuscript of poems, entitled Leaves of Grass. After reading a few pages, which he found perverse and ungodly, Harlan had the clerk, Walt Whitman, fired, despite

Whitman's protestations that he was a hard worker and had been spending his spare time volunteering as a nurse in local military hospitals. Later, after Leaves of Grass became a bestseller, Harlan insisted that he fired Whitman over concerns with the quality of his government work, not due to the content of his poems. Whitman became one of the country's most beloved poets despite his virulently racist views about Black Americans and American Indians.

It soon became clear that the Southern states would not allow Black Americans to attend colleges under their control, certainly not together with White students. Therefore, Harlan, with Lincoln's consent, decided to support two colleges in some states. For example, in Louisiana, Southern University in New Orleans was paired with Louisiana State University in Baton Rouge, the former serving Black students and the latter limited to White students. Similarly, the University of Arkansas was reserved for White students while the University of Arkansas at Pine Bluffs was open to Black students. In Northern states, it was usually not necessary to establish two schools. The University of Wisconsin, which was founded in 1848, was designated as Wisconsin's land grant university in 1866, which required it to establish its agriculture school that same year. In 1909, in recognition of his contribution to the University, a statue of Abraham Lincoln was erected near the top of Bascom Hill, home to the University's earliest buildings, including North Hall, a dormitory that housed Union soldiers during their Civil War training. The program was generally successful although it did little to reduce Southern states' hostility to the Lincoln government, and they did not similarly honor Lincoln with statues at their land grant schools.

Reconstruction—both political and economic—occupied most of the government's attention throughout 1866. Luckily, no major international crises occurred. The worst was probably tension between Great Britain and the United States over the Irish Fenian invasions of Canada that were launched from the northern United States after the failure of an effort by Irish emigres in the United States to supply weapons to rebels at home in Ireland. More difficult for the administration was the ongoing fighting with Indian tribes, including numerous clashes over the territorial limits established by the Fort Laramie Treaties. Lincoln shared the predominant view that the United States government had a right to occupy Indian land through conquest, and throughout his two terms the expansion of White settlement and the confinement of Indians to reservations continued. Lincoln extended his humanitarian instincts to the Indians, for example by issuing pardons to most of the Indian men condemned to death in 1862 during the war with the Dakota Tribe in Minnesota, allowing only thirty-eight of 303 captives to be hanged. But longstanding corruption in the Indian Office persisted throughout Lincoln's administration, hampering the distribution of aid that Lincoln favored. Fighting in 1866 culminated in a December battle known as the Fetterman Fight, named for Captain William Fetterman. After numerous attacks on U.S. Army forts and White settlers, a group of ten warriors from a confederation of Tribes tempted Fetterman to disobey his orders and follow them into a trap they had laid in a valley, resulting in the deaths of eighty-one U.S. soldiers, with estimates of Indian dead as low as thirteen and as high as 160. Rumors circulated that Fetterman and another officer had shot each other in the head to avoid capture, but in truth Fetterman's throat had been slit, and that was identified by the Army as the official cause of his death.

As resistance to Lincoln's lenient Reconstruction plans grew in Congress, the Joint Reconstruction Committee got to work on legislation to combat what the states were doing. The Radicals refused to accept the traditional crabbed view of federal power over individual rights. Their view, shared by many congressional Republicans, was that once it was ratified, the Thirteenth Amendment's grant to Congress of the power to "enforce this article by appropriate legislation" authorized Congress to pass sweeping legislation attacking all vestiges of the slave system. State racial restrictions on the mobility of labor, the ownership of property and the right to bring suit to enforce their contracts constituted continuing "badges and incidents of slavery" that Congress had power to eradicate, even if it meant legislating in areas that had previously been reserved to the states.

Even before ratification of the slavery-ending amendment, Members of Congress began pushing legislation to counteract the

Black Codes. Massachusetts Senator Henry Wilson put forward an initiative in December, 1865, to prohibit state denial of full "privileges and immunities" based on race. Wilson would likely be a better known historical figure if it were not for the notoriety of his larger-than-life Massachusetts colleague Charles Sumner. In 1861, as chairman of the Senate's Military Affairs Committee, Wilson skillfully steered important war-related legislation through the Senate, and when the Senate's session ended he returned to Massachusetts and quickly raised and equipped an entire regiment of volunteers, which he commanded in the early days of the war.

Wilson argued that his initiative was within the federal war power. It did not get serious consideration due to doubts about Congress's power to act, at least until ratification of the Thirteenth Amendment. Although ratification was certified only a few days after Wilson introduced his proposal, it was not revived. Four other proposals, made in January, 1866, received much greater attention in Congress. The first was a bill granting Black suffrage in the District of Columbia. The House was generally in agreement that suffrage should be extended, but there was disagreement over just how far. The controversy did not involve questions of federalism or Congress's power, since that body undoubtedly possessed full legislative control over the District. Radicals advocated simple universal suffrage for all males over the age of twenty-one while more conservative Republicans pushed for racially neutral qualified suffrage, granting voting rights only to those people who could read and write, were taxpayers, or had served in the military. The conservative view was defeated by a coalition of those favoring complete suffrage for Black Americans and those opposed to disenfranchising Whites who had voted in the past but would not meet the new qualifications. The bill passed the House easily but was never taken up by the Senate, where attention for the remainder of the first half of 1866 focused on Reconstruction of the Southern states.

The first proposal to come out of the Joint Reconstruction Committee was a bill to extend the Freedmen's Bureau and ratify some of its more controversial practices. Although Democrats attacked it as an unconstitutional interference with the internal affairs of the states, the bill passed the House of Representatives by a wide margin, but the 30-18 vote in the Senate was less than veto-proof. In addition to the extension of authority and funding to the Bureau for two more years, the bill added two notable provisions. One authorized the Bureau, "where the local courts do not treat all claimants the same as white citizens" to "establish tribunals to grant suitable remedies in civil cases brought by or against black citizens." The other authorized the military, in consultation with the Bureau, to take "all necessary steps to ensure that the civil rights of freedmen are respected." These provisions essentially ratified practices in which Howard and his assistant commissioners, with the help of the occupying federal military when necessary, were already engaged. Additionally, the bill confirmed the Bureau's power to distribute abandoned and vacant land to the freedmen and explicitly asserted the supremacy of title granted under federal authority.

Even before the bill extending the Freedmen's Bureau reached Lincoln's desk, opposing forces lobbied the President fiercely over whether he would sign the bill. Lincoln himself had mixed feelings. On the one hand, he very much wanted to help the freedmen and thought the Bureau was doing a good job. On the other hand, he was concerned that the Bureau was interfering with affairs that should be left to the states, and he feared that the Bureau, and the political loyalty it was spawning, might soon become an impediment to restoration of Southern local autonomy and provoke violent resistance. Democrats and some conservative Republicans howled at the bill's suggestion that local land ownership laws were subject to federal override and rejected the notion that a federal military tribunal could supersede state civil courts on matters touching contract and property disputes. Seward urged Lincoln to veto the bill and send a message promising to sign a bill that funded the Bureau's activities, provided help for Black veterans to secure military pensions and material aid such as food, clothing, shelter, medical aid, and educational opportunities without interfering with traditional state functions. Seward suggested that Lincoln could deflect some criticism by citing concerns over the cost of the expanded program.

Lincoln was inclined to agree with Seward, but felt that he could not reject the bill without speaking in person to General Howard and his Deputy Frederick Douglass. Conveniently, Douglass had already traveled to Washington from South Carolina, where he had been working on a schools project, to help Howard lobby for the bill's passage, so Lincoln's request that they come see him reached both at Bureau Headquarters in the War Department. Douglass and Howard arrived at the White House in the morning of February 18, 1866, and were immediately shown into the Oval Office. Douglass was by now a familiar face at the White House, having come a long way from the day in March, 1865 when, with an invitation in hand, he was refused entry to a White House Inauguration reception until the President himself interceded. Lincoln greeted the two men with a big smile and a friendly handshake and then, after hearing from them briefly about the Bureau's activities, turned the conversation to the bill.

Lincoln began by frankly acknowledging his doubts about the bill in its present form. He expressed grave concerns about federal intervention into matters of contract and property law and he asked whether the bill's appropriation of funding for economic aid and education might not be sufficient. Howard answered Lincoln with the old saw that if you give a man a fish, you satisfy today's hunger, but if you teach the man to fish, you feed him for a lifetime. Mr. President, said Howard, the bill as it stands provides us with the tools we need to enable our charges to become self-sufficient so that we may happily go out of existence at the earliest possible time. Without intervention into the economic matters, the freedmen would be doomed to a life not much distinguishable from their situation before the war.

The President turned to Douglass. "What's your view Fred?"

Douglass answered by recounting a story of a family of six named Culpeper he encountered in South Carolina. "Before the war, they had lived as slaves on a farm near Culpeper Virginia, but when the war broke out their owner and his family moved to live with cousins near Conway, South Carolina, taking their slaves and animals with them. In Virginia, Mrs. Virginia Culpeper, the mother, had been a house servant and the family seamstress while Mr. Randolph Culpeper, the father, managed the stables, and the family lived together in relative comfort. In South Carolina, the

63

parents and older children were put to work in the fields, and all were thrown into overcrowded slave cabins that were alternatively sweltering and freezing, depending on the time of year. The parents were frequently rented to other farmers in the area, leaving the children lonely and fending for themselves. The oldest son, a boy of 11, was periodically sent to a quarry to engage in backbreaking work. In the fall of 1864, the Confederate Army took slaves, male and female, who were old enough to the front lines to assist the infantry's vain attempts to hold off the advancing Union army, and one of their daughters had been wounded and nearly bled to death."

Douglass continued. "At war's end, the family was reunited and provided by the Bureau with a small plot of land, some chickens for eggs and meat and a goat for milk. The Bureau helped them build a small house which they furnished nicely, paying in part by selling clothing made by Mrs. Culpeper. They planted corn and squash, with seed provided by the Bureau. In late summer, when the crops were nearly ready for harvest, a nephew of the former owner of the land petitioned the Horry County Court in Conway to recognize his title to the land as the rightful heir of the former owners who had died childless in the war, the husband in the Second Battle of Fort Wagner and the wife of dysentery in Charleston where she moved when her husband enlisted. The county judge refused to hear testimony from Randolph, declaring that 'no Negro may speak in this courtroom in a case against a white person,' and decided that the claimant's state land title prevailed over the deed the Bureau had provided the family. The new owner allowed them to retain a small share of the crop, but he took their house, saying the crop was not sufficient to pay rent on such a nice dwelling, and forced the entire family to move to a small former slave cabin connected to the barn. Their new home was cold and cramped. I met the family while visiting a Bureau school which some of their children were attending. When this honorable man recounted the story, I had the sense that his dreams had been crushed by what had happened to him, and knowing of our friendship, he asked me to 'talk to Mr. Lincoln to see if he could help.' Virginia Culpeper was holding a baby in swaddling, and Randolph introduced this beautiful infant as 'Abraham William Lincoln Culpeper,' named in honor of you and your beloved lost son Willie."

Douglass concluded, "This is what we face, Mr. President, without power to override local laws. Every time my people find themselves able to stand on their own two feet, they are knocked back down by the forces endeavoring to put them where they were before the war."

The President sat quietly listening to Douglass until the mention of Willie, whose death in 1862 still left a dull ache in Lincoln's heart. Lincoln looked away, and after Douglass concluded, he remained silent for a good long bit, eyes closed. It was unclear whether he was thinking of Willie or the bill, but he was evidently in deep contemplation.

As he turned back to face Howard and Douglass, he said, "Thank you gentlemen. Your views are of great help and always welcome in this place as long as I am here."

The next morning, Lincoln signed the Freedmen's Bill and sent a message to Howard and Douglass pledging his support and urging them to continue their efforts. Although local resistance still posed serious obstacles, over the next few years the Bureau improved the lives and future prospects for innumerable freedmen and poor Whites, who received land, supplies, schooling, and other support as part of the effort to rebuild the Southern economy and infrastructure. And the Culpeper family thrived.

7

THE CIVIL RIGHTS ACT

Around the same time that the D.C. suffrage proposal emerged from the House committee with jurisdiction over District affairs, the Joint Committee put forward another proposal for a constitutional amendment regarding Black suffrage throughout the country. In addition to their views on the justice of their cause, Republicans understood the political benefits that would inure to their party if the franchise were extended everywhere to Black Americans. The committee quickly determined that any national reform would require a constitutional amendment, but the majority of the committee would not support a straightforward prohibition on racial discrimination in voting. Opposition had two main bases. First, there was genuine concern over the extension of federal power to such a basic traditional state function. Second, there was also the strong sense that it might not be practically feasible to enforce voting rights for Black Americans in the volatile conditions across much of the South. There was also the embarrassment that not all Northern states allowed Black Americans to vote. In fact, a referendum to grant Black Americans the right to vote in Connecticut failed in October, 1865, leaving it as the only New England state not allowing Black suffrage. The proposal that emerged from the committee focused on an area that Congress felt much more comfortable regulating, namely representation in Congress. The proposal that would have been the Fourteenth Amendment to the Constitution had it been enacted provided, in part, that:

> whenever the elective franchise shall be denied or abridged in any state on account of race or color, all persons of such race or color shall be excluded from the basis of representation.

In other words, the number of Blacks living in states that denied them the right to vote would not count toward the states' population when the number of seats in Congress was determined. Thus, rather than remove racial restrictions on voting, the proposal would pressure states to do so themselves. Reduced representation in the House of Representatives would not only decrease their power in the national legislature, but it would also minimize Southern influence in presidential elections given that the number of electors is the same as each state's number of Senators and Representatives.

Despite unanimous opposition from Democrats and grumbling among some Republicans that it did not go far enough by actually granting suffrage, this proposal won quick and easy passage in the House of Representatives. In the Senate, though, it ran into the buzz saw that was Charles Sumner. Sumner realized that the proposed amendment tacitly recognized that states have power to deny citizens the right to vote based on race, provided that they were willing to accept reduced representation in Congress.

When pressed to accept this as a compromise—as a first step in the right direction—Sumner proclaimed, "I had hoped that the day of compromise with wrong had passed. A moral principle cannot be compromised."

The proposal was defeated on the floor of the Senate on March 16, 1866, leaving the issue of Black suffrage at least temporarily in the hands of state governments.

More successful was the Joint Committee's effort to craft and pass a Civil Rights Act that would attack some of the provisions of the Black Codes. The Civil Rights Act was written by Senator Lyman Trumbull of Illinois, Chairman of the Judiciary Committee, a moderate but prominent Republican figure, and presented to the Committee for approval, which it granted with little dissent. Trumbull had an ever-evolving attitude about racial matters. For example, he once proclaimed that the Republican Party was a "White man's party," but later he became a vocal advocate for equal rights, and a strong supporter of the efforts of the Freedmen's Bureau. His bill included far reaching provisions that would overrule the Dred Scott decision, invalidate the Black Codes, and even override some discriminatory laws outside the South. After some amendments, the bill that emerged provided:

All persons born in the United States and not

subject to any foreign power, excluding Indians not taxed, are hereby declared to be citizens of the United States;

Such citizens, of every race and color, any law, statute, ordinance, regulation, or custom to the contrary notwithstanding, shall have the same right in every State and Territory in the United States, to make and enforce contracts, to sue, be parties, and give evidence, to inherit, purchase, lease, sell, hold, and convey real and personal property, and to the full and equal benefit of all laws and proceedings for the security of persons and property, as is enjoyed by white citizens;

And such citizens shall be subject to like punishment, pains, and penalties, as white citizens, and to none other;

No person shall knowingly and willfully obstruct, hinder, or prevent any officer or other person from enforcing the Act.

Moreover, any person acting "under color of any law, statute, ordinance, regulation, or custom" found to have subjected any "inhabitant of any State or Territory" to a violation of the Act was declared to be guilty of a misdemeanor, punishable by a fine up to $1000 and imprisonment of up to one year. A similar penalty was provided against any officer or other person who might "knowingly and willfully obstruct, hinder, or prevent any officer or other person from enforcing the Act." The federal district courts were granted exclusive jurisdiction over violations of the Act, and federal jurisdiction was also granted over cases alleging violations of the Freedmen's Bureau Act. The bill also empowered and required federal marshals and deputy marshals to enforce it. A refusal to do so entitled the victim of the alleged violation of the Act to a bounty of $1000 assessed against the recalcitrant federal marshal. Finally, the Act granted the President of the United States power to direct federal marshals, judges and district attorneys to attend enforcement proceedings at a place designated by the President, and it authorized the President "to employ such part of the land or naval forces of the United States, or of the militia, as shall be necessary to prevent the violation and enforce the due execution of this Act."

One reason for the sweeping extension of federal jurisdiction over cases arising out of the Act was a Supreme Court decision which cast doubt on the status of military tribunals that had been established under the auspices of the Freedmen's Bureau Act. On April 3, 1866, in the midst of Congress's consideration of the Civil Rights Act, the Court decided Ex Parte Milligan, 71 U.S. 2 (1866), which held that a military commission could not try civilians for conspiracy to aid the rebellion when civilian courts remained open. The decision, written by the President's friend David Davis, was distinguishable from the current situation on several grounds, including the existence of congressional authorization for tribunals constituted by the Freedmen's Bureau and the occurrence of an actual state of war in areas covered by the Bureau's tribunals, but it created uncertainty sufficient to convince enough Members of Congress to expand the jurisdiction of the federal courts.

Both the substantive and enforcement aspects of this bill were portrayed by Democrats and some moderate Republicans as extraordinary injections of federal power into areas traditionally reserved to the states, but the Act was actually more moderate on both scores than it appeared. The genius in its drafting was, like the apportionment proposal, that it did not mandate any substantive change to state laws on property, contracts, crimes or evidence. Rather, by setting "white citizens" as a benchmark, it preserved state autonomy over these matters, merely requiring that all covered state laws must be applied in a racially neutral manner. Only the citizenship provision made a direct change to the law, and that law was federal, not state, for the Act did not even require states to recognize all of their inhabitants as state citizens.

The enforcement aspects of the bill greatly expanded federal power, but a careful understanding of the Act reveals that even in this aspect, the bill was moderate. First of all, despite accusations that the Act federalized private violations of state law, its enforcement provisions applied only to official actions, i.e., actions taken "under color" of state law and private actions directed at preventing state and federal officials from executing their duties. No Member of Congress understood the bill as reaching purely private acts of racial discrimination such as a White person's refusal to sell his property to a Black person or to hire a Black farmhand. Second, the jurisdiction of the federal courts was expanded only to reach matters of federal law; there was no "wholesale removal of state court competence" as some critics charged. Third, states could avoid any intrusions by simply enforcing their laws in a nondiscriminatory manner, and federal enforcement and suits were not likely except in clear cases of need. Finally, no President of the United States was likely to get personally involved or employ the military in the enforcement of the Act except in extremis when a national consensus in favor of such action appeared.

Because Senator Trumbull drafted it, the bill was introduced first in the Senate. There, passage was virtually assured, but there was concern over whether the margin would be sufficient to withstand a possible veto by President Lincoln. Trumbull made great efforts to achieve a two-thirds majority in the Senate, even setting aside his enmity for Charles Sumner and enlisting him in the effort to whip up support. When they counted up the votes, they realized they might be one vote short (or at least one vote too many in opposition) due to possible negative votes from both of the Democratic Senators from New Jersey. One was home ill and the other, John P. Stockton, a third generation New Jersey Senator and conservative Democrat, had only been provisionally seated because he was elected by a plurality, not a majority of the New Jersey state senate. Sumner convinced Senator Lot Morrill of Maine, a one-time Democrat turned Republican, to vote against seating Stockton, while Senator William Fessenden, Chairman of the Joint Committee and also from Maine, convinced Nevada Senator William Stewart, a Republican who had voted in favor of Stockton in the Judiciary Committee, to be absent for the vote. The Senate vote was held before New Jersey's other Senator, Democrat William Wright, could return from the illness that ultimately killed him later that year, and it appeared that Wright would not be able to return for an override vote either. The vote still appeared to be a draw but then the body resolved that Stockton's own vote in favor of himself did not count and thus Stockton was not seated. Not only did Trumbull's bill pass the Senate, it did so by a two-thirds majority, shielding it from a possible veto.

Stockton's most lasting service as a temporary Senator was, in a bid to illustrate that state autonomy over selection methods should be respected, to prepare a report on the various procedures states followed for selecting Senators. After the dust settled, the Judiciary Committee used Stockton's report as the basis for legislation, which passed both Houses in July, requiring all state legislatures to elect their Senators by majority vote. This bill was signed by President Lincoln and remained in effect until 1913 when direct popular election of Senators was required by the Seventeenth Amendment to the Constitution.

In the House, the Civil Rights Act ran into even less trouble than it had in the Senate and, after some relatively minor amendments, easily passed by greater than a two-thirds vote. The House's amendments required another vote in the Senate, with the same result. The question now was whether the President would sign it.

It arrived on his desk on March 17, 1866. Lincoln was torn. Although he vehemently disagreed with the Dred Scott decision, he did not see how Congress could override the Supreme Court's interpretation of the Constitution without a constitutional amendment, which the Joint Committee was already working on. He understood from everything he heard during the debate over the Freedmen's Bureau bill that federal intervention was becoming increasingly necessary to protect the rights of freedmen, but he was concerned that coming on the heels of that bill, relations with Southern governments would worsen even more if he signed this bill. He also realized that Congress appeared to have the votes to override a veto, and he thought that perhaps his best strategy might be to veto it, send a message to Congress expressing his constitutional concerns, and then if two-thirds of Congress disagreed with him, he could enforce the Act without taking too much of the blame. Vice President Andrew Johnson, who had been virtually a non-presence at the White House since the failed assassination attempt, paid a call on the President and threw a bucket of cold water on that thought, telling him that enforcement of the Civil Rights Act would cause great dissension throughout the South including the border states, and that Lincoln should "send it back to Congress without encouraging them to take any further action along these lines." He said, "Mr. President, successful Reconstruction according to your plans, which I endorse, would be significantly impeded by this proposed federal intrusion into state affairs." Lincoln made no reply, simply thanking Johnson for his input and wishing him well.

Looking for legal advice and friendly counsel, Lincoln called Attorney General James Speed into the Oval Office to discuss the bill. Lincoln began the conversation by stating his "inclination to reject it at this point, and wait for progress on the constitutional amendment Congress is contemplating." Lincoln also expressed the hope that the newly invigorated Freedmen's Bureau would make enough progress that the Act would be unnecessary.

Lincoln said the passage of this Act, so soon after the reauthorization of the Bureau reminded him of the story of Queen Esther. "After the defeat of Haman's evil plot to wipe out her people, Haman and his ten sons were hanged on a public gallows. When the King asked his beloved Queen the next day if there was anything more he could do for her, she asked him to hang Haman's sons again. I never quite understood the point of this second request. It always seemed to me that Queen Esther might have waited for the effect of the first hanging to take hold before requesting another."

When he asked Speed for his thoughts, he was surprised at Speed's vehement endorsement of the Act and all it stood for. At that time, the Attorney General was much more independent of the President than in later years, and without frequent contact in recent weeks, Lincoln had not realized that the passage of the Black Codes and other events in the South, including some acts of violence directed against Black Americans for merely asserting their rights as free men and women, had moved Speed firmly into the Radical camp. In Speed's view, it was vital for the national government to prevent the Southern states from denying the basic rights of citizenship to the freedmen "and all of their colored citizens."

He advised Lincoln that in his opinion the Thirteenth Amendment and its enforcement clause provided Congress with "ample power to recognize freedmen's citizenship and endow them with the full rights as such. I do not view the Court's rejection of Dred Scott's petition for freedom as precedent for denying Congress authority to read the Constitution differently."

Speed then took the opportunity to express disagreement over Lincoln's lenient policy of Reconstruction, stating that "although I agreed with your view at the outset favoring quick restoration of normal governmental structures throughout the country, events have convinced me of the necessity of firm action, even revolutionary change to the previous relationship between this government and those of the states."

By not implying that Lincoln had been wrong to initially adopt a lenient policy, Speed exhibited his skill as both an advocate and friend, as well as providing Lincoln with a basis for altering his own views. Speed was looking to the future, too. He foresaw a strong Republican victory in the 1866 elections, and he was positioning himself as a Radical for an effort to become a Senator from his home state of Kentucky. An open seat there was likely because the incumbent was seriously ill and would therefore retire.

As Lincoln contemplated whether to sign the bill, he was also considering the 1866 election. Although he had been convinced in 1864 that he was likely to lose the presidency, his victory in the Civil War alongside continued doubts over how many Southern votes would be counted in the upcoming election made Lincoln confident of a sweeping Republican victory. The only open question in his mind was whether the new Congress would be dominated by the moderate or Radical wing of his party. Lincoln continued to prefer a more moderate course than the Radicals would pursue and even though his political instincts may have been second to none in American history, he did not have a firm sense of how his action on the Civil Rights Act would affect voters. Signing it might reinforce the sense that moderates would do enough and turning to the Radicals was unnecessary, or it might signal victory for the Radicals and open the floodgates to even more extreme measures.

Ultimately, Lincoln put politics aside and signed the bill, putting into effect the most sweeping federal Civil Rights Act in the nation's history. This Act, in one fell swoop, invalidated numerous provisions of state Black Codes and promised federal intervention on behalf of racial minorities across the country. Although Lincoln did not know it at the time, this Act would become intimately associated with his legacy.

Of course, passing a law and enforcing a law are two quite different things. Lincoln was not inclined to send federal marshals or troops across the South or take other aggressive action to ensure obedience. He continued to allow General Grant to determine the appropriate military presence in the South. There was nothing he could do about Congress's unwillingness to admit representatives selected under the Southern governments authorized by the President. As far as the effects of the Act on the election, other events soon overshadowed the Act and led to a Northern groundswell toward the Radical position. These events occurred in Memphis and New Orleans, both illustrating the perilous situation people of color found themselves in at the time.

8

RACE WARS

The stories of racial unrest in Memphis and New Orleans recounted here actually began in April 1865 at Appomattox Court House, when Grant and Lee agreed to join forces to pursue national reconciliation in the aftermath of the war. Their efforts along these lines had been delayed by the press of events that required Grant's immediate attention.

A year on, in April 1866, after lengthy correspondence, they met in Chicago to map out a tour of cities in Illinois and then south along the Mississippi River. Their plan was to meet with the local press and speak in lecture format, urging their fellow citizens to embrace the reunified country and work together to rebuild their society. They agreed to convey the message that the freedmen deserved to be treated as full citizens of the United States and, if not embraced by their White neighbors, should at least be let alone to pursue their own ambitions. In Northern cities, Grant would speak first and introduce Lee while in Southern locations, the reverse order would be observed. They both understood that this pursuit entailed some danger, and they would be accompanied wherever they traveled by a substantial security detail. This was to be a trial run, with stops in Chicago and Springfield and then the river towns of St. Louis, Memphis, Greenville, Vicksburg, Baton Rouge, and New Orleans. Grant had his eyes on the 1868 presidential election and thus viewed the tour as an early opportunity to make his case for the Republican nomination.

The tour began in Chicago on April 17, 1866, at a hall called the Chicago Auditorium, a large wooden structure later demolished to make way for the grand Auditorium Theater that still stands on the site. The hall was packed with men anxious to see both Grant and Lee. Although most of the attendees were White, there was a smattering of Black faces in the crowd, interspersed throughout the seats on the hall's main floor and many more in the crowd standing in the balcony where tickets went for half the price.

Grant was in full dress uniform while Lee wore morning clothes (coat black, not grey), with only the sword strapped around his waist as a sign of his military past.

Grant began his talk by disclaiming the intent to revisit the glories that had propelled him into his current position of prominence: "At events such as these, I am asked to recount our successes on the battlefield in the late war, and as proud as I am of the valor that our boys showed in that theater of war, it was as well a theater of blood, and it was American blood that poured forth on both sides. Therefore, on this occasion, I would rather our thoughts look forward toward peace than backward toward those awful times." He continued with remarks aimed at convincing his audience to "welcome our Southern brethren back into our union, as President Lincoln pledged, 'with malice toward none,'" stating that "I view it as my sacred duty to carry out the work of Reconstruction along the path charted by the President and Congress, with firm insistence on loyalty and an unbroken commitment to justice for all, but with an open heart to the feeling of brotherhood that is encapsulated by our Constitution's common pledge to form a more perfect union, ensure domestic tranquility and secure the blessings of liberty to ourselves and our posterity."

After lauding General Howard and Frederick Douglass's work for the Freedmen's Bureau and describing some of the successful efforts of Reconstruction that had already taken place— including the settlement of thousands of freedmen across the South, the establishment of schools for the education of young Black Americans and the sowing of a new cotton crop—Grant went on to describe his great respect for General Lee. He recounted how they had fought together in the Mexican War and proclaimed, "We are now fighting together in an effort to restore our country to its previous greatness." He pointed to the sword at his hip, saying, "I wear here General Lee's sword, and General Lee wears mine, as symbols of the unity we seek. I hope you will welcome him and listen to what he offers for our common future." With that, he turned the podium over to General Robert E. Lee, for Lee's first post-war speech before a Northern audience.

After several minutes of thunderous applause for Grant, the crowd became very quiet as Lee arose from his seat and approached the lectern. They were anxious to hear what he had to say. Lee began by reminding the audience that his father fought in the Revolutionary War and that, as General Grant had said, Lee himself had served in the U.S. Army for many years, including their common service in the Mexican War. He said that he had opposed secession but, as a proud and loyal Virginian, felt compelled to join with his state. He said it was his greatest current ambition to help knit the country together. He urged his listeners to visit the South, reopen business with the South, and support the President's efforts to reconstruct the Union as quickly as possible. He concluded by praising General Grant as a great leader and thanking him for the respect he showed the Army of Virginia "at the end of our common tragedy" and hoped it would serve as a model for the nation's future. Lee did not mention the end of slavery or the plight of Southern freedmen, omissions that were noticed by some of those in the audience who were predisposed against Lee, including members of Chicago's Republican press. Overall, however, Lee's remarks were well-received and the audience applauded politely, if not enthusiastically, at their conclusion.

Events were similar in Springfield, although Grant's efforts to secure an invitation for the pair to speak to the Illinois legislature were unsuccessful. Instead, the pair gave a brief afternoon talk in the capitol building's Supreme Court chamber before those lawmakers who chose to attend, mainly from Illinois' southern reaches. Grant noted that Abraham Lincoln had argued numerous cases to the court in that chamber, had served in the Illinois legislature, and had delivered his famous "House Divided" speech there after winning the Republican Party's nomination for Senate. Lee delivered the same remarks he made in Chicago, adding only a brief message acknowledging Springfield's connection to the President.

Things got more interesting in St. Louis. Missouri had been a slave state, and although it remained in the Union and sent over 100,000 troops to fight in the War, tens of thousands of Missourians went South to fight for the Confederacy. Moreover, a

Confederate government-in-exile was created after the Union took firm control of the state. Further, as the gateway to the frontier, St. Louis was a rough and tumble place under any circumstances. Thus, Grant and Lee and their security detail were a bit concerned as they prepared for the event at the St. Louis Municipal Theater, where tickets sold out far in advance. The city's mayor and police commissioner were aware of the potential for a ruckus and they provided a large contingent of policemen to secure the area. Once the crowd began to gather, the potential for trouble appeared even greater. Some spectators had dared to wear Confederate military jackets and wave Confederate flags, while others arrived in Union blues waving the stars and stripes. It was a hot April afternoon getting hotter by the minute.

As the crowd filled the hall, there was a great deal of shouting back and forth and a few minor skirmishes involving some pushing and shoving. All flags on poles or sticks of any kind were confiscated at the door for fear they might be employed as clubs or missiles. Luckily, the opposing factions did a pretty good job of separating themselves, Union on the left and Confederate on the right, and Black Americans occupied their customary place at the back of the hall's tiny balcony. As Grant began to speak, chants for Lee began. Lee stood to great applause. When quiet was restored, Lee asked the audience to hear Grant out and he would deliver his remarks in full afterward. Otherwise, he exclaimed, neither would be able to talk. Lee's wish was granted, and except for a few catcalls and boos when Grant mentioned federal aid to the freedmen and such things, Grant was allowed to speak without further interruption. Union supporters in the crowd rewarded Grant's words with enthusiastic applause and shouts of approval. The good feeling among Grant's supporters continued as they politely listened to Lee's remarks, which the other side applauded with fervor equal to that shown by their opposites to Grant.

The next stop on the tour was Memphis, the first stop in a state which had actually seceded and fought against the United States in the Civil War. The party, with their security entourage, traveled from St. Louis to Memphis on the Natchez. (That steamer, in 1870, famously participated in a race up the river from New Orleans to St. Louis against the Robert E. Lee, a steamer under construction in Indiana at the time of the Grant-Lee unity tour.) They made special arrangements for a daytime trip down to Memphis, and Grant and Lee spent hours together on the balcony of Lee's cabin, smoking and reminiscing. Grant refused Lee's generous offers of alcoholic refreshments, observing one of his many periods of abstinence but for a nip just before bed. It was a glorious late April day and they got up from the west-facing balcony only to cross to the other side of the boat to see the confluence of the Mississippi and Ohio Rivers at Cairo Illinois. Lee told Grant that although he missed the military life, he was enjoying his new role as President of Washington College in Lexington, Virginia, where "we educate Virginia's finest." The College was named for George Washington after he endowed the struggling school in 1796, and in just a few years, the name would be changed again to Washington and Lee. Grant confided in Lee that he was happy to be away from Washington, where "contestation over our policies toward the Southern states has become the city's favorite pastime." He told Lee that he was frustrated with the slow pace of Reconstruction and that the aftermath of the plot to assassinate the President distracted attention from the need to rebuild and expand the economy after the end of the war. Grant also confided that he feared that without progress on equal rights in the near future, Congress might soon take stronger measures to gain control over Southern governments.

The entourage arrived in Memphis on the evening of April 29, with the plan to hold an event sponsored by the Mid-South Cotton Growers' Association on May 1 at the 600-seat Calvary Episcopal Church on Second Street. There was one problem—the church had never welcomed Black Americans to worship there, and many Black residents of Memphis wanted to attend the lecture. In fact, the Church founders and early benefactors had been slave owners and slave auctions were sometimes held on Church property. Grant did not want to participate in an event that excluded Black Americans. In the morning of the 30th, he asked the Cotton Growers whether they could arrange for at least a small section for them. They were dead set against it, and they also reported that the Church's pastor would not allow it in any case. After more back and forth, during which Grant asked the organizers to look for an alternative site, the organizers and the pastor finally agreed to reserve the last row of pews for a delegation from the Collins Chapel, a church founded in 1841 by Black Americans, both slave and free, under the leadership of Pastor Joseph Collins.

As the crowd gathered later that day, when a few Collins Chapel members attempted to join the line entering the church, they were told by a White man behind them that "you niggers can wait until we get inside, and we'll see if there's place for you." Once the freedmen stood off to the side, the White crowd went back to figuring out which of them were Union men and which had supported secession and the Confederacy.

The latter group, including a large contingent who considered themselves some of the Vice President (and Tennessean) Andrew Johnson's staunchest supporters, outnumbered the former by nearly three to one. This imbalance actually helped preserve the peace because, after some vocal back and forth while in line, the Grant supporters quieted down, realizing how badly they were outnumbered. As the crowd streamed into the church's knave, informal lines were drawn with the Southern men at the front and then Union men behind them. True to their word, the back row was reserved for the Black Americans who had waited patiently for their turn to enter. Although there was space inside for only thirty of the Collins Chapel members, the entire congregation had turned out, with many men, women, and children remaining outside, singing spirituals and hymns.

Lee rose to speak first, with Grant seated behind and left of him on the pastor's ceremonial throne-like chair. Lee began by thanking General Grant for arranging the event, but at the mention of Grant's name, boos and hisses erupted from the front of the crowd. After the noise died down, Lee implored the crowd, "in the interest of our common futures and in the name of Southern honor," to listen with politeness to both speakers. Then, in these friendlier environs, in a calm tone, Lee launched into a lengthy review of the history of Southern grievances that justified the split with the Union, not mentioning slavery by name but referring to "our practices and our traditions" more than once. He asked his crowd to forgive the Confederate military for failing in their mission to preserve their new nation, insisting that "our men fought with valor, and our leaders provided all support necessary, but the resources and numbers of our adversary were just too much to overcome." Grant's expression during Lee's remarks quickly became a look of concern, and then of relief as Lee returned to more conciliatory themes. He recounted how Grant had shown him great respect at Appomattox Court House and kindness to his entire Army, how he had fed his hungry troops for three full days and had released them quickly, allowing them to return home with their horses and their side arms. After telling of their exchange of swords, he said, "We should view General Grant and our fellow citizens up North as having reunited with us after a family feud, and we should leave our old feelings behind and look only to the future." He continued, "Remember, gentlemen, I myself, as many of you, served for years in the Union Army, and I fought beside General Grant in Mexico, and led the Military Academy at West Point. I return now to a familiar place, and so can we all. Even more," Lee said, "we should renew our commitment to the ideals of our national Constitution and work together to restore American greatness."

Grant rose to cheers and huzzahs from the rear of the hall, including the Black Americans seated in the back row, and general murmuring and dismissive gestures from the front. Grant spoke briefly, as Lee had done in Chicago and Springfield. He began by thanking the good people of Memphis for their hospitality, singling out the Cotton Growers' Association and the Calvary Church pastor and congregation. He recounted his long acquaintance with General Lee and the high regard he always held for him. Then, with the best of intentions, he veered into territory that was more dangerous than he realized. He said that the Lincoln administration was anxious to reknit the country with a policy that promised opportunity for all. His first mistake was mentioning Lincoln's name. The second mistake was using the phrase "opportunity for all." He may as well have said "voting rights and property ownership for Blacks." The crowd erupted into shouts of disapproval that took Lee several minutes to quiet down. Sensing that his error was likely unrepairable, he concluded quickly, thanking General Lee once again and proclaiming him "a trustworthy guardian of the sword of unity I exchanged for his at Appomattox."

As the crowd emptied onto the street, some Black Americans in the crowd, sensing trouble, urged their fellow Collins congregants to leave the area quickly. In the confusion, there was a collision between two horse drawn wagons, one driven by a White passerby and the other driven by a departing Black spectator. Racial unrest broke out immediately and ultimately led to violence and riots. This continued for three days, until the arrival of sufficient Union troops to put it down.

The collision was more the occasion for than the cause of the rioting. During the War, the Black population in Memphis had increased dramatically once the Union Army took the city in 1862. The presence of thousands of free Black Americans, including escaped slaves and troops stationed at nearby Fort Pickering, created friction, especially with the Irish community who were in competition with Black Americans for unskilled employment. Incidents of violence against Black Americans by Irish mobs were common, and police abuses were legion. There was general racial hostility by White Memphis toward Black Americans and resentment that Black troops at Fort Pickering had been used during and after the war to patrol Memphis as part of the effort to secure Union control. Over time, hostility had grown to the point that the 20,000 Black residents of Memphis found it increasingly difficult to engage in commerce of any kind or even lead a normal life.

It was no surprise, then, that after the traffic incident, the White crowd grew hostile. Seeing the potential for violence, Grant sent a message to Fort Pickering demanding help, and Grant and Lee departed to a hotel near the riverfront for supper. Over a pleasant meal of fried oysters, baked potatoes, warm rolls, and waffles, accompanied for Lee by fine French champagne, they discussed the day's events and agreed that they should discontinue their tour.

In place of further personal appearances, they asked Grant's clerk who had accompanied them throughout, to write a summary of their remarks at their four stops for them to edit and publish in newspapers and in pamphlet form. This was accomplished, although the pamphlet never became widely available outside of Washington and Philadelphia, and many Southern papers, including the New Orleans Picayune and every paper in Virginia, printed only Lee's portion of the remarks and even omitted Lee's conciliatory comments and statements complimenting Grant.

Meanwhile, violence continued on the streets of Memphis after the police arrested the Black driver and let the White driver alone. The gathered Collins Chapel members, including numerous Black war veterans, attempted to prevent the police from taking the Black driver into custody. The four White officers on the scene exchanged gunfire with the Black veterans. One officer was killed and another was wounded, although the wound may have been accidentally self-inflicted. After this initial skirmish and a couple hours of rumblings, things calmed down enough that a small squad of troops sent from nearby Fort Pickering were ordered back to their barracks. However, after their departure, a mob composed mainly of Irish police officers and firefighters, along with some of the Calvary Church crowd, went looking for the Black veterans. Finding neither them nor any other federal troops or Black civilians, they went down to South Memphis where many of the families of Black troops stationed at Fort Pickering lived. Their first target was the empty Collins Chapel itself, which they ignited with the help of a group of the city's firefighters. Then, in their race-fueled rage, they destroyed the entire area, burning homes, churches, and schools, killing Black Americans indiscriminately and raping women and girls, including the wives and daughters of some of the Black soldiers. The violence continued virtually unimpeded for more than forty-eight hours. Only on the third day did sufficient federal troops arrive in South Memphis to end the violence, but not before forty-six Black Americans and two Whites had been killed.

Across the North, critics used what they called "the Memphis Massacre" to discredit Lincoln's lenient Reconstruction policies. They pointed out that while former Confederates had been disenfranchised under Lincoln's guidelines and the Tennessee legislature had not passed a Black Code like other states, control over the Memphis government and Tennessee society had simply reverted to a new group of White supremacists who used their discretion under existing laws, including vagrancy and forced apprenticeship provisions, to exert economic and social control over Black Americans. In Memphis, the disenfranchisement of the former Confederate elite left power largely in the hands of lower-class natives and Irish immigrants. If anything, Black Americans were worse off than they might have been if more experienced former Confederate officials had been in power, for they might have controlled the mobs in the interests of the overall welfare of the city.

9

CONSTITUTIONAL AMENDMENT AND POLITICAL EVOLUTION

The Memphis riot and events that followed forced Lincoln
to question his moderate inclinations. By late May, Northern
popular opinion began to swing in the Radical direction. Lincoln
was disturbed by the Memphis reports, and in a meeting with
Stanton and General Howard, with Speed also in attendance, he
asked them to use Bureau and military resources to do whatever
they could to protect Black Americans in the South. He expressed
frustration that it took so long for the military to respond in
Memphis. He asked Howard and Speed whether there was
anything in the Civil Rights Act that could be used to seek justice
against the instigators of the riot, but Speed said that he did not
think so because nobody had denied the victims any of the rights
enumerated in the Act. Prosecutions for murder, assault, and
destruction of property were for the state and local authorities,
not the federal government. Howard chimed in that the Bureau
would work with the military and Stanton promised to instruct
General Grant to order local commanders to intervene more
quickly in the future, if necessary.

Although fewer people died, similar events in New Orleans that
July moved political sentiment even further toward the Radical
camp—perhaps because Lincoln had pushed so hard for the
recognition of Louisiana's Reconstruction government. Despite
Lincoln's plea for voting rights for at least some Black Americans,
he had allowed Louisiana's new government to assume power
under a constitution that included no such guarantee. Further,
by early 1866, the state legislature had begun to restore pre-war
officials to power over Governor James Wells's objections. The lack
of voting rights coupled with enforcement of the Black Code and
related customs of exclusion and segregation caused great worry in
Louisiana's community of color, and even the relatively privileged
gens de couleur could see their special social status disappearing.

Radical Republicans, both White and Black, took aim at the
Louisiana constitution and, with Governor Wells's support,
reopened the 1864 constitutional convention with a view

toward establishing voting rights and full legal equality for Black Americans. The effort, which ended in disaster, was kicked off on July 27, 1866, when a group of Black Americans, mainly Civil War veterans, met at the Mechanics Institute near the French Quarter to hear speeches by leading advocates for equal rights. On July 30, the convention's racially diverse delegates convened and the July 27 group staged a march, complete with a band, to the site. When the session ended early due to lack of a quorum, the delegates left the hall. As they filed out, they and the marchers were set upon with clubs and firearms by a hostile crowd of White Democrats, many of them former Confederate soldiers now serving as police officers. Most delegates and marchers were unarmed; some retreated back into the building. Those who could not make it back inside were beaten mercilessly on the street while other members of the White mob fired at those inside through the Institute's windows. When people tried to escape the building, they were shot, stabbed, or beaten, and this often continued long after the victim was dead. The mob showed no mercy. It was a massacre, leaving thirty-seven people dead and more than one hundred wounded. It took the belated arrival of federal troops to stop the violence, and it was later revealed that Secretary of War Stanton did nothing when he received advance notice from local commanders that violence was likely to break out if the convention reconvened.

Upon hearing of this episode, Lincoln called a meeting of his Cabinet and informed them that he was inclined to suspend recognition of Southern governments that enacted Black Codes and would use the full strength of the federal government to squelch the reactionary forces at work across the South. In short, Lincoln's views began to evolve as he saw the consequences of his moderate treatment of Southern governments.

Even before the Memphis riot, the Reconstruction Committee had been hard at work crafting a new constitutional amendment to attack the Black Codes, support the 1866 Civil Rights Act, and enact some of its favored policies that had failed earlier in the year. One version was offered as early as December, 1865, by Ohio Republican Representative John Bingham. Serious consideration did not begin until late April, when his proposal was presented to the Reconstruction Committee together with a plan formulated by former Indiana Representative Robert Dale Owen, who had been first elected as a Democrat but later became a leading advocate for emancipation.

After complicated discussions and numerous separate votes on each issue, what eventually became the Fourteenth Amendment contained five sections, corresponding to eight separate substantive concerns: federal citizenship, state citizenship, equal rights, apportionment and voting rights, government service for former rebels, validity of federal and state debts, compensation for lost slaves, and congressional power to enforce the amendment.

Section 1 constitutionalized the Civil Rights Act's grant of American citizenship to "all persons born or naturalized in the United States" and, for the first time, required states to recognize state citizenship for all Americans residing within their borders. Section 1 also granted important civil rights including the rights to due process and equal protection of the laws and the privileges and immunities of citizenship. Significantly, the rights enumerated in Section 1 were not textually limited to discrimination against Black Americans or even racial discrimination more generally, but rather applied some of the protections of the Bill of Rights directed at the federal government to state and local governments as well.

Section 2 took up the apportionment issue, providing that any state that denies males over the age of twenty-one the right to vote would lose a proportion of their representation in Congress equal to the proportion of men denied the right to vote.

Section 3 prohibited anyone who had taken an oath to support the Constitution of the United States as a federal or state official and then participated in or aided the rebellion from serving as a state or federal official, unless this disability was removed by a two-thirds vote of each House of Congress.

Section 4 guaranteed the validity of the public debt of the United States government and declared void any debt incurred in aid of rebellion and any debt based on compensation for the loss or emancipation of any slave.

Section 5, like Section 2 of the Thirteenth Amendment but with minor grammatical differences, provided that "Congress shall have the power to enforce, by appropriate legislation, the provisions of this article." Absent were Owen's provisions regarding the readmission of Southern states and his proposal that would have required states to grant suffrage to Black Americans by July 4, 1876.

Debates over the meaning of the Amendment's provisions revealed the dangers of including vagaries such as "privileges or immunities," "due process of law," and "equal protection of the laws." Such language invited countless meanings.

For example, one question that immediately confronted the Framers of the Fourteenth Amendment was whether the Amendment's Privileges or Immunities Clause or the Equal Protection Clause mandated nondiscriminatory voting eligibility rules, or whether Congress might have the power to regulate voting under Section 5. In other words, the question was whether this was an attempt to enact a stealth voting rights provision.

The Framers unanimously rejected both possibilities. Bingham insisted that the mere presence of Section 2, given that it reduced federal representation for states denying Black Americans the right to vote, was sufficient to establish that no other provision of the amendment should be understood as touching the voting issue. Others chimed in that the history of the inclusion of Section 2 provided even more evidence because just before the Committee approved the draft amendment and sent it to the full House for consideration there, Section 2 was inserted as a replacement for Owen's voting rights proposal. There was also general agreement that without a substantive voting rights provision, Section 5 did not give Congress the power to regulate what was considered at the time a central element of traditional state authority.

But nothing would stop a future Congress or a creative Supreme Court from reading into those elastic words powers and standards far from the imaginings of their Framers. Democrats on the

Joint Committee, including Reverdy Johnson, argued this point, but the majority was unmoved and sent the proposal to the full Congress for consideration.

The House approved the Fourteenth Amendment by the required two-thirds majority on May 10, 1866, and sent it to the Senate for deliberation. Debate in the Senate on the amendment took nearly a month, mainly because of controversy over a provision in the House's proposal. In addition to disqualification from federal and state office, the House proposed that former rebels be prohibited from voting until 1870, adding insurance to Republican hopes to retain control of Congress in the 1866 election and the presidency in 1868. This proposal was attacked by moderate Republicans on two scores—first that it was needlessly vindictive and undemocratic, and second that it amounted to a direct intervention by the national government into state voting qualifications. Some Democrats opposed removing the disenfranchisement clause from the amendment not because they favored it but because they thought its inclusion would guarantee rejection by the states, where three-fourths agreement was required. Charles Sumner managed to slow down the proceedings with a lengthy speech attacking Section 2 as an endorsement of disenfranchisement of Black Americans. Outside the Senate, advocates for women's suffrage were unhappy with legislators' repeated insistence that "equal protection" did not refer to equal rights for women, and with Section 2's express reference to the voting rights of "male inhabitants" which, for the first time, constitutionally credited discrimination against women regarding the right to vote. On June 6, Senate Republicans mustered a two-thirds majority for an amendment that substituted what became Section 2 for the House's disenfranchisement proposal, and the amendment was re-passed by the House as altered on June 10, and sent to the states for ratification. That process took two years, and on July 28, 1868, Secretary Seward proclaimed that the Fourteenth Amendment had been ratified by the required number of states and had become part of the Constitution. But this process was not easy, and ratification was accomplished only after significant prodding by Congress that is described below.

Words on paper, such as the Civil Rights Act of 1866 and the putative Fourteenth Amendment, may gratify the heart's yearning for justice but cannot on their own accomplish material change. Human action must bring the words to life.

Although President Lincoln had signaled his support for enforcing the Civil Rights Act, he remained reluctant to push for the level of federal intervention that everyone knew would be necessary to do so. His views were evolving, but slowly. Further, enforcement infrastructure was not in place, especially now that the new state governments had taken over from the officials who had been installed by federal military authorities. The Joint Committee considered this and resolved to craft legislation taking control of Reconstruction from the President. Readmission of rebellious states to representation in Congress and the Union more generally was uncharted territory, and this legislation would require careful drafting and sober consideration. Before that could happen, Members of Congress had something equally pressing to attend to—an election.

The election of 1866 had been shaping up to be a referendum on the nature and political purpose of the Reconstruction project. Would voters be lenient along the lines originally suggested by President Lincoln and favored by moderate Republicans like Seward and most Democrats, or would the electorate turn Radical as advocated by the likes of Charles Sumner and Thaddeus Stevens? This understanding of things, though, was thrown into uncertainty by the continuous evolution of Lincoln's views, especially after the violence in Memphis and New Orleans. Lincoln now recognized the need for firm action, and this left conservative Republicans scrambling for a way to anchor their alliance with Democrats.

After much planning and with the support of Vice President Johnson, in August 1866 proponents of a lenient Reconstruction held "The National Union Convention" in Philadelphia, which portrayed itself as an extension of the National Union Party, the name adopted by Republicans for the 1864 election. Because Johnson had been elected Vice President on the National Union Party ticket, his participation in this gathering was technically appropriate, but it placed him in clear opposition to mainstream Republican sentiment as well as Lincoln's shifted stance on

Reconstruction. Johnson hoped to emerge from the convention as leader of its political movement and a potential unity candidate for President in 1868.

The convention turned into something of a pep rally for those who disliked Lincoln, whether Northern or Southern, and those who preferred a lenient approach to Reconstruction. The breadth of perspectives, however, prevented the sort of unity that would comprise an effective counterpoint to the likely Republican domination of the Northern and Western vote. The keynote speech was delivered by New York delegate Henry J. Raymond, who surprisingly spoke in favor of the Fourteenth Amendment and criticized slavery, and the convention's Committee on Resolutions would not include his statements in the party's draft platform. Other delegates were as diverse as Judge David L. Wardlaw, author of South Carolina's Black Code, and Interior Secretary James Harlan, who was in the midst of coordinating the establishment of Land Grant Colleges with state governments across the country. No consensus sufficient to establish a political movement would arise out of this meeting.

Andrew Johnson was frustrated by the failure of the convention and felt that he needed to try something else. What he did became an unmitigated disaster. In late August, Johnson embarked on a speaking tour by train, called the Swing around the Circle. It was an odd idea: the Vice President, in the guise of campaigning for congressional candidates who were at best loose allies of the administration (and at worst out-and-out opponents), in actuality campaigning to be President two years in advance of the election. Recognizing the appearance of impropriety in what he was doing, Johnson and his supporters invented a basic excuse for the trip as well as a strategic device to deflect criticism. The excuse was that Johnson was traveling to Chicago to participate in a ceremonial laying of the cornerstone of the monument to former Senator and presidential candidate Stephen A. Douglas, who had died in 1861, that was being erected in a park near Chicago's lakefront. (Lincoln himself could not attend due to fears for his safety.) The device was that when the train stopped along its (rather indirect) route from Washington to Chicago, Johnson would disclaim a desire to speak and allow his companions and hopefully the crowd to draw him into giving more than brief remarks of greeting.

The tour began fairly well in Philadelphia, Newark, and eastern New York, where Johnson had sufficient support to ensure a friendly reception. However, as the train headed west through upstate New York and then through a sliver of western Pennsylvania into Ohio, Johnson confronted hostile crowds. In places like Indianapolis and Kalamazoo, organized Republican crowds chanted "Grant, Grant" whenever the Vice President attempted to speak. In other places, spectators led cheers for Lincoln and for Congress and booed Johnson heartily when he spoke. Johnson grew testy and at one point proclaimed that he was surprised to find so many traitors in the North.

As time went on, when hecklers did not drown him out, his speeches became thinly veiled endorsements of Democratic candidates in the upcoming election. Even those who were inclined to agree with Johnson's policies were put off by his vulgar manner and divisive spirit. Apparently, Americans were not ready for Johnson's arrogance, ineloquence, and dismissiveness toward those who dared disagree with him. Things got so bad that in a few instances the conductors and engineers pulled the train out of the station before Johnson finished speaking, fearing for the safety of their equipment and its passengers. Fortunately, dignity was maintained at the dedication in Chicago, but even there, as news of the disastrous trip spread, many Illinois politicians, Republican and Democrat, who might have otherwise attended, if only to show respect for Douglas, stayed away.

If Johnson's Swing around the Circle had any effect on the election, it was to excite more voters to support candidates who favored aggressive action on Reconstruction. State Republican nominating conventions had already been turning in the Radical direction and once it became clear that local Republican organizations were overwhelmingly nominating Radical candidates, the evolving Lincoln felt stuck in the middle between them and the moderate wing of his party, which, along with Democrats, even unionist Democrats, favored quick and easy readmission with minimal ancillary changes to the law. Although there was little risk that the Democrats would gain a majority in either House of Congress, Lincoln would still need the support of his fellow Republicans to govern effectively, and thus he could not come out strongly against even their most extreme positions.

Elections for the fortieth Congress began as early as June 4 in Oregon and ran as late as September 6 the next year. When the votes were counted, it was a rout. Huge Republican majorities were elected to both Houses, dominated by the Radical wing. In total, Republicans won 147 House seats while Democrats took only 44. State governorships and legislatures also swung in the Radical direction. The Democrats' only glimmer of hope came in California where, in an election that was delayed until September 1877, two Democrats took seats previously held by retiring Republicans. In the Senate, state legislatures awarded fifteen seats to Republicans and only two to Democrats, resulting in a 57-9 Republican majority. Congressional elections were not held in the former Confederate states, which strengthened Northern control over Congress. Even more important than the effect this would have in Congress was that the momentum toward the Radical position would likely sweep up Lincoln, Stanton, and Grant, moving both political branches closer and closer to the Radical position.

The clearest signal of Johnson's waning influence was in his home state of Tennessee, which had been readmitted to the Union in 1866 after quickly ratifying the Fourteenth Amendment. Even though Johnson had openly campaigned for Democratic candidates there, Republicans swept all eight districts. Part of the reason for the Republican victory was that as soon as it was readmitted to the Union, the Tennessee General Assembly passed a law granting suffrage to Black Americans, and they turned out in large numbers in the 1866 election to vote for Republican candidates. Tennessee, having been the last Southern state to secede and the first to be fully readmitted, greeted the policies of its native son with hostility—a hostility, however, that would last only until Tennessee was later "redeemed" along with other Southern states and reverted to the strictures of Jim Crow.

Johnson's speaking tour and his political activity in support of Democratic candidates further infuriated the ever-outraged

Charles Sumner. Sumner denounced Johnson on the floor of the Senate and took to openly airing his suspicions that Johnson had been in league with the assassins of 1865 to anyone with the patience to listen. Sumner's attacks on Johnson were so intemperate that he risked another beating, either in the Senate chamber or on his way to or from the Capitol Building. Sumner's saving grace was that he was so consistent in his rabble-rousing that most people had either stopped paying attention or thought that he was not credible enough to be taken seriously. However, Johnson was so badly damaged by the accumulation of everything concerning him that he would not even secure the Democratic nomination for President in 1868.

10
WASHINGTON'S GRIP

With the 1866 election season over, the business of governing resumed. Reports on the conditions for Black Americans in the South were not good. Despite the passage of the Civil Rights Act, states continued to enforce their Black Codes; local customs of exclusion, segregation, and forced labor were strengthened, if anything. Although the Freedmen's Bureau was having some success distributing land and supplies to freedmen and providing educational opportunities, in December 1866, Frederick Douglass provided Lincoln, Stanton, Speed, and the leaders of the Reconstruction Committee with a lengthy, comprehensive report detailing the mistreatment of Black Americans and the malfeasance of state and local authorities. In addition to depressing news about working conditions for Black Americans, the report detailed numerous small acts of violence that had drawn little outside attention, unlike the larger occurrences in Memphis and New Orleans, and accounts of a number of cases in which state judges issued writs of habeas corpus to free criminals who had been convicted of crimes against freedmen by military tribunals in cooperation with the Bureau. Additionally, by the first week of December as Congress reconvened for a brief period before the holiday break, the legislatures of Texas, Georgia, and Florida had rejected the Fourteenth Amendment.

After talking over the report and related news with Speed and Stanton, Lincoln invited Senator Ira Harris of New York to meet with him at the White House. Harris, a frequent visitor, was the President's longtime friend and confidant, and father of Clara Harris, one of the Lincolns' Ford's Theater companions. Harris was a respected lawyer and New York state judge before his service in the Senate, and he was also a member of the Reconstruction Committee, where he distinguished himself for sober and careful contributions. He continued to teach law while in the Senate and was known as an expert in equity jurisprudence. Lincoln liked to discuss important matters with Harris because he was not shy about offering his opinions, even in direct opposition to the President's, yet he remained friendly and cordial.

As always, Lincoln greeted Harris warmly on his arrival at the Oval Office. It was always a relief to see a friendly face rather than another job-seeker or angry politician. After asking after Harris's wife Pauline, his daughter Clara, and her fiancé Henry Rathbone—who was also Pauline's son by a prior marriage— Lincoln asked Harris whether he had seen Douglass's report. Since the President had informed Harris the day before that he wanted to talk to him about the report, Harris had obtained a copy from the committee chairman and had read it before traveling to the White House. Harris was disturbed by what he read, but he was not sure what advice he might offer the President and he was curious to hear the President's reaction.

If Abraham Lincoln had any single extraordinary ability aside from eloquence, it was his prowess as a political operator. He understood perhaps better than any President either before or after how to employ Washington's political machinery to get things done, and he was a master at sensing the limits of what was politically feasible at any given moment. Lincoln's sixth sense was telling him, now, that progress required a united front of the legislative and executive branches. He was hoping to enlist the Reconstruction Committee as an ally in what he had come to believe was necessary for the good of the nation, a comprehensive plan for Reconstruction that would reestablish state sovereignty while recognizing and protecting the citizenship rights of the freedmen and all people of color. He could see now that federal power was still necessary, and that firm national resolve coupled with benevolent treatment for cooperative former adversaries was the only promising course of action. The only other possible course of action would be to evacuate all Black people from the South to Northern and Western states and territories, but that was not a viable alternative for numerous reasons, including the need for labor to rebuild the Southern economy and infrastructure.

Senator Harris told Lincoln "this report persuades me that strong federal action is necessary to ensure a just and effective transition to a reunified nation. While the Civil Rights Act was a good start, it seems to me that local hostility makes it very unlikely that enough civil or criminal cases could be brought under it to make a difference. From what I have heard, the views of many of our local United States Attorneys are more in line with the White opposition to civil rights than with the sentiments underlying the Act." Harris concluded by suggesting that Lincoln consider invoking his authority under sections 8 and 9 of the Act to employ the military to prevent violations.

Lincoln's reaction revealed deep skepticism over the current political feasibility of unilateral presidential action involving the power of the military. Lincoln said "I appreciate your views, but I fear that if I bring out the troops now, my sense is that resistance will only increase and may not calm down until federal power is banished and the old guard regains control down there." Lincoln added that in his previous, more lenient Reconstruction policy. "I was misled by early optimistic reports from Louisiana and Tennessee and I misjudged the depth of Southern opposition to civil rights for the freedmen. Even in Louisiana, with so many educated and wealthy people of color, I was surprised at the violence that greeted even the smallest steps toward political equality."

Harris responded: "I believe our Reconstruction Committee is willing and even anxious to cooperate with the President on Reconstruction." "Do you think," Lincoln asked, "the committee, and the Congress as a whole, might favor legislation instituting a formal system of federal oversight of Southern states that would impose more stringent requirements for gaining full political autonomy and their readmission to Congress?" Harris said "yes, and in fact we have already begun discussing a 'Reconstruction Act,' and support for a strong federal response is growing."

Lincoln ended the meeting by thanking Harris for his input and expressing hope that Harris would continue to be a liaison between him and the committee. Lincoln also advised Harris that he would be happy to work with the committee on formulating a policy going forward.

Harris said he would be glad to help, and then he asked the President whether he agreed with those who were saying that the country might never be truly reunited, that the Union as we know it might fail even after the military victory.

Lincoln answered with a story that he had used more than once. "I was boarding with the deacon of a local church in New Salem, Illinois, a quite elderly man. Once, in the middle of the night, I awoke to the sound of the house's door opening and the old man crying out 'arise Abraham, judgment day is here.' I looked outside to see the most impressive shower of falling stars I had ever witnessed. It appeared that the sky was on fire. But then, as the haze of sleep left my eyes, I could see that all of the familiar stars and constellations remained in the background where they always were." He concluded by expressing confidence that the Union will survive and that in the long run it will thrive.

When Congress reconvened on December 3, pressure for action on Reconstruction was coming from numerous directions. There were calls from Republicans across the South to suspend the operation of state governments and substitute direct federal rule, either via the military or by treating the former Confederate states, other than Tennessee, as territories. Thaddeus Stevens had brought such a bill before the Reconstruction Committee in the prior session, and he renewed his proposal on December 19. His proposal was to allow current Southern governments to function "for municipal purposes" only while a mandatory new constitutional convention was convened in each state that included delegates elected with full Black suffrage. The resulting state constitutions must guarantee equal rights to all and they must be presented to Congress for approval. Stevens's bill did not refer to ratification of the Fourteenth Amendment. Others, such as Charles Sumner, wanted full military government and reoccupation, with Black suffrage and protection of privileges and immunities as minimum conditions for renewal of Southern states to representation in Congress. More moderate Republicans, including John Bingham, Benjamin Wade, and John Sherman, who soon would find themselves in a clear minority when the new Congress was sworn in, argued that the Radicals were breaking their promise to readmit states upon ratification of the Fourteenth Amendment.

Democrats and moderate Republicans soon realized that they

were unlikely to have any influence on the terms of Reconstruction legislation, especially when the Republican majority was strengthened by the arrival of new members in January. They adopted a strategy of obstruction, which included placing every possible obstacle in the way of legislation and attempting to play the President's moderate views off against those gaining currency in Congress. It became clear, however, that although they might be able to slow the process down, there was little if any likelihood that they would prevent legislation from emerging. As far as pitting the President against Congress, their efforts were in vain because they failed to appreciate how much Lincoln's views had moved toward a more radical position. As the process unfolded, some of the more conservative Members of Congress came to regret their decision not to participate more in the creation of the bill that emerged as the Reconstruction Act of 1867.

After a flurry of activity beginning in December, it was Lincoln's input that shaped the legislation that ultimately emerged. In early January, 1867, Harris briefed the President on the range of proposals being discussed by members of the committee and Lincoln expressed his preferences in clear terms.

In Lincoln's view, while Congress had control over its own membership, and thus could establish whatever conditions it saw fit for allowing the formerly rebellious states to send representatives to Congress, the President had control over the recognition and operation of the governments of the formerly rebellious states. Lincoln explained that Congress should not attempt to use its legislative power or its control over membership in Congress to interfere in the details of the executive branch's superintendence of state governments. In Lincoln's view, the executive branch of the government, including the Freedmen's Bureau and the military, were agents of the President and must be under his exclusive control. Lincoln told Harris he would be inclined to veto any legislation that did not abide by these principles, although in truth Lincoln was not sure what he would do because he thought it was important for the federal government to present a united front against Southern recalcitrance on the treatment and rights of Black citizens.

After a good deal of back and forth, and despite warnings that it would meet significant resistance in the Senate, the Reconstruction Committee sent to the full House Stevens's bill to institute military rule in all Southern states except Tennessee and Louisiana, with reestablishment of Southern governments contingent on Congress's permission. On Louisiana, another committee investigating the New Orleans riot reported a bill disenfranchising former Confederates there and establishing a framework for a new Louisiana government, to be elected pursuant to universal male suffrage, Black and White, but excluding the ineligible rebels. Although Stevens's bill had been rejected by the House on a procedural vote just two weeks earlier, this time it and the Louisiana bill passed the House. In the Senate, as would be expected, Sumner greeted both bills enthusiastically, but passage in the Senate without any amendments was not to be.

The Senate's amendments rejected the abolition of existing Southern state governments, choosing instead to place them under federal supervision and control. Further, the Senate bill promised representation in Congress to any Southern state that adopted (in a process that included Black male suffrage for electing delegates) a new state constitution providing for universal male suffrage without regard to race and ratification of the Fourteenth Amendment. The reaction among the Radicals in the House was negative. At the same time, they realized that they did not have the votes to get everything they wanted, so they tried again.

Because it seemed that abolishing the Southern governments was a sticking point for moderates in the Senate, a new draft preserved those governments but made them subject to abolition if warranted by future events. Moderate Republican Senators signaled their agreement with this proposal. Amendments to the bill as approved in the Senate were soon drafted and were ready to be sent to the full House, when Senator Harris suggested a brief delay so that he could discuss the matter with the President. Stevens agreed, and Harris went to the White House bearing a copy of the bill. Lincoln asked Speed and Stanton to join them as they pored over the 900-word proposal.

Section 1 divided the South, excluding Tennessee but including

Louisiana, into five military districts.

Section 2 required the President to appoint as commander of each district, an Army officer "not below the rank of brigadier-general."

Section 3 specified the duties of the district commanders to protect persons and property, to suppress insurrection and violence and to employ military commissions for criminal trials when "in his judgment, it may be necessary."

Section 4 prohibited cruel and unusual punishments in military tribunals and required the commander's approval before any sentence thereof may be carried out, except that the President must personally approve any sentence of death.

Section 5 set forth the requirements for readmission of states to representation in Congress as specified above, including Black male suffrage, disqualification from voting for or participation in required state constitutional conventions for anyone "excluded from holding office by the pending amendment to the Constitution of the United States," and ratification of the Fourteenth Amendment.

Section 6 provided that until a state is readmitted to representation in Congress, its civil government is "deemed provisional only, and in all respects subject to the paramount authority of the United States at any time to abolish, modify, control or supersede the same." It also specified that persons not entitled to participate in a constitutional convention under Section 5 may not vote or hold office in the provisional governments.

Lincoln expressed concern over two of the provisions.

As a matter of principle, he did not like congressional imposition of a minimum rank for any position. Stanton encouraged the President not to worry about that requirement for two reasons, first because anyone appointed to that position was extremely likely to be of that rank or higher and second because if Lincoln wanted someone of lower rank to serve, most likely a colonel, he could simply order their promotion even presumably by brevetting them.

Second, Lincoln was concerned over the immediate grant of suffrage for Black Americans. He felt it would create great resentment across the South and wondered whether a more gradual introduction of suffrage might be possible, perhaps with a set of qualifications involving education and military service. Speed said that he agreed with Lincoln, but did not see how Lincoln had much choice but to sign the bill. With the imminent inception of the new Congress, the Radical majority might become so strong that an even more extreme bill might emerge as a response to the veto of this one. Harris corrected Speed's "might" to "would" but otherwise assented to what Speed had said. Lincoln saw the wisdom in Speed's advice and told Harris to let the leaders in Congress know that he would sign the bill.

With permission signaled by the President, Republicans in both the House and Senate— conservative, moderate, and Radical— joined together and passed the bill without a single dissenting vote from Republicans, and without a single favorable vote from Democrats. On March 2, 1867, two days before the beginning of the new Congress, Lincoln signed it.

With that, Black Americans in the South were granted the right to participate in the election of delegates to constitutional conventions and to vote in elections conducted under the provisions of the constitutions promulgated by them.

This was recognized as a momentous occasion. President Lincoln took the opportunity to give an impromptu speech from the balcony of the White House.

Lincoln's words were full of hope:

"It is nearly two years, now, since I stood in this place and proposed readmission of Louisiana to full participation in our national government, with suffrage extended to all whose education and loyal military service warranted it. Since that time, we have encountered many difficulties in making the transition away from the slave system that so tore apart our nation. This Reconstruction law that the Congress has sent to me carries with it the hope that we will not be back here again two years hence announcing yet another attempt. Now, with our Negro brethren fully admitted into participation in their political communities, we expect to see steady and certain progress toward our common national goal of restoring our precious Union, for which we endured so much pain and sorrow in the late war."

The Freedmen's Bureau and the military set out to enforce the Act, which brought about significant improvements for the daily lives of Black Americans in many areas. General Grant, in consultation with General Howard, appointed military commanders for each district: in Virginia, General John Schofield; in North and South Carolina, General Daniel Sickles; in Georgia, Florida, and Alabama, General John Pope; in Texas and Louisiana, General Philip Sheridan; and in Arkansas and Mississippi, a joint command shared by Generals Edward Ord, Alvan Cullem Gillem, and Adelbert Ames.

Sheridan and Sickles were especially zealous in their assertions of federal authority, provoking significant resentment among Whites (and numerous complaining letters to Grant and Lincoln), but the Black communities under their control thrived. This was especially so in Louisiana, where before the war, free people of color had already attained more economic, social, and political power than anywhere else in the country.

Frederick Douglass's efforts during this period were also very productive. He visited numerous Black communities to see for himself where resources such as schools and housing assistance were needed, and he identified Black community leaders who were best suited to liaison with the military authorities. Congress provided sufficient funds and authority for the Bureau to operate efficiently.

Although things went as smoothly as could be expected, the Bureau and the military encountered significant obstacles. Cooperation between Black Americans and the military proved difficult for most Southern Whites to accept, and the Bureau's efforts were most fruitful when they were conducted out of the public eye. This was difficult where Black and White Americans lived in close quarters, but not in the countryside and in places where shanty towns full of freedmen had sprung up on the outskirts of settled areas.

Douglass personally stayed away from large public gatherings to avoid attracting the attention of Whites who resented federal aid to the freedmen, and of the growing network of White supremacist organizations such as the Ku Kluxers and the White Leagues that were springing up across the South. Friction was, however, unavoidable especially in areas where Black Americans were in the large majority and could elect local officials from among their ranks who would also have authority over Whites. Many Whites could not bear the thought, much less the sight, of a Black police officer arresting a White person no matter what the circumstances.

The extent of the district commanders' authority was also somewhat unclear, as was the procedure for conducting the elections for membership in the constitutional conventions. At Howard and Grant's urging, Congress passed three additional Reconstruction Acts in 1867 and 1868. One in March 1867 authorized district commanders to hold elections for representatives to state constitutional conventions. Another in July 1867 authorized district commanders to remove from office uncooperative state and municipal officials, including voting registrars, and assign their duties to a member of the U.S. military or other person. The next, in March 1868, specified that the new state constitutions would be ratified by a simple majority vote in each state even if the draft constitution provided otherwise.

Lincoln signed all three bills. He trusted Grant, Howard, and Douglass, and moreover, he thought it important that he and Congress present a united front such that Southern White resentment toward federal policy would focus solely on either him or the Congress.

Although 1867 did not see any events like the violence in Memphis and New Orleans in 1866, there was still racial tension which occasionally erupted into public demonstrations. Many events arose out of discrimination on streetcars, including protests in Charleston, Richmond, and New Orleans. On March 27, a small group of Black Americans amidst a larger crowd violated the transit company's rules and attempted to ride a segregated streetcar in Charleston. When the conductor refused to continue driving, some members of the crowd tried to push the car forward. Although the police refused to arrest them at first and ordered the conductor to move ahead, the conductor drove instead to a guard house where they were arrested. Protests continued for several days resulting in multiple arrests, and the military had to be called in to restore the peace. Within two months, General Sickles ordered the end of discrimination on all modes of transportation in his district, including the streetcars.

In Richmond, on April 23, a Black man named Christopher Jones, with a ticket, was denied a place on a streetcar and arrested for disturbing the peace after a crowd gathered to support him. The crowd of Black Americans made it clear that they were protesting not only for Jones but for their rights, calling out slogans like "let us have our rights" and "let's teach these damned rebels how to treat us." Jones was charged the next day by local authorities on allegations that he "feloniously and maliciously conspired with a large number of colored persons, to wit to the number of one hundred or more, to incite the colored population of said city and state to make insurrection by acts of violence and war against the White population of the city and state and against the peace and dignity of the Commonwealth of Virginia." In New Orleans, protests broke out on April 28 when William Nichols was arrested for attempting to ride in a car reserved for Whites. Since at least 1865, Black Americans had been resisting that city's "star car" system under which passengers considered "colored" were confined to special cars marked with large stars that were often overcrowded and few and far between. After charges against Nichols were dropped to avoid a test of the star car system's legality, protests only intensified and on May 5, when opposing groups of White and Black men appeared on the verge of all-out battle, the Chief of Police ordered desegregation of the streetcars, ending, at least temporarily, segregation of New Orleans' streetcars.

The nation's biggest news in 1867, other than Reconstruction, was the purchase of Alaska from the Russian Empire. The Russians had approached the Buchanan administration before the Civil War, but no agreement was reached and the war put the potential sale on hold. In March, Tsar Alexander II instructed his minister to the United States, Eduard de Stoeckl, to reopen the negotiations. De Stoeckl reached out to Secretary of State William Seward who, with Lincoln's blessing, accepted. On March 17, the parties agreed to a treaty transferring Alaska to American sovereignty for $7.2 million, or approximately 2 cents per acre. Except for some partisan opposition, including from a few Radicals who were suspicious of anything involving Seward, the purchase was very popular among Americans, and Lincoln viewed it as a symbol of the return of the United States to its place among the nations of the world. The purchase was finalized on the American side by ratification of the treaty on April 9 by a vote in the Senate of 37-2, and a ceremony marking the official handover took place in Sitka, Alaska, on October 18.

The process of framing new constitutions had also begun in earnest across the South. Black suffrage and disenfranchisement of former rebels resulted in the election of Black and White Republicans to state conventions, which produced more progressive constitutions than had ever been seen before in the American South.

In South Carolina, in an election held in late 1867, the first in South Carolina in which Black Americans were allowed to vote, 124 delegates to the upcoming election were elected, of which 76 were Black and 48 were White. The resulting 1868 constitution of South Carolina provided that "[e]very male citizen of the United States, of the age of twenty-one years and upwards . . . without distinction of race, color, or former condition . . . shall be entitled to vote for all officers that are now, or hereafter be, elected by the people[.]" Further, all people eligible to vote were made "eligible to any office which is now or hereafter shall be elective[.]" (The constitution preserved disqualifications based on the federal Constitution but provided that "[n]o person shall be disenfranchised for felony, or other crimes committed while such person was a slave."). The constitution also provided for mandatory public education and stated that "[a]ll the public schools, colleges, and universities of this State supported in whole or in part by the public funds, shall be free and open to all the children and youths of the State, without regard to race or color." One of the first acts of the legislature elected under this constitution was to ratify the Fourteenth Amendment, and after Congress approved the state's new constitution, President Lincoln proclaimed on July 18, 1868, that South Carolina had fulfilled all requirements and was once again a full member of the United States.

In Louisiana, after its 1864 constitution was declared invalid by federal authorities and Congress rejected President Lincoln's attempt to readmit the state later that year, a constitutional convention was held in 1867 and 1868 to produce a constitution that met the requirements of the Reconstruction Act. This convention was dominated by Black Americans—both freedmen and the always free—as well as White Republicans. Their constitution granted citizenship to all, extended voting rights to Black men, repealed the Black Codes, prohibited public school segregation and aggressively excluded former rebels from voting and office holding. Louisiana's large population of pre-war free people of color had experienced a hardening of racial lines after the war, including increased exclusion from restaurants, theaters, and modes of transportation. In reaction, they included a wide-ranging provision in the new constitution requiring "equal rights and privileges upon any conveyance of a public character" and further that "all places of business, or of public resort, or for which a license is required by either State, parish or municipal authority, shall be deemed places of a public character, and shall be opened to the accommodation and patronage of all persons, without distinction or discrimination on account of race or color." White Republican Henry Clay Warmoth was elected governor in 1869, along with Lieutenant Governor Oscar Dunn, a former slave, who was the first Black lieutenant governor in any state. The legislature ratified the Fourteenth Amendment and President Lincoln declared it fully restored as a member of the Union on July 9, 1868.

On July 20, 1868, Secretary of State Seward declared that the Fourteenth Amendment was part of the federal Constitution, after having been ratified by 28 states as of July 9. He issued a formal proclamation to that effect on July 28, adding two additional states to ratification, Alabama and Georgia. New Jersey had attempted to rescind its ratification in March, but Seward declared that action invalid. (Oregon rescinded its ratification in October, after the amendment had gone into effect.) The final seven ratifying states did so pursuant to the Reconstruction Act, giving rise to a persistent claim that ratification was invalid as coerced. With the Fourteenth Amendment in place, doubts about the constitutionality of the Civil Rights Act of 1866 evaporated. Further, contrary to the Supreme Court's infamous Dred Scott decision, all persons born in the United States were now citizens of the country and their home states.

Throughout 1868, racial tension simmered across the South but rarely festered into open conflict. This tentative peace resulted from a combination of factors—strict rule in many areas by district commanders whose forces remained in place as peacekeepers even after states were readmitted to the Union, the sense among resentful Whites that resistance was futile with the governments firmly in the hands of Black Americans and Republicans, the focus on rebuilding, and finally, growing sentiment in favor of equal rights, even in the South. While the vast majority of Southern Whites insisted on segregation, more than ever before had adopted an attitude of "live and let live." Continuing armed conflict with the Indians remained a major focus of energy throughout 1868, even as General Sherman negotiated the new Treaty of Fort Laramie to replace the 1851 treaty that had failed after the United States government reneged on most of the commitments made in that treaty, such as protection of Indian territory and annuity payments to the tribes.

Part III: Chief Justice Abraham Lincoln

11

PRESIDENT CHASE?

The machinations leading up to Grant's victory in the 1868 presidential election are among the most interesting in the history of American politics. Early in 1868, Abraham Lincoln began testing the waters for a bid for an unprecedented third term as President. Over lunch on the veranda outside the Oval Office, he asked his closest confidants in the White House, John G. Nicolay and John Hay, what they thought about the idea. He offered the delicacy and incompleteness of Reconstruction, and the nation's instability, as his reason for considering a run that would violate the precedent first set in 1796 when George Washington declined to seek a third term that he almost certainly would have won.

Some of Washington's reasons for not running again applied equally to Lincoln—his exhaustion, his longing to return home, and then of course the never-ending attacks on his performance and character that came mainly from the Democratic press but sometimes emanated from dissatisfied Radical circles. Although Lincoln did not have pressing business matters calling him back to Springfield like those that constantly weighed on George Washington during his absences from Mount Vernon, Lincoln was concerned about the stress that the political life placed on his wife Mary, who never felt that she was quite accepted into Washington social circles.

Nicolay and Hay, Lincoln's most loyal friends and staffers, told Lincoln that they would support whatever decision he made, but Hay had his doubts that Lincoln was up to another four years of the stress of the presidency.

After Nicolay left the table to attend to some other business, Hay told Lincoln his concern and asked, "Have you not expressed a desire to return to the law in some capacity?"

Lincoln let that question hang, but it got him thinking about alternatives to the presidency. Later that week, in separate meetings, he mentioned the possibility of a third term to Seward and Stanton, asking each whether they would be willing to continue their service in such an event. Both were noncommittal—they had already served longer than virtually any cabinet members in history. Seward served from the very beginning of Lincoln's presidency, and Stanton since early in Lincoln's first term.

Although the sting of losing the 1860 nomination to Lincoln had faded, Seward still felt as if he had never reached his true potential as a leader and a statesman under Lincoln. Moreover, he wanted to travel, especially to Alaska to see the territory he had helped acquire, where he could explore his interest in whaling. But he told Lincoln that if the President felt that he was still needed, he would serve, and Seward, ever the patriot, meant it.

Stanton was more reluctant, owing to poor health and financial difficulties. In fact, Stanton thought that Lincoln confided in him not with the idea that he would actually continue as War Secretary, but rather just to see his reaction to the idea. Stanton had another reason for alarm. Ulysses S. Grant had previously asked Stanton to support him for President in 1868, and Stanton had agreed, not imagining that Lincoln might go for a third term.

Over the next several days, Lincoln bandied the idea around with a number of others—never wanting to seem too serious—asking whether "I have overstayed my welcome at the White House" or if "the rail splitter ought to spend a few more years in Washington." When Frederick Douglass came to the White House with General Howard to give the President a progress report (and, as usual, to request increased funding), Lincoln asked Douglass, "How do you think we would do down South if I ran for re-election with you on the ticket?"

Douglass, who over their long years of collaboration had become comfortable with the President's banter, answered, "I'm sure we would do fine among the freedmen, but what makes you think I would accept if you asked me?"

They shared a good laugh at this, but Douglass was serious

about the freedmen vote. Throughout 1868, the Bureau had very successfully registered Black Americans across the South to vote.

Later that day Lincoln recounted Douglass's quip to his friend Noah Brooks, and Brooks asked the President if he was really considering another run.

Lincoln answered, "Well, once the fish got good at riding his bicycle, he never again saw a good reason to return to swimming."

Brooks extended the metaphor by replying that there were other interesting swimming holes in Washington, including over at the Supreme Court. He reminded Lincoln of their long talks in recent years about Supreme Court decisions on a variety of subjects. These included decisions regarding Lincoln's suspensions of habeas corpus, and also the railroad cases, which still interested Lincoln from his days as a lawyer. After they parted, Lincoln pondered this idea. What better place for a country railroad lawyer than on the Supreme Court?

Back at the War Department, Stanton told Grant what he had heard from the President. Grant dismissed it as just talk. "If there's one thing the President is good at, it's talking."

But Grant was concerned. Although he thought he might have a chance of defeating Lincoln at the Republican convention, and he was certain he would win in November, he did not want to appear disloyal to the President who had guided the country through so much and who had shown so much confidence in him personally. That night, Grant told his wife Julia what Stanton had said. Julia reassured him, saying that all the Washington ladies were already talking about him as if he had been elected and was just waiting to move into the White House. Even Kate Chase Sprague, Chief Justice Salmon Chase's daughter, had told Julia that as much as she thought her father ought to be President, she was certain that Grant would be elected and would do a fine job. According to Kate, who was perhaps the leading lady in Washington society and had worked on her father's behalf to oust Lincoln from the 1864 nomination, her father had even said so, remarking once that the rise of Grant was the final nail in the coffin of his hopes of ever being President.

However, Kate also told Julia (which she reported to her husband) that her father was prepared to leave the Court if he had a realistic chance in the 1868 election, perhaps if Grant decided not to run. This mollified Grant a bit, but after a sleepless night considering various strategies, Grant decided that a frontal assault was his best strategy and decided to call on the President to talk it over directly. Although he would have liked to gather some intelligence before the engagement, Julia and Mary Lincoln were still not on great terms, so he decided not to ask Julia to accompany him.

In response to Grant's morning request for a meeting, Lincoln suggested that Grant come by late that afternoon after the bustle of business and the line of visitors would calm down for the dinner hour. Grant arrived at the White House at about 5 pm in the afternoon of May 11.

Grant found Lincoln busily working through some correspondence with John Hay concerning matters in the State of Nevada and a possible position as postmaster there for one Orion Clemens. Orion was the older brother of Samuel Clemens, who was just then getting famous out West under the pen name Mark Twain. Orion had left Nevada for California, but with business ventures there faring not better than what he left behind in Nevada, he had requested an appointment as postmaster, but Lincoln could not provide one because all of the positions in Nevada had been filled by candidates identified by Nevada's two Republican Senators, elected in the new state's first election in 1864.

Grant and Lincoln met the more famous Clemens, but not until some years later, and Grant and Twain eventually became close friends.

Grant's first formal meeting with Twain was an odd affair. In 1870, Twain, already a well-known humorist and travel writer, was introduced to Grant at the White House. The meeting began with an awkward silence, and after about thirty seconds, Twain said to Grant "Well, I'm quite embarrassed. Are you?" Grant laughed and said, "Well yes I am, but there's really no need to be." They then talked in earnest. Grant told Twain that he and Lincoln had enjoyed some good laughs over Twain's published stories— "especially the one about the frog"—and a lifelong friendship was initiated. The next day, Grant brought Twain to meet Lincoln, when again an awkward silence began the encounter. Twain started the ball rolling by saying, "Mr. President, I hear from this fellow here" (indicating Grant with a wave of his cigar) "that you enjoyed my jumping frog story," to which Lincoln replied, "Yes I did Mr. Clemens, and many others I have read in the papers. As you may have heard, I like to spin a yarn or two myself, but I am afraid to tell you one, not only because I am afraid it might not measure up but because I fear I have purloined more than a few of yours and I don't think I can at the moment recall which ones of mine are yours." All three had a laugh over Lincoln's quip which was followed by a lengthy conversation during which Twain and Lincoln expressed their admiration for each other.

After Grant's death, Twain's publishing company, Webster and Company, published Grant's memoirs to critical acclaim and unprecedented financial success, earning Julia Grant more than $400,000 in royalties, finally, albeit posthumously, allowing Grant to provide financial security for his family.

Back to the present. After completing his letter informing Orion Clemens that he would not be getting an appointment as a postmaster, Lincoln turned his attention to Grant. He said, "Well General, I suppose you have good news and want to deliver it in person."

Grant chuckled and then demurred, saying, "Not exactly, Mr. President. I am here actually to make an inquiry concerning the upcoming party convention, whether I might have your support when the delegates meet in Chicago next month."

Lincoln knew that Stanton must have told Grant that he was mulling over a third term, and he understood that this was Grant's way of discerning Lincoln's intentions. Lincoln remained silent for some time. He said, "Well General, I have been thinking some about both of our futures, and something has caught my eye. My friend Noah has been telling me I would make a good Chief Justice, but with our friend Chase in that position, the only way I can imagine that happening is if he beats you at the convention and steps aside thereafter. Otherwise, I might just stay where I am, as I am finally getting used to this place. I cannot imagine serving simply as one of many on the Court—they'd probably give me all the work they didn't want for themselves. Fred Douglass tells me there are plenty of Republican votes down South to make up for whatever I might forfeit in Ohio or New York"

Grant asked, "What if Chase stepped aside to run for President?"

Lincoln replied simply, "Interesting thought General, interesting thought."

Grant said, "One thing I can say without reservation, Mr. President. If I were so fortunate to be in position to make the choice, I cannot imagine a better choice for Chief Justice."

After this meeting, Grant went home and talked it over with Julia. He told her that he now understood that Lincoln would give up the idea of a third term if he had assurances of an appointment as Chief Justice, and he was confident that Lincoln understood that he had made the promise. It was vital to figure out a way to get Chase out of the way. Julia suggested that she have a talk about it with Kate Chase. General Grant agreed, and that night Julia sent a message to Kate, who was known to be visiting Washington, inviting her to lunch the next day. There had already been talk that one of the reasons Kate was spending so much time in Washington away from her family in Rhode Island was that her father had asked her to make inquiries about his presidential prospects. (Another presumed reason was a rumored intimate relationship with her husband's successor in the Senate Roscoe Conkling.) Kate accepted, and on May 12, over lunch at the Grant residence, Julia played the opening gambit in the Grant plan.

After asking after Kate's husband, their son, and Kate's father, Julia got to the point. She said that she and her husband had been talking about the upcoming Republican convention and that General Grant thought that if Kate's father committed himself to being a candidate, he would be a strong candidate and Grant himself might even take himself out of the running. When Kate then asked Julia if she thought her father should run, Julia said that in her opinion, he should, but, as General Grant had suggested, any effort at securing the nomination while remaining Chief Justice would seem tentative, not a sufficient commitment in such turbulent and dangerous times to convince people to support him or the delegates to nominate him. She also reminded Kate of how his 1864 bid to quietly unseat Lincoln had backfired. Kate was taken aback by Julia's directness. She replied that she found Julia's thoughts interesting and was supposed to dine with her father that evening, when she was sure the convention would be an important subject of conversation.

Kate's dinner with her father that evening was pleasant. She and her father were very close, and Kate had always been her father's biggest, and most influential, political supporter. She began the political discussion by reporting that many people were still saying that he would make a great President and that the steady hand he showed at the Treasury during the Civil War bodes well for his ability to steer the country through the straits of Reconstruction. All, however, thought that General Grant was a very strong candidate with wide support among the delegates to the upcoming convention and would be the overwhelming favorite if he stood for election. Unknown to Kate, Chase was so desperate to be President he had already made inquiries to prominent Democrats about leading that party's ticket, but their replies were not promising. Chase sighed and said something like, "Once again, the country will be given the choice between a disastrous Democrat and an unqualified Republican." He then asked, "Kate, do you really think that if I announce my candidacy, General Grant will step aside?" Kate said she was not sure, and they decided to each make discreet inquiries with trustworthy friends.

Chase himself approached two people, Elihu Washburne of Illinois and George S. Boutwell of Massachusetts. Washburne had been a Member of Congress since 1853, set to become Dean of the House in 1869. Chase sought him out because he had a longstanding, close relationship with General Grant, dating back to when they both lived in Galena, Illinois. Washburne had enthusiastically backed Illinois's Abraham Lincoln for President, and he was also likely to be a strong supporter of a Grant candidacy. Over drinks at Washburne's Washington home, he promised Chase that he would speak to Grant and report back. Boutwell had served under Chase as the first Commissioner of Internal Revenue, after which Boutwell was elected to Congress. Chase admired Boutwell's work at the revenue office and the two became friends as a result of working together closely on the design and implementation of that office. Boutwell was an ardent pre-war abolitionist turned Radical Member of Congress, and he had always supported Chase's presidential aspirations. Chase told him that he was thinking of running and asked Boutwell whether he thought he should leave the Court to do so. Boutwell answered Chase's question in the affirmative, stating that it would be difficult for Chase to be a serious candidate while still serving on the Supreme Court. Boutwell said that the only way to have any chance would be to do it openly and enthusiastically, and the sort of politicking he would have to do was not compatible with service on the Court.

Chase received an answer from Washburne two days later. Washburne paid a call on Grant at the War Department, told him about his conversation with Chase and asked Grant about his plans. Grant replied that Washburne should keep it to himself, but he might just step aside if it looked like Chase was a serious candidate for the nomination. Washburne then asked, "General, what should I tell Chase?" Grant said you should try to dissuade him from running because, and you can tell him I said this, I do not see him as a significant factor at the convention if he remains on the Court. Washburne, eager for Chase's approval in case Chase should get elected and have the power of making Cabinet-level appointments, told Chase everything, even adding that he thought Grant wanted him to discourage Chase from running because he feared the strength of Chase as a candidate. Little did Washburne know that what he feared might be viewed as a betrayal if Grant learned of this conversation was exactly what Grant hoped Washburne would tell Chase.

Kate Chase was not sure who to ask. That evening, she told Senator Conkling what her father was considering, and he was negative—vehemently so—regarding the idea of Chase resigning from the Court to run. He told Kate that in his opinion, support for Grant was overwhelming and that Chase's only real hope would be to run as a Democrat. Even then, if he got the nomination, he would almost certainly not prevail in the election. Kate pressed him to ask Abraham Lincoln for his view on the matter, and when Conkling got back to her the next day, Conkling said that the President was "more open to the thought than I had expected given how his relationship with your father had soured at the end of his service at the Treasury." Lincoln told Conkling that he had thought earlier that Grant had the nomination sewn up, but that he had heard some misgivings due to Grant's well known "issues," which Conkling took to mean his reputation for drinking to excess, and some Republican leaders were looking for an alternative. Conkling reported that the President agreed with the view that, given the shortness of time (the convention was less than a month away), Chase would have to come right out and campaign hard before the convention and that this might be difficult for a sitting Chief Justice. While campaigning did not necessarily mean speaking before large gatherings, which Presidential candidates of the day rarely did before the convention, it would mean numerous meetings with party leaders where promises of Cabinet positions and commitments to elements of a party platform would be made. Conkling concluded the discussion by saying, "I regret having to say it Kate, but I do not think your father's prospects at the convention are great, and I don't trust what is going on. I would urge him to stay where he is, at the pinnacle of the legal profession."

The next morning, over breakfast, Kate told her father what Conkling had said, stressing his doubts but also his somewhat surprising report on what Lincoln had told him. Chase's presidential dreams were growing by the minute, and they prevented him from comprehending the wisdom in Conkling's doubts. All be damned, he thought: I am going to see Lincoln myself and get a sense of what's going on.

Chase called on Lincoln that afternoon, making a valiant effort to hide his dislike and resentment. Lincoln, for his part, was extremely cordial, inquiring after Kate and asking Chase whether he was enjoying life in the basement of the Capitol. Chase reminded the President that they had moved upstairs several years back, to the old Senate chamber, and quipped that they now were literally (not just figuratively) a coequal branch of government.

Then, Chase cut to the chase. "Mr. President," he said, "you know that I have always been willing to serve my country in whatever capacity it needed me, and I fear that in the treacherous times lurking ahead, my greatest value to the country may be as your successor. I am interested to hear your opinion on that."

Lincoln was pleased at this confirmation that Chase was taking the bait. He could sense that the Chief Justice's hope to be President was now paramount in his mind. He did not want to lie to Chase, but perhaps a bit of misdirection was in order.

Lincoln replied, "If you could repeat the way you steered our finances through the war, I am confident that you would be a trustworthy pilot for the entire ship. You are aware that I am not in a position to get involved directly in the convention, but if the convention had the wisdom to choose you, I would do whatever the dignity of my office allows to ensure victory in November and a continuation of our party's policies."

In his state of excitement, Chase came away from this meeting sensing that he had received a virtually unqualified endorsement from the President, and on his way home, he resolved to make the move.

Upon arriving home, Chase wrote out a letter of resignation addressed to President Lincoln that he planned to have delivered the next morning. Kate came for dinner and when her father told her his plans, she confessed her mixed feelings. On the one hand, she said, this was probably his last best chance at the presidency. On the other hand, it was still a long shot, and he would be giving up a position that most of his peers dared not even dream about. She again stressed Conkling's doubts, and his suspicions that political machinations like those of 1860 and 1864 were at play behind the scenes. Kate asked him to wait another full day and think before he leapt.

Chase held out until late the following afternoon, when he buckled under the weight of his ambition and asked a messenger in the Supreme Court Clerk's office to deliver his letter to the White House, informing the President that he would step down as Chief Justice on June 15. This was the day before the Republican convention was scheduled to convene in Chicago. Just two weeks had elapsed since Kate's lunch with Julia Grant, and Salmon Chase's presidential dreams lived only a few days more before he understood the terrible mistake he had made.

On the morning following the submission of his resignation, he called on Representative Thaddeus Stevens to inform him of his plans. Stevens was still a leader of the Radical wing of the Republican Party and as chairman of the House Ways and Means Committee, he and Chase had worked together closely on financing the war effort. Chase expected Stevens to be an influential presence at the convention.

When Chase made his pitch, Stevens looked at him as if he had grown two heads. "As far as I know," Stevens said, "General Grant is going to be the overwhelming choice of the convention."

Chase asked Stevens whether he had heard any talk of Grant not standing for nomination, but Stevens said that he had not. Stevens also informed Chase that due to ill health, he was unlikely to travel to Chicago anyway. He did promise that he would let Chase's interest in the nomination be known, but he was not optimistic.

Chase next called on Schuyler Colfax, Speaker of the House. Colfax confirmed what Stevens had said, saying that he had spoken with General Grant a few days earlier and was given no reason to think that he had changed his mind about the presidency. Colfax did not inform Chase that Grant had let Colfax know that he was under consideration for inclusion on the ticket, asking whether he would be willing to serve if asked. Colfax had agreed and was

119

the leading contender for the Vice-Presidential spot on Grant's Republican ticket.

On the Senate side of the Capitol Building, Chase paid calls on Charles Sumner and Jacob Howard.

Sumner was suspicious of Grant and was critical of his abortive tour with Robert E. Lee. He was concerned that Grant would resist important elements of the Radical Reconstruction program. He gave Chase a glimmer of hope, telling him that he certainly preferred Chase—as a committed Radical—to Grant for President, but he added that he did not have much influence with his fellow Republicans.

Jacob Howard's comments echoed Stevens's. He said everyone on the Reconstruction Committee, Republican and Democrat, expected Grant to secure the nomination and be elected in November. Even committee members who disliked Grant thought that he had a virtual lock on the nomination and election unless Confederates were re-enfranchised and all Southern states were allowed to participate in the election.

That evening, Chase asked his daughter to meet again with Julia Grant and also ask Senator Conkling what he was hearing. Her father was unaware that she had already planned to see Senator Conkling that evening, and when they met, she asked him whether he had heard any talk about her father's candidacy.

Conkling replied that several of his Senate colleagues said the same thing, that Grant's support across the country was overwhelming and that even though they might prefer Chase, they did not see a way to stop Grant at the convention. He was so likely to win the nomination that even those who were most disposed to oppose Grant would not, if only to preserve their standing with the next President and in the party more generally. And when Conkling spoke again to the President, he reported that Lincoln told him it looked like Grant all the way and he saw no point in getting personally involved at this stage.

Julia Grant received Kate's invitation to lunch and put her off for a couple of days, claiming that she was too busy to see Kate any sooner. Kate took this as a bad sign. In the meanwhile, all public signs pointed toward Grant as the Republican candidate. There were numerous articles reporting speeches and statements of Republican political figures, many of them convention delegates, all indicating support for Grant. Grant himself had not suggested that Chase's entry into the field made any difference to him. When Kate and Julia finally met, all of Kate's worst fears were confirmed. Julia said that her husband had spoken to several leading Republicans about Chase's resignation, and they all told him both that they still supported Grant and that they expected the convention to go for him by a wide margin, if not unanimously.

When confronted with this reality, Salmon Chase considered two options. The first was to rescind his resignation. The second was to seek the Democratic nomination. He rejected the first option because, clinging to some small shred of hope, he wanted to be available as a candidate in case something changed before or during the Republican convention. Maybe Grant would renew his well-known acquaintance with strong drink, or simply decide he did not want to endure the rigors of the presidency. As far as the second option was concerned, because the Democratic convention was not scheduled to take place until July, Chase could wait before exploring that less attractive possibility.

Meanwhile, as soon as Chase's resignation became public, Lincoln began receiving letters urging him to promote Associate Justice Samuel Miller to Chief Justice. Miller had been appointed by Lincoln in 1862 and quickly became the Court's intellectual leader and workhorse, authoring more opinions than any other Justice in the history of the Court. Further, he had generally been supportive of broad presidential power during the Civil War. He was somewhat of a judicial minimalist, which helps explain why some of his later opinions were criticized for taking narrow positions on the effects of the Fourteenth Amendment. But his merits were beside the point. As Miller's supporters would soon learn, Lincoln had other plans regarding the appointment of the next Chief Justice.

12

CANDIDATE GRANT

The Republican Party convened in Chicago on June 16, the day after Chief Justice Chase officially left the Supreme Court. The leading Radical Republicans were in attendance, except for Thaddeus Stevens, whose worsening health left him unable to travel to the Windy City (so named because of its history of 'windbag' political speeches).

As was the custom of the time, Grant himself stayed away, but his Vice-Presidential choice Schuyler Colfax was omnipresent, seeking support from the delegates for his candidacy. While Grant's nomination was a foregone conclusion, the Vice-Presidential slot was contested by a number of candidates, including three who would receive more votes on the first ballot than Colfax: Ohio Senator Benjamin Wade, who out balloted Colfax for the first four ballots; New York Governor Reuben Fenton; and Massachusetts Senator Henry Wilson.

On the morning of June 16, when Grant's victory was apparent, both Wade and Chase informed the convention that they did not wish their names to be placed in nomination for President. After Grant was nominated on the first ballot by acclamation, it was considered an oddity that the convention did not automatically accept his choice of Colfax as running mate. Colfax had apparently made plenty of enemies as Speaker of the House, and some delegates were also concerned about his unremitting support for full suffrage for Black Americans in every state, North and South. Rather, that decision took what is best characterized as five and one-half ballots—in the midst of the fifth ballot all of Wilson's supporters as well as most of Wade's and Fenton's switched to Colfax, which put him well over the number of votes necessary for the nomination.

The suffrage issue was both constitutionally and politically fraught. Many of the Radicals favored Black suffrage in every state, while others felt that the federal government lacked the power to impose that as a requirement except in the previously rebellious states. Some of the more cautious delegates feared that a platform that included federal imposition of Black suffrage would strengthen the Democratic opposition and endanger Republican candidates in state and congressional elections, even if Grant was a shoo-in for the presidency. In the end, the moderates prevailed and the platform favored "equal suffrage to all loyal men at the South," presumably including Black Americans, but also provided that "the question of suffrage in the loyal States properly belongs to the people of those States." The 1868 platform also condemned British and European claims that their people who had emigrated to the United States remained their subjects and declared that "foreign immigration" and "asylum of the oppressed of all nations should be fostered by a liberal and just policy."

Once Grant's selection was finalized, Chase turned his attention to the Democratic Party, which was much less unified than its Republican counterpart. Southern Democrats were returning to the convention for the first time since 1860, and they brought with them more extreme views on race and Reconstruction than many in the Northern branch of their party. Chase, once a leading Radical Republican, had no chance at securing their support, or even the support of more than a few Northern Democrats. In Democratic eyes, he had committed numerous unforgiveable sins: defending fugitive slaves while practicing law in Ohio; coauthoring an 1854 anti-slavery manifesto with Charles Sumner among other heretics, which had helped spur the founding of the Republican Party; adamantly opposing slavery and secession; supporting both the war effort and Republican Reconstruction policies; and admitting a Black man, John Rock of Massachusetts, to practice before the nation's highest court.

Perhaps his gravest political sin was the opinion he wrote while riding circuit in the case In re Turner, an action for habeas corpus brought in 1867 on behalf of a Maryland girl who had been forcibly placed into an apprenticeship two days after Maryland abolished slavery. Chase ruled that the apprenticeship violated the Thirteenth Amendment and the Civil Rights Act of 1866, which he concluded was a valid exercise of Congress's constitutional power. He also explicitly stated that Miss Turner was a citizen of the United States, in direct contradiction with the Dred Scott decision. He thus ordered that Miss Turner be released from the person to whom she had been indentured and restored to freedom.

Chase contacted several leading Democrats only to be rebuffed. Vice President Johnson did not even bother to answer his letter requesting a meeting, and his name was never placed in nomination. The real question confronting the Democratic Party in 1868 was whether its campaign would be overtly racist, or only indirectly so. This struggle for the soul of the Democratic Party played out over six days in July, culminating in the unlikely nomination of New Yorker Horatio Seymour for President and Missouri's Francis Blair for Vice President after twenty-two and one-half ballots. Before the shift toward Seymour, the convention was deadlocked between Thomas Hendricks of Indiana who as a U.S. Senator had voted against both the Thirteenth and Fourteenth Amendments, and General Winfield Scott Hancock, a Civil War hero and the man who carried out the death sentences imposed on the assassination conspirators, despite his opposition to executing Mary Surratt. Vice President Johnson's best showing was on the first ballot when he received 65 votes, placing him a distant second to former Ohio Representative George Pendleton, who led the voting through the first fifteen ballots.

Johnson accused Seymour of scheming for the nomination all along, but Seymour truly was a reluctant candidate, having rejected similar efforts to draft him in 1856, 1860, and 1864. Although Seymour was opposed to Republican Reconstruction policies, and may have actually opposed the Civil War as some accused, the party platform reflected Blair's views more than Seymour's, calling for immediate restoration of all states to the Union, complete amnesty for all "past political offenses," state control over the franchise everywhere, and abolition of the Freedmen's Bureau "and all political instrumentalities designed to secure negro supremacy." The enumeration of grievances against the Lincoln administration was reminiscent of the Declaration of Independence's accusations directed at King George III.

The official party election motto, appearing on numerous campaign posters and handbills, was "This is a White Man's Country; Let White Men Rule." Blair contributed mightily to his own ticket's defeat by embarking on a speaking tour which in its negative impact was reminiscent of Johnson's Swing around the Circle. He advocated military action to expel the current "illegitimate" Southern governments and characterized Black Americans as "a semi-barbarous race who are worshippers of fetishes and poligamists [sic]."

By contrast, Grant's campaign slogan was "Let Us Have Peace."

After the Democratic convention, Chase was crestfallen and watched the election campaign from afar. The election resulted in a resounding victory for General Grant in the electoral vote. The Grant-Colfax ticket won twenty-six states while Seymour and Blair took only eight including New York, the nation's most populous state. The popular vote was much closer than most people expected, with 52.7 percent for Grant and 47.3 percent for Seymour. This may have been due in part to violent efforts in many Southern locales to suppress the Black and Republican vote. Congress had readmitted seven Southern states into the Union between the Republican convention and the November election, expecting large Republican majorities from a combination of freedmen voting for the first time and the continued disenfranchisement of many former rebels. These states participated in the presidential election and sent Senators to the new Congress, but their representatives were not seated in the House when the new Congress convened in March, 1869.

The Republican ticket did receive substantial support across the South, but in Georgia and Louisiana, which the Democrats won, as well as in other areas within a few Southern states, White supremacist violence prevented most Republicans, Black and White, from voting. This presaged things to come. Hundreds of people were killed in pre-election violence including White Republican James M. Hinds, a Member of Congress from Arkansas. In one massacre in St. Landry Parish, Louisiana, more than 200 Black Americans were killed after a local Republican newspaper, citing Democratic violence, urged all Black Americans to support the Republican Party. After killing twenty-nine Black Americans they had taken as prisoners, including numerous Black Republican activists, the mob went on a killing spree throughout the area resulting in the killing of an estimated 200 to 300 more. The killing was facilitated by provisions of local law that prohibited Black Americans from owning guns, leaving them unable to defend themselves, and the lack of sufficient federal troops to prevent violence everywhere that it might arise among enraged Whites.

In addition to the White House, the Republican Party retained its majority in both Houses of Congress, although the Democratic Party did gain a few House seats. When the lame duck Congress returned to session following the election, its main order of business was the issue of Black suffrage. The Democrats had made suffrage a major issue in the 1868 campaign, accusing congressional Republicans of usurping state control over voting rights. Although many of the Southern states had been forced to allow Black Americans to vote as a condition for approval of new constitutions, Radicals in Congress were pushing for a federal suffrage amendment for several reasons, the first two of which were closely related. First, White resentment of Black voting was so widespread that it appeared likely that once federal supervision was gone, Southern states were likely to revert to White-only suffrage. Second, just as the first sentence of the Fourteenth Amendment was a response to constitutional doubts over Congress's power to regulate citizenship, principles of federalism created doubt over the constitutionality of a federal statute creating Black suffrage, even in elections for federal office. Third, it was unclear whether the Republican majority in the next Congress would be strong enough to pass the amendment, as it was still unknown whether Southern representatives would be seated in the House. Fourth, there was a genuine concern that the longer Congress waited to pass the amendment, the less likely it would be that Republicans would have control of enough state legislatures to achieve ratification. Finally, Republicans wanted to get the issue settled as quickly as possible so sentiment against it would die down long before the next congressional or presidential election.

Republican sentiment in favor of a suffrage amendment was not unanimous, with some Radicals preferring a statute. Charles Sumner was as usual the outlier, taking the odd position that a constitutional amendment in favor of Black suffrage would affirm state control over everything else, thus validating all other aspects of official discrimination. He declared, "Anything for human rights is constitutional, and there are no states' rights against human rights." Sumner and his colleagues abandoned their statutory effort only when it became clear that too many moderate Republicans disagreed with them on Congress's power to act. Attention then turned to constructing a constitutional amendment.

Crafting a constitutional amendment extending the right to vote to the freedmen and other people of color turned out to be a complicated process, which proponents felt they had to complete before the end of the Fortieth Congress on March 3, 1869. From the outset, there were competing proposals ranging from a simple ban on voting qualifications based on race or color to more complex federal prohibitions on property tests and poll taxes regardless of race. The competing factions often agreed in principal but had different views on the likelihood of passage and on the propriety of federal intervention beyond the simple question of race. A plethora of proposals in both Houses resulted in complicated and lengthy parliamentary maneuvers that led ultimately to the need for a conference committee of the two Houses, where a simple proposal emerged, prohibiting the denial or abridgment of the right of citizens of the United States to vote "on account of race, color, or previous condition of servitude" and granting Congress the power to enforce the amendment "by appropriate legislation." There was no reference to national origin and no prohibition on race-neutral devices that might be used to suppress Black voting. The balm for these omissions were that the reference to "citizens of the United States" presumably encompassed all naturalized citizens regardless of their national origin, and the grant of enforcement power to Congress would provide Congress ample power to override any state laws or practices that might undercut the spirit of the amendment. One observer characterized the whole process as a "congressional somersault" since Congress effectively ended up exactly where it began, essentially adopting language proposed at the outset of the process by Massachusetts Representative George Boutwell.

Ratification was hotly contested in many states, but ultimately the required twenty-eight states assented less than a year after Congress sent them the amendment. Opposition was concentrated mainly in Democratic strongholds and Southern states. Supporters of women's suffrage, outraged that their cause had not been included, were also among the most vocal opponents of the amendment. Elizabeth Cady Stanton became the first woman in United States history to testify before a congressional committee, when she appeared before the Joint Committee on Reconstruction to oppose passage of the Fifteenth Amendment unless it included women's suffrage.

Some states ratified the amendment quickly, including most of the New England states, Nevada, and the Southern states governed by Reconstruction legislatures, Louisiana, South Carolina, and Arkansas. By the end of March, 1869, twelve states had ratified the amendment, with three more coming into line by the end of May. Thirteen more states were necessary for ratification, and after May, the process slowed down but never really stopped. Connecticut and New Hampshire ratified during the summer, and Iowa became the twenty-eighth state to ratify on February 3, 1870. Alabama, Mississippi, and Georgia had ratified the amendment by then, Georgia acting only after Black members of the Georgia General Assembly who had been expelled in September were reinstated by an act of Congress.

If enforced, the Fifteenth Amendment had the potential to initiate fundamental changes to Southern politics. Black voters were likely Republican voters, and in many places they constituted a high enough percentage to determine the outcome of elections, especially if former participants in the rebellion remained disenfranchised. Because Southern White society was so committed to reasserting White supremacy, this was a big "if." Leading Radicals such as Sumner and Shellabarger, who had not stood for reelection and was seeking an appointment in the new administration, reached out to President-elect Grant and pressed him to commit to long-term military supervision of Southern political activity, including federal voter registration and a heavy presence of federal troops during election campaigns and on election days.

The lame duck Congress continued to meet until the day before Grant's inauguration, passing numerous bills and resolutions, mostly grants of military pensions and military pay for various persons who had served during the Civil War without an official authorization for compensation. For example, on March 3, 1869, the Fortieth Congress's last day, a Joint Resolution was adopted granting Ella E. Hobart "the full pay and emoluments of a chaplain in the United States army, for the time during which she faithfully performed the services of a chaplain as if she had been regularly commissioned and mustered into service." Mrs. Hobart was the first woman to serve as chaplain in the United States military.

In preparation for his inauguration as Vice President, Schuyler Colfax resigned as Speaker of the House on March 3 and was succeeded, for one day, by New York Representative Theodore M. Pomeroy, who also left Congress the next day, not having stood for reelection. He had plenty of work during his short tenure, with Congress passing 31 bills on March 3, including several appropriations bills, a bill designating dozens of post roads and a bill repealing an 1868 prohibition on the establishment of militias in North Carolina, South Carolina, Florida, Alabama, Louisiana, and Arkansas.

One very important bill that was passed in the waning hours of the Congress was the Judiciary Act of 1869, which established the position of United States Circuit Judge and reset the membership of the Supreme Court at nine.

13
LINCOLN TO GRANT TO LINCOLN

Anticipation over the end of Lincoln's presidency was rampant nationwide. Gifts and letters of congratulations poured in from across the world. Lincoln had given no clue concerning his post-presidential intentions, and the purchase by supporters of a home for him in Washington had been kept quiet. Even his wife Mary could not get a straight answer to her questions about their future plans. He told her only that he thought the family should remain in Washington for the time being so Tad could stay close to his friends. She would have preferred to move back to Illinois to be closer to her family and their son Robert, who was in Chicago, first studying and now practicing law. She was also concerned that if their income faltered, her debts for extravagant purchases of clothing and household goods would cause even more friction with Lincoln than there already was at home due to her frequent trips to New York to shop and spend time with her friends there.

Lincoln had hoped to give a major speech shortly before departing the White House, but the press of business kept him busy, and he was barely done signing bills and resolutions from Congress when it came time to join President Grant for the inauguration. Normally, an outgoing President would leave the White House two or three days before his successor was inaugurated, to allow the new President to begin life at the White House immediately after inauguration. In this case, however, Grant, anxious to portray the transition as one of continuation, insisted that the Lincolns remain at the White House until the morning of March 4. Rather than leave the White House, Mr. and Mrs. Lincoln sent most of their belongings to their new home and spent the night of March 3, with Tad, in a two-room suite on the southeast corner of the White House, with the President sleeping in a room that since that day forward has been known as "the Lincoln bedroom" even though he slept there only once.

Although no festivities were planned, people began to gather at the White House in the afternoon of March 3, hoping to see the President and wish him a fond farewell. Lincoln was busy at work signing bills and making last minute appointments to positions across the country, including numerous postmasters in western areas that were being rapidly settled and developed throughout the 1860s and 1870s. One of the last bills he signed was the Judiciary Act which in effect re-created the position that he was set to occupy. By about 6 pm, the crowd was enormous, and an army band had arrived. The band and the crowd began serenading Lincoln and at about 7 pm, he rose from his work and went to the window in the portico where he had appeared so many times before. For a time, he stood back, appearing from below only as a vague shadow, and took in the scene and the music. Accompanied by his loyal secretaries Nicolay and Hay, Lincoln stood quietly, his hair and beard showing only the slightest hints of the grey that would overtake it in the coming years, tears gathering and flowing over and through the wrinkles that marked his aging features. He turned to the two men and said, "Gentlemen, we shall do this one last time." He stepped outside onto the balcony into the roar of a crowd that had at this point grown to nearly twenty thousand men, women, and children.

It took five long minutes for the cheering to subside, and only then because the President raised his hands, indicating he was going to speak. He composed himself and made the following brief statement:

"Fellow-citizens: I am very glad indeed to see you to-night, and I do most sincerely thank Almighty God for the occasion on which you have called. More than ninety years ago, for the first time in the history of the world, a nation by way of its representatives assembled and declared self-evident the truth that 'all men are created equal.' The two most distinguished men in the framing and support of the Declaration were Thomas Jefferson and John Adams—the one having penned it and the other sustained it the most forcibly in debate—the only two of the fifty-five who signed it being elected President of the United States. That the Almighty chose me to follow them to bring their words into fruition I would not presume to say, but I was privileged to find myself in their shoes, and I have been even more privileged to witness and preside over the gallant efforts and self-sacrifice of so many of our fellow citizens in our late effort to preserve and extend the blessings of liberty throughout our land. Gentlemen and Ladies, this is a glorious occasion, fit for a memorable speech, but I fear I am not prepared to make one worthy of it. I would like to speak in terms of praise due to the many brave officers and soldiers who fought in the cause of the war and to the brave people now who struggle to secure the blessings of peace and liberty for all of our fellow citizens. There have been and will likely be trying occasions, not only in success, but for the want of success. My confidence in General Grant's ability to carry forward the work on which we have embarked is complete, and I can only thank all of you for the confidence and affection you have shown me in what may be the longest eight years in the still short history of our Republic. Having said this much, I will now take the music."

Of the many changes that occurred in Washington in the transition from Lincoln to Grant, one that was personally important to the outgoing and incoming Presidents involved Mary Lincoln and Julia Grant. After the election, as was customary, Mary invited Julia to the White House for lunch and to tour the premises. Given the past bad feelings between the two, Julia accepted the invitation with trepidation. But when Julia arrived at the White House, Mary was more than gracious, telling her how happy she was that "such a fine family as yours will be in this great house" and saying, "I hope any differences we might have had in the past can be put behind us and that we can now enjoy a pleasant luncheon." This guaranteed a festive mood, and an even more pleasant tour, including a walk around the gardens. Mary introduced Julia to all of the servants they encountered including the kitchen staff whom she surprised by bringing Julia directly into the kitchen after they finished their lunch. It was at the conclusion of this January afternoon that Julia broached the subject—dependent on their husbands' agreement—of the Lincolns remaining in the White House until the morning of her husband's inauguration.

With no Chief Justice in place, protocol would have been for Associate Justice Samuel Nelson, the Court's senior member, to administer the constitutionally-prescribed oath of office to Grant. Grant, however, did not want to be sworn in by someone who had joined with the majority in the Dred Scott decision, and nothing in the Constitution required that Nelson, or any judge for that matter, administer the oath. Grant, not realizing just how deeply Chase resented what had been done to him, sent a note to the former Chief Justice, wishing him well and asking whether he would accept his invitation to administer the oath. Chase sent back a note saying simply, "No thank you." When he told Julia what he had done, she was mortified, but she had not told him that Kate Chase had stopped answering her letters after Grant was nominated at the Republican convention.

Julia made a suggestion that both surprised and intrigued the President-elect: why not ask President Lincoln to administer the oath? President-elect Grant liked the idea and immediately sent Lincoln a note to that effect. Lincoln replied, "I appreciate the request but I wonder if the sunshine on that day shouldn't be reserved for illumination of the future." Grant understood that Lincoln was concerned that the outgoing President would overshadow him, but he had plans for the grandest inauguration in the nation's history. Once eight army divisions finished parading in front of the Capitol Building in Grant's honor, the incoming President believed that Lincoln's thirty seconds administering the oath would fade somewhat from memory. And anyway, Grant was savvy enough to recognize that he could only benefit if the public tied him to Lincoln. Lincoln, on Grant's second request, agreed and for the first time in U.S. history, a new President would be sworn in by his predecessor. Both Lincoln and Grant hoped and expected that four years later, Lincoln, as Chief Justice, would once again administer the presidential oath to President Grant.

On the morning of March 4, 1868, the largest crowd in the history of Washington gathered in front of the east portico of the Capitol Building to witness the inauguration of Ulysses S. Grant as the Seventeenth President of the United States. After Lincoln spent the entire morning furiously signing the papers that were put before him, he and Grant took the traditional carriage ride together from the White House to the Capitol building while their wives, along with Ella Wade Colfax, Schuyler Colfax's wife of less than four months, stayed behind to wait for them to return. Schuyler Colfax's swearing in as Vice President took place precisely at noon, in the Senate chamber where both the outgoing and incoming Senators were assembled along with the Members of the House of Representatives who had continued voting on bills and resolutions until the clock struck them out of office. Colfax gave a brief address promising the Senators that he would faithfully and impartially administer the rules of the Senate. The seat reserved for Vice President Johnson remained vacant. In a break with tradition, a petulant Johnson refused to accompany Colfax to the ceremony or attend Grant's inauguration and instead left Washington the previous evening to return by train to Tennessee. Johnson spent the rest of his life trying to regain influence in Washington, and after several unsuccessful attempts at election to the House, he was elected by the Tennessee legislature to the Senate in 1875, where he served for only a few months before suffering a fatal stroke in July of that year.

As they stood before the vast sea of people on the platform erected at the Capitol, Lincoln leaned over and whispered to Grant, "You're already more popular than I ever was, but don't worry: half of them will hate you in a month." Grant smiled and looked around, trying to take in the scene as best he could. Lincoln approached the dais first, holding a Bible that belonged to Grant's family. Grant stood before Lincoln and took the constitutional oath of office, swearing that, "[I will] faithfully execute the office of President of the United States, and will to the best of my ability, preserve, protect and defend the Constitution of the United States."

Grant gave a very short address, promising to handle issues arising out of the "great rebellion . . . calmly, without prejudice, hate, or sectional pride, remembering that the greatest good to the greatest number is the object to be attained." He spent more words on debt and revenue than any other topic, pledging to collect revenues owed to the government and pay the country's debts in gold. In a brief mention of the situation of American Indians, he proclaimed, "I will favor any course toward them which tends to their civilization and ultimate citizenship." He also urged the states to ratify the Fifteenth Amendment to remedy what he portrayed as the wrong of excluding "a portion of the citizens of the nation . . . from its privileges in any State" without, apparently, a thought to the majority—women—who were excluded from electoral franchise throughout the nation.

He ended his speech with surprising news, that later that day he would send the Senate the name of his nominee for Chief Justice, Abraham Lincoln. Those near the front and on the dais who could hear him erupted in cheers, and the cheering spread throughout the crowd as the news was relayed to those out of earshot.

Grant and Lincoln rode by carriage back to the White House. Along the way, troops accompanying the procession found it difficult to keep the path clear. Colfax, for security reasons, took a second carriage along with Wade and other leading Republican Senators. When they arrived, the entire group and other invited guests assembled in front of the White House to observe the largest parade in inauguration history. Throngs of people lined the parade route, and many paid hundreds of dollars to rent rooms with windows overlooking it. As the parade reached the White House, the Lincolns left quietly from the back of the White House in a carriage that took them, Tad and the last of their belongings to their new home about two miles from the White House. Mary asked her husband whether he was going to accept the appointment as Chief Justice, and he replied, "If the Senate will have me, I suppose it to be a good option for an aging country lawyer."

True to his word, upon arriving at the White House that very afternoon, Grant sent papers to the Senate formally nominating Abraham Lincoln of Illinois to be Chief Justice of the Supreme Court of the United States. The only thing that marred an otherwise perfect day was that Grant's father, Jesse Grant, became separated from the inaugural party and fell down a flight of stairs at the Capitol Building while being guided by John F. Driggs, outgoing representative from Michigan. Driggs himself died less than ten years later after falling on ice back in Michigan, but Jesse Grant was not seriously hurt and was eventually brought to the White House to rejoin his family for the festivities.

As was the custom of the time, in the days immediately following the inauguration, the complete text of Grant's address was printed in hundreds of newspapers across the country. While some papers noted that Grant's address was notably bland and pleasantly brief, many focused their attention only on Lincoln's appointment.

The Western Reserve Chronicle of Warren, Ohio, a Republican paper, praised the nomination and most of Grant's cabinet appointments, saying, "There is no single lawyer in the United States more fit to be Chief Justice than the Hon. Mr. Lincoln."

The New Orleans Picayune, a Democratic White supremacist news organ, by contrast, characterized the appointment as "nothing but a blatant effort to extend the tyrant's rule with Gen. Grant as his General in Chief. If it has even a shred of honor, the Senate will turn this scheme away."

Ohio Democratic papers, like the Cincinnati Daily Times, took the opportunity to criticize Grant and Lincoln for their apparent treachery in deceiving Ohio's Salmon Chase to give up his position as Chief Justice, and it urged the Senate to reject Lincoln's nomination to "teach the scoundrels a lesson." The Daily Times was never a big Chase fan either, but the opportunity to criticize the Republicans in power could not be missed.

Despite the protests from Democrats and the Democratic press, approval of Lincoln's nomination was guaranteed by the massive Republican majority in the Senate, and it was accomplished by voice vote on March 5, along with most of Grant's cabinet nominations. The only vocal opposition came from the Senate's few Democrats, most notably from Ohio's newly-elected Democratic Senator Allen G. Thurman, who later became the Democrats' leading voice in opposition to Republican Reconstruction policies. Thurman was simultaneously a strident orator, and a well-liked man who could put his arm around the shoulders of a Republican adversary and laugh with him immediately after slinging accusations of the basest of political sins. Very impolitely on the second day of a new President's term, he lambasted Grant and Lincoln for their deception of Chase and the alleged impropriety of placing a former President on the high Court. Charles Sumner, Thurman-like in speech but without the personal charm, and without the ability to hold his tongue when appropriate, spoke not so much in opposition but to express concern that Lincoln would be overly deferential to executive power and would revert to his prior leniency toward the former rebels. Nonetheless, the Senate spent less than two hours deliberating, and opponents did not even bother to request a call of the roll.

In the early morning of March 6, 1869, at 61 years of age, with greying hair and beard, Abraham Lincoln arrived at the Supreme Court to be sworn in as the Court's seventh Chief Justice. Lincoln brought with him his now-extensive collection of law books, as well as his favorite chair, the rocker that had been made a gift by the Ford brothers after the unsuccessful attempt on his life. The oath was administered by his old friend, Court-appointee and former campaign manager Associate Justice David Davis. Lincoln had appointed Davis as a Republican, but during his years at the Court, Davis declared himself an independent and behaved like one, siding with liberals and conservatives depending on his view of the merits of the particular case. At the beginning of Lincoln's Chief Justiceship, Davis served as an informal mentor on Court procedures, but Lincoln was a quick study and called on Davis for advice only a few times. After taking the oath in the morning and hearing arguments, Lincoln hosted a luncheon for his new colleagues, of which there were seven, one seat being open that would not be filled until 1870 when William Strong of Pennsylvania became President Grant's second Court appointee. Strong would become Lincoln's reliable ally on the Court on matters of economic regulation, but they often clashed on civil rights matters.

By and large, Lincoln was among friends on the Court. He had appointed four of its members, though not all of his appointees were legally or ideologically compatible with the views that Lincoln came to adopt as Chief Justice. Aside from Davis, Lincoln became personally closest to Justices Noah Swayne and Samuel Miller. From the beginning, Lincoln placed a high value on personal harmony among the Justices, and he was successful with nearly all of his colleagues, save perhaps the notoriously cantankerous pro-slavery Nathan Clifford of Maine, who had been appointed by President James Buchanan in 1858 and who often seemed to disagree with everyone about everything. In particular, he had voted against Lincoln in the Prize Cases, in which now-ailing Associate Justice

Robert Grier had written an opinion recognizing the President's power to blockade Southern ports during the rebellion. Clifford joined Justice Nelson's dissenting opinion, which argued that federal seizure of ships of neutral countries pursuant to a blockade was illegal unless Congress declares war. Lincoln and the majority in Congress did not want to declare war against the Confederacy because they feared that such a declaration would amount to a recognition that the Southern states had left the Union, given that a nation cannot declare war against itself. Grier's opinion agreed with Lincoln's view, while Nelson's opinion stated that seizure was legal only if pursuant to an express invocation of the war power following a declaration of war.

Regardless of the legal disagreements that marked this and every period of the Court's history, all of the Justices except Grier attended Lincoln's luncheon as they had attended the inauguration. Grier, who had been appointed by President James Polk in 1846, was suffering the ill effects of three strokes he suffered in 1867, and his colleagues had been urging him for months to step down. He was rarely able to attend oral argument and had written only 15 opinions for the Court since the beginning of 1867. By contrast, Justice Miller wrote 75 Court opinions during that same time period and Justice Field wrote 55. When Grier finally stepped down in 1870, Grant quickly nominated Strong to replace him.

The luncheon was such a success that Lincoln resolved to make it a tradition, reminiscent of Chief Justice John Marshall's practice of boarding and dining with members of the Court during his time in that office. During most of Lincoln's service as Chief Justice, the Justices dined together on Monday evenings whenever the Court was in session. Lincoln immediately recognized that as a member of the Court he would miss the constant contact with people from all walks of life and he would lack outlets for his favorite pastime, storytelling. Not surprisingly, then, Lincoln took the opportunity to spin a yarn or two at these gatherings, and most of his colleagues appreciated the stories and the break from the Court's serious work, which at times could press all the joy out of life.

Lincoln was sensitive to the appearance that his leadership of the

Supreme Court might be perceived as undermining the separation of powers, at least between the Judicial and Executive Branches of government. Moreover, he was not particularly happy with the Supreme Court's cramped quarters in the Capitol Building. He thus adopted as his pet non-judicial project the construction of a separate building to house the Supreme Court. He envisioned a grand structure and thought the perfect location would be the site of the Old Capitol Prison, just east of the Capitol. Lincoln lobbied for this throughout his chief justiceship but was never able to convince Congress, and it was not until more than fifty years later that the Supreme Court moved to its own building, on the exact site proposed by Lincoln.

14

THE COURT

The first few months of Lincoln's service as Chief Justice brought unprecedented crowds to the Court's bleak courtroom, as members of the public wanted to see their beloved former President in action on the bench. By and large, these court-watchers were disappointed. Even in the Supreme Court, most cases are to the average person boring and technical affairs. For example, on Lincoln's first day at the Court, in the presence of as many spectators as could be jammed into the Court's chamber, the Court heard argument in Lynch v. Carmen S. de Bernal, an appeal of an action brought to enforce title to land in San Francisco that had been granted by the government of Mexico. Less than a month later the Court ruled in favor of the claims based on Mexican title, but in light of his lack of opportunity to prepare, Lincoln's only comments at oral argument were to thank his new colleagues for their warm welcome and invite each lawyer in turn to commence their presentations.

On March 19, 1869, Chief Justice Lincoln was more vocal as he presided over the arguments in Ward v. Smith, a dispute over $14,000 worth of securities in which the questions included whether the Civil War's disruptions to banking altered the parties' legal rights and obligations. From his early days representing railroads, Lincoln was well-versed in the technicalities of bond law, and he also had views on the implications of the Civil War for the continuity of legal obligations. But Lincoln's close questioning of the lawyers in the case were likely unintelligible to the assembled laymen, and he exhibited none of his folksy charm until the very end when he complimented the lawyers for making the Court's job "significantly easier by presenting their cases so ably, but it would have been even easier if only one of you had done so."

That same day, March 19, 1869, the assembled got their money's worth when, after Lynch, the Court took up Ex parte McCardle, the second appearance at the Supreme Court of McCardle's attempt to be released from military custody. McCardle was being held awaiting trial by military commission for publishing newspaper editorials in the Vicksburg Times critical of the Reconstruction-era government in Mississippi and the national authorities and military. The charges included disturbing the peace, incitement to insurrection and disorder, libel, and impeding Reconstruction.

A good sample of McCardle's handiwork is the following excerpt, in which after listing a number of military officials he opined that "they are each and all infamous, cowardly, and abandoned villains who, instead of wearing shoulder straps and ruling millions of people, should have their heads shaved, their ears cropped, their foreheads branded, and their persons lodged in a penitentiary." He urged White Mississippians to boycott upcoming elections to choose members of what would be a bi-racial constitutional convention, and said that any tax collector hired by the government established under that constitution should know that "they will be shot down like dogs, as they are!. . . They know that [this] convention has no power or authority to tax them, and they are determined not to be robbed! The men who attempt it will certainly get hurt, for they will be treated as all robbers and highwaymen deserve to be treated."

While extremely partisan journalism was commonplace in nineteenth century America, this rhetoric strayed outside its usual bounds and threatened to inspire disobedience to law and even violence under the volatile circumstances in many Southern states. The most apt metaphor would be pouring gasoline on a fire, had gasoline existed at the time.

On remand after a prior visit to the Supreme Court in which McCardle's right to seek habeas corpus relief had been established over the government's objections, a lower federal court denied his petition for release, affirming that military authorities had jurisdiction over him and that the charges against him were legally sound. While his appeal to the Supreme Court was pending, Congress passed a statute repealing an 1867 statute which had granted the Supreme Court jurisdiction over cases like McCardle's. Congress relied on the clauses of the Constitution that allow Congress to suspend the writ of habeas corpus and make exceptions to the jurisdiction of the Supreme Court. This new statute, by repealing jurisdiction over "appeals which have been, or may hereafter be taken" was aimed directly, if not exclusively, at McCardle's pending appeal. The legislative history reveals that Congress knew exactly what it was doing.

The oral argument on March 19 addressed only the effect of this new statute—argument on the constitutional merits and pre-amendment jurisdiction had been held more than a year earlier. Former Illinois Senator Lyman Trumbull, the Radical Republican author of the Civil Rights Act of 1866, who had argued earlier that the Court had jurisdiction over the case, argued again for the government, this time urging the Court to obey the amendment and dismiss the appeal. After leaving the Senate in 1873, Trumbull became one of the nation's most respected lawyers and later ran for Illinois governor as a Democrat. McCardle also had distinguished counsel including President Buchanan's Attorney General Jeremiah Black and Justice Field's brother David Dudley Field. The arguments, which lasted more than four hours, began with technical arguments concerning the Supreme Court's constitutional jurisdiction and Congress's power to make exceptions to it.

After Black's jurisdictional argument, Field took over and made an impassioned plea against the notion that Congress could prevent the Court from hearing a challenge "to the most blatantly unconstitutional and un-American policy imaginable, the use of a military commission to dispense rough justice against a civilian after hostilities have ceased and the civilian courts are open and perfectly capable of enforcing the law. If this Court stands for anything, it stands for preserving the great writ against political attacks like the one before the Court today."

At this point, Chief Justice Lincoln interjected, stating, "Counsel, I am inclined to agree with your minor proposition, but only in order to deny the major one, that the federal military authorities are powerless to impose necessary discipline on the remnants of the rebellious forces that would have destroyed our union to preserve their slaves."

Lincoln's outburst inspired Field to even greater rhetorical heights, "reminding" the Chief Justice that "the war is long over, and loyalty has been fully and repeatedly pledged. Nothing that happens in this Court or in any courthouse across the country can alter that reality. What courts can do, if they so choose, is provide justice and relief from the unconstitutional assumption of military power that continues now, nearly four years after the cessation of the shooting."

Lincoln took this as a personal challenge and responded with a lengthy disquisition on the situation, both "during the War in areas held by our forces and ever since, in those same areas and in many more that outwardly seem at peace but inwardly are fighting to extend the vestiges of their failed dream. Disloyalty comes in many shades of grey, and vigilance is our only hope for hindering the creeping re-imposition of our past sins that led us into the great and bloody calamity so gently referred to as 'civil' war." Lincoln expressed "no discomfort in confining this Court to imposing its will in ordinary times while allowing the government ample latitude to combat the extraordinary challenge that, we must hope, will be but infrequently encountered."

Throughout this exchange, which went on for nearly an hour, the other members of the court sat quietly, recognizing that Lincoln was defending not only Congress's prerogative to determine the Court's appellate jurisdiction but also his view of the powers of the military and its commander in chief to take decisive action to put down rebellion. The large crowd filling the gallery remained attentive throughout, with none of the usual shuffling of hands and feet and mid-argument departures that had created distractions during Supreme Court proceedings in the nearly two weeks since Lincoln took the bench.

When Senator Trumbull began his argument by reciting the history of the 1867 Act and its recent amendment, the crowd relaxed. His voice on the former was authoritative since he was that statute's primary author and as such his views on the effects of the 1877 amendment garnered respect from the Justices as well. In addition to the text of the amendment, he pointed out that Congress's underlying motivation clearly was to defeat McCardle's claim, and thus the Court had no choice but to dismiss the appeal as beyond its jurisdiction.

It was only after Trumbull had laid out his statutory arguments that the other Justices began to pose questions, most of which Trumbull handled with little difficulty. That is, until Justice Samuel Nelson, Democrat from New York, challenged Trumbull most energetically by asking how far Congress might go in stripping the Court's appellate jurisdiction.

Trumbull responded, "We look to the words of our Constitution, and those words, admitting of no limits, the scope of this Court's jurisdiction is to be determined by the political, not legal, organs."

Nelson grew animated and exclaimed that Chief Justice Marshall would be appalled to think that this Court would even contemplate abdicating its role as voice of the Constitution in such a delicate case as this.

Lincoln rejoined the fray, asking Trumbull if "my recollection is correct that in the great Chief Justice's opinion in the Marbury case he hadn't determined that the Court was without jurisdiction to right what it had already found to be a legal wrong?"

Trumbull responded, "Yes Mr. Chief Justice, because your esteemed predecessor understood that his first duty was to the law as written, because that is the only certain formula for preserving our Republic as the Framers, in their wisdom, designed it."

When the Court issued its opinion only a month later, it ruled 8 to 1 against McCardle, with only Justice Nelson dissenting, but without opinion. Lincoln and Justice Robert Grier, Democrat from Pennsylvania and a consistent advocate of expansive presidential military power during the Civil War, joined Justice Clifford's uncharacteristically brief opinion finding that Congress had stripped the Court of jurisdiction over McCardle's case, but they appended a statement that they "agree with Justice Clifford's conclusion but had they been forced to reach the merits," they would have held that "the decision to try McCardle before a military commission was, in the absence of legislation to the contrary, well within the powers allocated to the Commander in Chief and delegated by him to the military authorities in

144

Mississippi."

15
MORE ENFORCEMENT

The public's interest in witnessing Lincoln's performance as Chief Justice remained high for years, and when in session the Court became almost a mandatory stop for tourists visiting the nation's capital. Yet the affairs of the other branches went on without him, with President Grant and Congress facing significant challenges in 1869 and 1870. Two issues were front and center: Reconstruction and the nation's finances, which were still suffering from the debts incurred in the war effort and which only grew during Reconstruction. In addition, the increasing nationalization of the economy brought about by improved transportation and communication raised concerns. The national government was at a crossroads between retreating to its traditional, relatively weak presence in day-to-day affairs and expanding into areas of state government and the economy upon which it had not previously tread. On economic matters, the Republican majorities in both Houses of Congress were not united, and the fractured 1870 Congress rejected proposals to create a national railroad commission and a national bureau of health.

There was more unity in Congress surrounding Reconstruction policy and the rights of people of color. Some Democrats charged that, under the guise of the Constitution's Guarantee Clause—which guarantees to states a "Republican form of government"—Republicans were attempting to impose a Republican Party government. This characterization was derived from the additional terms for readmission imposed on Texas, Virginia, and Mississippi, which included Black suffrage and office holding, free and open access to public education, and wide-ranging disqualification of former rebels from voting and holding office. Charles Sumner led the charge to impose these conditions, provoking Illinois Senator Lyman Trumbull, one of the authors of the Thirteenth Amendment, to charge Sumner with always championing "the least practical and most inflammatory measures imaginable." Trumbull, however, was in a small minority, resulting in a rare case of Sumner leading the Republican majority.

Republican control of the national government did not translate into complete domination of Southern and border states. Although federal troops were stationed throughout the South, organized terror groups like the Ku Klux Klan were nonetheless able to interfere with Republican and Black political activity in many areas. The realization that there were not enough troops to keep the peace everywhere came slowly, and in some areas, the violence was not sufficiently overt to warrant a military response. In Arkansas, Georgia, and Louisiana, violence and intimidation had delivered those states' 1868 presidential vote to the Democrats. And there were foreboding signs that state governments in border and Southern states were going to become less enthusiastic about enforcing rights for Black Americans. For example, in Tennessee, the new and nominally Republican governor, with urging from former Vice President Johnson, appointed election commissioners who looked the other way as scores of ex-rebels registered to vote with support from a Tennessee supreme court decision placing procedural hurdles in the way of disenfranchisement. Voters in the state elections held in August 1869 firmly rejected Radical Reconstruction policies and installed a government set on restoring White rule in Tennessee. Kentucky had previously elected a Democrat as governor, and the entire government was populated by Confederate sympathizers. The governor, John W. Stevenson, was a strong believer in states' rights, and he vehemently opposed the Fifteenth Amendment and enforcement of the 1866 Civil Rights Act's requirement that Black Americans be allowed to testify in court against Whites.

Radicals in Congress took note of the resurgence of White supremacists and, in late 1869, began to formulate legislation to combat it. They urged President Grant to send more federal troops to areas suffering from Klan violence. At first he was reluctant, hesitant to antagonize politicians and voters he would depend on for future support, and concerned for his government's financial situation. But in relatively short order, Grant came to the realization that only decisive action would rescue Black Americans from a fate nearly as bad as slavery.

Violence and intimidation in states like Louisiana and Georgia that prevented many people from voting made it evident that federal legislation should follow the ratification of the Fifteenth Amendment, which would provide Congress with "power to enforce this article by appropriate legislation." Some Members of Congress were looking into whether and how they could invoke the Fourteenth Amendment to reduce representation in the House for states where Black Americans, either by law or de facto, along with White Republicans, were unable to vote. This would also reduce those states' influence on the presidential election because electoral votes were based on the number of representatives in Congress.

The first of several bills aimed at enforcing civil rights against recalcitrant state and local governments and terror groups like the Klan was introduced in the House by Ohio Representative John Bingham in February 1870, shortly after the ratification of the Fifteenth Amendment. Ratification set off nationwide celebrations among Black Americans. Black and White veterans paraded in Boston alongside jubilant Black civilians, and similar parades were seen in numerous cities including Baltimore, St. Louis, and Philadelphia. Frederick Douglass spoke at a celebratory meeting in Albany, New York, proclaiming, "It means that you and I and all of us shall leave the narrow places in which we now breathe and live in the same comfort and independence enjoyed by other men. It means industry, application to business, economy in the use of our earnings, and the building up of a solid character. . . . It means that color is no longer to be a calamity; that race is to be no longer a crime; and that liberty is to be the right of all." These celebrations, however, could not mask the reality that Klan violence and the connivance of White officials at the state and local level stood in the way of full realization of Black suffrage. Whether Black Americans would be allowed to vote in all elections—federal, state, and local—was unclear even in relatively liberal Northern states like Ohio.

Bingham had quietly received advance support from President Grant to do something once the voting rights amendment went into effect. His February proposal was short and to the point. It would criminalize any action by federal, state, and local officials that interfered with any citizens' right to register and vote. It would punish anyone, public official or private citizen, who used force or violence to prevent Black citizens from voting or registering. Enforcement was through criminal and civil actions in the federal Circuit Courts, with fines and statutory damages of $500 assessed against violators. The bill took the broad view of the scope of the Fifteenth Amendment as applying to elections at every level of government. It also contained a provision enforcing Section 2 of the Fourteenth Amendment's promise that if any male inhabitants of a state are denied the right to vote, representation in the House of Representatives "shall be reduced in the proportion which the number of such male citizens shall bear to the whole number of male citizens . . . in such State."

In the Senate, the effort to craft an enforcement bill was led by Vermont Republican George Edmunds. His proposal was more comprehensive and with stronger built-in enforcement mechanisms. The Senate bill created several new criminal offenses related to interference with voting and conspiracies related to that conduct. The Senate bill would authorize federal judges to appoint supervisors with power of arrest to supervise voter registration and the elections themselves, it extended voting and office-holding disqualification for former rebels and authorized the President to use military force in furtherance of the provisions of the bill.

These proposals were extremely controversial, with Democrats and some conservative Republicans characterizing them as massive federal intrusions into traditional state functions. Democrats singled out for particular derision the potential for reduction in representation in the House, complaining that Republicans were aiming to enshrine themselves as a permanent and unassailable majority. Ohio Democrat Allen Thurman led the charge against the bills in the Senate, complaining that the federal government was usurping the power of the state courts and positioning the federal military as the supervisor of the most vital aspect of state autonomy. Maryland Senator George Vickers joined in the Democratic chorus against the proposals, stating simply that the Fifteenth Amendment was not intended to enlarge Congress's power to "rule over the White race." On the other side, one of the more interesting contributions to the debates over this first Enforcement Act was a brief floor speech by Mississippi Senator Hiram Revels, the first Black member of the United States Senate.

Revels was elected by Mississippi's Reconstruction legislature to serve out the unexpired term of former Senator (and later Confederate President) Jefferson Davis. He was seated in the Senate over the objection of Southern Democrats that he did not meet the nine year citizenship requirement for membership in the Senate because, although he was born in the United States, due to the Dred Scott decision, he became a citizen only with the ratification of the Fourteenth Amendment two years earlier. Debate on the objection occupied two days of the Senate's time in January, after which he was seated before a packed Senate chamber. He was a brilliant man with moderate and optimistic instincts but with a firm resolve to confront prejudice against his race.

Revels did not speak often during his brief time in the Senate, but when he did, his words were admired and often moving. His first extended remarks as a Senator came on March 16, 1870, during a discussion of the bill imposing conditions on the readmission of the State of Georgia. He rose to urge his colleagues to invalidate action by the Georgia legislature that expelled those elected to it with more than one-eighth African blood and pleaded for Congress to protect the loyal and defenseless members of his race there. After recounting how during the Civil War, rather than rebel, slaves across the South protected the women and children who were left behind, he proclaimed that the members of his race "bear toward their former masters no revengeful thoughts, no hatreds, no animosities. They aim not to elevate themselves by sacrificing one single interest of their White fellow-citizens. They ask but the rights which are theirs by God's universal law, and which are the natural outgrowth, the logical sequence of the condition in which the legislative enactments of this nation have placed them."

On May 17, Senator Revels entered the debate over the 1870 Enforcement Act, briefly but with words that garnered the admiration of colleagues. After expressing reluctance to speak, which he only rarely overcame, he began by flatly stating, "I am in favor of removing the disabilities of those upon whom they are imposed in the South just as fast as they give evidence of having become loyal and of being loyal." This was a consistent theme for him, at least partly because he thought that punitive action from Washington against Whites would, in the long run, make life worse for Black Americans in the South. He pointed out that in his state of Mississippi, the Republican Party had campaigned on a platform of universal amnesty, and he thought his Republican colleagues in Congress should make good on that promise. He credited the Republican Party's conciliatory stance toward former rebels with helping to keep the peace in Mississippi, boasting that in Mississippi "the people now I believe are getting along as quietly, pleasantly, harmoniously, and prosperously as the people are in any of the formerly free States." He thus positioned himself as a moderate on how Congress should treat former rebels. His comments led Nebraska Senator John Milton Thayer to state, "I wish that the speech of the Senator from Mississippi just made in this Chamber may be spread all over this land, in every town and in every hamlet. He, in a five minutes' speech, has presented the whole doctrine of the question of the removal of disabilities."

After the typical congressional wrangling involved in passing important or controversial measures, and with steadfast opposition from Democrats, the bill which emerged from Congress and was signed by the President incorporated most of the proposals from each House, resulting in 23 sections spread across seven pages of the Statutes at Large. The Act promised unprecedented federal involvement in elections, including the registration process and voting itself. The key provisions of the bill that became the Enforcement Act of 1870 are as follows:

Section 1 proclaimed that all qualified citizens have the right to vote in all federal, state, territorial and local elections "without distinction of race, color, or previous condition of servitude."

Section 2 placed a duty on "every person or officer" involved with the process of voter qualification to give all citizens the equal opportunity to become qualified to vote "without distinction of race, color, or previous condition of servitude."

Section 3 provided that after each election for Congress, the Freedmen's Bureau, with help from the military, would prepare a report on the number of Black Americans prevented in each state from voting by any improper means, private or official, so Congress could determine whether to reduce a state's representation in the House of Representatives.

Section 4 made it unlawful for any person to obstruct or prevent a citizen from voting or qualifying to vote by "force, bribery, threats, intimidation, or other unlawful means."

Section 5, attacking the economic weapons used to prevent Blacks and Republicans from voting, created criminal liability against "any person who prevents or attempts to prevent a person from voting through bribery, threats, or threats of depriving such person of employment or occupation, or of ejecting such person from rented house, lands, or other threats, property, or by threats of refusing to renew leases or contracts for labor, or by threats of violence to himself or family."

Section 6, aimed directly at the Ku Klux Klan and similar terror groups, created a felony carrying up to a $5000 fine and ten years imprisonment (and disqualification from holding any federal office) for persons who, in groups of two or more, "go in disguise upon the public highway, or upon the premises of another, with intent to violate any provision of this act, or to injure, oppress, threaten, or intimidate any citizen with intent to prevent or hinder his free exercise and enjoyment of any right or privilege granted or secured to him by the Constitution or laws of the United States, or because of his having exercised the same."

Section 17 made it a crime for any person acting under color of state law to deprive any person of rights secured by the Constitution.

Section 18 reenacted the Civil Rights Act of 1866 in its entirety.

Sections 19 and 20 criminalized vote fraud, including allowing ineligible persons to register or vote.

The remaining sections were procedural or structural in nature, creating federal jurisdiction, specifying civil damages and criminal penalties, mandating enforcement of the Fourteenth Amendment's voter disqualification provisions and making clear that all officials, federal, state and local were duty-bound to enforce the Fifteenth Amendment and the Act, under pain of criminal penalties. Other provisions provided for the employment of commissioners and use of the United States military, local militia and even the posse comitatus to aid in enforcement of the Act and the Fifteenth Amendment. The Act's final provision provided for a cause of action in federal court to overturn an election in which ineligible persons were allowed to vote. This was strong medicine for what many saw as a serious illness that was sweeping across the South.

The first major test of the Enforcement Act of 1870 came in state and congressional elections that fall, and on the whole it met its goals. More Black Americans voted in this election than any in the country's history, aided to a great extent by the presence of election monitors assigned by the Freedmen's Bureau and staffed largely by military troops. The presence of federal troops allowed for a largely peaceful campaign, although there were certainly areas in the South where Black Americans and Republicans feared for their safety and refrained from public political activity. Sentiment was turning against Grant due to scandals among members of his administration, but Republicans retained control of both Houses of Congress. In the Senate, Republicans suffered a net loss of four seats. Most Southern states continued to be represented in the Senate by Republicans, with only Alabama rejecting a Republican incumbent in favor of a Democratic challenger. In the House, Republicans suffered greater losses. Democrats made gains in many areas, including the South where the Democratic Party was successfully regrouping.

In formerly Confederate states where Democrats made their strongest gains—North Carolina, Tennessee, and Texas—Freedmen's Bureau investigations revealed widespread suppression of Black voting, mainly through violence and intimidation in rural counties where Black Americans made up a substantial majority but barely voted, as well as through racially neutral devices such as the poll tax. For example, in Tennessee, one observer reported that "a wave of banditry and Ku Kluxism washed over the region." The violence and intimidation there led to the election, in early

1870, of a strongly Democratic constitutional convention which produced a constitution designed to further White supremacist rule while also appearing to be race-neutral so it would not be disapproved by Congress. When the constitution was sent to the people for a vote, Klansmen stood guard at many polling stations to prevent Black Americans and other Radical Republicans from voting. Numerous voters were disenfranchised by officials' refusal to recognize voter registration certificates that had been issued under a previous Republican state government. Similar conduct swung Tennessee's November congressional election to the Democrats, and when Congress reconvened in December, Congress adopted a resolution on the recommendation of the Reconstruction Committee pursuant to Section 2 of the Fourteenth Amendment, giving Tennessee two choices: either it hold a new election administered by federal authorities, or lose half of its six Representatives in the House and see only three highest vote-getting candidates seated. Realizing that a new election, with Black Americans and Republicans voting in full force, might cost them even the three seats they would gain without holding one, Tennessee's governing Democrats opted to acquiesce in the reduction of their representation in Congress. Similar events occurred in North Carolina and Texas; consequently, in March, 1870, each of those states saw its representation in the House cut in half, the first time that Section 2 of the Fourteenth Amendment was enforced. In North Carolina, clever drafting of the resolution allowed the two elected Republicans to take their seats, while all three Democrats were disqualified, as were two of four Democrats elected in Texas.

Even with its reduced majority, the Republican Congress was demonstrating its resolve not to abandon the cause of Black suffrage. Undoubtedly, the motivation was partly or even largely self-preservation, but Republicans could at least assure themselves that their cause was just and in line with what would have resulted from free and fair elections. Southern Democrats, of course, were also convinced that preservation of White rule was a just cause, sanctioned by God, and universally accepted among true Southerners.

Republicans also suffered losses in some Northern states,

including Pennsylvania and New York. In New York City, it appeared that Democrats in control of the city government were issuing fraudulent voter certificates to newly arrived immigrants before they were truly eligible under state law, along with providing government financial support designed to make them loyal Democratic voters. Congress attempted to put an end to this by, for the first time in United States history, taking control of naturalization away from state and local authorities and placing it in federal hands—mainly federal judges who from then on were given exclusive authority to naturalize citizens. A statute to this effect was passed by Congress and signed by President Grant in mid-1870.

In early 1871, amid signs that vagaries in the 1870 Enforcement Act were muddying its enforceability in some areas, Congress began work on a supplementary statute. In February, John Bingham brought forward a new proposal from the House Judiciary Committee, adding detailed instructions on the administration of federal voting requirements, strengthening criminal penalties for violations, and increasing federal judicial supervision of elections in cities with populations larger than 20,000. Despite complaints from Democrats that Republicans were using the race issue as a sham to perpetuate their rule, the bill passed both Houses of Congress within a week of its introduction in the House and was immediately signed by the President, who directed federal authorities to enforce it "with determination."

More pressing were continued reports of increasing Ku Klux Klan violence across the South, aided by the active connivance of state and local government officials. The results of the 1870 elections and Congress's refusal to seat all elected Democratic representatives enraged Whites and inspired even greater reaction. Despite reinforcements, there were still not enough federal troops to pacify the entire South. State militia could not be depended upon because too many White men of military age were sympathetic to the cause of overthrowing Black and Republican rule or perpetuating existing White dominance, and it was too dangerous to leave the task to Black militia alone.

Meanwhile, the issue of whether to adopt a statutory amendment requiring school segregation in Washington, D.C., came before Congress. It was on this subject that Senator Revels made his most extended and impassioned comments. Against the backdrop of what he perceived as increasing prejudice against his race, the theme of his speech was that official endorsement of segregation would further encourage and legitimize that prejudice. He said, "The prejudice in this country to color is very great, and I sometimes fear that it is on the increase. [I]t matters not how colored people act, it matters not how they behave themselves, how well they deport themselves, how intelligent they may be, how refined they may be . . . the prejudice against them is equally as great as it is against the most low and degraded man you can find in the streets of this city or in any other place. [I]t is the wish of the colored people of this District, and of the colored people over this land, that this Congress shall not do anything which will increase that prejudice which is now fearfully great against them." He denied, in religious terms, the morality of race prejudice: "[I]f this prejudice has no cause to justify it, then we must admit that it is wicked, we must admit that it is wrong; we must admit that it has not the approval of Heaven."

Senator Revels insisted that his moderate attitude was shared by Black Americans across the country: "[I]f this amendment is rejected, so that the schools will be left open for all children to be entered into them, irrespective of race, color, previous condition, I do not believe the colored people will act imprudently. I know that in one or two of the late insurrectionary states the legislatures passed laws establishing mixed schools, and the colored people did not hurriedly shove their children into those schools; they were very slow about it. . . I do not believe that it is in the colored people to act rashly and unwisely in a manner of this kind. . . . I desire to say here that the white race has no better friend than I. [D]uring the canvass in the state of Mississippi I traveled into different parts of that state, and this is the doctrine that I everywhere uttered: That while I was in favor of building up the colored race I was not in favor of tearing down the white race. Sir, the white race need not be harmed in order to build up the colored race. The colored race can be built up and assisted, as I before remarked, in acquiring property, in becoming intelligent, valuable, useful citizens, without one hair upon the head of any white man being harmed. And I believe God makes it the duty of this nation to do this much for them; but at the same time, I would not have anything done which would harm the white race."

One consistent argument that was made by White supremacists against integrated schools was that it would lead to social mixing between Black Americans and Whites, ultimately culminating in White supremacists' greatest fear: interracial marriage between Black men and White women. Revels even addressed this issue, albeit in gentler language about "social equality" which was the phrase used by Whites in polite conversation. Particularly interesting is that "social equality" was apparently defined simply as White and Black Americans associating in social settings, rather than involving a claim by Black Americans that they are entitled to the same social privileges as Whites or some other claim to equal social status.

Revels recounted a conversation with a White man who had expressed opposition to school integration based on opposition to social equality:

"'[P]lease tell me this: does not social equality result from mixed schools?'

"'No, sir; very far from it,' I responded.

"'Why,' said he, 'how can it be otherwise?'

"I replied, 'Go to the schools and you see there white children and colored children seated side by side, studying their lessons, standing side by side and reciting their lessons, and perhaps in walking to school they may walk together; but that is the last of it. The white children go to their homes; the colored children go to theirs; and on the Lord's day you will see those colored children in colored churches, and the white family, you will see the white children there, and the colored children at entertainments given by persons of their color. I aver, sir, that mixed schools are very far from bringing about social equality.'"

Moderation, he was arguing, would lead to segregation in social life that would not be undermined by children attending school together.

Revels' speech reflected the views of many people of color at the time, most of whom took a realistic view of the relations between Black and White. Few Black Americans thought that emancipation and federal civil rights laws would suddenly obliterate the color line so deeply entrenched in American society. They understood that actions that Whites would perceive as challenging the separation of the races in most social situations would aggravate rather than alleviate the difficulties they were experiencing. While some may have aspired to complete social equality, and might have dreamed of a day when Black and White Americans would routinely share dining tables and church pews, their immediate goal was to have the equal opportunity to determine their own destinies and realize their own potential through educational, economic, and political activity. Unfortunately, even this more modest vision of a just post-war society was beyond what White Americans, especially Southerners, could bear.

Ultimately, Congress left school segregation to the discretion of the local Washington government, and while new schools for Black students were established during the 1870s, they were segregated, if not by law then by custom.

The Grant administration devoted substantial resources to enforcing the 1870 Act, bringing dozens of prosecutions and employing numerous officials across the South to protect the rights of Black Americans and Republicans, including military lawyers and contractors hired as outside counsel. Success in court was modest but significant enough to create a sense that the Act was likely to be effective in the long run. Most of the cases brought to court were brought by federal authorities because individuals were afraid to go public with their grievances against their oppressors. Defendants were entitled to trial by jury in criminal prosecutions and damages actions, and whenever Whites were included on the jury, it was virtually impossible to achieve a unanimous verdict against a White defendant. Some prosecutors brought actions for injunctions, which would be tried to a judge sitting in equity without a jury. Injunctions, if violated, could be enforced through fines and imprisonment, also without a jury. This plan was stymied by judicial decisions in more than one federal Circuit Court determining that the Enforcement Act did not provide for injunctive remedies. These courts reasoned that the Act was very specific on the civil and criminal remedies it allowed and thus must not have intended to allow injunctive suits as well. Several local prosecutors joined together to take this issue to the Supreme Court, but delays there meant a possible two-year wait for a decision.

Another problem was reluctance of some local United States attorneys to bring cases under any of the civil rights or enforcement acts. Under the Judiciary Act of 1789, United States Attorneys were independent of the Attorney General and had exclusive authority over all prosecutions within their districts. The U.S. Attorneys received as compensation whatever fees and costs were assessed by the judges in the cases they litigated, making them dependent on those judges. Further, many of them maintained private law practices, making it even more important for them to safeguard their standing in the local community. The Attorney General, who received a salary appropriated by Congress, had authority to litigate cases in the Supreme Court and the obligation to advise the President and Department Heads on legal issues but could not intervene in local prosecutions. In 1870, President Grant's first Attorney General, E. Rockwood Hoar, previously a Justice of the Massachusetts Supreme Judicial Court, suggested that Grant address this problem by supporting efforts in Congress to create a legal department and place the U.S. Attorneys under the supervision of the Attorney General.

16
DEPARTMENT OF JUSTICE

Representative Thomas Jenckes, Republican of Rhode Island, had already proposed the establishment of the Department of Justice in 1868. The effort began to pick up steam in 1870 while Congress was considering the Enforcement Act. Consideration of creating the department raised three sets of fears among skeptics: first, the expense; second, the fear that the proposed department would become a tool for presidential domination of the administration of the law; and third, the realization by Democrats and conservative Republicans that it might invigorate the enforcement of civil rights law against the wishes of local (White) communities.

Surprisingly, once Jenckes's proposal received the backing of the Grant administration, it sailed through Congress, but instead of supporting civil rights enforcement, it became an impediment. Here's how.

When Congress established the Department of Justice in July 1870, it was by far the smallest of any of the federal departments. Congress's act authorized the employment of only one new permanent lawyer, the Solicitor General, and severely restricted the ability of local U.S. Attorneys to hire outside counsel. The coalition in Congress that passed the bill was more concerned with budgetary matters and professionalization of the federal government's lawyers than with enforcement of federal law of any kind, civil rights or otherwise. Spending on lawyers by the federal government declined substantially, and somehow no one realized that restricting the hiring of outside counsel for local cases would negatively affect civil rights enforcement. Local U.S. attorneys remained loyal to their local benefactors and local communities. If anything, the Attorney General's attitude of independence was strengthened by the creation of the Department of Justice making it more difficult than ever for the President to exert control.

Hoar himself never had the chance to oversee the District Attorneys' prosecution of civil rights cases. Due to political controversy, he was not destined to remain as Attorney General for very long. At the outset of his administration, Grant had shocked Washington by nominating a cabinet without consulting the Republican Party leadership. His nominee for Secretary of the Treasury was Alexander Stewart, owner of A.T. Stewart & Co., one of New York City's most successful retail store chains. The Senate confirmed his nomination along with all of Grant's initial appointees, but after some of Grant's opponents protested, Hoar ruled him ineligible to serve because of a 1789 statute that prohibited anyone in "trade or commerce" from serving as Treasury Secretary. Grant then appointed Massachusetts Representative George Boutwell. This was problematic for Hoar because at the time it was considered politically inappropriate for the President's cabinet to include two members from the same state. Grant first tried to deal with this problem by nominating Hoar to an open seat on the Supreme Court, but the Senate would not confirm him on the ground that he had refused to approve their choices (i.e., patronage) for judicial appointments to the new United States Circuit Courts. There was also concern that Hoar was too devoted to the law and might not carry out Republican policy on the Court. Former Secretary of War Edwin Stanton was nominated to the Court and confirmed instead, but Stanton died before taking his seat.

Hoar's Massachusetts background was not his only problem for Grant. Although he was a loyal Republican, it quickly became clear to Grant as well as Radicals in Congress that he was relatively conservative and would not be very enthusiastic about bringing civil rights enforcement cases across the South. Thus, just before the legislation establishing the Department of Justice was due to go into effect, Grant requested and received Hoar's resignation. Hoar stayed on until November, when his successor Amos Akerman of Georgia was appointed. Akerman had been a Colonel in the Confederate Army, but after the war he became a strong supporter of equal rights for Black Americans and energetically prosecuted the Klan and other terror groups during Reconstruction, so much so that he lasted only a little more than a year as Attorney General before being run out of office by opponents of his civil rights policies and his attacks on abusive financial business practices.

The presence in the South of federal troops and other officials at this time did lead to a decline in the level of violence and an increase in the ability of Black Americans to engage in political activity and vote in elections.

But it was a constant struggle, like a game of whack-a-mole. In some regions, whenever one area was pacified, trouble flared elsewhere. Louisiana, for instance, was mainly peaceful, and the Black community there was thriving. Then, without warning, the White League would attack a political meeting in Iberville Parish or the Ku Kluxers would set fire to the crops of a Black planter in St. James Parish. Or a planter known to be a Republican would be murdered for hiring Black workers without permission of their former "owners." In parts of South Carolina, violence and boycotts made it virtually impossible for Black Americans to work their own land, and they were forced into sharecropping, often moving their families back into former slave quarters. The governor of South Carolina reported that in the northern part of the state, where federal troops were plentiful, political activity was conducted in relative peace, but in the southern part of the state, in some areas there was a "general reign of terror and lawlessness" that prevented Black Americans from voting and participating in politics more generally. The terror was designed to further two goals—restore or retain White supremacist political power and maintain Black Americans as a source of cheap labor. There was just enough terror there to substantially advance both aims.

The new social reality, with millions of free Black Americans across the South, created novel situations that sparked the development of new social norms. There had always been free Black Americans everywhere, although in some places their status was tenuous. Before the war, more than one state required that any freed person leave the state. Even relatively liberal states like Illinois made residence by free Black Americans difficult or illegal in the years before the war. In Southern states, norms of race-based exclusion and segregation developed quickly and some Northern locales were not far behind. White-owned establishments such as theaters would exclude Black Americans completely, or segregate them into inferior accommodations such as standing room behind the back row, or an upper balcony section constantly filled with tobacco smoke. In New Orleans, where mixed-race French-speaking residents had enjoyed a special "middle race" status, attitudes hardened. Restaurants and bars excluded even well-known and respected elected officials of partial African descent—people they would have served before the war and in the years immediately following it. Even courthouses were segregated, with Black spectators either excluded from courtrooms entirely, or confined to a standing room in the rear.

Transportation continued to be problematic for Black Americans. On the rails, as Hiram Revels detailed in his comments on school segregation, Black Americans were relegated to the smoking car "where men are cursing, swearing, spitting on the floor; where she is miserable, and where her little children have to listen to language not fitting for children who are brought up as she endeavored to bring them up to listen to." This treatment was without regard to sex, age or social class, and regardless of whether the traveler had purchased a first-class ticket. On steamboats, an important mode of transportation especially on the Mississippi River, Black Americans were placed in what was referred to as "the Bureau," a sarcastic reference to the Freedmen's Bureau, where the accommodations were often far inferior to those afforded to Whites, and where there was no effort to separate the sexes, placing women of color traveling alone at risk of sexual assault and other terrors.

Continued Klan violence, the unavailability of effective judicial remedies, the failure of state and local officials to enforce civil rights laws, and the development and application of norms of exclusion and segregation led Radicals in Congress to look once again at legislative action. Focusing specifically on exclusion and segregation, Charles Sumner introduced a "public accommodations" law to prohibit race-based exclusion and segregation by any business serving the public. This bill, which became Sumner's greatest cause as a Senator, was drafted in 1870 by Sumner and John Mercer Langston, a Black lawyer and one of the founders of Howard University Law School and was first introduced by Sumner in 1871. Whenever it was even remotely relevant, Sumner would rail at his fellow Senators for not passing his bill immediately. On more than one occasion he recounted

Frederick Douglass's humiliation, including at least one moderate beating, at being forced in the 1850s to ride in the smoking car on the train that ran between Boston and Newburyport, Massachusetts, as he traveled from his home in Lynn to make speeches at places like Boston's Faneuil Hall and Newburyport's Prospect Street Church. The negative reaction to the bill from Democrats and some conservative Republicans was not surprising. Not only did they claim that Congress had no power to legislate social equality, they found the idea abhorrent. Many Republicans viewed this bill as politically poisonous and as soon as Sumner introduced it, it was referred to the Committee on the Judiciary where it languished.

A set of proposals for yet another Enforcement Act, again from John Bingham's

Judiciary Committee, was brought before the House in March 1871. After lengthy debates in the House and Senate it became law with President Grant's signature on April 20, 1871. Among numerous efforts to reinforce federal authority over civil rights, the core of this bill created two new civil and several criminal actions in federal court, and in an effort to mute the jury nullification effect, both civil actions included equitable remedies, which meant that cases could be tried to the judge without a jury. The first civil remedy, directed against state and local government officials, gave a cause of action for damages and injunctive relief against any person who, acting "under color of" state or local law, "subjects" "any person within the jurisdiction of the United States to the deprivation of any rights, privileges, or immunities secured by the Constitution of the United States." This provision remains in force and is the method used to bring police brutality cases to federal court. The second civil remedy, directed against the Klan and similar private persons and groups, created a damages and injunctive claim on behalf of parties injured when "two or more persons go in disguise on the public highway or upon the premises of another for the purpose, either directly or indirectly, of depriving any person or class of persons of the equal protection of the laws, or of equal privileges or immunities under the law" or for the purpose of hindering local authorities from protecting equal rights or disrupting the due course of law in such matters. Each of the civil remedies was reinforced with a criminal counterpart declaring violations "high crimes" punishable by "fines of not less than five hundred nor more than five thousand dollars, or by imprisonment, with or without hard labor, as the court may determine, of any person, for a period of not less than six months nor more than six years."

The Act, which became known alternatively as the Civil Rights Act of 1871 and the Ku Klux Klan Act, also criminalized intimidation of jurors in cases arising out of any of the Enforcement or Civil Rights Acts, prohibited complicit persons from serving on such juries, and more dramatically, it created an entire class of crimes out of any activity designed to overthrow the government of the United States, hinder state and federal authorities from enforcing federal law, and activity designed to prevent voting or other political activity in favor of candidates for federal or state office. The Act also declared that if the state or local authorities, and federal agents operating in the area, were overwhelmed by conspiracies to hinder their operations, the President was authorized to suspend the writ of habeas corpus and employ military force to restore order.

The Senate added two amendments to the House bill that were ultimately defeated when the House would not agree. First, Charles Sumner moved to append his public accommodations law to this bill. Second, Senator John Sherman proposed amendments making municipal governments liable for damages resulting from any violations of the provisions of the Act within their territory, and allowing victorious plaintiffs to satisfy their damages judgments by seizing any public or private property within the city or town. After the Senate approved both of these additions and sent the bill back to the House, the House Republican leadership instructed members to vote them down, resulting in a conference to work out the differences between the views of the two chambers. Although the House action was taken with no debate, reasons for this action emerged in the discussions in the Conference Committee. On the Sumner proposal, House Republicans feared that any public accommodations legislation would cost the party dearly in future elections by alienating moderates who favored equal rights but opposed social equality. On what became known as the "Sherman

Amendment," the House conferees explained that even the most committed Radical Republicans in the House were concerned that it was unconstitutional to impose a duty to keep the peace on municipal governments who might lack sufficient power to do so under state law, and they questioned the fairness of allowing victorious plaintiffs to levy on the private property of potentially innocent residents. In place of the Sherman Amendment, the conferees substituted language imposing civil liability on persons aware of violations of the Act who were able, but failed to, prevent them. This was still a fairly radical concept and would prove virtually impossible to enforce.

Despite repeated bitter protests from Sumner over the rejection of his public accommodations proposal, the Senate concurred with the House's views. Consequently, the bill passed in both Houses of Congress and was signed into law by President Grant on April 20, 1871, without either the Sherman Amendment or Sumner's proposal. Sumner vowed to re-introduce his bill in the next session, and he went on to do so every year until his death in 1874.

As soon as he had taken office in November, 1870, Attorney General Amos Akerman began a vigorous effort to effectuate the goals of the Enforcement Act as well as previous statutes such as the 1866 Civil Rights Act. Numerous federal prosecutions were brought in federal circuit and district courts throughout the South. Much of the effort was designed to reinforce the efforts of state and local authorities that often found themselves overwhelmed by opposition—both violent and non-violent, open and insidious. The 1871 Act enhanced Akerman's weapons against the Klan and other White supremacist groups, both organized and disorganized: groups that were terrorizing Black Americans and their Republican allies so as to suppress Black political and economic activity.

And Akerman's efforts soon paid substantial dividends. Federal authorities and federal judges were less susceptible to local political pressure than state or local authorities, so there were dozens of prosecutions and convictions under the Enforcement Act and the Ku Klux Klan Act.

Even a few local United States Attorneys embraced their mission. For example, U.S. Attorney Wiley G. Wells of the Northern District of Mississippi regularly rode with the U.S. Marshal to make arrests. In 1871, he went up to Tishomingo County and "captured five KKK with disguises." He took photographs of them in costume, which were published in Harper's Weekly and presented to a congressional committee investigating Klan violence. When things got particularly bad in South Carolina, President Grant suspended the writ of habeas corpus there and a cadre of prosecutors brought dozens of cases under the 1870 and 1871 Acts. Federal juries which were invariably multi-racial did not shy away from convicting defendants, in large part because even Whites were tired of the constant societal disruption caused by Klan terrorism. After Wells was elected to Congress, Wells's successor as U.S. Attorney, Thomas Walton, picked up where Wells left off. Walton was a Mississippi native, a former Democrat, and a soldier in the Confederate army, but shortly after the war, he became a Republican. He declared that the Democratic Party had become "the party of violence and ought to be rejected by all right-thinking Southerners."

The Freedmen's Bureau, whose mission had repeatedly been extended and funded by Congress, was also having more and more success. This was mainly in areas pacified by the presence of federal troops and the efforts of federal marshals and prosecutors. Hundreds of schools established by the Bureau across the South were educating Black children and young adults. Black-owned businesses were beginning to thrive and there was land available for farming. The Bureau helped Black farmers become established and break away from the chronic poverty inherent in sharecropping. There was peace, but at times, it was an odd peace, because regardless of the changing political and economic realities there nonetheless remained entrenched norms of exclusion and segregation. It was as if Southern Whites viewed social equality as the one fight they could ultimately win and thus need not give up.

17
LINCOLN'S COURT

Lincoln's Supreme Court buzzed with activity from day one. The Court's caseload was substantial, and while as always many cases involved important but mundane affairs, a few were radically momentous, especially those implicating Reconstruction.

One of the first matters related to Reconstruction to reach the Lincoln Court was litigation concerning Texas's status during the rebellion. In the case, Texas v. White, Texas's Reconstruction government brought suit within the Supreme Court's original jurisdiction to challenge the Texas Confederate government's sale of United States bonds owned by the state. The Confederate state government had used the proceeds to finance state operations, including the war effort, and the Reconstruction government sought to reclaim the bonds from their putative owners.

Here's the background: In 1850, the State of Texas purchased $10 million in federal government bonds. A Texas statute in effect through the onset of the Civil War prohibited the alienation of the bonds without the endorsement of the state's governor. During the Civil War, the Confederate government of Texas sold at least $135,000 of the bonds to two people, White & Chiles, without, allegedly, the endorsement of a lawful governor. Then in 1866, the new Texas Governor J.W. Throckmorton instructed the state's attorneys to sue to recover the bonds. The case had been filed, briefed, and argued in 1868, and Salmon Chase drafted an opinion for a 5-3 Court majority finding in favor of the current government of Texas. The Court decided three issues: first that Texas is and always was a state of the Union because no act of secession from the Union could be valid without the consent of the United States; second that the Reconstruction government of Texas was a lawful government because it was established by Congress in exercise of its power under the U.S. Constitution's Guaranty Clause, which guarantees states a "Republican form of government;" and third that the contract of sale of the bonds was void as "in aid of the rebellion."

The opinion had not been issued before Chase's resignation, mainly because the Court was waiting for a promised dissent from Justice Robert Grier, who would have held that Texas could not bring suit in the Court's original jurisdiction because it had not yet been readmitted to the Union and thus was not a "State."

Once Grier's dissent arrived and all Members of the Court reaffirmed their initial votes, Lincoln issued Chase's opinion under his own name, noting that it had been drafted by Chief Justice Chase and that, "as it cannot be improved upon, there was no reason to discard it and begin again." Chase's opinion in the case was generally consistent with Lincoln's views on the status of Confederate state governments. The most interesting part of the opinion was its discussion of the insolubility of the American union, meaning that Texas continued to be one of the United States throughout the period of rebellion whatever its avowals otherwise.

It has often been observed that the Framers of the Constitution illegally disregarded the Articles of Confederation when they drafted a new Constitution and specified that it would go into effect upon the ratification of nine states. The Articles declared themselves perpetual and required unanimous consent for alterations; yet clearly that was missing. If those nine states could form a new union in disregard of the Articles, why couldn't the Confederate states similarly ignore the U.S. Constitution and adopt the Confederate Constitution?

The Court, in a discussion of this puzzle that Chase may have included to answer the argument for secession that he must have heard dozens of times during the rebellion, characterized the Articles of Confederation as indeed having created a perpetual union which was transformed into "a more perfect Union" by the adoption of the Constitution. The Confederacy, by contrast, was an effort to dissolve, rather than perfect, that union and thus should be disregarded by the government of the United States whenever appropriate.

Another holdover from the Chase court was Paul v. Virginia, which provided the Court with its first opportunity to apply the

Privileges and Immunities Clause of the Fourteenth Amendment. At issue was a Virginia statute that prohibited out-of-state insurance companies from operating within the state without obtaining a license which required the company to post a bond of up to $50,000. No such requirement applied to in-state insurance companies. The statute was challenged by a New York insurance corporation and its local agent, a citizen of Virginia, as violating the Privileges and Immunities Clause and intruding on Congress's exclusive authority to regulate interstate commerce, a doctrine that became known later as the "dormant" or "negative" commerce clause. The Court, in an opinion by Justice Field, unanimously upheld the statute, holding that a corporation is not a citizen and therefore is not protected by the Privileges and Immunities Clause, and further that the business of insurance is not commerce subject to regulation under the Constitution's Commerce Clause. The Court appeared to be taking a relatively narrow view of the scope of the Privileges and Immunities Clause. By dodging the commerce power question, the Court did not indicate its attitude toward the purported exclusivity of Congress's power in that domain.

Chief Justice Lincoln often found himself ruling on actions that were taken during his presidency, or in relation to it. The President-turned-Chief Justice did not perceive any problem with this. Recalling his days as a lawyer riding circuit in Illinois and acting as judge when the actual judge was ill or otherwise unavailable—he felt he could adopt the proper judicial attitude at will, even when his private views might run contrary to the law he was required to apply. And he was also confident of the legal soundness of his views on perpetuating the country's recovery from the war and on Reconstruction, though they grew out of his experience as Chief Executive during the country's darkest hours.

Griswold v. Hepburn raised an important issue with vast economic implications: the status of paper money. In 1862 and 1863, with the full support of President Lincoln, Congress authorized the printing of $150 million in United States notes, the original "greenbacks," and declared those notes legal tender for all debts. Griswold sued Hepburn on a promissory note made before the existence of the U.S. notes and demanded payment in gold or silver coins rather than paper money. A Kentucky trial court held Griswold was legally required to accept Hepburn's payment in U.S. notes, but the appellate court reversed and declared the 1862 statute void as to debts contracted before its passage.

On appeal to the Supreme Court, Griswold—being a creditor in many transactions entered into both before and after the Act in question—argued for a broader proposition that the Constitution does not grant Congress the power to issue notes at all but rather authorizes only the coining of money, i.e., the fashioning of valuable material into coinage of an established worth. Chief Justice Lincoln, who as President had signed the bills making paper money legal tender, told his colleagues in conference that he had favored the law because it was vital to the country's financial health. Without paper money, he argued, the ability of thousands of debtors to settle their accounts would be thrown into grave doubt causing a ripple effect that would cause incalculable economic damage.

Unfortunately, Lincoln failed to convince enough of his colleagues of his position. Only six Members of the Court voted on the case: Justice Grier's former seat was empty after the death of his confirmed replacement, Edwin Stanton, and there were two additional open seats. Lincoln, Swayne, and Davis voted to reverse. Justices Field, Clifford, and Nelson voted to affirm, and Justice Miller did not vote because he was personally involved in litigation over the acceptance of paper money in repayment of a loan he had made to a business in his adopted home state of Iowa. Thus, the judgment was affirmed by an equally divided vote—albeit without a precedential ruling—but the status of paper money was thrown into doubt.

President Grant was surprised by the decision in the Hepburn case, having been assured by Lincoln that the Court would rule the other way. Lincoln himself was surprised at Justice Miller's recusal because in conference, Miller had indicated he would vote to reverse. On February 7, 1870, the same day that the decision was announced Grant nominated William Strong to replace Grier and nominated Joseph P. Bradley of New York (a distinguished and wealthy lawyer) to a new seat on the Court created by legislation that established the Court's membership at nine where it has remained fixed ever since.

The paper money paper issue came back before the Court's new, and apparently more receptive lineup, later that same term in two separate cases. Congress's power to issue paper money and render it legal tender even for preexisting debts was upheld by the Court in a 7-2 vote, with Chief Justice Lincoln now joined by his two new colleagues, Justices Strong and Bradley, and Justices Swayne, Davis, Miller, who had settled the case that had previously caused his recusal, and Nelson, who had changed his mind on the issue.

Greenbacks were thus and thenceforth the coin of the realm.

In 1871, two Lincoln Court decisions had important impacts on Reconstruction.

The first, United States v. Klein, concerned the effects of blanket pardons that Lincoln had issued to Confederate supporters in his role as President at the end of the Civil War. His first proclamation of pardon and amnesty—conditional on the recipient's taking the Ironclad Oath of loyalty to the Union—was issued in 1863 as part of an effort to help smooth the path to peace. Lincoln reiterated this general pardon and amnesty in 1865 and again in 1868, with fewer conditions than earlier versions.

Klein was the administrator of the estate of a man named V.F. Wilson who had owned the King of Prussia Cotton Company. In 1867, Klein sued in the United States Court of Claims to recover the proceeds of the sale of cotton that the U.S. government had seized during the Civil War. The Court of Claims decided in Klein's favor. However, Congress failed to appropriate funds to pay the judgment, which was required at the time before payment would be made. Then, in 1870, while the case was still open due to nonpayment of the judgment, Radicals in Congress pushed through a statute providing that if a claimant brought evidence of a pardon to the Court of Claims as evidence of loyalty, that court was required to treat the pardon as conclusive evidence of disloyalty and dismiss the case. Attorney General Akerman took the case to the Supreme Court, asking it to dismiss the case because the 1870 statute had deprived the Court of Claims of jurisdiction.

After oral arguments, the Justices met in conference. The discussion normally went around the table in order of seniority aside from Lincoln, who as Chief Justice spoke last. But in this case Lincoln decided to break protocol and hear the views of his colleagues in reverse order. First up, his two newest colleagues, Bradley and Strong, expressed strong support for the government's view of the case—that the government had the power to confiscate rebel property and Congress had the power to prevent compensation for it. After Bradley and Strong, the tide began to turn. Justices Field and Davis expressed support for Klein's arguments that Congress could not change the effect of a presidential pardon and deprive Wilson's heirs of their property. Justice Miller said that while he agreed with the legal principles cited by Field and Davis, he did not think the record established that Wilson's property had been taken wrongfully, and thus he was likely to vote with Bradley and Strong. Swayne said simply that he agreed with Field, and then the ever-prickly Clifford lengthily harangued his colleagues about the injustice of the government having to pay compensation for property that had been taken only because its owners had engaged in rebellion. Although he did not expressly say so, it appeared that he would vote with the government, and when Nelson said he agreed with Field, the Court was divided 4-4 when it became Lincoln's turn to speak.

Lincoln began by stating his conclusion that he would vote to declare the statute of 1870 unconstitutional and that he would write the opinion explaining why.

"Back in Illinois, when the facts were against me, I knew to argue the law. When the facts were with me, I knew I had the easier argument." He continued by explaining that in this case, the facts were clearly on the government's side. "No one wants to reward the rebels or even make it appear that rebels were being rewarded. But in this case, the law and policy are so clearly against the government, that I would feel that I was neglecting my duty if I ruled in its favor. Congress's statute treads on the President's power to use the pardon power at the most important time—

173

during wartime—and it treads on our branch's power to determine the effect of evidence brought into court. I cannot countenance either of these intrusions."

When Lincoln later circulated his opinion, it was joined without reservation by everyone but Miller and Bradley. And even they, in an opinion written by Miller, agreed with Lincoln's statement of the law. But they said they were not convinced that Klein had presented sufficient evidence to justify a monetary award. Lincoln's invocation of presidential power in wartime, and the Court's authority in ordinary times, were apparently what persuaded them.

Blyew v. United States, also decided in 1871, was the first case to reach the Court which hinged on applying the Civil Rights Act of 1866. The case presented an issue that was somewhat tangential to the central provisions of the Act: whether criminal cases in which state law disallowed testimony by Black witnesses could be brought in federal court to avoid that restriction. Two White men—John Blyew and George Kennard—had attacked a Black family and killed four of them, husband and wife Jack and Sallie Foster, their sixteen-year-old son Richard and Jack's elderly and blind grandmother. Richard died after making a dying declaration identifying the murderers, and the crime was also witnessed by the Fosters' eight-year-old Laura and her six-year-old sister Amelia. Laura hid and was unharmed; Amelia was struck repeatedly on the head but survived. There was evidence that the killings were racially motivated.

Due to their race, a Kentucky statute disqualified Laura from testifying against the defendants and rendered Richard's dying declaration inadmissible. It provided, "That a slave, negro, or Indian, shall be a competent witness in the case of the commonwealth for or against a slave, negro, or Indian, or in a civil case to which only negroes or Indians are parties, but in no other case."

The 1866 Civil Rights Act provided exclusive federal jurisdiction over "all crimes and offences committed against the provisions of this act, civil and criminal, affecting persons who are denied or cannot enforce in the courts or judicial tribunals of the State or locality where they may be any of the rights secured."

The local United States Attorney, with Akerman's approval, procured indictments under the Civil Rights Act of 1866 charging Blyew and Kennard with the murders. The prosecutor claimed federal jurisdiction on the theory that the witnesses who were disqualified from testifying were among the persons "affected" by the violation of the 1866 Civil Rights Act. After the defendants were convicted, the Commonwealth of Kentucky at the urging of its legislature intervened in their appeal to argue that a federal indictment for a murder committed in Kentucky "was an insult to her dignity and an outrage on the peace of a community which, by the organic law of the land, was placed under her sole protection; that none but she had a right to enter into judgment with the perpetrators of it; that no other state, sovereignty, prince, or potentate of earth had made or could make any law which would punish that offence at that place; and that it was no more an offence against the United States than it was against the republic of France or the empire of Germany."

Attorney General Akerman's response included the following: "The thirteenth amendment to the Constitution worked a radical change in the condition of the United States. But it did not execute and was not meant to execute itself. Appropriate Congressional legislation was provided for. No man is really free who is not protected, by law, from injury. So long as he is denied the right to testify against those who violate his person or his property he has no protection, and is denied the power to defend his own freedom. The condition of things in Kentucky under its law excluding the evidence of blacks where white persons have committed crime is disgraceful to a Christian community. A band of whites shall set upon and murder half a congregation of blacks, their minister included, and though a hundred blacks who saw the massacre survive, and can identify the murderers, conviction is impossible. The murder did affect persons who were denied in the State courts rights which the act of Congress secured. It affected the murdered negro, the negro witnesses in the case, and the whole negro population of Kentucky."

Akerman's brief was viewed by some as infected by hyperbole: who could imagine that even the most committed White supremacist would murder Christian ministers and congregants engaged in prayer or bible study?

When the Justices met to discuss this case, Chief Justice Lincoln opened the judicial conference by urging his colleagues to look at the case in the context of the social realities in places like Kentucky, and against the backdrop of the purposes of the statutory and constitutional changes "recently made."

The next Justice to speak was Bradley, and he pointed out that Justice Swayne, in an 1866 Circuit Court decision United States v. Rhodes, agreed with the Attorney General's arguments and allowed a similar prosecution to go forward in federal court. Swayne, sitting as Circuit Justice on the Seventh Circuit, which at the time included Kentucky, realized the gravity of the issue and had written a nearly thirty-page opinion explaining why he and his colleagues had concluded that federal jurisdiction was proper in such cases. Swayne spent only a few pages on the meaning of the statute, with the remainder of the opinion focused on the constitutional issue of whether people of African descent born slaves were citizens of the United States and thus protected under the 1866 Act. He concluded, in apparent direct conflict with the Dred Scott decision, that all slaves born in the United States became citizens at the precise moment they obtained their freedom and that therefore they were included in the 1866 Act's references to "citizens" even before the adoption of the Fourteenth Amendment clearly overruled Dred Scott.

Lincoln recognized that his position had three votes right off the bat. To his dismay, immediately after Bradley spoke, Justice Strong professed disagreement on the basis that witnesses to crimes are not "affected" persons within the meaning of the Act. Strong was open to federal jurisdiction in cases brought by federal prosecutors on behalf of the victims of violations on the Act, or by civil cases brought by the victims themselves but not when the issue concerned witnesses or other non-victims of the particular crime charged.

The battle lines were drawn, but when the discussion reached Lincoln, his position had a bare 5-4 majority, with Davis and Nelson joining Swayne, Bradley and the Chief Justice. Lincoln concluded the discussion by announcing that he would write a majority opinion upholding the indictments on the basis that the witnesses and indeed all "colored" persons in Kentucky were "affected" within the meaning of the 1866 Act by the refusal of Kentucky to ensure the personal security of a class of its citizens merely on account of their membership in the "African race."

When Lincoln's proposed majority opinion was circulated to the other Justices, even those that agreed with him were shocked.

Lincoln began, "Our citizens of the African race did not arrive on our shores voluntarily. They were seized, chained, and dragged across an ocean of tears to a new and strange place. Those 'lucky' enough to survive the journey were subjected to depredations that would be unimaginable had not many of us witnessed them with our own eyes. The unwillingness, now, of some of our state governments to protect the most basic liberties of these newly freed citizens—including the Commonwealth of Kentucky in this case—should be a cause of national shame, and it is our sacred duty, as its highest court of justice, to do what we can to remedy this failure and follow the path of justice wherever it may lead."

Lincoln's draft opinion went on to explain why a proper understanding of the 1866 Act, in both language and purpose, compelled the conclusion that racially motivated murders in states with laws like Kentucky's may be prosecuted by the United States Department of Justice within the jurisdiction of the national courts because such states denied to Black citizens "equal benefit of all laws and proceedings for the security of persons . . . as is enjoyed by white citizens."

On the narrow but fundamental linguistic issue of whether the statutory requirement that the violation "affects" a person whose murder cannot be effectively prosecuted in state court for racial reasons, Lincoln stated that "[i]f it would have been a cause affecting him when living, it will be a cause affecting him though dead. The object of prosecution and punishment is to prevent

177

crime, as well as to vindicate public justice. The fear of it, the anticipation of it, stands between the assassin and his victim like a vindictive shade. It arrests his arm, and loosens the dagger from his grasp. Should not the colored man have the aegis of this protection to guard his life, as well as to guard his limbs, or his property? Should he not enjoy it in equal degree with the white citizen? In a large and just sense, can a prosecution for his murder affect him any less than a prosecution for an assault upon him? He is interested in both alike. They are his protection against violence and wrong. It cannot be denied that the entire class of persons under disability is affected by prosecutions for wrongs done to one of their number, in which they are not permitted to testify in the State courts."

Justice Strong wrote a dissenting opinion joined by three colleagues. His dissent was brief but to the point. He stated that "the 1866 Act did not, and could not, grant the federal circuit court jurisdiction of the crime of murder committed within the district of Kentucky." On the 'did not,' he stated simply that witnesses are not among those encompassed by the language of the Act, which grants rights only in favor of those "affected" by the violation. On the 'could not,' Justice Strong argued that "the Court's decision overthrows the federal structure of our government. It recognizes and authorizes the seizure of state authority by the central government in a way never imagined by the architects of this Republic. As much as I sympathize with the victims of terrible crimes like those recounted in the indictments before us, the citizens of Kentucky must look to her authorities for protection and satisfaction, and not to Washington or the federal tribunals over which this Court presides."

The Court's decision in Blyew was applauded by Radicals in Congress as well as by Black American leaders. Frederick Douglass, who paid the former-President a visit in his Supreme Court chambers to thank him for "recognizing our nation's responsibility to my people," was especially gratified to see the change in Lincoln's attitude toward enforcement of racial equality. Lincoln greeted Douglass enthusiastically and introduced him to those of his colleagues who were in their chambers at the time. This raised some eyebrows among Court staff who were not accustomed to seeing a Black man treated as a visiting dignitary. Back in Lincoln's chambers, Douglass asked the Chief Justice whether he remembered hearing from him about the Culpeper family of Virginia. Lincoln said that he did, and Douglass told the him that the 1865 infant, Abraham William Lincoln, who goes by the nickname Willie, was "now a strapping seven-year-old who attends a school set up by the Bureau whenever work on his father's small farm allows. When I saw him last month, he asked me if it was true that I had written a book, and I promised I would send him a copy. There are stories like that across the South. Wherever there is peace, the people are thriving and getting educated like never before." As they parted, the Chief Justice said to Douglass "this Court can be a lonely place. Stop by for a visit whenever you can."

Black-owned newspapers like the Richmond Virginia Planet hailed the Blyew decision and the Chief Justice's opinion as "a giant step forward toward a just and peaceful future for our people." The White Southern press, though, was livid and portrayed the decision as a continuation of everything they hated amid the Lincoln presidency. As the Lexington Kentucky Daily Press put it, "We had hoped that in the role of Chief Justice, Mr. Lincoln would feel the restraints of the Constitution and laws. Instead, he has transformed his esteemed position into yet another instrument of federal tyranny, designed to displace the lawful local authorities in a quiet judicial revolution. A call to resistance is the only reasonable response to this outrage."

Thus, although some improvement was evident—with more Black children in school, more independent Black-owned businesses and farms, more Black state and local officials, and better relations between Black Americans and White Americans in more places than ever before—the old battle lines had not disappeared. They had simply gone below the surface. There was no guarantee whether or when they might re-emerge.

18
GRANT: SCANDAL AND RE-ELECTION

The year 1872 brought another worry to the Grant administration—the upcoming presidential and congressional elections. After accepting 1870's reduction in congressional representation, the states of Tennessee, North Carolina, and Texas each had a change of heart and abandoned, at least for outward appearances, the vote suppression techniques that had led Congress to exclude half of their representatives from the House. White Democratic political leaders in those states determined that although they might lose some seats in a more open election, they would retain control of state government regardless of Black suffrage, and the loss of representation in Congress simply was not worth it, if only because of the lost control over political patronage hiring. Greater protection of Black voting rights thus guaranteed millions of eligible Republican voters across the South, but actually getting out the vote would take significant work. Whites would continue to overwhelmingly support Democrats, and with the reforms it was highly likely that Congress would restore full representation to all of the Southern states. To shore up support among the Black community, and to get out the vote, Grant's campaign sent Frederick Douglass on a speaking tour across the country from which Douglass earned an estimated $30,000 in speaking fees and Grant received badly needed votes.

Grant remained highly popular and would not have had much to worry about had repeated financial scandals not tainted his administration. Although Grant was an honest and devoted public servant, his personal loyalty to friends and longtime associates made him blind to the corruption around him, and his precarious financial condition led some of his critics to assume that he must be involved in financial shenanigans. Officials in his administration were involved in numerous scandals, great and small. The largest financial scandal during Grant's first term involved a scheme by financiers Jay Gould and James Fisk to profit from higher gold prices by convincing the administration to halt sales of treasury-owned gold. Gould bribed an assistant treasury secretary to keep him apprised of the government's plans and paid the President's brother-in-law to participate in the scheme. To make a long story short, the plan backfired, the price of gold crashed, the entire economy was sent into a months-long tailspin, and the scandal touched Grant both professionally and personally due to a warning he sent through his wife to friends to get out of the gold market, as well as a package of money sent to Julia which reportedly contained $25,000 in gold profits. The only saving grace was that the economy recovered by 1872, though no one then knew what was in store in 1873, when panic struck again.

Three additional, albeit smaller, financial scandals occurred during Grant's first term, none of which caused anything like the far-reaching economic consequences wrought by the gold scandal. In 1871, Grant's ambassador to England, Robert C. Schenk, participated in a scheme hatched by Nevada Senator William Stewart and a trio of private owners to defraud English investors by selling them shares in an exhausted Utah silver mine. Schenk's name on promotional material lent credibility to the investment plan and was typical for the economic chicanery that often surrounded Grant. After the fraud was discovered, Schenk disassociated himself from the group, but not before investors had been duped out of more than $5 million.

Corruption discovered in 1872 at the New York Custom House, engineered by two Grant customs-collector appointees, also reflected badly on the administration. This plan involved steering storage of unclaimed imported goods to expensive warehouses in exchange for payments from warehouse owners. Customs collectors at the time did not receive a salary but instead earned commissions on duties paid by importers on goods that went through their ports of entry, and the earnings from the corrupt rental arrangements were often much greater than their official earnings. (In reality, customs collectors often made more money from 'gratuities' paid by importers for favorable service than from their official fees.) Treasury Secretary Boutwell investigated this scheme, which came to an end only after Grant appointed a new customs collector, Chester Arthur, who later became the twentieth President of the United States when, in his first year as James Garfield's Vice President, Garfield was assassinated by a disappointed federal office seeker. The third smaller scandal during Grant's first term involved fraudulent bidding for lucrative postal contracts out West that had been procured by bribing Grant's appointed Postmaster General John Creswell. Damage to Grant's reputation was minimized when, in 1872, a congressional investigation found no wrongdoing by him personally, but it later became known that the investigation itself had been affected by a $40,000 bribe, and the postal fraud continued for ten more years, until Chester Arthur's administration stepped in and shut it down.

Grant should not have worried about his reelection prospects. The only real casualty of his administration's scandals was Vice President Schuyler Colfax, who was not re-nominated due to allegations that he had received bribes in what became known as the Credit Mobilier scandal. Credit Mobilier was a shell company set up by directors of the Union Pacific Railroad so they could profit personally from the construction of the railroad. At the time, it was considered improper for railroads themselves to do the construction; they were supposed to earn their profits by operations. The company bribed numerous Members of Congress to support subsidies for the construction, including Colfax when he was Speaker of the House. Then, after the Republican convention selected Senator Henry Wilson of Massachusetts to replace Colfax on the ticket, it was revealed that Wilson had purchased shares in Credit Mobilier in his wife's name, which would be improper since he was voting government subsidies to the company at the same time. When the scandal came to light, he cancelled the transaction and later claimed to have paid the profits he earned as a shareholder to the corrupt Member of the House of Representatives from whom he had purchased the shares.

Despite all of these scandals Grant won the popular vote by more than eleven percentage points and won every electoral vote that was counted in the election.

The Democrats' poor showing was due in large part to three factors, one of which should have caused concern for the future. First, Grant was still an immensely popular war hero whose policies were favored by a large segment of the populace. Second, the Democratic candidate Horace Greeley, was an outstandingly weak campaigner who simply could not muster any enthusiasm for his ticket even among people who were concerned over the incumbent administration's corruption and its aggressive Reconstruction policies. Third, Greeley ran on behalf of a coalition of Democrats and the so-called "Liberal Republicans," (actually the conservative wing of the party) revealing a more serious split in the Republican ranks than might have been evident given Grant's popularity among mainstream Republicans. As the glow of Civil War victory dimmed, the alliance between Democrats on the one hand, and conservative Republicans skeptical of continued federal intervention in Southern states on the other, was a sign that without moderation the Republican dominance of the presidency and Congress might slip away in the not-too-distant future.

Not surprisingly, the results of the congressional election followed the presidential results, with Republicans more than making up for their losses in the 1870 mid terms. Republicans made their biggest gains in New York and Pennsylvania, picking up nine seats in each state. This included two newly-created seats that expanded the size of the House so that New Hampshire and Vermont would not lose seats due to the census.. Democrats also took a beating in Andrew Johnson's home state of Tennessee, where Republicans picked up five seats, including both additional seats it received after the census. Democrats gained multiple seats in Georgia, Missouri, and Texas, but overall lost thirteen House seats while the Republicans gained forty-nine in the expanded House.

In the Senate, Republicans lost two seats, but kept their majority. Of particular interest, Illinois Senator Lyman Trumbull lost his reelection bid in the Illinois General Assembly to Republican Richard Oglesby after Trumbull threw in his lot with the Liberal Republican-Democratic Party coalition that was trounced as badly in Illinois as it was nationwide. Oglesby was elected Illinois governor, but only on the understanding that he would resign in favor of Republican Lieutenant Governor John Beveridge once he was elected to the United States Senate. Thus ended Trumbull's Senate career. Although his views on race were often in flux, he was the author of the Thirteenth Amendment and a primary architect of the Civil Rights Act of 1866, but by 1872 he had become disillusioned by the Radicals' Reconstruction policies and no longer felt comfortable in the Republican Party.

The country had never seen anything like President Grant's second inauguration. More than a hundred thousand people came to Washington to witness the ceremony, but temperatures in the teens—the coldest ever for a March inauguration—coupled with a harsh, biting wind convinced many potential spectators to avoid the outdoor ceremony. Still, a large crowd witnessed former President Abraham Lincoln, now Chief Justice, again swear in his successor, now for Grant's second term.

Another first was Frederick Douglass's presence on the dais. Grant planned to mention Douglass's work leading the Freedmen's Bureau's educational and vocational training efforts in his speech, and he wanted Douglass there to exemplify his progressive views on race. Douglass had a good seat in the crowd for Lincoln's second inauguration ceremony, and he had managed to make it into the official reception at the White House, but this time he occupied a place of honor on the dais, a first for a man of color.

In light of the weather, Grant kept his address short and to the point. He covered two major themes: economic recovery, and what he saw as an overriding need to protect the rights of freedmen and other people of color. On the economy, Grant hailed the telegraph, the railroads, and new post roads as facilitating a national economic recovery that he observed was gathering steam after the downturn caused by the gold scandal. On the rights of Black Americans, he proclaimed that although the slaves had been freed and made citizens, they were "not possessed of the civil rights which citizenship should carry with it. This is wrong, and should be corrected. To this correction I stand committed, so far as Executive influence can avail." However, he did not mention the violence that in some places still prevented many people of color from fully exercising their rights, and he made clear his stance that "social equality is not a subject to be legislated upon, nor shall I ask anything be done to advance the social status of the colored man, except to give him a fair chance to develop what there is good in him, give him access to the schools, and when he travels let him feel assured that his conduct will regulate the treatment and fare he will receive." Grant thus declared that his administration's policy would focus on legal rights, not social rights.

The weather also affected the size of the crowd for the inaugural parade and fireworks display, which were both the largest and most elaborate in history. Most of the crowd made it to the inaugural ball, which was held in a large temporary structure built just for the occasion on Judiciary Square, about halfway between the Capitol Building and the White House, but nearly all left their overcoats on for the entire evening. The President and his wife Julia were resplendent in their formal attire, and both were clearly enjoying themselves. Everyone who was anyone in government and Washington society was there, including Frederick Douglass and his wife Anna.

The Douglasses were the first Black invited guests at an official inaugural ball. It came about only after a concerted effort by friends and supporters of Douglass, including Senator Charles Sumner, who had bitterly criticized Grant for not inviting Douglass to a White House dinner held for the commissioners on an ill-fated mission to Santo Domingo to explore the annexation of that nation as a state, even though Douglass was a commissioner. One of the more memorable scenes at the ball occurred when Mary Lincoln, Julia Grant, and Anna Murray-Douglass gathered together in a small group chatting amiably while their husbands were a few yards away, also carrying on what appeared to be a pleasant conversation. As usual, the Chief Justice did most of the talking, and Grant and Douglass did most of the smiling and laughing. At one point Grant directed the attention of the group toward the women, and said to Lincoln, "What a nice thing to see" to which Lincoln responded simply, "Yes sirree," clearly happy to see the often-troubled Mary enjoying herself.

When Charles Sumner saw Grant, Lincoln, and Douglass together, he injected himself into the conversation and wished Grant "a hearty congratulations." He asked Lincoln how life was treating him on the Court, and clapped his "old friend" Douglass on the back.

After this round of pleasantries, Sumner asked Douglass to report on the need for his proposed civil rights bill. "On your travels south, are you able to take meals at many establishments, Mr. Douglass? Do you find it easy to find lodgings?"

Douglass did not want to mar the occasion by complaining about his treatment, which was consistently very bad wherever he traveled. He said simply, "Mr. Sumner, you know nothing in that regard has changed much, but I am focusing on the people who need me, not the people who would rather I disappear. But tonight, I am beyond overjoyed at the prospects for our country and my people."

Sumner replied that the Douglasses' presence at the inaugural ball is "but another bit of evidence of the injustice of the exclusion of his people from so many public places and activities, and makes the case for my bill." Sumner had apparently not comprehended the words on social equality contained in Grant's address. Or maybe he had, and this was his response.

Another notable presence at the Inaugural Ball was Oliver Wendell Holmes, Jr.—the Union army soldier who had once warned Lincoln that he was liable to get shot as he stood on a rooftop to watch the fighting near City Point in 1865. Holmes was in Washington at Lincoln's invitation, to work as the Chief Justice's "law secretary," a precursor to the law clerks who, in future years, would assist the justices in the drafting of their opinions. After the war, Holmes had studied law at Harvard and then begun a legal career which soon brought him national attention, not only as a practitioner, but as a budding scholar whose case summaries were used by lawyers across the country.

Lincoln, always prone to bouts of melancholia, found his solitary work at the Supreme Court stressful, and Mary suggested that he hire a lawyer as his secretary so he would have someone he could engage with over the cases, more than a copyist or librarian. Holmes traveled to Washington in 1872 to meet with a group of legal scholars working on creating a legal history archive at the Smithsonian Institution. During that visit, he called on Lincoln at the Court. After they shared a laugh over their first meeting back in 1865, Lincoln asked Holmes whether he would like to spend some time with him at the Court. Holmes agreed on the understanding that the position would be part-time, so he could continue his scholarly work as well as his law practice in Boston. Over the next several years, Holmes traveled frequently between Boston and Washington, assisting Lincoln on some of his most difficult cases. This arrangement continued until 1882, when Holmes was appointed to a professorship at Harvard Law School. On that occasion, Lincoln sent Holmes a letter of congratulations and a box containing a top hat with what looked like a bullet hole near the top.

19
COLFAX, LOUISIANA

Although Grant resoundingly won reelection in 1872, complaints over federal meddling in Southern affairs grew ever louder throughout 1873. Whites resented the Freedmen's Bureau's educational and economic aid to Black Americans, and many remained vehemently opposed to Black suffrage and Black political activity more generally. There was constant friction in the transportation area, as Black Americans resisted being relegated to the second-class smoking cars on trains and low-quality cabins on steamboats. In some quarters, the opposition to civil rights spawned general resistance to all of Grant's policy initiatives, and despite his personal commitment to equal rights, he sometimes asked himself whether it was worth it. Although some Black Americans were prospering economically, it was only the presence of federal troops and other law enforcers that kept Klan violence down to a tolerably low level. And Blacks were humiliated every day by the segregation and exclusion they suffered at the hands of restaurants and other places of public amusement.

It often seemed like it would take only one small spark from one side or the other to set off a spasm of violence.

An especially violent incident—perhaps the most deadly of the period—occurred on Easter Sunday, April 13, 1873, in Colfax, Louisiana. After a largely Black Republican ticket prevailed in Grant Parish elections held earlier in the month, White supporters of the Conservative Democratic Party's candidates claimed the election had been stolen. They refused to accept the results and ultimately attacked the county courthouse in Colfax to expel Black office holders and their allies who had arrived to protect them and safeguard their hold on the local government. The attack was inspired by a Klan leader who proclaimed, "This is a struggle for white supremacy." The armed assault took very little time, and once they took the courthouse, the White attackers executed prisoners taken inside the courthouse and those they captured while attempting to flee the area. In total, they killed upwards of 150 Black Americans, while three White men died in the battle. Federal marshals reported burying sixty-two dead the day after the battle but no search for the perpetrators was conducted until the arrival of federal troops on April 18. By then, most of the attackers had fled the area, and very few Whites were arrested in the immediate aftermath of the Colfax Massacre.

President Grant reacted forcefully to the massacre, which he called "a butchery of citizens." Disturbed by the lack of local efforts to apprehend the murderers, he ordered military action, and within two weeks Army Captain Jacob Smith's troops had arrested eight White men for murder. A federal grand jury was convened, and indictments were handed up charging more than 100 men with seventy-two violations each of the 1870 Enforcement Act. The charges tracked many of the provisions of the Act, including conspiracy to deprive victims of their lives, conspiracy to deny them the right to assemble, conspiracy to deprive them of the right to engage in political activity and to vote, and conspiracy to deprive them of the right to bear arms for lawful purposes. In Louisiana, the federal prosecution was made somewhat easier by the inclusion of Black Americans on juries. Federal courts generally drew their jury pools from local voting lists, and Black Americans were registered to vote in Louisiana in greater numbers than in other Southern states.

After a lengthy trial of eight of the defendants in a federal Circuit Court presided over by Supreme Court Justice Bradley riding Circuit, all were convicted on each charge alleged in the indictment. Justice Bradley then stunned the federal prosecutors by vacating the convictions. He ruled that, as private citizens, none of the defendants could violate the federal constitutional rights of the victims. Bradley supported his ruling by pointing out that the indictments did not allege the races of the defendants or the victims, implying that perhaps a racial motivation would be actionable under the Thirteenth or Fifteenth Amendment. This ruling, if it stood, could severely limit the reach of the Enforcement Act, and by analogy the Civil Rights Act of 1871, especially its provision directed at the Klan and other private organizations that might "go in disguise on the highway or the premises of another."

Charles Sumner's recently-enacted public accommodations law

was also at risk. Sumner had died in March 1874. His last words, spoken to Rockwood Hoar, Grant's former Attorney General, were reportedly "take care of my civil rights bill" and in 1875, the bill became law, making racial segregation and exclusion illegal in "inns, public conveyances on land or water, theaters, and other places of public amusement."

Attorney General George Williams, who had replaced Amos Akerman in 1871, appealed Bradley's decision to the Supreme Court, which heard arguments in 1875 in the case that became known as United States v. Cruikshank. Williams, a former Senator from Oregon and the first West Coast cabinet member in U.S. history, was a strong advocate for enforcement of civil rights in the South. He argued the case on behalf of the government, with aid from Solicitor General Samuel Phillips, who, as speaker of the North Carolina House, had worked to protect and expand the rights of Black Americans. The defense assembled a distinguished group of lawyers for the Supreme Court arguments, including Reverdy Johnson and Robert H. Marr, who was a leading Democratic Party opponent of rights for Black Americans in Louisiana and later became a justice on the Louisiana Supreme Court.

The briefs and arguments at the Supreme Court centered on the two points that Justice Bradley had found decisive: first, whether constitutional rights such as the right to life, to assemble, to vote or to bear arms could not be violated by private citizens; and second, whether any power Congress might have under the Enforcement Clauses of the Thirteenth and Fifteenth Amendments was implicated even though the indictments did not allege that the victims were Black or that the crimes were racially motivated.

At the Supreme Court, a majority overruled Justice Bradley's Circuit Court ruling on all counts except for the alleged violation of "the right to bear arms for lawful purposes." At the conference table, several of the Justices expressed reluctance to allow what they viewed as federal usurpation of the traditional state power to keep the peace, but Lincoln persuaded them not by legal argumentation, but rather by eloquently pointing out that the failure to recognize federal power would enable White supremacists to reassert power across the South and subjugate the Black population through violence and terror.

The Court, in an opinion by Chief Justice Lincoln, stated that *"the Enforcement Act is but one of the many products of a vast transformation away from the concepts of federalism that had prevailed in this country before the late war. With the passage of the Thirteenth, Fourteenth and Fifteenth Amendments to the Constitution, and the laws enforcing them, the federal government has assumed responsibility for the protection of the rights of the freedmen and all persons of color. Those rights certainly include the right to live free from fear of racially-motivated violence, the right to engage in political and social activity, including the right to vote and the right to hold office when elected. When the local authorities are unable or unwilling to protect those rights, as was the case when the terrible events that led to these prosecutions occurred, the federal government has both the power and the duty to act. These are federal rights and the federal government is their appropriate protector."*

Lincoln's opinion brushed aside the failure to allege the race of the victims by stating that *"the want of an allegation that the victims here were of African descent is of no moment. The events were notorious, and judicial notice suffices where, as here, there is no conceivable lack of understanding by those people brought to the bar of justice for their alleged participation in the acts alleged."*

The opinion was not very precise on the source of Congress's power to enact the 1870 Enforcement Act or on the application of the Bill of Rights to cases not directly involving the federal government, except to state that *"with the recent Amendments, the Constitution places direct constraints on how states treat their citizens, and provides Congress with express power to enforce those constraints. With these powers, the federal government has a responsibility to see that all citizens, regardless of their descent, are able to enjoy the blessings of liberty recognized in the Declaration of Independence and protected by the Constitution of the United States."*

The defendants' only victory was on the charge that they had deprived the victims of their right to bear arms. Here, Lincoln agreed with Justice Bradley's opinion at the Circuit Court that "the Second Amendment has no other effect than to restrict the powers of the national government. The right to bear arms involves preservation of state militia, nothing more." Justices Bradley and Clifford dissented from the decision except for the holding that the second amendment could be violated only by the federal government. Bradley reiterated the conclusions he had reached at the Circuit Court, while Clifford's dissent read as if he had attempted to draft a majority opinion affirming the Circuit Court but on technical grounds concerning the precision of the language of the indictments.

Popular opinion, even in the North, questioned the wisdom of Lincoln's "transformation" language. The Chicago Tribune lamented that "our Chief Justice may have strayed beyond the limits of the federal judicial power, and sound policy, in proclaiming that the Union has been transformed." Southern papers were less diplomatic, with the New Orleans Picayune proclaiming that "the tyrant, now in judge's robes, has overthrown our system of government in favor of the rule of the jungle, with federal game wardens now free to roam about capturing white people seeking to preserve our form of government."

The Court's decision, announced early in 1876, might have spurred the Department of Justice to quickly bring more cases against Klan violence, but unfortunately, Grant had appointed former Democrat Edwards Pierrepont to replace Williams as Attorney General, and although Pierrepont was a strong supporter of Grant, he failed to bring any new prosecutions under any of the Civil Rights or Enforcement Acts. Prosecutions were resumed when Pierrepont was replaced in May, 1876, by Alfonso Taft, father of future President and Chief Justice William Howard Taft, who, for the remainder of Grant's time in office energetically pursued civil rights cases, especially those involving voting rights and discrimination in violation of the Civil Rights Act of 1875.

The period between the Colfax Massacre and the Supreme Court's decision in Cruikshank was pivotal in more ways than one. On the political side, even though Grant himself remained popular, the continuing stream of corruption scandals in his administration hurt the Republican Party all over the country and cost the party control of the House of Representatives in the 1874 election. The administration's worst scandal to date came to light in 1874 when a newly-appointed Treasury Secretary, William Richardson, was found to have steered lucrative delinquent tax collection contracts to an associate, John Sanborn, and then instructed government revenue agents not to try too hard to collect excise taxes so that Sanborn would have more delinquent accounts to go after. Sanborn, who by contract kept fifty percent of his collections, allegedly shared his bounty with Secretary Richardson and Senator Benjamin Butler. The scandal, Grant's aggressive civil rights enforcement actions, and his veto of a bill to increase the money supply, which would be good for debtors but costly for creditors, cost Republican candidates dearly in the 1874 election. Among Southern states, only South Carolina sent a majority of Republicans to the House, while up North things were so bad that even voters in Massachusetts elected a majority of Democrats. While they had the legal right to vote, and in some areas were well-protected by federal troops, without a secret ballot, many Black Americans in the South remained afraid to vote for Republican candidates and thus their turnout was relatively low.

Legally, Lincoln's Supreme Court was consistently friendly toward Reconstruction-related legal reforms including favorable readings of the Reconstruction-era constitutional amendments in several cases. Federal enforcement activity and Democratic efforts to gain Black support meant that Black Americans enjoyed unprecedented freedom and prosperity, although there were dark clouds on the horizon, especially with the 1876 Presidential election looming.

20
SLAUGHTERHOUSES, WOMEN LAWYERS AND BASEBALL

The year 1873 provided the Supreme Court with two opportunities to apply the Privileges and Immunities Clause of the Fourteenth Amendment. Both cases called for the Court to construe the clause to limit the power of states to regulate the practice of professions.

The first case challenged the refusal of the Supreme Court of Illinois to admit a woman, Myra Bradwell, to the practice of law. The Illinois court relied on two grounds for its denial of her petition: first that, because women were not ordinarily thought to be qualified for the practice of law, the legislature's delegation of power to the court system to grant licenses for legal practice could not have been meant to include a delegation of power to afford that privilege to women; and second that, as a married woman, Mrs. Bradwell could not make a legally binding contract without her husband's consent and thus was not reasonably equipped to perform the duties of an attorney.

Bradwell argued that the Illinois' court's decision deprived her of the privileges and immunities of United States citizenship because those privileges and immunities included the right to engage in her chosen profession. Notably, Bradwell did not raise an equal protection argument, which in later years became the prevalent basis for challenging this rule and other classifications based on gender. At the time, though, the consensus was that the framers of the Equal Protection Clause did not intend to address discrimination against women.

The Court denied Bradwell's claim in an opinion authored by Justice Miller. The Court held, *"The right to admission to practice in the courts of a state is not a privilege or immunity of citizens of the United States. This right in no sense depends on citizenship of the United States. It has not, as far as we know, ever been made in any state, or in any case, to depend on citizenship at all. Certainly many prominent and distinguished lawyers have been admitted to practice, both in the state and federal courts, who were not citizens of the*

United States or of any state. But on whatever basis this right may be placed, so far as it can have any relation to citizenship at all, it would seem that, as to the courts of a state, it would relate to citizenship of the state, and as to federal courts, it would relate to citizenship of the United States."

Justice Bradley concurred but rather than rely on a narrow conception of the rights of citizens, he relied on the regulatory powers of the state as they relate to the treatment of women. He wrote, "The civil law, as well as nature herself, has always recognized a wide difference in the respective spheres and destinies of man and woman. Man is, or should be, woman's protector and defender. The natural and proper timidity and delicacy which belongs to the female sex evidently unfits it for many of the occupations of civil life including, in the judgment of the State of Illinois, the practice of law. We have no occasion to upset that judgment, belonging, as it does, to the police power of the state."

Chief Justice Lincoln dissented, without opinion.

The Court's second opportunity to construe and apply the Privileges and Immunities Clause concerned Louisiana's regulation of slaughterhouses in New Orleans. The case involved the civil rights of Black Americans, but only tangentially. For years, slaughterhouses in New Orleans were the source of major health and sanitation problems, in large part because butchers discarded unused animal parts and bodily fluids with no regard for sanitary practices. Some left their waste in piles to rot out in the open and be scavenged by wildlife, while others dumped their waste into the Mississippi River and therefore tainted the main source of drinking water for city residents. This contributed to annual outbreaks of cholera and other diseases, which, along with the heat and humidity and odors emanating from the slaughterhouses rendered New Orleans virtually uninhabitable in the summer months.

To address these issues, the Louisiana legislature, which was dominated by Republicans and included many members of color, passed a statute granting the newly-formed Crescent City Live-Stock Landing and Slaughterhouse Company a monopoly over the business of slaughtering animals in New Orleans. The statute also moved all slaughterhouse operations downriver and to the other side of the Mississippi, where waste and odors would not affect the City of New Orleans. The connection to the civil rights of people of color was that this company was required to accept all animals for slaughter regardless of the race of the animal's owner. Previously, Black Americans found it nearly impossible to get their animals slaughtered in New Orleans and often had to sell their livestock to Whites at a discount. This aspect of the new law was consistent with the anti-discrimination provisions of the 1869 Louisiana constitution and numerous other anti-discrimination laws passed by the Louisiana legislature during this period of Republican rule.

This statute was challenged by New Orleans butchers and slaughterhouse operators, who argued that it violated the Thirteenth and Fourteenth Amendments by creating an involuntary servitude, abridged their privileges and immunities as citizens of the United States, denied them equal protection, and deprived them of property without due process of law. Their claims could be summarized quite simply as contending that the statute deprived butchers in New Orleans "of the right to exercise their trade." In effect, White butchers were seeking to employ constitutional amendments adopted to protect Black Americans to perpetuate their own purported right to exclude Black Americans from the business of slaughtering animals and to foul the local environment. This was consistent with the worldview of many Southern White supremacists, who often portrayed reforms meant to provide Black Americans with equal rights as establishing Black domination and subjugation of the White race.

After the Slaughterhouse Cases were argued, it was clear among the Justices that the majority of the Court would reject the plaintiffs' claims, but on what basis remained to be seen. Only three Justices expressed the view that the Act was unconstitutional. All Justices agreed that neither the Thirteenth Amendment nor the Fourteenth Amendment's Due Process and Equal Protection Clauses supported the plaintiffs' claims.

That left the Privileges or Immunities Clause. In conference,

Justice Miller expressed a view, initially shared by some of his colleagues, that the Privileges or Immunities Clause should be understood very narrowly. In his understanding, it would protect only rights that "owe their existence to the Federal government" such as the right to vote in national elections, the right to assemble for the purpose of petitioning the federal government for the redress of grievances, the right to seek federal habeas corpus, and the right to travel across state boundaries.

Miller suggested that the Court declare that the right to engage in a trade or occupation was not a privilege or immunity of federal citizenship, in large part to head off future litigation anytime a state or local government regulated that activity. Justice Field argued to the contrary, that the Privileges or Immunities Clause of the Fourteenth Amendment protected the rights of citizens of "free governments" which clearly include "the right to pursue a lawful employment" and that the Court should take a stand against government-created monopolies over what ought to be free, private businesses.

Chief Justice Lincoln was torn. On the one hand, as a lawyer he had seen the harm that regulation could do to business, which inclined him to read the Privileges or Immunities Clause to protect the economy from burdensome regulation. He was also concerned that a narrow reading of the clause would hinder governments' ability to accomplish the primary goals of Reconstruction, to provide security and full and equal opportunity to all Americans regardless of race or color. On the other hand, he also recognized the necessity of government regulation to protect the market and public health and welfare, which disinclined him from reading the Privileges or Immunities Clause so broadly that it would interfere with state and local governments' traditional police powers. In this case, ruling against the plaintiffs was consistent with both of Lincoln's instincts, but he did not want the Court to write the protections of the Privileges or Immunities Clause out of the Constitution with a broad opinion rejecting the butchers' claims.

Lincoln asked Holmes for his input, and was surprised when the young man launched into an energetic defense of state and local regulatory powers. Holmes explained, "The Court ought to leave it to those in the local community to determine what's best for them. Interference with health and welfare rules based on legal principle would almost always do more harm than good. If it doesn't work as hoped for, the locals will fix it with no help from a court in Washington." In a phrase Lincoln loved but felt he could not use in an opinion of the Court, Holmes said, "Experience and practicality is much more important to the law than its internal logic."

On the Privileges or Immunities Clause, Holmes said that a decision against these plaintiffs would not prevent the Court from reading the clause more broadly in a case presenting a direct threat to the constitutional values underlying the Fourteenth Amendment. It was during the pair's long discussions of the Slaughterhouse Cases that Lincoln recognized Holmes as not only a true genius but a revolutionary in the law.

Lincoln set out to write an opinion denying the butchers' claims while leaving the door open to reading the Privileges or Immunities Clause to protect a broad range of rights, especially the rights of freedmen. He hoped that his opinion could achieve a majority. He began his opinion by stating that *nothing in the Constitution, before or after the adoption of the recent Amendments, disables the state of Louisiana from playing the traditional role of protecting and pursuing the health, safety and welfare of her citizens. Specifically, there is no privilege or immunity to endanger the health and safety of the residents of the State, nor is there a privilege or immunity that overcomes the judgment of the State of Louisiana that this particularly vital industry should be organized as specified in the Louisiana Act of March 8, 1869."* He then went on to describe what he saw as the content of the Privileges or Immunities Clause, reading it much more broadly than Justice Miller had suggested so that its effectiveness as a protector of civil rights would not be dampened. While some of this language might appear to support the butchers' claims, the Chief Justice went on to explain that these rights and freedoms are not absolute:

> *The Amendment undoubtedly protects the rights we all hold dear. The right to liberty clearly protects the right to practice one's profession and the*

privileges and immunities of citizenship granted by the national government must be respected by all States of our Union. States may not deny rights, privileges or immunities to a sub-class of citizens, but when the State acts to restrict the exercise of these rights, the particulars of the situation are vital to the performance of our duty to measure the restrictions against the words of the Constitution. Here, the government's interests are clear. They are aimed at protecting the health of the residents of New Orleans and at ensuring equal opportunity in the trades of raising livestock and marketing the resulting products. While under some circumstances, government-created monopolies may be considered obnoxious to the genius of the law, that is not the case when they are awarded by representative bodies that are presumed to be acting in the public interest, rather than in favor of monarchical power that our Constitution abolished for all times. The monopoly in this case has been awarded in pursuance of pressing and vital aims, and it is not for us to disturb the judgment of the Louisiana assembly that this is the most efficient manner of pursuing those aims. It is both the right and the duty of the legislative body— the supreme power of the State or municipality—to prescribe and determine both the localities where the business of slaughtering for a great city may be conducted and reasonable regulations governing it.

In a concurring opinion, Justice Miller argued for a narrower understanding of the Privileges or Immunities Clause under which only the rights inherent in federal citizenship were protected and only when the rights of the newly freed slaves and perhaps other racial minorities are threatened. He commented, *"In his zeal to set forth an expansive understanding of the Fourteenth Amendment, I am afraid that the Chief Justice has strayed beyond the judicial function by opining on hypotheticals that are not presented by the case before the Court. I fear he has laid out a map to a place in our government that no one envisioned for this Court to occupy."*

Justice Clifford joined Justice Miller's opinion, leaving Lincoln with a plurality of four, but not a majority. This rendered the precedential value of his opinion weak, although when combined with the dissenters' expansive views of the reach of the Privileges or Immunities Clause, as detailed below, a majority joined him in rejecting Justice Miller's crabbed view of the clause.

Justice Field's dissenting opinion, joined by Justices Swayne and Bradley, agreed with the Chief Justice's view that the Privileges or Immunities Clause protects *"all of the rights that belong to the citizens of all free governments,"* but parted company with Lincoln on the proper application of that principle. He agreed that the provisions of the Act requiring slaughtering downriver from New Orleans and inspections of livestock before slaughter were proper regulations; the others were, to Miller, in gross violation of fundamental rights. To him, government-granted monopolies outside of a narrow area of necessity, such as *"ferries, bridges and turnpikes,"* violate the freedom *"to acquire property and pursue happiness. Indeed, upon the theory on which the exclusive privileges granted by the act in question are sustained, there is no monopoly, in the most odious form, which may not be upheld."*

Around the same time, a more obvious example of racial discrimination emerged in the nation's capital. The city of Washington, D.C., had one foot in the North and the other in the South with regards to racial segregation. Rails, streetcars, and other public facilities, such as inns and theaters, were integrated by law but often segregated by customs enforced by their owners. And public schools were segregated by decision of the local government pursuant to authority delegated by Congress.

A challenge to equal rights for Black Americans occurred in 1873, right next to Grant's White House and involved the game of baseball, the popularity of which was growing across the country by leaps and bounds. Nationally, professional baseball associations had voted in 1871 to exclude Black Americans from their teams and to prohibit member teams from playing games against teams with any Black players. Washington's premier team was the Creighton Base Ball Club. In 1871 and 1872, despite the ban, the Creightons played games against the Washington

Mutuals, an exclusively Black team on which Frederick Douglass was an honorary member. The games were played on the Creightons' home field, the White Lot, so named because of its proximity to the White House. Douglass's son Charles ran and played on another Black team, the Washington Alerts, and there were several additional Black teams in Washington, including the Metropolitans (known as the "Mets") and the Arlington Base Ball Club.

Douglass convinced President Grant to attend a Creightons/ Mutuals game in summer 1872. The small stands were full to overflowing, with the President and Douglass sitting in the front row behind the plate. Thousands of enthusiastic spectators stood along the foul lines and in the outfield and when the Mutuals took the lead in the last inning, the Black Americans in the crowd broke into jubilant cheers which continued long after the Creightons, unable to make up a three run deficit in the bottom of the ninth, had gone down to defeat 13-10. After the game, the President congratulated both teams on "a fine display of sporting abilities," but declined offers of champagne and whiskey from both sides.

An article about the game in the next issue of the Sunday Herald, a paper that reported frequently on baseball, contained more details about the behavior of boisterous Black Mutuals fans than on the game itself. After scolding the vocal fans, the reporter editorialized that it was time to close the field to "the gangs of lazy Negroes and other vagrants that infest it whenever a Negro team is invited to play on the White Lot." Sure enough, a few days later, in a chain of events engineered by the Creightons' management, the superintendent of parks in Washington announced that the White Lot was to be placed under the exclusive control of the Creightons, and the Creightons informed the Mutuals and the Mets that their upcoming games were cancelled because the Creightons were not willing to risk their ability to play against other (White) professional teams. Apparently, the manager of the New Orleans Lone Star Base Ball Club, the South's best team, read about the game between the Creightons and the Mutuals while in Philadelphia to play the Athletics there, and let it be known that his club would not keep its upcoming dates with the

Creightons if they continued to play games against Black teams.

As soon as they heard about this pair of edicts, Frederick and Charles Douglass went to see President Grant to complain. Grant was livid, and although technically he lacked authority over the administration of Washington City, he summoned the parks superintendent to his office for a good old-fashioned verbal horse whipping. The superintendent, a meek Irishman named John O'Grady, was startled to receive the invitation and even more shocked when the President demanded that he explain his decision "to exclude my friends the Douglasses and their base ball clubs from the field over yonder," gesturing with his cigar in the general direction of the White Lot. O'Grady stammered that he hadn't meant to exclude anyone—certainly not any friends of the President—and he would be sure to inform the Creightons that all teams were entitled to sign up to use the Lot. In reaction to the news, the Creightons moved their remaining home games to a more distant field at Simpson Park outside Alexandria. They also kept their dates with the Mutuals and the Mets, but they wore uniforms emblazoned with the name "Nationals" and kept their true identities an open secret so as not to jeopardize their relations with other professional teams.

21
THE ROUGH SQUIRREL

Resistance to integration remained throughout the South, but it receded somewhat in the face of hundreds of prosecutions and civil suits brought under the various civil rights acts. The 1875 Act was a powerful weapon in the hands of federal prosecutors and citizens of color alike.

In a case typical of dozens more, in April 1876, John Hartfield, the editor of The Messenger, a newspaper catering to Black Americans in Meridian, Mississippi, went for a drink at his favorite tavern, the Rough Squirrel. He had been there many times before because the owner of the tavern, Steven Rogers, was a progressive on race and had served him and his Black friends many times before, usually in a side room not visible to others in the tavern. Hartfield was returning from a trip to Laurel, Mississippi to cover the opening there of a Black-owned timber mill there which went badly when a group of White business owners tried to prevent the mill from opening because it would compete with one owned by a White man. Serious violence was averted when the inaugural mayor of the newly-incorporated town persuaded the Whites that there was "enough of that yellow pine for us and the Negroes." There had also been a bit of racial unrest in Meridian itself a few months earlier after a Black church burned down in a suspected Ku Klux Klan attack aimed at the preacher whose sermons urged militancy in the face of discrimination. The congregants marched down Main Street demanding justice, but no real investigation was conducted and no one was ever charged.

Hartfield entered the Rough Squirrel and seeing that no one else was there walked right up to the bar in the main room. Rogers' brother Jimmie was tending bar and when Hartfield asked for his usual "rye with a glass of water" Jimmie mumbled something about talking to Steven, who would be right back, gave Hartfield his water and asked him to wait in the back room until Steven returned. A few minutes later, Steven sat down at the table with Hartfield and explained that "ever since the trouble at the church" his other customers had been complaining about him serving "colored folks like you." He said he would be happy to sell him a bottle of rye that he could take home or drink at a picnic table in back of the building, but he couldn't accommodate him in the tavern any longer. Hartfield reminded Rogers that it was against the law to refuse to serve him, but Rogers held firm.

The next edition of The Messenger included an article about the Rough Squirrel and the mill in Laurel, and an editorial urging "all right thinking people of Mississippi" to respect the rights of all citizens to equal treatment. At the same time, Hartfield went to the local office of the Freedmen's Bureau and complained to a friend who worked there that the Rough Squirrel was violating the law by refusing to serve him and other Black Mississipians. The Freedmen's Bureau employee took Hartfield to see the United States Attorney, James Howard, and on April 19, 1876, after procuring an indictment from a local grand jury composed largely of freedmen, Howard filed the case of United States v. Steven Rogers in the United States Circuit Court in Meridian, Mississippi. The one-count indictment, in language identical to dozens more that had been procured across the South, alleged a single violation of the Civil Rights Act of 1875 based on Rogers' refusal to serve James Hartfield on April 12. The Messenger reprinted the complete text of the indictment.

Rogers brought the indictment to his lawyer, Frederick Phelps, who realized that although he could try to dispute the facts or argue that Rogers' willingness to sell bottles of whiskey to Black customers satisfied the law, he was pretty sure that his only real hope of winning was to attack the constitutionality of the Civil Rights Act of 1875. Thus, Phelps filed a motion to dismiss the indictment raising his legal defenses including arguments that Congress lacked the power to regulate discrimination in a privately owned tavern, that it would violate Rogers's Fourteenth Amendment rights as a business and property owner to force him to serve persons he preferred not to serve and that his offer to sell Hartfield a bottle of whiskey satisfied any obligation he might have under the Civil Rights Act. Luckily for Rogers, the Supreme Court Justice assigned to the Fifth Circuit, which included Mississippi, was Joseph Bradley, who was more than sympathetic to Phelps's arguments.

After holding a hearing on the matter, Justice Bradley took less than two weeks to issue his ruling dismissing the indictment. His opinion noted that the only possible sources of power in the Constitution to support the Civil Rights Act of 1875 were the enforcement clauses of the Thirteenth and Fourteenth Amendments. He offhandedly dismissed any other source of power such as Congress's power to regulate interstate commerce, stating that "[o]f course, no one will contend that the power to pass it was contained in the Constitution before the adoption of the last three amendments."

Justice Bradley rejected the Fourteenth Amendment as the source of Congress's power on the ground that the amendment reached only state action, not the actions of private business owners such as Rogers. As Justice Bradley concluded:

> *Individual invasion of individual rights is not the subject matter of the amendment. Until some State law has been passed, or some State action through its officers or agents has been taken, adverse to the rights of citizens sought to be protected by the Fourteenth Amendment, no legislation of the United States under said amendment, nor any proceeding under such legislation, can be called into activity.*

After laying out his understanding of the Fourteenth Amendment's state action requirement, Justice Bradley explained what he viewed as the mischief that would result if the state action limitation on Congress's power to enforce the Fourteenth Amendment were not strictly followed:

> *If this legislation is appropriate for enforcing the prohibitions of the amendment, it is difficult to see where it is to stop. Why may not Congress, with equal show of authority, enact a code of laws for the enforcement and vindication of all rights of life, liberty, and property, superseding those of the States on every subject imaginable? Why should not Congress proceed at once to prescribe due process of law for the*

protection of every one of these fundamental rights, in every possible case, as well as to prescribe equal privileges in inns, public conveyances, and theatres? This eventuality is certainly unsound. It is repugnant to the Tenth Amendment of the Constitution, which declares that powers not delegated to the United States by the Constitution, nor prohibited by it to the States, are reserved to the States respectively or to the people.

In other words, Justice Bradley thought that if Congress had power under the Fourteenth Amendment to prohibit private discrimination, it would necessarily have the power to displace entirely all state laws affecting life, liberty, and property.

Justice Bradley had more difficulty explaining why the Thirteenth Amendment did not grant Congress the power to legislate against private discrimination in places of public accommodation. The Thirteenth Amendment abolished the private relationship of master to slave, and was not limited to counteracting discriminatory state laws or state action. And, as Justice Bradley recognized, *"the power vested in Congress to enforce the article by appropriate legislation clothes Congress with power to pass all laws necessary and proper for abolishing all badges and incidents of slavery in the United States."* The question then became whether a private refusal to serve a Black patron was a badge or incident of slavery, which Justice Bradley answered with a resounding "no":

> *It would be running the slavery argument into the ground to make it apply to every act of discrimination which a person may see fit to make as to the guests he will entertain, or as to the people he will take into his coach or cab or car, or admit to his concert or theatre, or deal with in other matters of intercourse or business. When a man has emerged from slavery, and, by the aid of beneficent legislation, has shaken off the inseparable concomitants of that state, there must be some stage in the progress of his elevation when he takes the rank of a mere citizen and ceases to be the special favorite of the laws, and when his*

*rights as a citizen or a man are to be protected in
the ordinary modes by which other men's rights are
protected. If the laws themselves make any unjust
discrimination amenable to the prohibitions of the
Fourteenth Amendment, Congress has full power
to afford a remedy under that amendment and in
accordance with it.*

While this last sentence's suggestion that state laws supporting
discrimination were unconstitutional and subject to congressional
override offered a glimmer of hope, the rejection of Congress's
power to enact the 1875 Act overshadowed any hope for corrective
action.

Bradley's decision was big news across the country. Republican
newspapers, especially those serving Black communities,
universally condemned it, calling it, among other things "an
abomination," "a stab in the backs of all loyal colored citizens,"
"potentially the greatest injustice perpetrated against American
Negroes since emancipation," and "the first step in what looks like
a march back into the slave quarters." One Republican Senator
exclaimed on the Senate floor that "Sumner is surely spinning in
his grave."

Frederick Douglass brought the decision to Chief Justice Lincoln's
attention, imploring him not to let it stand. Not surprisingly,
many Southern newspapers applauded Justice Bradley's decision,
one calling it "a victory of reason over the tyrannical imposition of
social equality." The leader of the Southern Presbyterian Church,
Dr. Rev. Benjamin Morgan, preached a sermon that was reprinted
in the New Orleans Daily Picayune in which he declared: "As the
words of scripture came from the mouth of the Lord through the
hands of the authors of his Gospels, Justice Bradley's words deliver
us from the evil of the mixing of the races, which all right-thinking
Christians understand as against the will of the Almighty." The
Jackson Democrat praised the decision, expressing "the hope that
the death of the abominable Sumner law will allow all businesses
to operate in peace and security from federal intrusion."

The Grant Administration's Solicitor General Samuel Phillips immediately decided to appeal Bradley's decision to the Supreme Court. Phillips was from North Carolina, a strong opponent of secession who after the war had become an even stronger supporter of full and equal rights for Black Americans. He filed a notice of appeal on May 15, 1876, and began work on a brief. The brief proclaimed that the case involved fundamental questions concerning the future of the "Negro race" in the United States. He asked, "What does it mean to be a citizen? What does it mean to be a former slave and become a citizen? What are the privileges of citizenship? It is these questions, the importance of which cannot be overstated, that we shall endeavor to answer in this memorial to this honorable Court." The brief included spirited arguments proclaiming that the Civil Rights Act of 1875 was supported by the Thirteenth and Fourteenth Amendments and was founded upon the moral obligation of the government of the United States to treat the freedmen with care and dignity. On the Thirteenth Amendment, Phillips asserted that discrimination in places open to the public was a "badge of slavery, incident to the utter deprivation of rights that constituted that dreadful institution." On the Fourteenth Amendment, Phillips argued that access to places of public accommodation was incident to the citizenship granted in the Amendment's first clause and was also an element of each citizen's entitlement to the privileges and immunities of citizenship and equal protection of the laws. Finally, Phillips urged the Court to adopt a broad view of Congress's power to enforce the two amendments, asserting that the Constitution allocated to Congress the authority to determine the appropriate scope of federal civil rights laws.

Phelps's job briefing the case for Rogers was much simpler because Justice Bradley had supplied his legal arguments. Further, being unfamiliar with Supreme Court practice, Phelps enlisted help from Reverdy Johnson who, as ever, was more than willing to do whatever he could to unravel Congress's Reconstruction program. Johnson took Bradley's conclusions and created a polished and comprehensive legal attack on the 1875 Act as beyond Congress's power as understood in Justice Bradley's opinion. Phelps devoted his energy to painting a favorable factual picture, portraying Rogers and the Rough Squirrel as welcoming to Black customers while maintaining local customary limits on social interactions between Black and White inhabitants. Phelps noted that "before local social custom compelled a change, on numerous occasions Rogers had served James Hartfield in his tavern. He remains willing to serve Hartfield and all other members of his race and he is among the few local victualers that do so, merely not inside his four walls. Mr. Rogers hopes that in time the custom will progress so that all may be peacefully welcomed together into his establishment, but until that time, no law of Congress will bring about the change sought by this indictment of a just and honorable businessman like Rogers."

Both parties asked the Court to schedule oral argument on the case, and the Solicitor General asked special permission to share his time with Frederick Douglass. Douglass was among the greatest orators in the nation and had obvious credibility on issues of slavery and segregation. There was one catch—he was not a lawyer, and non-lawyers were strictly forbidden from officially addressing the Supreme Court on the merits of a case, even in writing. Thus, even though the Chief Justice would have loved to have Douglass appear, the request was denied without explanation.

When the Court assembled in late June to hear arguments, with a full gallery that included Douglass, the fault line among the Justices was clear. Based on questions and statements made at the argument, Chief Justice Lincoln had solid support from Justices David Davis, Samuel Miller, and Noah Swayne, all of whom he had appointed to the Court. Justice Bradley led another group of four Justices who expressed skepticism over the constitutionality of the 1875 Act, composed of himself alongside Justices Nathan Clifford, Ward Hunt, and Stephen Field. Justice Clifford was especially vocal, asking Solicitor General Phillips repeatedly whether he thought that "Congress could legislate against the human nature that keeps the races in their preferred spheres." Only Justice William Strong, a Grant appointee, gave no indication of his leanings. However, when the group assembled to discuss the case after the argument, Strong made his views clear: he was firmly on Lincoln's side and would vote to uphold the Act. In fact, he let it be known that he was ready and willing to draft an opinion that, in his view, would convince more than one of the dissenters to join the majority. The Chief Justice considered Strong's request for a few long moments and then said, "William, as always, you are welcome to share your views on the case in writing, but I view it as my responsibility to write the main opinion in this case. I would, of course, welcome your input on the Court's opinion at any time."

Chief Justice Lincoln set to work on drafting an opinion in United States v. Rogers, relying primarily on the Citizenship Clause of the Fourteenth Amendment for Congress's power to prohibit racial discrimination in public places but finding support also in the Thirteenth Amendment. He wrote in sweeping language, with the same passion he showed as President for preserving the Union. Justice Strong read early drafts and provided significant input, contributing several sentences that Lincoln used in the portion of the opinion addressing the power of Congress to enforce the recent constitutional amendments.

Lincoln began his opinion by declaring, *"This case presents matters as fundamental to the future of our nation as those that came before the great men who assembled in Philadelphia in 1787 to repair the defects in our original confederating articles. We must now determine whether our national efforts to expiate the collective sin of slavery will be sufficient to earn our redemption or whether we will continue to suffer the collective guilt we so deservedly experienced through war and destruction."* After recounting the facts, and charitably absolving James Rogers for *"having done nothing out of the ordinary for the time and the place and in reality treating the colored residents of Meridian perhaps better than most local merchants and victualers,"* Lincoln addressed the legality of the Act:

> *Congress relied on its power to enforce the Thirteenth and Fourteenth Amendments to support the constitutionality of the Act. Whether its power to regulate commerce "among the several States" might also lend support is a question we need not answer, for we find ample authority in the two late additions to our Constitution.*
>
> *The first sentence of the Fourteenth Article of*

addition to the Constitution declares that "All persons born or naturalized in the United States, and subject to the jurisdiction thereof, are citizens of the United States and of the State wherein they reside." These words, as simple as they are, made a great change to our national community, for they welcomed into it those who this Court had previously excluded in the Dred Scott case due to their ancestral slavery. What is citizenship? As the former Chief Justice explained in that regrettable decision, the lack of citizenship for our Negro brethren meant that they were "altogether unfit to associate with the white race, either in social or political relations; and so far inferior, that they had no rights which the white man was bound to respect; and that the negro might justly and lawfully be reduced to slavery for his benefit." When the Congress and the states, through ratification, declared that all persons born in the United States are citizens of the United States and their state of residence, it reversed this state of being and made the Negro absolutely fit to associate with the white race, socially and politically; it required the white man to respect the Negro's rights; above all, it prohibited the white man from reducing the Negro to slavery in form or in substance, which includes pinning a badge of inferiority on him through exclusion from places of business and public amusement. In short, the grant of citizenship created a new American Republic, a more perfect Union, in which all men are created equal and endowed by their Creator with certain unalienable rights, and in which all shall enjoy the sacred gifts of self-government, opportunity and dignity that this Republic has bestowed upon those of us fortunate enough to call it our home.

We have heard the argument, ably presented by counsel for the defense, that the Act of Congress before us bestows upon our Negro citizens rights and privileges well beyond those contained in the Article itself. This contention, in our view, ignores the wisdom of the framers of the constitutional Article, and its language, in which Congress has been charged with enforcing the Article by appropriate legislation. Chief Justice Marshall, in the McCulloch case, taught us that Congress's power to "make all Laws which shall be necessary and proper for carrying into Execution . . . all . . . powers vested by the Constitution in the Government of the United States" entrusts Congress with judging the wisdom and advantage of the measures it finds necessary, proper and appropriate. The Amendment purposely enlarged the power of Congress, not the power of the Courts. Whatever legislation is appropriate, that is, adapted to carry out the objects the amendments have in view, whatever tends to enforce submission to the prohibitions they contain, and to secure to all persons the enjoyment of perfect equality of civil rights and the equal protection of the laws against State denial or invasion, if not prohibited, is brought within the domain of congressional power. Unless the Congress transgresses clearly marked limits on its authority, which we judge in this case not to have transpired, our obligation is to enforce, and not oppose, Congress's will.

Although what we have already said is sufficient to reverse the judgment of the Circuit Court, we feel constrained by the gravity of the matter to state our conclusions regarding additional grounds relied upon by Congress for its authority to promulgate the Act. Plaintiff below and in error argues strenuously that Congress may rely upon the Equal Protection Clause as authority for requiring that Negroes be admitted to all places of public accommodation. The defense argues with equal vigor that the Equal Protection Clause constrains only government, and that therefore Congress lacks power over the policies and practices of private businessmen in their choice of who to serve or admit to their establishments.

In our view, the truth of the matter lies somewhere in between. While it may be that the requirement of equal protection does not reach purely private relations such as intimate social assemblies and even intimate political relations, it is universally understood that the institutions reached by the 1875 Act are not of that variety and are closely regulated by state and local authorities. Many are licensed. Further, in many states, laws that required all such businesses to serve any member of the community willing to follow its rules and pay its price were altered recently so that business owners would not be required to extend those privileges to the freedmen. The states are thus, unfortunately, complicit in the exclusion of the Negro citizen from the equal protection of the laws enacted to create and shape our economic institutions. The authority to exclude the Negro thus comes from the state, and the Act merely reverses that legal circumstance and renews the preexisting state of being in which all citizens, including Negroes, enjoy the same legal protections. As our discussion of Congress's power to enforce the Article of amendment establishes, whether this reform goes beyond the bare words "equal protection of the laws" is beside the point. It is undoubtedly adapted to that end, transgresses no explicit limitation on Congress's power and thus is encompassed in the power allocated to Congress under the Amendment. We have upheld the application of fugitive slave laws to private individuals. It would be a sad irony indeed if our Constitution would be of greater efficacy in preserving slavery than in its abolition.

Finally, but certainly not of lesser importance, the Solicitor General presses the Thirteenth Amendment's abolition of slavery as a basis for the 1875 Act. As the Circuit Court recognized, not only did that amendment abolish the relationship of slave to master, it empowered Congress to wipe from existence all of the badges and incidents of slavery as they existed in the pre-War period. There is no question of state action here, since the Amendment works directly on private arrangements. The question we must address, then, is whether the exclusion of Negroes from places of public accommodation is a badge or incident of slavery, a relic of the time when Negro slavery was an accepted social and legal practice. The Circuit Court, led by our colleague Justice Bradley, answered this question in the negative, pronouncing that "it would be running the slavery argument into the ground" to understand the abolition of it to include application of traditional public accommodations rules to require the admittance of Negroes to private places of business. In our view, the answer to these arguments is the simplest of all of the issues before us. Before the late War, there were two classes of persons in this Republic, one with the freedoms and privileges for which the Republic was established, and one in bondage and thus lacking those freedoms and privileges. The abolition of bondage brought with it the unification of citizenship, the unification of humanity, and any effort to reimpose the dual caste system is an effort to label the lower caste with a badge of slavery as bright as the sun in the sky and the stars in the heavens. It is surely an incident of slavery to tell a man that because of his membership in the Negro race he is not entitled to the privilege of visiting his local tavern, enjoying a theatrical presentation or riding with others on the rails. When Mr. Hartfield was denied service at Mr. Rogers' establishment, he was labeled with a badge legible to all who understand its meaning, "here comes a lesser citizen, one afflicted yet with the defect of a legacy of bondage and a stain of race, one not entitled to enjoy the pungent blessings of liberty that define the Republic that is the United States of America." In our Republican form of government, there can be no such lesser citizen, or we cease to be a Republic.

> *Bereft of all legal technicalities, Congress and those who ratified the three most recent additions to our Constitution created a new reality, a reality of full and equal citizenship for all regardless of race and previous bondage. They granted all persons born in the United States a share in the dreams and hopes of our still-young Republic. They are no longer on the outside looking in but rather are in the midst of this noble experiment in self-government that we hope, and trust, will endure for the ages.*

With these words, Abraham Lincoln exorcised the spirit of his earlier views on race, that the Black and White races could not live together and that the best course would be for Black Americans to resettle in Africa. He proclaimed a vision of a multi racial society, which he understood as a new experiment, for while other nations had followed the example of the United States and moved toward a more democratic form of government, none had done so with anything approaching the racial diversity present in the United States. It is one thing to rally a nation of virtually all-White Frenchmen around the concepts of liberté, égalité, fraternité; it is quite another thing to extend that vision to a community of diverse origins, traditions, beliefs, values, and skin colors, and with a history that included periods and pockets of unbridled enmity.

Justice Bradley wrote a dissenting opinion, surprisingly joined only by Justice Clifford. Although Justices Hunt and Field had indicated at argument and in conference afterwards that they agreed with Justice Bradley's opinion for the Circuit Court, when Chief Justice Lincoln circulated his opinion to the Court, they joined it. Alongside Justices Strong, Miller, Davis, and Field, this gave the United States a 7-2 victory in Hartfield's case against Steven Rogers.

Justice Bradley's dissenting opinion was virtually identical to his Circuit Court opinion, except that he expanded significantly on his view that the 1875 Act was beyond the limits of the power Congress had been granted to enforce the recent constitutional amendments. He focused on the word "enforce" in each of the empowering clauses to distinguish his view from the more expansive powers Congress was granted in the body of the Constitution to make all laws "necessary and proper" for carrying into effect the powers of the national government. In his view, the power to "enforce" the amendments is limited to legislation addressing actual violations, not transgressions that may be such only in the view of Congress. As he put it:

The concluding section of each amendment invests Congress with power to enforce it by appropriate legislation. To enforce what? To enforce the prohibition contained therein. To adopt appropriate legislation for correcting the effects of such prohibited practices and State laws and State acts, and thus to render them effectually null, void, and innocuous. This is the legislative power conferred upon Congress, and this is the whole of it. Contrary to the Chief Justice's pronouncement, it does not invest Congress with power to legislate upon subjects which are within the domain of State legislation, but to provide modes of relief against State legislation, State action, or in the case of the Thirteenth Article, of private action of the kind referred to in the amendment itself. Of course, these remarks do not apply to those cases in which Congress is clothed with direct and plenary powers of legislation over the whole subject, accompanied with an express or implied denial of such power to the States, as in the regulation of commerce with foreign nations, among the several States, and with the Indian tribes, the coining of money, the establishment of post offices and post roads, the declaring of war, etc. In these cases, Congress has power to pass laws for regulating the subjects specified in every detail, and the conduct and transactions of individuals in respect thereof. But where a subject is not submitted to the general legislative power of Congress, but is only submitted thereto for the purpose of rendering effective some prohibition, whether against particular State legislation or State action in reference to that subject, or some previously existent private relation, the power given is limited by its object, and any legislation by Congress in the matter must necessarily be corrective in its character, adapted to counteract and redress the operation of such prohibited relation, State laws or proceedings of State officers.

22
THE DAVIS PLAN

The reaction to the June 1, 1876 decision in United States v. Rogers and the release of these opinions was dramatic and virtually instantaneous. Conservative Southern politicians and newspapers condemned it as "a new war of Northern aggression against our way of life," "authorizing the basest intrusion into matters rightly in the hands of the states," and moreover "a vain attempt to force social equality of the races on the people of this country when no such equality has, does, or will ever exist as long as there are right thinking men treading the ground of these United States." Conservative Northerners also reacted negatively. Northern Democrats seized on it as "yet another reason to end Republican rule in Washington, soon, before it is too late to save our Union from yet another conflagration." Even conservative Republican papers criticized it, but in a more measured fashion, asking whether "the Chief Justice and his allies have considered the consequences of their decision" and questioning whether the decision would be enforceable.

By contrast, Black Americans were overjoyed. Frederick Douglass proclaimed, "We are on the road to the promised land of America. We see the way, charted by Congress and illuminated by the Supreme Court. We need only press on and we will arrive in a new country of freedom, opportunity, equality, and good will towards all men, regardless of color." Black-owned newspapers celebrated "President Lincoln's second emancipation proclamation, and this one will take effect immediately and without bloodshed on either side." Privately, however, even liberal Republican politicians feared a backlash that would have dire consequences for Republican candidates in the upcoming election. While violence and terror had receded in the South, even a few incidents might convince Black and other Republican voters to stay home out of fear for their safety. Leading Republican presidential contender, Speaker of the House James G. Blaine of Maine, was concerned enough to urge President Grant to be gentle in civil rights enforcement until after the November election, and although Grant communicated these concerns to the Attorney General, there were so many prosecutions already underway, all of which were brought by local United States Attorneys, that from the Southern White perspective, it felt as if the South was under the occupation of federal troops and the racial police.

In some places, the days and weeks that followed were revelatory to Black Americans, who felt a new freedom to enjoy life as full and equal members of society. They were welcomed, often grudgingly, into many restaurants that had refused to serve them before, and even though they were allocated tables in an informally segregated portion of the dining room, they didn't seem to mind. Likewise, they could attend theatrical presentations and musical performances, knowing that it was not by chance that their tickets placed them in a section occupied by other Black patrons, but they were in the hall and that was, at least for now, progress.

Change was not universal, though. There were still plenty of places across the South where Black patronage was not welcome. On riverboats and the rails, segregation continued, and violence against Black Americans asserting their new-found rights to ride in the first class rail car and occupy rooms in the first class cabin still occurred, though less commonly. In the face of this continued but dwindling resistance, local United States attorneys brought criminal prosecutions against prominent targets to make examples of them. In other areas, with less sympathetic federal prosecutors and strong White resistance, there was little or no enforcement. When violence broke out, local White police officers took sides and escorted Black patrons to the city jail on charges of disorderly conduct or trespass.

In Louisville, Kentucky, Wallace Davis, the owner of the well-known Blue Boar Inn along the Ohio River, had an idea.

The Blue Boar included a popular restaurant on the ground floor and about a dozen sleeping rooms on the second floor. It was close to the riverboat landing, so in addition to locals and their guests, the inn catered to travelers. The only Black people allowed inside were workers, including cooks and dishwashers in the kitchen and the maids who took care of the rooms upstairs. Behind the building, beyond the view of the other patrons, there were tables where Black travelers and locals could eat meals purchased out of a rear door to the kitchen, but none had ever been allowed to stay at the inn or eat in the dining room. Davis himself appeared often at the back door to thank his Black customers for their patronage.

During the week after the Supreme Court's Rogers decision was announced, brothers John and Cyrus Adams—Black publishers of the Bulletin, a local newspaper catering to a Black readership—arrived during the lunch hour and asked to be seated in the dining room. The host, as instructed by the owner, said he was sorry but the restaurant was closed and he could not accommodate them. They stood aside and then watched as several White diners were led to tables. When they received no answer from the host as to why these patrons were being seated if the restaurant was closed, they walked past him and took a seat at an empty table in a prime location along a window overlooking the river. Of course, the staff ignored them, but they were prepared. After about fifteen minutes without attention from a waiter, one of their assistants at the Bulletin, also a Black American, walked into the dining room carrying a basket of food that he had purchased from the back door of the kitchen. The Adams brothers spread their lunch out on the table and began to eat.

As soon as the pair started eating, the White patrons at nearby tables stood up and began to leave. Soon, the dining room was nearly empty, but the Adams brothers continued to enjoy their lunch, largely in silence. After another half an hour, they rose and walked quietly out of the dining room and into a jeering crowd of White men who were waiting outside to be seated after they left. The crowd included some tough-looking crew members of nearby riverboats who had been encouraged to come down and help teach the Adams brothers a lesson. However, before the assembled had the opportunity to set upon the brothers, Davis came outside and asked the crowd to leave them be out of fear of the attention all this would bring to his establishment. His offer of free whiskey persuaded the group to stand down. After a few moments the Blue Boar Inn was back to normal—until the next day, when the Adams brothers returned for lunch.

This time they walked briskly to an empty table without asking to be seated or speaking to anyone at all. And they brought their own lunch because they knew that the Blue Boar's back door would close as soon as they approached. Once again they spread their lunch on the table and began to eat. Once again, the restaurant emptied out. Davis came to their table and begged them to leave. He said that he would like very much to serve them, but White Kentuckians were not ready to share a dining room with them. "You know I pay my Black workers well and I serve a fine meal out back. Give the people some time to get used to it," he implored. Cyrus answered, "The people have had two hundred years to get used to us" and went on eating his lunch. After they finished their lunch, they calmly departed the restaurant and showed no reaction to the jeering crowd that had again assembled outside.

The next evening, the Adams brothers escalated the situation by appearing at the Blue Boar at supper time, when men would be dining with their wives and children. This provoked an even stronger reaction from Southern White men concerned with protecting their ladies from exposure to Black men. Moreover, it was even more disruptive and costly to Davis, who faced losing his lucrative evening business when diners ordered expensive bottles of fine French wine and nearly every table would be filled. The Adamses had engaged in subterfuge to gain entry—they had a White friend, Republican United States Attorney Marcus Clay, reserve a table. Clay and another man entered the restaurant at the appointed time, ordered a lavish meal and then stood up and left when the Adams brothers appeared to take their seats.

The brothers had correctly calculated that the White men present would not become violent in the presence of their families, and as at lunchtime, the dining room emptied out until, after about a half an hour, the Adamses finished their meal and left. As planned, they headed straight to the Bulletin's office where they completed a favorable review of the food they had been served at the Blue Boar, recommending sarcastically that their readers give the place a try—readers who knew full well that the Boar would not welcome them. The only thing that marred the evening was that rocks were thrown through the Bulletin's windows, no doubt by someone upset that the publishers were asserting their right to nondiscriminatory treatment.

After the Adams brothers departed the restaurant, a group of White patrons cornered Davis and demanded that he do something to stop them from entering the restaurant. "Why not hire a guard? There are plenty of dock workers who could do the job," one man asked. Davis explained that he risked arrest under federal law if he didn't serve everyone. "Marcus Clay would see to it. My only choice is either to serve them or to close the restaurant."

As he said these words, he had an idea. Why not close the restaurant and re-open as the Blue Boar Supper Club, limited to members and their guests? He could sell membership cards for a nominal price, say 5 cents, and simply not accept any Black applicants. And members would be allowed to bring as many guests as they wanted. Everything else about the place would stay the same. He also promised that the 5-cent membership charge would be deducted from every new member's first bill, at a time when a sirloin steak dinner went for fifty cents at lunch time and one dollar in the evening.

The brothers returned the next day at lunch hour and were turned away by the host, who pointed to a handbill that spelled out the club's membership requirement. They asked for a membership card, but the host said they were not eligible: "Membership is limited to members of the white race." Anticipating that the Adams brothers might insist, Davis had offered a half dozen dock workers free lunch if they would stand by in case there was trouble. The brothers, seeing this assembly, left quietly and went straight to Clay's law office to tell him about Davis's ploy. Clay immediately went to the Blue Boar and informed Davis that a 'club' open to any member of the White race willing to pay a nickel for the privilege was no club at all—that he would consider it a restaurant and charge the Blue Boar with violating the Civil Rights Act. Davis traveled by coach to his lawyer's office in the center of Louisville to ask him for advice. The lawyer told him that to make it a real club he ought to establish a membership committee that would decide on each new applicant. That would give him at least a fighting chance if Clay brought charges. Davis then went back to the restaurant and appointed his host, the head chef and himself as the membership committee, and told them that agreement of two committee members was required before a new member could be accepted.

Word of Davis's scheme quickly spread through Louisville, and most restaurants, taverns, inns, and theaters soon transformed themselves into private clubs that accepted only Whites as members. Some places that had historically been more liberal also allowed Black Americans, as non-members, to occupy designated areas such as the rear of a theater balcony or a dining area in the cellar or outdoors behind the kitchen. Many charged only one cent for membership and assigned a single employee to serve as the membership committee, such as a restaurant's host or a theater's ticket seller. After a front-page story in the Louisville Courier, and an editorial praising the "Davis plan" as a "wise and sensible manner of dealing with intrusive and abusive federal intervention into our local affairs," news of the Davis Plan spread throughout the South. Some proprietors printed handbills proclaiming themselves adherents to the Davis Plan that included a drawing of Jefferson Davis, misleading some Southerners into believing it was the brain child of the former Confederate President.

By the second half of 1876, the Davis Plan became standard practice wherever the local U.S. Attorney seemed likely to prosecute violations—from Virginia south to Florida, and west to Louisiana and Texas—with most establishments in the nation's capital and even some in a few Northern cities, such as Chicago and New York, adopting it. In other areas, where there seemed to be little or no risk of federal prosecution, establishments continued to exclude Black Americans or relegate them to inferior accommodations. The only establishments covered by the Civil Rights Act that could not take advantage of the Davis Plan were modes of transportation which could not turn away Black travelers. On the rails, steamboats, and coaches, segregation was maintained with Black Americans relegated to inferior accommodations where possible and at a minimum they were separated from the White riders. A few successful prosecutions were brought, but by and large, Black Americans were happy to be admitted and did not want to take the risk inherent in challenging White supremacist practices. Thus, many unhappily suffered their relegation to smoking cars, cars just behind the locomotive where smoke and ash made travel nearly unbearable, steerage-like areas below deck on boats and uncovered seats on the roofs of horse drawn coaches. The social forces behind segregation in transportation were virtually impenetrable.

23
A JOURNEY NORTH

Nationwide resistance to the Civil Rights Act presented the Grant administration with a dilemma. Grant's commitment to equal rights for Black Americans was unwavering even in the waning days of his presidency, but he was a realist and was equally concerned with the election prospects of the Republican Party, which were important to the future of equal rights. His new Attorney General, Alphonso Taft, father of future President and Chief Justice William Howard Taft, was even more adamant in his support for equality, and was especially interested in enforcing voting rights. But Taft also knew that there would be resistance to any Department of Justice enforcement effort and might cause moderate support to migrate to the Democratic Party's candidates, which in the long run would be even worse for the cause than the costs of a currently less energetic enforcement program. As Grant put it, "We might win Louisiana by losing Ohio, but we can't win both." They both knew that it would be unwise to take the Black vote for granted, either; they had to deliver on their promises or the Republican Party's Black constituents might simply stay home on election day, or even favor some Democrats who had been courting them with promises of favorable treatment.

In the end, Grant and Taft agreed that enforcement should continue through the discretion of local U.S. Attorneys. Taft wrote a letter instructing them to "bring cases challenging violations of the Civil Rights Act whenever local conditions allow." This was understood by the recipients to leave it to them to judge whether local opposition would make enforcement counter-productive or even risky to the local Black community. Consistent with his priorities, Taft's letter also urged U.S. Attorneys to be "ever vigilant in preventing the deprivation of voting rights based on color or party." In some places, like Louisville, numerous prosecutions were brought while in others, with less committed U.S. Attorneys and a clearer potential for violent resistance, few if any cases were filed and the twin practices of exclusion and segregation took hold. Even in Louisville, Clay's prospects for attacking the exclusion of Black Americans from "private clubs" like the Blue Boar were dimmed by defendants' right to a jury trial. A single White juror voting for acquittal would preclude a guilty verdict, which Clay understood would make convictions very difficult to procure.

Meanwhile, the campaign for the election of 1876 was heating up, nationally in the presidential race and locally in the bi-annual election for the U.S. House of Representatives.

Grant was certain to leave office after serving the customary two terms. Even if he sought a third term, all agreed that he could not have been reelected due to the taint of scandal. Three more scandals that became public in 1875 and 1876 sealed the Grant administration's reputation as one of the most corrupt in the nation's history. These were the Whiskey Ring, in which Treasury officials were bribed to help distillers evade taxes, the Fort Sill scandal in which Secretary of War William Belknap extorted funds for himself and his wife from a government contractor and the Cattell & Co. scandal in which Secretary of Navy George Robeson was bribed by the Cattell company in exchange for Navy contracts. Belknap became the first, and to the date only, Executive Branch official other than the President to be impeached by the House. The Senate held a trial even after he resigned, but he was acquitted because, contrary to the view of leadership, a number of Senators concluded that they lost jurisdiction once Belknap resigned. Although Grant himself was not implicated in any of the scandals, and in fact acted forcefully against conspirators when the corruption came to his attention, he would always be remembered for having presided over an extraordinarily corrupt administration.

Democrats were in control of the House, largely due to disillusionment in the North with the Grant administration's rampant corruption and violent suppression of the Black vote across the South. Because the House was in Democratic hands, there was no possibility that the Fourteenth Amendment's representation-reducing penalty would be invoked again, which freed Southern White supremacists to increase their campaign of terror. Even before the 1876 campaign got underway, it was clear that the situation would continue to deteriorate unless the federal government intervened forcefully. In early 1876, there had already been serious political violence in many places including Mississippi.

One of the worst incidents happened in Yazoo City, Mississippi, the seat of the county of the same name. The local "Colored Republican Committee" was having a meeting and barbecue to celebrate the reelection of Sheriff Albert Morgan. Morgan, originally from Wisconsin, had settled in Yazoo County with his brother Charles after the Civil War. Although he was White, he was beloved in the Black community for many reasons including his marriage to a local Black schoolteacher, made possible by his statewide campaign to legalize interracial marriage. He also hired numerous Black deputies, including Zachariah Collingsworth, whose brother Jacob, a moderately successful tenant farmer, was chairman of the committee. With the scent of roasting pigs as background, Jacob had just begun his welcome remarks to a jubilant crowd of more than 300 mostly Black Republicans, including men, women, and children, when a small group of masked White men overwhelmed the sentries that had been posted to protect the assembly and rode directly to the stage, firing pistols to ward off efforts to stop them, quickly killing four men and wounding several more. In silence, they snatched Jacob from the stage, rode to the perimeter of the assembly and fired their rifles over the heads of the crowd.

As the gunfire subsided, the leader of the gang of marauders, who could be identified by voice as the former Democratic sheriff Francis Hilliard, took a rope with a noose on one end from his saddlebag and hung it from a tree at the edge of the picnic ground. Two of his comrades then placed Jacob on a horse under it and wrapped the noose around his neck.

The leader said, "This is a mighty fine piece of rope, and we will use it if you keep agitating the colored folks round here. Stay home where you belong." He then yanked the rope from around Jacob's neck and shoved him off the horse to the ground. The masked attackers rode off as the assembly began to attend to its dead and wounded. Morgan himself escaped injury by crawling under the wooden stage, but the next day, after his telegraphed request for help from the State government in Jackson was turned down, he resigned his position as sheriff. One month later, when an election was held to fill the vacancy, only about a dozen Black Americans even dared to vote, and his previous Democratic Party opponent Hilliard was elected with over 90 percent of the vote. Morgan left politics and public service for good and moved to Jackson where he and his brother operated a successful dry goods store that catered to a largely Black clientele.

Zachariah Collingsworth also resigned his position as deputy sheriff and convinced his brother that they should try their luck in Chicago, where a small number of Black Americans from the area had migrated during and after the war to find work and escape Southern violence and discrimination. Despite their love for their native Mississippi, and the dozens of friends and family they would leave behind, they agreed it was worth a try. The brothers set off a week later by rail with clothes and money they had saved, leaving their wives and children behind, promising to send for them once they got settled into gainful employment.

Travel was by steamboat to St. Louis, where they were provided sleeping accommodations below deck in the area known as the "colored bureau" and then by rail up to Chicago. On the train, run by the Chicago & St. Louis Railway, they purchased second class tickets and were happy to be accommodated in a roughly appointed but clean car populated by other Black travelers, including men, women, and children. Their car was served by a Chicago-based porter, Edwin Morse, who shared with them the names of the biggest employers in Chicago including the McCormick Company that made farm equipment, the Pullman Company that made rail cars including the one on which they were riding and the Union Stockyards, where thousands of animals were slaughtered every day and enough meat to feed the entire midsection of the country was processed. He warned them that most of the well-paying jobs were reserved for Whites. As he put it, "They'll hire the most ignorant German speaking roughneck before they'll consider a Black man, even cultured and well-spoken folks like you two." When they asked Morse about railroad jobs, he told them they could apply—Black Americans were hired as porters and as assistants to the fireman to shovel coal—but jobs were scarce. He gave them advice on where to look for lodging and warned them to stay away from the sharpies who would be waiting at the train station to steal their belongings and money with offers of employment assistance.

When Jacob and Zachariah stepped off the train in Chicago they headed to the area just west of the station where Morse said lodgings were to be had. They found themselves in the midst of the most bustling mass of humanity and construction they had ever seen. There were thousands of people on the walkways, mainly White, dressed in all manner of work attire from the finest tailored suits to blood spattered aprons and mud-coated coveralls. A layer of greasy smoke hung low in the air and the odors emanating from the various industrial plants nearly overwhelmed them. Brick buildings stood interspersed among construction sites where larger structures were replacing those that had burned down in the Great Chicago Fire just a few years before. Between and behind houses and the small workshops and taverns, they could see fenced off back and side yards that served as animal pens filled with dozens of sheep and pigs who seemed to be looking suspiciously at the human passersby. And just as Morse had told them, after crossing a short bridge over a smelly canal, they came to a narrow road that seemed to be populated exclusively by Black Americans. They found a small room in a house that had apparently been constructed as a rooming house in the immediate wake of the fire. Their room provided just enough space for the two of them to stretch out on the floor and stash their traveling bags in opposite corners. The window was a blessing for the light it provided but a curse when the southwesterly wind carried the stockyard and factory smells in their direction.

The brothers set out on their job search bright and early the next morning. Their first stop, because it was the closest, was the McCormick factory which they heard was always in search of unskilled labor. They arrived at the gates and as they watched men speaking various European languages being ushered inside, they were turned away with three simple words, "no colored here." They received the same message at numerous smaller establishments despite the "help wanted" signs nailed to front doors or posted on gates. They heard talk that the Union Stockyards and neighboring meat processing plants would hire Black Americans, but they preferred what they considered better work in industry. After a long unsuccessful day searching for work, they dined at a small tavern near their room with a Black clientele, although they did notice several American Indians eating there as well, dressed in blood-stained clothes that indicated they were employed at the stockyard.

The next morning, they rose before the sun and ventured south to the Pullman company town to seek work at the largest rail car factory in the country. The town, just south of Chicago, was owned and operated by the company with housing for the workers and shops that accepted company scrip rather than greenbacks. This journey was unpleasant, running as it did largely over rough and muddy roads by horse drawn car amid the stench of rotting animal flesh emanating from piles left by the roadside or dumped into any available waterway in the area near the stockyards. They rode on the roof of the car with the driver while White passengers rode inside away from the wind and cold. When they arrived after their three-hour journey, their fate was foretold by the lack of a single Black face in the long line of men waiting to seek employment. One young Black man—a teenager, really—was waiting to board the coach for a return trip and as the brothers climbed down from the roof, he told them not to bother: they wouldn't find work with Pullman. Although Jacob wanted to try, Zachariah convinced him to reboard the coach and head back to the heart of the city.

On the way back to the city, back on the top of the coach, the young man told them that he had heard a rumor that Pullman was hiring "colored workers" but it turned out not to be true. "The only jobs for colored in Chicago," he said, "are as waiters and washers in restaurants, domestics, and as cleaners at the yards." Except for the cleaning shifts at the yards, these were the lowest paying jobs in the city. And cleaning at the stockyards and meat processing plants, where the wages were decent, offered backbreaking and nauseating work. Jacob decided to try the yards, while Zachariah ate lunch at their local tavern.

While Jacob was gone, Zachariah was surprised to see a Black police officer patrolling the neighborhood. He approached the

man and introduced himself as a former police officer from
Mississippi, and Chicago Officer James Shelton greeted Zachariah
warmly. Zachariah offered to buy Shelton lunch, which Shelton
accepted, and over sausages and onions, they talked about police
work and Shelton described the destruction wrought a few years
before by the great fire. Shelton encouraged Zachariah to seek
work with the police department. "They're looking for colored.
We get paid less than the white patrolmen, but they assign us to
the colored neighborhoods to keep us away from white folk who
wouldn't take to being ordered around by a Negro."

Both Jacob and Zachariah were successful in their job searches.
Zachariah became a Chicago police officer and lived the rest of
his life in Chicago with his wife and family, who had joined him
a few months on. During his career, there was a great deal of
labor unrest in the city as workers went on strike and protested,
demanding better wages and working conditions. The number of
Black residents in Chicago remained fairly small, with just a few
hundred migrants from the South arriving each year. Jacob found
work at the yards, first as a cleaner and later at the rendering
vats of a large meat producer. The work was horrible. Cleaning
involved scooping masses of odiferous entrails and gelatinous
waste products into vats, loading them on wagons and then
dumping the whole mess into the canals and streams that ran
through the area, sometimes directly into the Chicago River. The
river became so fouled with this waste that a few decades later, in
a major engineering feat, authorities had to reverse its flow to keep
the waste out of Lake Michigan, the source of Chicago's drinking
water. After a few days as a cleaner, the nauseating work led Jacob
to move to a rendering plant, where fat and other byproducts of
meat production were turned to lye for soap and other products.
This work paid less but was not as unpleasant except for the heat
from the fires. The meager wages, however, were barely enough
for him to live on alone and he realized after just a few weeks
that he would never be able to support his family in Chicago, so
after an emotional farewell with his brother, Jacob boarded the
train and headed back to Mississippi, via St. Louis once again,
and resumed life as a tenant farmer in Yazoo County, less free but
more content to be home with family and friends.

Part IV: The End of Reconstruction

24

HAYES-TILDEN

At the beginning of 1876, House Speaker James Blaine was the clear favorite for the Republican nomination to succeed President Ulysses S. Grant. Soon, however, the well-known tales of corruption doomed his candidacy among Republicans anxious to nominate a reformer after years of constant scandal surrounding the Grant administration. It did not help when it became known that Blaine himself had legislatively aided a railroad in which he held a financial interest and had stolen documents that would prove his guilt from a congressional investigating committee's star witness. So although Blaine pursued the presidency through the Republican convention and led the delegate vote until the seventh and final ballot when the other candidates in a crowded field threw their support to Ohio Governor Rutherford B. Hayes, he had to settle for appointment and then election as Senator from Maine, where he served until 1881 when President James Garfield appointed him Secretary of State. Blaine finally secured the Republican nomination in 1884 and then, owing largely to the continued taint of old scandal, lost the presidency to Democrat Grover Cleveland, marking the first time a Republican would not occupy the White House since the onset of the Civil War and only the second time any Republican presidential candidate had been defeated.

Hayes's victory at the convention came as a surprise to observers and even many of the delegates. In addition to Blaine, there were several candidates with more support going in, including Treasury Secretary (and formerly the nation's first Solicitor General) Benjamin Bristow, Indiana Senator (and former Governor) Oliver P. Morton, and New York Senator Roscoe Conkling (Ira Harris's successor). Hayes lacked the charisma and oratorical ability normally associated with presidential candidates, but his reputation as a reformer and his success in the key state of Ohio, where he had won three terms as governor, made him a logical choice when it became clear that Blaine could not secure enough delegates to win the nomination. Former New York Representative William Wheeler, with a sterling reputation for honesty, was nominated for vice president on the first ballot. Hearing the news, Hayes admitted that he had no idea who his running mate was. Personal chemistry between the candidates was not an important factor in those days.

The Democrats had an easier time choosing their nominees. New York Governor Samuel Tilden won the required two-thirds convention majority after only two ballots against a field in which his strongest opponent, Indiana Governor Thomas Hendricks, received about one-third of Tilden's count on the first ballot. A ceremonial third ballot made Tilden's nomination unanimous, as was Hendricks's selection as vice presidential nominee in a single ballot. Tilden was loyal to the Union and loyal to the Democratic Party, and he had amassed a sizable fortune in the private practice of law while staying involved in politics throughout his career. Tilden's strengths as a candidate included a deserved reputation as a reformer, leading investigations into Tammany Hall and successfully rooting out corruption in public works contracting in New York, as well as a record of electability, based on him roundly defeating the Republican incumbent in the 1874 state gubernatorial election. The only oddity was that such a calm, reasonable, and accomplished man would be the leader of the movement to put an end to Reconstruction's efforts to recognize the humanity of America's subjugated race. Politics makes strange bedfellows.

The election campaign was hard fought and contentious from the beginning. After years of constant scandal in the Grant administration, Tilden's reform candidacy resonated with the American public, as did his economic platform, which included a return to the gold standard and the elimination of unsecured paper currency in the form of greenbacks. Hayes's campaign was largely a "get out the vote" operation and relied heavily on Civil War history, with attacks on allegedly disloyal Democrats and reminders of Republican Civil War success, labeled by the Democrats as "waving the bloody shirt." When the votes were counted, Tilden had secured an outright majority of popular votes, defeating Hayes by about a quarter of a million votes, 50.9

per cent to 47.9 percent. Tilden also appeared to have won the electoral vote by a margin of 203-167, but Republicans challenged the tabulations in three very close states—Florida, Louisiana, and South Carolina—and claimed an additional electoral vote in Oregon, where the Democratic governor had ruled a Republican elector ineligible and appointed a Democrat in his place.

In all four contested states, competing electoral vote certificates were prepared by factions claiming to hold key state offices, including governorships, placing the outcome of the election in doubt. This dispute revealed a flaw in the Constitution: it contains no procedure for resolving controversies over the authenticity of electoral vote certificates. The Twelfth Amendment, which was necessary to correct the original Constitution's failure to provide for the separate election of the President and Vice President, specifies only that "[t]he President of the Senate [usually the incumbent Vice President] shall, in the presence of the Senate and House of Representatives, open all the certificates and the votes shall then be counted." With no further specification, the best reading of the amendment is that the President of the Senate decides whether to include a certificate in the tally, perhaps subject to challenge in federal court by a candidate who loses the election due to the failure to count a certificate or a decision to count what appears to be a defective certificate. Congress's only apparent role is to witness the tally and, in case no candidate receives a majority of the votes, elect the President (in the House) and the Vice President (in the Senate) as specified in the amendment.

The controversy over the 1876 election would not be resolved until March 2, 1877, two days before the constitutionally-prescribed transition to a new administration. Because Tilden had clearly won 184 of the 185 electoral votes necessary to be elected President, Hayes needed to win all of the disputed votes to prevail. Fraud and violent voter suppression tactics aimed mainly at Black Republicans most likely cost Hayes Louisiana, South Carolina, and possibly Florida, and Hayes had clearly defeated Tilden in Oregon, which made the appointment of a Democratic elector there illegitimate. Events in Florida illustrate how tainted the election was in the three disputed southern states. During the campaign, election-related violence threatened to erupt at any moment. The chairman of the Florida Republican state executive committee relayed reports that armed militia from Georgia were going to invade Florida on election day to prevent Black Americans in the northern part of the state from voting. Republicans, meanwhile, encouraged their people to vote "early and often," which was possible in an era without reliable voter lists and polling procedures. One trick that Democrats successfully deployed in Jackson and Columbia counties was to print Democratic ballots with a Republican symbol, tricking some illiterate voters into casting their votes for the wrong party. The incumbent Republican governor, who was defeated in the 1876 election, alleged in a post-election statement that there were 600 fraudulent Democratic votes in Jackson County; a wreck, blamed on "ku-kluxers" involving a train carrying couriers with election returns; reports of Black Georgians brought into Florida to vote Republican; reports of armed Democrats forcing large numbers of Black Americans to vote Democratic; and widespread reports of fraudulent vote tallies contributed to a general distrust of the outcome in Florida among supporters of both parties.

Tilden's supporters urged him to do whatever he could to ensure he was not cheated out of the presidency, including violence if necessary. There were plenty of Democrats ready to take up arms to force the Republican authorities in Florida, South Carolina, and Louisiana to concede and certify Tilden as the winner of their states' electoral votes. But regardless of their abstract commitment to the rights of the freedmen, White Republicans were not anxious to risk their lives to preserve the rights of people of color. Sporadic violence had already broken out and numerous Republican officials in the contested states, especially those involved in the election process, lived in constant fear for their lives. However, no matter how much Tilden firmly believed that his presidency would go a long way toward restoring faith in the American government and solving the persistent economic problems of the 1870s, and that if all votes were counted properly he had won the election, he dreaded the chaos and bloodshed that would result if the outcome of the election was determined through violence. Thus, he discouraged it and instructed his followers to let the political process play out. He was barely involved in his party's efforts to preserve his electoral victory.

In contrast to Tilden, Hayes was actively involved in plotting the Republican effort to thwart what his opponents saw as the will of the voters. Hayes argued that the constitutional solution was for the President of the Senate to decide which votes to accept. Because Vice President Henry Wilson had died in 1875, the president pro tempores of the Senate, Republican Senator Thomas W. Ferry of Michigan was in charge of the process, and the Hayes campaign's position was that Ferry, and Ferry alone, had the power to determine the outcome of the election by choosing which state certificates to accept. Ferry was a loyal Republican, and there is virtually no doubt that he would have declared Hayes the winner, but he and many other Members of Congress viewed it as imprudent to place the outcome of the election in the hands of a single man. Without constitutional guidance, it was up to Congress and perhaps the outgoing administration to figure out what to do.

The lame duck Congress convened on December 6, 1876, faced with ongoing disputes and extreme delay over counting the votes in the presidential election. As noted, under the Constitution, the President of the Senate, either the Vice President of the United States or, in the absence of a Vice President, the president pro tempores of the Senate, opens state election certificates and presides over their tabulation before a joint session of Congress, but it is silent on how disputes over the validity of these certificates should be resolved. Does the Vice President alone decide which certificate to accept, or is it put to a vote of Congress? As the date for counting the electoral votes drew near, these unanswered constitutional questions came to be viewed as unanswerable.

Agreeing that a process acceptable to both the electorate and to the political establishment in Washington was needed, each House of Congress established a committee to design one. Although this was not officially a joint committee, the two groups cooperated and designed a process very quickly. During the last week of January, with Hayes's reluctant acceptance and apparent indifference from Tilden, Congress passed and President Grant signed the Electoral Commission Act, which authorized the formation of a fifteen-member commission with the power

235

to decide which electoral vote certificates to accept, subject to override only by a Joint Resolution of Congress, which was unlikely given that the House was in the hands of the Democrats while the Senate was controlled by the Republican Party. The commission would comprise fifteen members, including five Senators chosen by the Senate (which chose three Republicans and two Democrats), five Representatives chosen by the House (which chose three Democrats and two Republicans) and five Supreme Court Justices, four of whom (two Republicans and two Democrats) were designated in the Act, not by name but by their assignments as Circuit Justice. The four designated Justices were empowered to choose a fifth Justice to serve, and the Members of Congress assumed that the choice would be David Davis of Illinois, who had renounced his membership in the Republican Party in 1872 and became the Court's only independent.

The planned bipartisan commission, with an independent Supreme Court Justice there to cast the deciding vote, was promising but not universally accepted. Some in the Tilden camp thought they should fight for their candidate in Congress, both on the floor and in the halls, where promises and threats might do the trick. Some Republicans feared that Justice Davis's departure from the Republican Party indicated that he might vote with the Democrats, perhaps to advance his own presidential ambitions. They then seized upon a plan to get Davis off of the commission, leaving only Republican Justices to take his place. Shortly after the passage of the Commission Act, the Republican-majority Illinois legislature elected Davis to the United States Senate, which Davis accepted as a better path to the presidency, making him ineligible to serve on the commission. The remaining Justices, lacking a neutral principle other than superior status, selected Chief Justice Abraham Lincoln to replace Davis and serve on the commission as its presiding officer, rejecting arguments from their Democratic colleagues that they should leave the position vacant to prevent the Republican Party from securing a majority.

The selection of Lincoln, which placed eight Republicans and seven Democrats on the commission, virtually assured that the outcome would favor Hayes. Democrats in Congress introduced a bill in Congress to reduce the number of commissioners to fourteen to exclude Lincoln and prevent a Republican majority. The bill, which had no hope of passage due to Republican control of the Senate, would have left it to Congress to make a final decision in case of a tie at the commission. Justice Clifford was also unhappy with the selection of Lincoln because without Lincoln, he would have been the senior Justice on the tribunal and would have been the natural choice to be its presiding officer, a role he had relished.

In preparation for the commission's proceedings, each candidate hired a team of distinguished lawyers. Tilden's team included Jeremiah S. Black, Attorney General and Secretary of State under James Buchanan and former member of the Pennsylvania Supreme Court, John Archibald Campbell, former United States Supreme Court Justice who resigned at the outbreak of war and later served as Confederate Secretary of War, Matthew H. Carpenter, former Wisconsin Senator, gifted orator, and distinguished lawyer who won landmark cases at the Supreme Court including Ex parte Garland (restoring the rights of former Confederates to practice law before the U.S. Supreme Court) and the Slaughter-House Cases (Carpenter also represented Myra Bradwell in her failed attempt to overturn Illinois' ban on women practicing law), Lyman Trumbull, former Senator from Illinois and author of the Thirteenth Amendment, and Charles O'Conor, a distinguished trial lawyer and close friend of Tilden who represented Confederate President Jefferson Davis in his treason defense and was appointed by President Franklin Pierce to be United States Attorney for the Southern District of New York in 1853, where he served briefly.

Hayes hired William M. Evarts, who had briefly served as Attorney General in the Johnson administration and would later serve again in that role and as Secretary of State and Senator from New York, Stanley Matthews, a talented lawyer who knew Hayes at Kenyon College and served under his command in the Civil War, read the law with Supreme Court Justice Salmon P. Chase and later became a Justice on that Court after serving as a Senator from Ohio, Samuel Shellabarger, former Representative from Ohio and drafter of 1871's Ku Klux Klan Act, and Edwin W. (E.W.) Stoughton, a successful patent lawyer and well-known supporter of the Grant administration's deployment of federal troops to keep the peace and protect freedmen's rights in Louisiana. This may have been the greatest assemblage of legal talent in a single proceeding in the history of the United States.

25
ELECTORAL COMMISSION

Commencing on February 1, 1877, with Chief Justice Abraham Lincoln presiding, the proceedings took on a magisterial air. The tone was solemn, reflecting the gravity of the issues. Procedural regularity was unfailingly observed. Lawyers made their presentations calmly, earnestly, insistently, and respectfully. Time moved slowly as the lawyers meticulously presented their evidence and made their arguments. The rules adopted by the commission provided that after each state's votes were examined, the commission would deliberate and vote on which slate of electors should be recognized. The commission's decisions, however, were not certain to be final, for the President of the Senate, and perhaps Congress, in its constitutionally-prescribed joint session, might decline to accept the commission's tally of the electoral votes. None of this was clearly covered by the Constitution or the Commission Act.

The dispute was framed in opening statements delivered by Stanley Matthews for the Hayes team and Charles O'Conor for the Tilden team. Matthews began by declaring that the only questions before the commission were "which set of electors, by actual declaration of the final authority of the State charged with that duty, has become entitled to and clothed by the forms of law with actual incumbency and possession of the office and whether the selection of those electors had been conducted in pursuance of each states' regulations pertaining thereto." In other words, his claim was that the commission should not look behind the certificates provided by state governors and inquire into alleged irregularities in the conduct of the election, but rather should ascertain only which certificates were provided by the governor of each state in dispute and whether the governor and other state officials had followed state law in doing so. And then he asserted that the evidence would show beyond a doubt that the Republicans were the legitimate governors of Florida, Louisiana, and South Carolina, that each government had scrupulously followed their states' prescribed procedures for certifying the results and that the governor of Oregon had improperly appointed a Democratic elector when Hayes had clearly won the election there.

O'Conor began, "I agree with Mr. Matthews on the proposition that one issue before the commission is whether each state followed its own laws on certification of the choice of electors pertaining to the selection of the chief magistrate." O'Conor then argued, contrary to the view urged by Matthews, that the Commission should delve into the accuracy of the returns that resulted in the competing certificates: "This tribunal can investigate, as political and legislative bodies may, touching all the facts and circumstances that are necessary to be known in order to enlighten their judgment and guide them to a just and righteous decision. The notion that this commission may not ascertain the truth for itself is a common plea among persons who set up a falsely and fraudulently contrived title." O'Conor was urging the commission to investigate allegations of vote fraud, which was likely rampant in many locations, including parts of Louisiana where, some months later, local officials were prosecuted for providing fabricated vote totals. O'Conor also declared that the certificates provided by the putative Democratic governments in the states at issue reflected an accurate tally of the votes and that it was they, and not their Republican counterparts, who were lawfully entitled to the gubernatorial offices.

Following these opening statements, the proceedings turned to examination of the vote tallies and electoral slates provided in each state, first Florida, then South Carolina, then Louisiana, and then Oregon, where the dispute was over a single, but potentially decisive, electoral vote. Congress had been presented with three competing slates of Florida electors, and each slate was objected to by members of both the House and Senate. As provided in the Act creating the Electoral Commission, rather than resolve the matter itself, Congress referred the dispute to the commission, which took it up on February 2, 1877.

After Chief Justice Lincoln gaveled the proceedings open, the Democratic objectors began their presentation. Their case on the merits was presented by David Dudley Field. He began by reciting Florida law on the choice of electors, and when he turned to Democrats' claim that the Republican slate of electors was tainted by fraud in the conduct of the election, Matthews rose and objected, arguing that the only issue properly before the commission was whether Florida law had been complied with, which turned mainly on who had been elected Governor of Florida in the 1876 election. President Lincoln inquired of Field how much evidence he intended to present, and he replied that, with the commission's indulgence, he thought the evidence on Florida would take three or four days to present, while that on Louisiana somewhat longer, and on South Carolina somewhat shorter. Oregon, he said, would take only a few hours.

Under commission rules, the objection would be determined by a majority vote of the fifteen commissioners. Before putting the matter to a vote, Lincoln asked the lawyers from each side to argue their views and, despite increasingly furious objections from Matthews, allowed Field to outline his evidence of fraud in the tally of votes underlying the Republican slate of electors. After some back and forth between the lawyers, Lincoln said, "Gentlemen, I think the issue has been presented and the time for us to rule has arrived." Rather than call for an immediate vote of the commissioners, Lincoln said, "I welcome debate among my fellow commissioners on this subject, recognizing, however, that we have been assisted by able counsel for both sides." Justice Bradley stated that as far as he was concerned, an immediate vote was preferable to further delay "which would simply amount to a rehash of counsels' arguments."

Seeing the other commissioners nodding their assent, Lincoln said, "Very well, but before we vote, I feel compelled to clarify just what it is we are voting on. If Mr. Matthews' intent is for us to hear nothing pertaining to the conduct of the election, I would oppose his objection. I am reminded of an experience I had as a young man flatboating in Illinois. I encountered many difficulties, one of which was the necessity of loading a few dozen unruly hogs onto a barge that was bobbing rather unsteadily on the Sangamon River. My partner had the ingenious thought that perhaps a blind hog would load easier than one who could perceive his surroundings, so he proceeded to sew seventy-two sets of eyelids shut, which turned out only to strengthen the resolve of our suilline cargo to remain on dry land. We were forced to sell those hogs for less

241

than we paid for them, since they were too many to slaughter on the spot and the labor of unstitching their lids would fall on their new owner, as we were constrained to depart before we could undo our doings. I have always found decisionmaking with eyes open preferable to that with eyes shut, and thus I am inclined to allow the commission to hear at least some of the parties' evidence on each states' election, even if the ultimate question is resolved largely by the factors urged by Mr. Matthews."

Exercising his prerogative as presiding officer, Lincoln offered the commissioners two options: a vote in favor of Matthews' objection to limit presentations to a preliminary review of the conduct of the election, or alternatively, a vote against Matthews' objection, which would allow the Democrats to offer full evidentiary presentations on election fraud and other misconduct in the tallying of the votes. When the vote was taken, it set the tone for the remainder of the commission's decisions: all eight Republicans sided with Matthews while all seven Democrats sided with Field. This meant that the Democrats would be able to offer only a small slice of their voluminous evidence that votes had been manufactured and mis-tallied in many locales, while Republicans would be precluded from offering their evidence of the intimidation that kept many Black Americans and Republicans away from the polls, especially in Louisiana. But the Republicans understood that their need for evidence was much weaker because they were confident that they would convince the commission that Republican governments had lawfully certified their electors for Hayes in all of the contested states.

This ruling took much of the wind out of the sails of the Democratic contestants. Yet the proceedings continued for four long weeks, punctuated by commission votes on the electors of each of the four contested states. Over time, Chief Justice Lincoln became a more and more lenient enforcer of his evidentiary ruling, and the proceedings ultimately consumed over 10,000 printed pages, including evidence and arguments supported by lengthy quotations from Supreme Court decisions and even Lincoln's own writings on the fruitless attempt of Louisiana to have its electoral votes counted in 1864. They were conducted in all seriousness, but as each consequential vote taken broke perfectly on party lines, doubt about the outcome dissolved. First the vote on Florida's electors went to Hayes eight to seven followed by eight to seven on Louisiana, eight to seven on South Carolina, followed by a final vote of eight to seven awarding the single disputed Oregon elector to Hayes. The Oregon decision was, in the eyes of Tilden supporters, particularly galling because in that state, the universally acknowledged governor's certificate was rejected after the commission inquired into the evidence and reasoning behind the governor's replacement of an allegedly ineligible Hayes elector with a Democrat. While in the other three states, the commission refused to look behind the certificates, it was necessary to take the opposite tack in Oregon if Hayes was to prevail.

No matter how hard Chief Justice Lincoln tried to keep up appearance, the commission had become a grotesque charade, with participants playing their roles en masque without connection to the reality of what was transpiring. As one observer described it, it was akin to the Oberammergau Passion Play—really far too long, with everyone in the village taking part and everyone knowing that "in the end, Tilden will be on the Cross, his presidential aspirations expiring slowly and, for the good of the nation, asking for renewed faith in our supreme protectors." For his part, Lincoln was the reluctant Pontius Pilate, fulfilling but not relishing his role. At one point, when Matthews vehemently proclaimed the truth of an assertion, Lincoln replied "quid est veritas," sensing that the commission's decisions would bear little relation to the truth. As the days moved forward Lincoln's countenance grew increasingly melancholy, understanding as he did the nature of the proceedings he was conducting.

As the commission's proceedings dragged on, lingering Democratic resistance to accepting the outcome emerged. Democratic leaders in Congress began planning efforts to obstruct the process of finalizing the election there, or to simply refuse to recognize Hayes as President in every way possible. One idea was that if proceedings in Congress dragged out past March 4, the presidency would be deemed vacant and the Democratic House of Representatives might elect Tilden. There was even talk of a renewed secession movement, or barring that, a confederation of Southern states that would ignore the federal government until the succeeding presidential election, including by forcibly preventing the collection of import duties and other federal taxes in their states. These plans went so far that there was serious discussion of sending a delegation to England to seek a trade agreement between the confederation and the United Kingdom.

As word of this maneuvering became an open secret among Washington politicians, Hayes instructed his supporters to talk to leading Southerners to see if an agreement could be reached. It was decided that an off-the-record, off-the-books meeting would be held to work on a compromise. Hayes's delegation included future President James Garfield, Stanley Matthews, John Sherman, and Charles Foster. Southern Democratic interests were represented by a group that included Henry Watterson, Lucius Q.C. Lamar, Benjamin Harvey Hill, and John Gordon. The parties agreed to meet at Wormley's Hotel in Washington, which they considered neutral ground because the proprietor James Wormley, a prominent Black hotelier, maintained friendly relations with all sides in every political dispute that arose in Washington. Wormley's hospitality was known world-wide, and he may have been the only Black man considered a friend by both Charles Sumner and Jefferson Davis. Frederick Douglass entertained guests there on more than one occasion, and successive delegations sent by the Japanese monarch considered Wormley's their Washington home. Sumner's affection for Wormley was so great that he presented Wormley with his personal original copy of the Thirteenth Amendment that had been signed by more than 150 of the Members of Congress who voted to send it to the states for ratification. It was at Wormley's that Abraham Lincoln first dined out after the heartbreaking death of his son Willie, and he chose the place because he knew that James Wormley would be a comforting presence in his time of distress.

The meeting took place beginning in the early afternoon of February 16, 1877, in an elegant dining room overlooking the Wormley property's beautiful grounds, including a willow-tree-lined pond that was used by guests for skating in a cold winter and fishing in the summer. The grand luncheon, served under Wormley's watchful eye, included, according to the printed menu, Oysters, Mock Turtle Soup, Chicken Patties, Sheep's Head in an Egg Sauce, Small Potatoes, Tenderloin of Beef with Wild Mushroom Gravy, Sweetbread Croquettes with Peas, Roman Punch, Duck Salad, Ice Cream and Cake, Fruit and Coffee, all accompanied by the finest wines and liquors available anywhere. In fact, the banquet was so distracting that the assembly did not get down to the business at hand until it was concluded. By then, the mood was buoyant and the alcohol nearly made fast friends of erstwhile political enemies.

After dessert, the group rose from the table and adjourned to the rectangle of couches under the hall's windows. No one noticed Wormley's framed copy of the Thirteenth Amendment hanging on a wall behind them. As the setting winter sun glinted weakly on the frigid surface of the pond, the discussion began amidst the alcoholic haze of cigar smoke, brandy or bourbon warming between the hands of some. Matthews made the opening gambit:

"I trust we are all in agreement that Mr. Hayes is President-elect and nothing we do here today can alter that reality. What we need to accomplish, then, is an understanding that will facilitate the renewal of a fully-functioning national government, free from the discord that has infected our country for far too long."

In response, Benjamin Harvey Hill, delivered what seemed to be a prepared speech of nearly fifteen minutes detailing the Democrats' grievances reaching back to the disenfranchisement of former rebels: "the indignity of submission to the will of Negro governments in rank conspiracy with carpetbaggers and scalawags who suppress the Southern white man and purloin every morsel of value they get their hands on, and the prolonged occupation of Southern territory by federal troops. Federal enforcement of the civil rights laws in our states is inconceivable and would likely be greeted either by renewed rebellion or at the least with resistance by whatever means right-thinking Southerners are able to muster. Gentlemen, despite our friendly personal relations, if these injustices are not addressed, Mr. Hayes will not find his ascent to power easy, and if he manages to arrive at the acme, the landscape below may not be an inviting sight."

Hill was the man to deliver this stern message. A unionist

Southerner who voted against secession, he had once been affiliated with the Whigs and initially opposed the Democratic Party in his home state of Georgia. His opposition to secession was born not of agreement with Northern ideals but of the realization that Civil War would end slavery. But more than an American, he was a loyal Georgian, serving in the Confederate Senate as a strong ally of Confederate President Jefferson Davis. After the War he returned to Congress, first in the House, and when this gathering took place he was on the precipice of entering the U.S. Senate. He was among the greatest orators of his time and was respected across the political spectrum for his political instincts and his honesty, but all knew that he had absolutely no sympathy for the view that Southern governments should respect the rights of Black people. And he even more strongly rejected the notion that the federal government had any business legislating or intervening in Southern affairs on these matters. He identified Chief Justice Lincoln's opinion affirming the convictions in the Cruikshank case as "the greatest heresy ever uttered by a Member of that esteemed body. Contrary to the esteemed Mr. Lincoln's pronouncements, responsibility for the protections of the rights of the citizens of each state lies with the states, not in the national governors who have no sense of local conditions and local sensibilities, and at war's end were not awarded the keys to our cities and villages."

Matthews was outraged by this presentation, replying, "The gentleman certainly does not mean to suggest that the recent amendments to our Constitution are not as much a part of that great document as the provisions in the original text. In the fourteenth and fifteenth articles, we find the words 'no State shall,' and it is certainly the province of the national authorities to ensure that the states shall not do as the text prohibits. The laws that the gentleman references were enacted in pursuance of those amendments and are effective throughout the country. Our Republican form of government does not admit of local variation on matters of the Constitution."

By the time Matthews' and Hill's argument progressed to this point, the mood in the room was as dark as the view from the windows, as the sun had set in the meanwhile. It suddenly seemed that their efforts at resolution might fail.

At this point, Ohio Senator and close Hayes ally John Sherman, ever the practical man among politicians, spoke up. "We are not a legal commission presided over by President Lincoln and his colleagues. Our job is to find a suitable route to navigate the shoals that confront all of us. As I see it, we are presented with two questions, one that admits of a single answer and one that presents possibilities for agreement. The former question is whether the Constitution and all the laws that have been passed under it, both predating the conflict and postdating it, are in full force and effect throughout the country. The answer to this must be in the affirmative lest we return to disunion and even conflict. However, the degree to which flesh and blood clothed in the uniform of the national government are the law's sole enforcers is another question altogether. It seems to me that if we can agree on these two principles—that all the laws are effective everywhere within the boundaries of the re-united United States of America and that the States should and will pledge their enforcement everywhere— we can also agree that the continued presence of federal troops in the Southern states is unnecessary and presents the potential only for interference and resentment."

Hill piped up immediately: "I can sign on to neither of Senator Sherman's two principles" but as soon as these words were uttered, Lucius Q.C. Lamar grabbed Hill by the sleeve and indicated to him that he ought to quiet down.

Lamar was one of the Southern delegation's most ardent secessionists, but he was also a shrewd political operator, and understood better than Hill what was on offer. He begged pardon and ushered his Democratic colleagues to the far corner of the room to confer.

Addressing Hill, he said, "Ben, what they propose is that we pledge loyalty to the United States, which we have already done at War's end or we would not be here, and they will leave us alone."

Although it took a bit of persuading from Lamar and the other Democrats, Hill finally agreed. "Lucius, if you are correct, then although we may have to admit defeat in the battle for the presidency, we will have won the war for our future."

Back at the couches, Matthews was berating Sherman. "This is an outrageous proposal. Would you sit back while our Black citizens, such loyal supporters and for whom we fought the bloodiest war in our history, are re-enslaved?"

James Garfield, who had remained virtually silent, until this time, supported Sherman's view. His words were prescient: "the fervor that supported national intervention into the affairs of the states has died down, and John's proposal, with which I know our leader endorses, is the only way we might achieve the unity and stability we need going forward. Further, as John knows better than any of us, the Treasury can no longer bear the expense without forcing the neglect of even more pressing needs. In my view, the law will sooner adjust to these practical constraints than our Southern brethren will adjust to the continued presence of uniformed outsiders in their midst."

When the Southerners returned to the table, little more was said. Both Hill and Matthews looked sullen yet resigned. The first to speak was Lamar. "As it appears we are in agreement on John's two principles, and we are assured that this commitment is shared by Mr. Hayes, we foresee no further disruption when the electoral votes are counted at the conclusion of the Electoral Commission's deliberations. We certainly agree to protect the legal rights of all citizens of the United States throughout the country."

Sherman replied. "I am grateful for these assurances and the spirit of national unity from which they are derived. You can be assured that one of the first actions of the new administration will be to acknowledge that there is no further need for forcible intervention into Southern affairs and the troops will be called home, where they will reengage in our nation's unified defense."

With these few words, uttered over final sips of brandy and bourbon among an overstuffed group of weary Washington insiders, the collective fate of millions of Black American citizens was placed at the mercy of White supremacists. It was perhaps the single largest slave sale in history.

26
ELECTORAL DECISION

The Electoral Commission completed its work on February 23, sending to Congress decisions in favor of Republican certificates in the three disputed states and designation of a Republican as the third Oregon elector, along with a lengthy statement by Chief Justice Lincoln, prepared with help from Senator Edmunds as well as Justices Bradley and Miller, outlining the commission's proceedings and explaining in detail the bases for its conclusions on each disputed elector.

Lincoln began by stating that he was initially surprised by Congress's decision to create the commission over which he presided. *"Insofar as previous circumstances led me to examine the process for electing our nation's chief magistrate, I had always understood that the President of the Senate was entrusted with sole discretion to open and tally the certificates provided by state governors, and that Congress's only role in the process was to bear witness to this solemn event, excepting of course the unlikely and unfortunate role of the lower chamber to select the President from among viable candidates in case no contestant received, in the tally of the Senate's presiding officer, a majority. After the weeks of hearings before this commission, in which the disputants were given every opportunity to make their cases, which were listened to attentively by a group of fifteen commissioners sworn to impartiality and fidelity to the Constitution, I have come to understand that the gravity, complexity, and dubiety of the situation begged for a solution as novel, as unanticipated and as carefully designed as this body, created as it was, by an act of Congress. Members of Congress had previously objected to the certificates chosen for tally by the President of the Senate, and we have been assigned the task of determining which of the certificates are the proper ones for including in the total."*

The Chief Justice continued by recounting the commission's proceedings in great detail, including its examination of state election laws, the facts underlying the disputes over the identity of the true holder of state gubernatorial offices and its acceptance of some evidence relating to the conduct of the state elections.

He then turned to the decision not to base the commission's determinations on the veracity of state election returns or activity within the states such as illegal casting of votes and violence and intimidation for the purpose of vote suppression. *"We recognize that both Houses of Congress and the whole country knew full well that there were in the contested cases charges of fraud, perjury and forgery, and that it was expected that those charges would be heard and a true judgment would be given thereon. However, we came to the conclusion that to inquire into all of this would have stretched the competence of this body beyond its limits, surpassed the constitutional role of the national authorities in determining the outcome of the presidential election and delayed our proceedings beyond the expiration of the current incumbent's term as President. We would have been placed in the discomforting position of deciding the country's most important political controversy possible in light of evidence that would have been by nature highly unreliable, as so much of the alleged improprieties would and could be testified to by only one side, by nature a partisan side, of the dispute. We have done our utmost to fulfill the function Congress assigned to us within the limits of the possible, guided by the signposts erected by the wise men who framed our Constitution."* He then explained that in each case, *"unfortunately, by a vote of only the barest majority of this humble commission, the ruling was in favor of the certificates offered by, in our view, the properly and legally elected governors of South Carolina, Florida and Louisiana, and, in the case of Oregon, the restoration of the original slate of electors selected by the people in their election."* The final tally, submitted to Congress, left Tilden stuck at 184 electoral votes, and put Hayes over the top with 185.

The Democrats on the commission also submitted an opinion roughly equal in length to that of the Chief Justice. It was signed by Justice Field but drafted, in large part, by Charles O'Conor and David Dudley Field, members of Tilden's legal team. It began by going all the way back to the maneuvering that left the commission with a Republican majority, which, they argued *"was clearly in defiance of Congress's intent to entrust this investigation to a group that would not be dominated by one faction or the other. Once the seat became vacant it should have remained unoccupied. No recommendation would have been better than the sham that this process became. A sober examination of the evidence surrounding*

251

the election in Florida, South Carolina, and Louisiana can lead to only one conclusion, that the voters have chosen Samuel Tilden as President, while the state governments, in their last gasp of power, chose otherwise and superimposed their selection on the people through blatant and visible fraud, evidence of which was placed before this commission which chose, for obvious reasons, to ignore it and pretend it could not be seen. This body's decision to ignore reality is, in my judgment, forbidden by every consideration of law and justice, and once revealed will shock the public sense, and when the knowledge of it reaches other lands, I will be greatly disappointed if it does not shock the wise and just throughout the civilized world. The refusal to hear and consider the most relevant evidence is a mockery, and amounts to an abdication of the responsibility assigned to us by the Congress."

The dissenting statement also alluded to the inconsistency between the majority's treatment of the disputes in the Southern states and the dispute in Oregon where no one disputed that the certificate, showing one vote for Tilden and two for Hayes, had been supplied by the state's legitimate governor. *"This Commission has disappointed public expectation in its decisions. By a vote of eight to seven, this Commission has decided on purely technical grounds that Florida, Louisiana and South Carolina voted for Hayes, and by the same vote of the same members have discarded these very same technical grounds to give the one disputed vote of Oregon to Hayes. I say this Commission has disappointed public expectation because the country expected of it that it would decide who had been elected President and Vice President by the people. They did not expect of us that we would merely confirm the judgment of corrupt and illegal returning-boards who in effect put the presidency up to the highest bidder in the public market."*

The commission's final votes, along with the statements in support and in opposition to the outcome, were sent to Congress on February 23. The next step according to the Electoral Commission Act was for Congress to reconvene its concurrent session and then, if objections to the certificates were renewed, for each House to separately vote on the objections. Even though Congress faced an Inauguration Day deadline (March 4 at the time, but March 5 in 1877 because March 4 fell on Sunday) for completing this process, it did not reconvene until March 1. This was risky because the Constitution is silent on what happens if no new President has been selected by Inauguration Day. News of the informal agreement reached at the Wormley's dinner had spread throughout Congress, but renegade Democrats sensed an opportunity, theorizing that if they renewed their objections, they might be able to delay the final determination until after March 4, at which point, their theory went, the presidency would either be decided by the House of Representatives as provided for in the Twelfth Amendment or, if the process of determining objections to certificates would continue, as of March 5 it would be in the new Congress which would be under complete Democratic control for the first since the presidency of James Buchanan. The electorate, it seemed, at least the White electorate, had tired of Republican policies and corruption and was ready to re-embrace White supremacy as a guiding principle in American society.

On March 1, when the proceedings before Congress began, Senate president pro tempore Ferry restarted the process of reading and tallying the state electoral vote certificates. When he reached Florida, he announced that, consistent with the decision of the Electoral Commission, Florida's four electoral votes are awarded to Rutherford B. Hayes. Immediately, James Throckmorton, former Texas governor and now a lame-duck Member of the House, and Florida Senator Charles Jones, both rose to object on the ground that, in Throckmorton's words, "This certificate, and those from Louisiana and South Carolina, as well as the allocation of all three of Oregon's electors to Hayes, represent, by overwhelming evidence, fabricated and fraudulent vote returns. I am joined by my colleague Mr. Jones in urging the Congress to reject the conclusions of the commission, which contrary to our expectations, turned out to be a partisan charade, and award Florida's four electoral votes to Samuel Tilden." In response, Ferry ruled that objections to the certificates that had been ruled on by the Electoral Commission were out of order under the provisions of the Electoral Commission Act, in which Congress had committed to abide by the commission's decisions. Therefore, he determined, there would be no separation of the Houses to debate and vote on the objections.

Most Members of Congress, even Democrats, were relieved that

Ferry had found a way to short-circuit the potentially lengthy and pointless process of debating and voting on objections. Things went along smoothly until Ferry reached Vermont. As soon as he announced that Vermont's five electoral votes were awarded to Hayes, by a certificate that had not been previously a subject of dispute, New York Congressman (and future Mayor of New York City) Abram Hewitt, the chairman of the Democratic National Committee, joined by Florida's Senator Jones, challenged the votes, although on just what grounds he did not say. Ferry had no choice but to direct that Senators reconvene in their chamber while the House debated the matter. In the Senate, only Jones, the Senator from Florida, insisted on being heard and his brief remarks focused on the fraud and intimidation that, in his view, rendered the Florida certificate of votes for Hayes "less trustworthy than the word of an imbecile." He never even mentioned Vermont. After a bit more grumbling, the objection was overruled by an overwhelming voice vote.

In the House, after seemingly endless debate on procedural motions that would have stopped Hewitt's effort in its tracks, Hewitt and Throckmorton engaged in a filibuster during which they read from affidavits and newspaper accounts detailing fraud, violence and intimidation in Florida, Louisiana, and South Carolina. They also read the Democrats' dissenting statement from the Electoral Commission report. As in the Senate, there was no mention of Vermont. After about six hours, Hewitt and Throckmorton abandoned their filibuster and allowed a vote in which the objection was overruled by an overwhelming voice vote. They decided to save their energy for another objection which they hoped would carry them past the inauguration deadline.

When the concurrent session reconvened at about midnight the morning of March 2, it was expected that the remainder of the tally, namely the announcement of the votes of three remaining states, would go smoothly and without further delay. And everything went according to plan when Virginia and West Virginia's votes for Tilden were announced, but when Ferry announced that Hayes had secured Wisconsin's ten electoral votes, Hewitt, joined again by Jones, rose again and made the same vague challenge to the certificate, forcing yet another vote in each chamber. This time, Hewitt considered a three-day filibuster, but when Throckmorton took the reins of the filibuster at about 3 am and began re-reading the packet of affidavits from Louisiana, House Speaker Randall cornered Hewitt and said, "It is time for us to confirm this election. On behalf of leadership, I offer you the carrot and the stick. Relent now and you shall have our support in your efforts to reenter this House or when you strive for other elective office. Continue for much longer and the barriers to your return will become insurmountable." Hewitt got the message and at about 4:15, pleading fatigue and hunger, he halted his efforts and allowed the House to take its vote to reject his objection. It was then, and only then, in the early morning hours of March 2, 1876, that Rutherford B. Hayes was declared the winner of the election of 1876 and would be inaugurated three days later as the eighteenth President of the United States.

In all of these proceedings and maneuverings, the Wormley's agreement remained unmentioned, but it was certainly on the minds of Members of Congress from the South, who looked with hope to Inauguration Day as the moment that their states would finally and absolutely throw off the yoke of "carpet-bag misrule," as they called it, and become, once again, masters of their own destinies—and the destinies of their fellow citizens unlucky enough to be members of the subjugated race.

27
INAUGURATION AND WITHDRAWAL

Outwardly, the Inauguration of Rutherford B. Hayes appeared typical for these grand quadrennial events. On the cold overcast morning of March 5, outgoing President Grant escorted the President-elect to the ceremony, where, after being sworn in by Chief Justice Lincoln, Hayes delivered a speech focused largely on familiar Republican principles, while recognizing that that work of rebuilding the economies and governmental structures of the South was far from complete. These "evils which afflict the Southern States can only be removed or remedied by the united and harmonious efforts of both races, actuated by motives of mutual sympathy and regard," and he promised "to protect the rights of all by every constitutional means at the disposal of my Administration." He proclaimed that "universal suffrage should rest upon universal education, [as] at the basis for all prosperity . . . lies the improvement of the intellectual and moral condition of the people. To this end, liberal provision should be made for the support of free schools." He also proposed a return to a currency backed by specie as a means to further economic progress. Recognizing the corruption that had plagued his predecessor's administration, he urged a "radical and complete" reform of the civil service where "the officer should be secure in his tenure as long as his personal character remained untarnished and the performance of his duties satisfactory. [A]ppointments to office [should not] be made nor expected merely as rewards for partisan services, nor merely on the nomination of members of Congress, as being entitled in any respect to control of such appointments."

In light of the controversy surrounding his election, President Hayes also found it necessary to defend the Electoral Commission, recognizing that in light of human nature the defeated were unlikely to be satisfied with either the process or the outcome: "That tribunal—its members, all of them, men of long-established reputation for integrity and intelligence, its deliberations enlightened by the research and the arguments of able counsel—was entitled to the fullest confidence of the American people. . . . For the present, opinion will widely vary as to the wisdom of the several conclusions announced by that tribunal. The fact that two great political parties have in this way settled a dispute in regard to which good men differ as to the facts and the law . . . is an occasion for general rejoicing." He stressed the importance of an end to the controversy to allow the nation to move forward: "Upon one point there is entire unanimity in public sentiment—that conflicting claims to the Presidency must be amicably and peaceably adjusted, and that when so adjusted the general acquiescence of the nation ought surely to follow."

That Hayes's claim to unanimity in this sentiment was not realistic was perhaps best exemplified by the actions of an otherwise serious newspaper, the New York Sun, which for four years consistently stamped the word "FRAUD" across the forehead of its frequent drawings of the President.

Behind the scenes, the inauguration was anything but ordinary. There were substantiated fears that Tilden supporters might disrupt the ceremony or, even worse, make an attempt on Hayes's life. Therefore, on March 5, security was incredibly tight and many people who viewed themselves as among Hayes's strongest supporters were unable to get close to the Capitol portico where the ceremony was held. Even more extraordinary was what happened on March 3 at a farewell/celebratory dinner at the White House hosted by President Grant, with numerous Members of Congress and Supreme Court Justices in attendance, including Chief Justice Lincoln. Lincoln, Hayes, and Grant were at the head table with their wives, and as the crowd took their seats, President Grant rose and said, "Ladies and gentlemen, we have a special event for you this evening. As you know, Mr. Hayes prefers not to take the oath of office on the Sabbath, and in view of the importance of an uninterrupted government, we thought we would provide a preview of Monday's events." Although continuity might have been an issue—in prior years when March 4 was a Sunday, the presidency may technically have been vacant for 24 hours—Grant did not mention the rumor that Tilden might take the oath of office on March 4 and claim to be the legitimate President or that disruptions by Tilden's partisans might derail the public event. (Tilden did not stage his own inauguration, but throughout 1877, he made speeches decrying the election as a fraud and characterizing Hayes as an illegitimate President. This served to limit Hayes's ability to get Democrats in Congress to cooperate with his initiatives, blunting the ability to advance even elements of his agenda on which there was otherwise general agreement.) Chief Justice Lincoln and Hayes then rose, an attendant handed Lincoln a White House bible, and Hayes took the oath of office. Hayes did not actually become President at that moment—this would not occur until the next day when Grant's term officially expired, but the Constitution does not specify the timing of the presidential oath, only that it be taken "before [the President] enter on the execution of his Office." Hayes made a few remarks thanking President and Mrs. Grant for their hospitality and promising "a fuller oration on Monday." Champagne flowed among those in attendance, but Hayes, a known teetotaler, did not partake.

Immediately after Hayes's public inauguration, President Grant and his family began traveling, first within the United States, mainly visiting friends, and then across the world. Grant was greeted as a hero wherever he went, including such far flung places as Jerusalem, Japan, China, and India. After two years they returned home, and President Grant flirted with the idea of running again for President, as Hayes had promised to serve only a single term. But financial issues also arose as his travels took most of his savings and no significant income was coming in. Ultimately, Grant joined the investment firm founded by his son, which, unknown to Grant, turned out to be a virtual Ponzi scheme before the birth of Charles Ponzi. The firm's failure wiped out what little of Grant's savings and other assets remained. It seems that corruption followed the trusting and loyal Grant wherever he went, whether in public service or private enterprise. Here is where Grant's friendship with Mark Twain paid off.

After successfully publishing several magazine articles about his military exploits, Grant had agreed with a publisher to write his memoirs for a paltry 10% royalty. When Grant told Twain about the agreement, Twain countered with an offer of an unheard of 75% royalty, which Grant accepted. Suffering from throat cancer, Grant wrote feverishly until just days before his death, fearing that without the income, his wife Julia would suffer financial embarrassment. Twain's creative and extensive marketing scheme involving agents personally soliciting orders across the country from military veterans and others resulted in 350,000 subscriptions and nearly half a million dollars in royalties, which kept Grant's widow Julia economically secure for the rest of her life.

After the dust kicked up by the election controversy settled, Congress set out to cure the defects in the Twelfth Amendment, not via a new constitutional amendment but rather by statute. This effort took ten years, and what emerged from Congress, not surprisingly, was a procedure under which Congress itself would resolve future controversies over whether any particular electoral vote certificates would be counted. The Electoral Count Act of 1887 provides that Congress meets in a joint session on January 6 following the November election to witness the opening and tally of the electoral vote certificates by the President of the Senate. If, during this process, a member of each House of Congress objects in writing to a certificate, the House and Senate debate and vote separately on each objection, with a majority in each chamber required to reject any challenged certificate. Just as the Electoral Commission refused to look behind the certificates into allegations of fraud, violence, and intimidation, the Act provides that "no electoral vote or votes from any State which shall have been regularly given by electors whose appointment has been lawfully certified from which but one return has been received shall be rejected." In other words, the only basis for refusing to accept a certificate is if the certificate was not provided by the lawful state electors selected pursuant to the state procedure for appointing them. In cases in which the President of the Senate receives more than one certificate purporting to represent a state's electoral votes, the Act leaves the decision to the same process in each House of Congress, but if the two Houses do not agree, then the President of the Senate is required to accept "the votes of the electors whose appointment shall have been certified by the executive of the State, under the seal thereof." The Act provides no guidance on how the determination is made if more than one person claims to be the "executive of the State." There are strong arguments that the Act is unconstitutional insofar as it assigns any role in the presidential election to Congress other than electing the President and Vice President when a majority is lacking. Fortunately, until now no controversy over electoral votes comparable to what arose in 1876 has happened again, so that Act has not been tested. Typically, the process of counting the electoral votes is entirely ceremonial and occupies less than an hour of Congress's time.

Not only had Hayes promised to be a one-term President, he began behaving like one almost immediately, taking actions that virtually guaranteed he would quickly lose the support of the Republican political establishment. For starters, he selected a cabinet composed largely of independent political figures. Two of his choices, William Evarts as Secretary of State and Carl Schurz as Secretary of the Interior, were viewed as a thumb in the eye to important Republicans who had helped Hayes get elected, such as Roscoe Conkling and John Logan. He also quickly launched his attack on the patronage system. A reluctant Congress refused to go along, which is not surprising since members derived a great deal of political support by handing out plum jobs. But Hayes did whatever he could unilaterally, forbidding federal officials from engaging in political activity and from exacting the customary monetary assessments in exchange for federal appointments. When New York officials, including Postmaster Chester Arthur, a staunch Conkling ally and future President of the United States, refused to go along and continued to use their positions to support Republican candidates, Hayes fired them, further alienating the powerful Conkling and numerous other Republicans.

In accord with the Wormley's agreement, Hayes also began to withdraw federal troops from deployments that propped up unpopular (with Whites) Southern governments, further alienating large segments of Republican officials and voters. Even though this had been agreed to at the Wormley's dinner, many Republicans, especially those who leaned Radical, opposed it, correctly viewing it as spelling disaster for the Southern wing of the Republican Party. In Louisiana and South Carolina, Republican governors had resisted being overthrown only due to federal military occupation of the state capitol buildings. The situation in Louisiana was especially precarious because the Republican governor Stephen Packard was confined to the statehouse and controlled only the immediately accessible executive organs of government while his Democratic opponent Francis Nicholls was in full control of appointments to the Supreme Court and all components of the executive branch that were outside of the statehouse. While President Grant had been unwilling to order federal troops to take offensive action against Democratic resistance, Hayes was willing to go one step further and remove the last impediments to a complete Democratic takeover of the South. Hayes's only line in the sand was that he would not order the troops home, at least not right away, but rather have them return to barracks, where they would remain as a symbol of legitimate federal authority in the former Confederacy.

In an action that broke the hearts of South Carolina's Black population, on April 10, only a few days more than a month into his presidency, Hayes ordered the withdrawal of federal troops from the South Carolina statehouse. This left the elected Republican governor Chamberlain with no choice but to abandon his office to Democrat Wade Hampton, who took over in perhaps the first federally-sanctioned statehouse coup in the history of the United States. Hampton's promise to respect the rights of Black Americans was as empty as had ever been made by an American politician. For Black Americans in South Carolina, their past became their future.

In Louisiana, with a much more developed and populous non-White political class, resistance to a Democratic takeover was robust, especially because Republican Packard had clearly won the election, garnering substantially more votes in the state than Hayes himself. Democrats had prevailed in the legislative election, but Republicans, knowing that the Democrats would recognize the Democratic candidate as governor, refused to attend legislative sessions, depriving the Assembly of the quorum necessary to do business. Hayes appointed a group of six commissioners to help in the agreed-upon transition to Democratic rule in Louisiana, and even though the commission was majority Republican, with false promises that the governorship would not be on the agenda, the commission tricked enough Republican state legislators to attend a legislative session that it achieved a quorum and officially recognized Democrat Nicholls as governor, the second, and so far last, federally sanctioned statehouse coup in American history.

In 1879, Louisiana adopted a new constitution that repealed the previous constitution's anti-discrimination provisions and imposed a poll tax that was employed largely to prevent poor Black Americans from voting. On paper, it promised compliance with the Civil War era constitutional amendments, but those promises were never fulfilled. Unchecked violence from White supremacist organizations filled the void left by nonexistent state enforcement of equal rights. As in South Carolina, and throughout the South, the legal rights of Black Americans, and their social status, steadily eroded until the situation was virtually indistinguishable from what had prevailed before the abolition of slavery. Resistance in Louisiana remained, exemplified by the activities of the Citizens' Committee that was formed almost two decades later to contest the legal imposition of segregation. But for the most part, people of color quickly came to the realization that their situation was hopeless and resistance was futile.

Hayes made a pair of appointments that gave people of color some comfort. With the end of federal protection for Black people in the South, the winding down of the activities conducted or sponsored by the Freedmen's Bureau left Frederick Douglass out of a job and in need of income due to failed investments. Hayes nominated Douglass to be Marshal of the District of Columbia, a position that included formally introducing foreign dignitaries to the President at official White House events. The nomination caused an outcry among members of the bar of the District of Columbia who did not want a man of color in such a prominent public position in their segregated city. Through back channels, Senators were reassured that Douglass would not assume that role in public, and with that, Douglass became the first Black man confirmed by the Senate to a position in the federal government. Although stung by the snub of not assuming the ceremonial role at White House events, Douglass did make private introductions of visitors to the President and reported that "I was ever a welcome visitor at the Executive Mansion on state occasions and all others, while Rutherford B. Hayes was President of the United States and never had reason to feel myself slighted by himself or his amiable wife."

The second was Hayes's decision to nominate John Marshall Harlan to the Supreme Court. Harlan provided at least a dissenting voice from the Court's own eventual turn away from protecting the rights of Black Americans. Harlan was nominated after the Senate rejected Hayes's first choice, Stanley Matthews, who was turned down because of his role in prosecuting people who had provided aid to fugitive slaves, an unforgiveable sin in the eyes of many. Hayes wanted Harlan as Attorney General, the role in which he was serving in his native Kentucky, but Senator Oliver Morton objected, concerned that as a Southerner, Harlan would be yet another nail in the coffin of Reconstruction. Although similar grumbling arose over Harlan's nomination to the high Court, he received a unanimous confirmation vote and began his service on the Court in early 1878.

28
THE BIRTH OF JIM CROW

The consequences of the Wormley's agreement slowly but steadily transformed the situation for Black Americans across the South. It's not that White supremacist violence and intimidation were not already having profound effects on Southern life for Black Americans. In the early 1870s, White supremacists were elected to state governorships and legislatures across the South. Events are perhaps best illustrated by the 1874 proclamation of the White supremacist governor of Virginia: "Any organized attempt on the part of the weaker and relatively diminishing race to dominate the domestic governments, is the wildest chimera of political insanity. Let each race settle down in final resignation to the lot to which the logic of events has inexorably consigned it." The Grant administration had repeatedly declined to authorize federal military intervention to protect the political rights and personal security of Black Americans and their Republican allies, save the two exceptions of Louisiana and South Carolina, where federal troops protected Republican governments until President Hayes withdrew them.

The techniques employed in post-Reconstruction society were familiar, as many of them had been used in the previous decade when White supremacists could get away with it. Vagrancy laws and harsh penalties for minor infractions continued to be used to force impoverished Black Americans into labor for little or no compensation. Draconian labor contracts and norms that prevented Black Americans from working elsewhere without permission from their former owners or employers kept them in virtual servitude to employers or owners of the land they worked as sharecroppers. And lynching, a tool long used in the United States by vigilantes to exact punishment for crimes, became racialized, with a significant portion of lynchings directed at people of color for real or imagined transgressions of racial norms or for suspicion of crimes that, in the United States, took on a racial character. Black men suspected of raping a White woman, or of even directing attention in a White woman's direction, were liable to be lynched, as were Black men who violated a minor social norm, such as failing to defer sufficiently to Whites in a social or business setting. Even innocent Black men might be beaten or lynched simply for being in a place where something triggered White animosity. Poll taxes and political violence and intimidation, usually with the official sanction of state and local governments, kept most Black Americans and many Republicans from voting, making it impossible for them to elect a government that would be willing to come to their aid. In cities with large Black populations where political violence was problematic, gerrymandering and other devices ensured White control.

The poor situation of Black labor was exacerbated by the federal government's harsh reaction to the nascent labor movement that arose in the post-Reconstruction period. The first major challenge involved an 1877 strike at the nation's railroads, which, pleading economic difficulty, had instituted wage cuts across the country, as had mining concerns earlier in the year. A general strike ensued and, when violence broke out in several cities, President Hayes did not hesitate to call out the troops against workers and threaten strikers and their allies with legal reprisals. Federal intervention on their behalf was encouraging to employers, as was the lack of a similar response to racial injustice was discouraging to its Black victims. With federal and state government backing, laborers, Black and White, were at the mercy of their employers, and with the economy continuing to suffer the aftereffects of the War and numerous financial disruptions that followed, there was a ready supply of replacements for workers who became dissatisfied with their meager wages and poor working conditions.

In cities and towns across the South, official and unofficial residential segregation hardened, leaving Black Americans to reside in areas with inferior infrastructure and little if any government services. Their de facto exclusion from voting left them powerless to do anything about government neglect and mistreatment, and widespread poverty, unavoidable for the first free generation, hampered private improvement efforts. Although there were numerous examples of successful Black-owned businesses in the late nineteenth century, many attempts by Black Americans to establish businesses that would compete with White-owned businesses, even when designed to serve the Black population, were rebuffed by violence, harassment, and the inability to obtain financing. While the situation for Black businesses improved somewhat during the 1870s and 1880s in the Upper South, in the Lower South, the number of Black American business owners declined precipitously. Although the number of Black-owned businesses, even in the Upper South, remained small, a number of success stories, including hoteliers James Wormley (Washington, D.C.) and Henry Harding (Nashville), and real estate baron James Thomas (St. Louis), were a beacon of hope to aspiring Black entrepreneurs.

Another impediment to progress for impoverished Black Americans in the post-Reconstruction period was the insufficiency of educational opportunities open to Black children, which became even more pronounced after Democrats took control of state governments. Black Americans hungered to educate their children, but Democratic control brought a wave of tax and spending cuts and severe reductions to funding for public education for Black Americans.

Only private funding from Northern donors and abolitionist missionary organizations helped keep the vestiges of the network of Freedmen's Bureau schools alive. For example, in the late 1860s, in Charleston, South Carolina, funds from the estate of the Reverend Charles Avery of Allegheny, Pennsylvania were used by Francis Cardozo, the mixed-race son of a wealthy Jewish businessman and a free woman of color (and distant cousin of future Supreme Court Justice Benjamin Cardozo) to establish the Avery Normal Institute, a teacher's college for Black Americans. Reverend Avery, who died in 1858, was an early Methodist minister and a pre-War abolitionist whose will established a fund to be used "for the education and elevation of the colored people of the United States and Canada." Before establishing Avery Normal, Cardozo had left his position as a minister in New Haven, Connecticut, to return to his native Charleston to become superintendent of an American Missionary Association (AMA) school serving Black children, and it was the AMA that secured the funds from Reverend Avery's estate. Teachers trained at Avery taught at primary and secondary schools across South Carolina, often to poor children in the most miserable school buildings imaginable.

After founding Avery Normal, Cardozo entered South Carolina politics as a Republican and, during Reconstruction, was elected secretary of state and then state treasurer. Like his counterpart in Louisiana, the mixed-race state treasurer Antoine Dubuclet, he was constantly harassed by Democrats for alleged corruption, but he staved off impeachment in 1874, and was reelected treasurer that year and again in 1876, even after Democrats had taken most other statewide offices and control of the state legislature. However, his career in state politics came to an end when, in 1877, he was prosecuted by Democrats for fraud in the election that brought Hayes to power. He served six months in prison before being pardoned in 1879 by the Democratic governor. He was then appointed by U.S. Treasury Secretary John Sherman to a position in the Hayes administration where he worked on education in the District of Columbia which, at that time, was administered directly by the federal government.

There were numerous institutions of higher education open to Black Americans in the post-Reconstruction period, including Fisk College in Nashville, Howard University in Washington, and Clark College in Atlanta, as well as the land grant colleges that catered to Black Americans in Southern states where authorities had insisted on establishing two in order to maintain segregation. But the lack of adequate primary and secondary education prevented many Black young people from taking advantage of these opportunities.

The only national governmental institution that remained committed to racial justice and equality through most the 1870s was the Supreme Court. Under the leadership of Chief Justice Lincoln, the Court had upheld Reconstruction-era civil rights laws and spoken in expansive language about the federal government's role in preserving the rights contained in the recent constitutional amendments. With the Enforcement Acts and the Civil Rights Act in force, it was inevitable that cases alleging violations would continue to reach the Court, and there was great curiosity over whether the Court would stick to its guns in the face of the end of Reconstruction. Not many Black Americans were willing to sue

Chief Justice Abraham Lincoln

given threats of violence and economic reprisal, but enough cases were brought that something was bound to satisfy the curious. But near the end of the decade, the first cracks in the Court's resolve emerged.

29
SEGREGATION TESTED

The first case raising issues of race to reach the Court during the Hayes presidency was an oddity, Hall v. Decuir, which arose out of segregation on a riverboat that ran passenger service between New Orleans and Vicksburg, Mississippi. Reconstruction-era Louisiana law prohibited racial discrimination on all forms of commercial transportation, so when Josephine Decuir, the sister of Louisiana treasurer Dubuclet, was not provided with a berth in the Ladies' Cabin due to her status as a mixed-race woman of color, she sued and prevailed in the state courts of Louisiana. The boat's owner, with financial support from associates and competitors, brought the case to the U.S. Supreme Court alleging that application of Louisiana's anti-discrimination law on the Mississippi River interfered with Congress's exclusive authority over interstate commerce.

Although the incident occurred in 1872 and case had been filed at the Supreme Court by 1874, for procedural reasons the Court did not reach it until October, 26, 1877, when, much to Chief Justice Lincoln's surprise, a majority agreed with the defendant's Commerce Clause argument and voted 5-3 to reverse the Louisiana court's decision, with Lincoln dissenting along with Justices Hunt and Strong. (Justice Davis's seat was still vacant at the time with nominee John Marshall Harlan awaiting confirmation.) At the October 26 conference, Lincoln expressed his astonishment that five of his colleagues had voted to reverse the judgment, but the only response he received to his pleas was an insistence that the case had nothing to do with racial matters and everything to do with keeping the channels of interstate commerce open, subject only to federal regulation. They also reminded him that with the Civil Rights Act of 1875 in effect, federal law would fill any gap left by this decision, at least with regard to cases arising now.

Justice Clifford, the senior justice in the majority, assigned the opinion in Hall v. Decuir to himself, and wrote a lengthy disquisition, made public on January 14, 1878, on the importance of uniform federal regulation on interstate waterways like the

Mississippi. However, the single-minded Clifford, apparently untroubled by the prospect of placing a legal stamp of approval on the racial segregation which was the prevailing custom on Southern riverboats and railroads, went further: *"If Louisiana may pass a law forbidding such steamer from having two cabins and two tables—one for white and the other for colored persons—it must be admitted that Mississippi may pass a law requiring all passenger steamers entering her ports to have separate cabins and tables, and make it penal for white and colored persons to be accommodated in the same cabin or to be furnished with meals at the same table. Should state legislation in that regard conflict, then the steamer must cease to navigate between ports of the states having such conflicting legislation, or must be exposed to penalties at every trip."* This opinion was heartbreaking to those who pursued racial justice, for in it they saw not only the rejection of Louisiana's law but acceptance of racial segregation as a legitimate object of state legislation. Otherwise, how could Mississippi's hypothetical law interfere with Louisiana's?

Chief Justice Lincoln wrote a dissenting opinion, ostensibly for him and his colleagues, Justices Hunt and Strong who, in October, had voted along with him to affirm. Lincoln's opinion began, *"This Court has only recently discovered that the Constitution's Commerce Clause itself, without congressional action, restrains the powers of the several States, and then only when State law was aimed directly at or discriminated against interstate commerce. I agreed with those decisions, but they were direct regulations of interstate commerce, while here we deal with a general prohibition of private discrimination not directed in any special way at interstate commerce, a matter that is at the heart of the police power of the States."* He was referring to the two previous instances in which the Court had struck down state laws for interfering with interstate commerce, one in 1870 and the other in 1875.

This legal theory was controversial because the Constitution's Commerce Clause is a grant of power to Congress, not, like some provisions, a limitation on the power of states, and there is no textual or historical hint of exclusivity underlying the clause. The prior cases involved a state tax directed at goods shipped through a state (1870) and a state law requiring peddlers of out-of-state goods to procure an expensive license when no such license was required to sell goods made inside the state (1875). Continuing on the commerce theme, Lincoln wrote *"I had not thought it necessary to remind my colleagues that only recently we upheld Iowa's requirement that railroads, even those traveling interstate, post annually their schedules of shipping rates in every station on their lines and adhere to those rates for the coming year."*

Lincoln then came to the heart of the matter as he saw it: *"What is most astonishing is that the Court seems unconcerned with the discrimination suffered by the defendant-in-error in this case and, in this I fervently hope I am mistaken, my colleagues appear willing to endorse the notion that a State of our union may, without legal repercussion, require racial segregation. I had thought this badge of slavery and supposed inferiority as a citizen, was abolished by the Thirteenth and Fourteenth amendatory articles to the Constitution. As the learned trial judge in the State court in this case so eloquently stated, 'I cannot conclude without expressing the fond and sincere hope, that the time may speedily come when . . . all distinctions germinating in prejudice, and unsupported by law, may be finally forgotten, and when the essential unity of American citizenship shall stand universally confessed and sincerely acquiesced in by the national family.' I had thought until now that this was the universal hope of all loyal Americans."*

When Lincoln circulated a draft of this opinion, he included a personal note to each member of the majority imploring them to reconsider their vote in light of his opinion, but none did. He did have some limited success—Justices Miller and Swayne, two of Lincoln's colleagues who shared his concern over racial justice, appended a statement to the majority opinion stating that *"we understand the Court's opinion to go no further than to determine that allowing each State to impose rules governing the treatment of passengers on interstate conveyances would lead to intolerable disuniformity. It is with that understanding that we join in reversing the decision of the Louisiana court."* And in late December, he sent a copy of the record and the draft opinions to the Court's newest member, John Marshall Harlan, along with a letter congratulating him on his November 29 confirmation and inquiring when the Court should expect him to arrive in Washington. Lincoln was gratified to receive a reply indicating Harlan's agreement with his position in the case. Thus, when Lincoln's opinion was announced on January 14 along with that of the majority, it concluded by stating *"I am authorized to note that Justices Hunt, Strong and Harlan are in accord with this opinion."*

Lincoln also included in his opinion a reference to the 1875 Civil Rights Act, and suggested that the Court's surprising decision might not cause much of a concern. This reality muted what otherwise might have been a furiously negative reaction from people of color and Republican Members of Congress. But on the ground, the reality was different. The custom of segregation, which had long prevailed on passenger boats and on the rails, became even more firmly entrenched than before. By and large, Black Americans were unwilling to risk the consequences of suing or even objecting, so most people acquiesced, with a few exceptions, most notably among Louisiana's gens de couleur, who could not accustom themselves to being treated as if they were Black. Not that they necessarily sued, as had the plaintiff in the Decuir case, but they tested the boundaries of the custom by insisting on riding in the first-class areas of boats and rail cars and asking to be served in restaurants and taverns that generally excluded non-Whites. By and large, these efforts were unsuccessful.

As much as the limits of propriety would allow, Lincoln kept up contact and friendships with many of his former political colleagues. Frederick Douglass visited him often as did journalist Noah Brooks, who even convinced the Chief Justice to accompany him to an occasional game of baseball. When Lincoln had traveled to Massachusetts in 1874 to attend the funeral of Charles Sumner, he had a chance to chat informally with numerous current and former Senators from across the political spectrum. He also paid a call on Oliver Wendell Holmes, Jr. who had taken up the practice of law in Boston while still traveling, now infrequently to Washington to advise Lincoln on some of his more perplexing cases. Lincoln and Holmes maintained a steady correspondence about Lincoln's cases until Holmes became a Justice of the Massachusetts Supreme Judicial Court late in 1882, but their in-person meetings had been rare for some time. Holmes did not assist Lincoln with his dissenting opinion in the Decuir case, but in a letter after it was released, Holmes wrote, "Although I found your opinion in the Hall case convincing, even here in Boston and Cambridge, the public tide seems to be turning against strenuous efforts to enforce civil rights laws in favor of unity and stability."

Radical Republicans, now constituting a small minority in Congress, were feeling similar winds of change and confided to Lincoln their concern that the Court might, as it often did, follow the trend. In one of his frequent conversations with his former secretary John G. Nicolay, who was now serving as Supreme Court Marshal, Lincoln observed, "It seems as soon as I boarded the train, everyone else started to disembark." Nicolay later remarked that Lincoln's expression and tone of voice reminded him of some of Lincoln's consternation during the Civil War. And Nicolay also noticed that the spirit of collegiality at what had become known as Lincoln's luncheons at the Court now seemed a bit frayed, as if some of the Justices sensed that their movement away from protecting the rights of Black Americans might be felt more personally than disagreements over more mundane matters.

Fissures created by disparate views on racial justice also affected the nation's religious denominations. Many churches had previously split in two over the issue of slavery, and after the end of that "peculiar institution," segregation and White supremacy were preached from the pulpit along with the Lord's Gospel in Southern churches, and segregation was the practice, if not the rule, in many Northern churches as well. The maintenance of segregation in Southern Methodist Churches after the Civil War gave the lie to that denomination's claim that its anti-abolitionist stance was founded upon the Biblical notion of religion staying out of civil affairs, that they must "render unto Caesar what is Caesar's." And the Southern Presbyterian church was also segregated, as its leaders found support in the Bible for their doctrine of strict and complete separation of the races. Segregationists throughout the South could rest assured that the exclusion of Black Americans from their social structure would not, when the time came, affect their entry into heaven. Although without doctrinal basis, many Catholic churches were also segregated, with Black Americans unwelcome at predominantly White parish masses.

30
LINCOLN'S DECLINE

The next several years were personally and professionally difficult, and sometimes disastrous for Chief Justice Lincoln. On the personal front, the youngest of his sons, Thomas "Tad" Lincoln, died suddenly and unexpectedly of heart failure while on a visit to Illinois with his mother Mary. Tad had been attending law school at the Columbian University in Washington after spending three years in the U.S. Army, stationed in Northern Virginia. Lincoln's grief was surpassed only by that of his wife, who never recovered from the shock of finding Tad dead in bed at Robert Todd Lincoln's lakefront home in Chicago, thinking he was sleeping peacefully until she was unable to wake him. Mary long suffered from periodic depressive episodes, sometimes accompanied by paranoia in which she believed that her son Robert or unknown thieves were plotting to steal her assets, and this latest family tragedy dropped her into a melancholy that lasted nearly a year. Her good spirits at Grant's second inaugural ball became a distant memory. She could not bring herself to attend Tad's funeral, held at the home in which he had died. The main eulogy was given by Lincoln's trusted secretary John Hay, who said, "There was never a son in the history of this Earth who admired his father more than Little Tad looked up to our President Lincoln, and never a son who was more loved in return." Hay also fondly recalled Tad, as a precocious twelve year old, holding court outside the Confederate White House in April, 1865, dispensing words of reassurance— "my father will take care that the South is rebuilt in no time, no time at all"—and offering to introduce bemused onlookers to his father "for a small payment of a silver dollar, Confederate notes not accepted."

After the funeral, Mary remained in a sanitarium in Bellevue, Illinois, to recover from the shock, while Chief Justice Lincoln returned to Washington to resume his duties at the Court. The couple would not live together again. As soon as she was well enough, she left for an extended trip to Europe, including nearly two years in Pau, France, keeping largely to herself and living off of a stipend sent through diplomatic channels by her husband.

Mary Lincoln's physical health began to decline, and when she returned to the United States in April, 1881, she went directly from New York to Springfield to live with her sister Elizabeth, without even stopping in Washington to see her husband or their son Robert, who was serving as Secretary of War under President James Garfield. That summer, for the first time as Chief Justice, her husband returned to their Springfield home both to be close to his wife and to escape what he experienced as an increasingly unpleasant legal and political environment in Washington. He arrived just before the July 4 holiday, and although he would have preferred to stay out of the spotlight, he felt compelled to accept the entreaties of Republican Illinois Governor Shelby Collum, a fellow Kentucky native, to lead Springfield's annual Independence Day parade and attend the celebration.

Mary was not well enough to accompany him to the festivities, but the next day she appreciated his minute-by-minute account, including the pie baking contest he was asked to judge. The winner he described as "a very fine Strawberry Rhubarb brought in by Molly Herndon, William's niece." (William Herndon was Abraham Lincoln's law partner in Springfield.) As he reported, "the problem was that it took me three or four tastes of several of the finalists' offerings to make a decision, and I don't think I'll be able to eat another bite for a week. And even the winners seemed a bit distressed at how little I left over, but I paid them no mind, although I felt so good after all of that pie eating that I suspect the bakers might have added some brandy or other liquor to augment the fruit flavors. Anyway, no one translated the annoyed looks on their faces to spoken words, so I got out of there without too much embarrassment." Mary seemed amused, but she remained very quiet and somber, asking her husband only to join her in looking once again at a well-known photo of her in mourning clothes that was taken shortly after Willy's death and appeared to show the image of Willy standing beside her. Only much later was the photographer's fraud discovered.

A bit more than a week later, Mary's health gave out and she died with her husband and sister at her bedside. The immediate cause was a stroke, but it had been some time since Mary had lived anything approaching a normal life, suffering from various physical ailments as well as bouts of anxiety, depression, and melancholy over the loss of her beloved sons. Robert left Washington for Springfield as soon as he got the news by telegraph of Mary's stroke, but by the time he arrived, his mother was gone, and he was left to console his father and help prepare for another family funeral. Lincoln insisted on speaking at the service, which was held at the local Presbyterian Church, and he eulogized her as a loyal, dedicated, and strong-willed companion "who I hope will be remembered for the support she gave to her husband through the most difficult time in our nation's history and for her devotion to family and country, which never wavered against great challenges."

After two weeks of mourning, Lincoln took to receiving visitors on the front porch of his Springfield home, seated as always in the rocking chair from Ford's theater. Even with Mary gone, because he enjoyed the comradery with his friends and former colleagues in Illinois so much, he resolved that he would return there every summer thereafter, and he did so again in 1883 and 1884, traveling back to Washington and his duties as Chief Justice sometime in early to mid-September, always regretting having to end his "porch hours" and leave his friends behind. As a bonus, the climate in Springfield, though not particularly nice, was somewhat better than the oppressive heat and humidity of the Washington summer.

On the professional side of Chief Justice Lincoln's life, he felt powerless as he witnessed the steady decline of federal executive branch protection of the rights of people of color occurring in tandem with the complete lack of support for civil rights in the Democratic Congress and in many Northern and all Southern state governments. Unlike President Grant, the Hayes administration had no interest in prosecuting civil rights cases, and Hayes probably could not have advanced a civil rights agenda if he wanted to. The real question was whether Congress would repeal the post-Civil War legislation that at least nominally prohibited both public and private racial discrimination. However, it soon became clear that repeal was not necessary, as the Supreme Court, to the Chief Justice's horror, would do the Democrats' dirty work for them, issuing rulings that dismantled the impact of the Reconstruction

Congress's handiwork. And even if some provisions of some of the laws remained, Black Americans were too intimidated by the twin threats of violence and severe economic consequences to take their cases to the courts, federal or state. It simply was not worth risking economic ruin much less lynching to bring a case before a court that might turn out to be just as hostile to claims for racial justice.

Hayes kept his promise and declined entreaties from many Republicans to run for a second term. Although he lacked the vision or ambition to do great things, Hayes had earned a reputation as a steady leader and a modest reformer. But truth be told, Republican dominance of the presidency had depended until now on the party's ability to "waive the bloody shirt," i.e., campaign on the party's Civil War legacy. As time passed, the centrality of this issue diminished, and Democrats, seeing an opportunity to blunt it altogether, nominated General Winfield Scott Hancock for President in 1880. Not only was Hancock a war hero, but he had presided over the executions of the conspirators in the plot against Lincoln.

The Republican Party was still badly split over the issue of civil service reform, which Hayes had failed to accomplish and which made it difficult for the party to settle on a nominee. After flirting with nominating Grant for a third term, the convention settled on James Garfield, mainly based on a speech he made in opposition to an effort by Senator Roscoe Conkling to expel West Virginia's delegates from the convention after they refused to promise that they would support a nominee from Conkling's pro-patronage faction. In an attempt to mollify Conkling and his group, Garfield selected New York Customs Collector Chester Arthur, a close Conkling ally, as his running mate. Party peace was ultimately achieved, Garfield was elected in an incredibly close election, and in six months Arthur was President after a disappointed federal office seeker assassinated Garfield. Republican policy was focused on economic development and tariffs, and civil rights was on the agenda only in an effort to improve educational opportunities for Black Americans. Garfield appointed Frederick Douglass to a new position, Recorder of Deeds for the District of Columbia, but by and large the business of governing the country remained an all-

White affair.

As enthusiasm for civil rights waned across the country, whenever and wherever Black Americans attempted to vindicate their rights, political or economic, they were met by violent opposition along both racial and political lines. Examples included the Jaybird-Woodpecker War in Texas, where the 1874 election had restored White supremacist rule at the state level, and the Thibodaux Massacre in Louisiana, where racist Democrats took control of the state in the aftermath of the withdrawal of federal troops in 1877.

In the Jaybird-Woodpecker War, a newly-formed faction of the Fort Bend County Democratic Party, the Jaybirds, refused to acquiesce in the results of the 1882 local election in which moderate Whites and Black Americans had joined together to reelect the Woodpeckers. After a few small violent incidents, the Jaybirds waged an all-out attack, killed nearly a dozen local residents, and all of the recently elected officials resigned in fear for their lives. The governor declared martial law and filled the open county offices with Jaybirds, in effect a county-level forceable coups, ending the last post-War attempt at biracial government in Texas.

The Thibodaux Massacre, although rooted in race, was provoked more by economics than politics. Louisiana sugar planters conspired to impose extremely low wages and keep their workers in virtual slavery through delayed payment of wages in company scrip redeemable only at company-owned stores and housing facilities. The national Knights of Labor viewed Louisiana as an opportunity to advance a pro-labor agenda, and, with promises of economic support and a better future, the Knights convinced nearly 10,000 sugar workers, across four sugar-producing parishes, 95 percent of them Black, to go on strike. In Thibodaux, the Parish Judge, who was also a sugar planter, declared martial law and then ordered his newly formed paramilitary organization, the "Peace and Order Committee," to round up and kill striking Black workers and their families. After between thirty and fifty Black Americans were murdered within a week, the workers returned to their jobs, and for several months afterwards, Committee members continued to hunt down and kill those Black Americans they viewed as instigators of the strike. Sugar workers made no further attempts to resist or organize for decades.

Despite the federal government's legal power to prosecute individuals who engaged in racially motivated violence, no one in either the Jaybird-Woodpecker War or the Thibodaux Massacre was arrested or prosecuted for the murders. Another incident of racial violence in Crockett County, Tennessee, did result in prosecutions, and the results were disastrous. In 1876, four Black men, George Wells, Patrick Wells, Robert Smith and William Overton, were arrested by County Sheriff Robert Harris for disorderly conduct after they attempted to hold a Republican Party rally on the plaza in front of the county courthouse in the city of Alamo, the county seat. Sheriff Harris, with the assistance of a pair of deputies, locked the four men in the county jail adjacent to the courthouse. Late that night, Sheriff Harris returned with nearly two dozen armed White citizens, including the two deputies, took them men out of the jail into a nearby field and beat the four of them, in the Sheriff's words "to show them that nigger Republicans ain't welcome in Crockett County." The four men were brought back to the jail where Patrick Wells died from his injuries while the other three recovered.

At the very end of the Grant administration, Harris and nineteen others identified as having taken part in the beatings were indicted by a federal grand jury, and in due course all were convicted in federal circuit court of criminal violations of the Ku Klux Klan conspiracy provision of the 1871 Civil Rights Act, which made it a criminal offense to "conspire together, or go in disguise upon the public highway or upon the premises of another for the purpose, either directly or indirectly, of depriving any person or any class of persons of the equal protection of the laws, or of equal privileges or immunities under the laws." Remarkably, the jury that convicted them was composed solely of White men. Apparently no one was particularly enamored of Sheriff Harris's brutal law enforcement tactics that were deployed against Whites as well as Blacks. Due to its heavy caseload, the Supreme Court did not rule on the defendants' appeals until 1883, with Garfield in the White House and Republicans William Woods, Stanley Matthews,

Horace Gray, and Samuel Blatchford recent arrivals to the Court, having replaced Justices Strong, Swayne, Clifford, and Hunt. (Matthews, appointed by Garfield, after failing to be confirmed when nominated by President Hayes, would, in 1886, write one of the Court's most important cases regarding race discrimination, ruling in the Yick Wo case that San Francisco authorities violated the Equal Protection Clause by selectively enforcing a building code provision against laundries owned by people of Chinese descent but not against White-owned laundries.) Despite dissents by the Chief Justice and Justices Harlan and Matthews, the Court held the Ku Klux Klan Act unconstitutional on the ground that Congress did not have power under the Fourteenth Amendments to punish private racial violence. Most disheartening to the Chief Justice was that both of Chester Arthur's appointees and one of Hayes's joined the majority.

In his dissenting opinion Lincoln lamented, *"The Court seems to have forgotten both that Sheriff Harris and his deputies are public officials and that we have only recently suffered through Civil War to protect our Black citizens from the sort of treatment these Ku Kluxers have inflicted upon them. We have failed our fellow citizens in this sacred duty."* The Court majority had nothing to say in response to Lincoln's dissent. It rested its decision on the notion that only state governments had the power to protect citizens from private misconduct, stating that *"It was never supposed that the section under consideration conferred on Congress the power to enact a law which would punish a private citizen for an invasion of the rights of his fellow citizen conferred by the State of which they were both residents on all its citizens alike."* The Court had also apparently forgotten that in the Decuir case it displaced state regulation of private discrimination in favor of exclusive federal power. From Lincoln's perspective, the dismaying march away from federal protection of Black Americans proceeded apace.

31
THE END OF CIVIL RIGHTS

The decisions in the Decuir and Harris cases combined were widely understood as the legal equivalent of Hayes's withdrawal of the troops from Southern states. The Supreme Court sent a clear message that it would no longer protect Americans of African descent from White supremacist activities, even of the most violent sort. As the news of these decisions spread across the country and the social realities across the South became firmly established, businesses that had grudgingly obeyed the Civil Rights Act of 1875 reasserted their right to segregate and exclude. In Louisville, Wallace Davis, owner of the Blue Boar Inn abandoned his membership pretense and erected signs proclaiming "Colored Not Welcome" at the entry to the dining room and hotel lobby. As soon as they heard about this, the ever-vigilant Adams brothers, John and Cyrus, whose newspaper remained the most widely read publication serving the Kentucky Black community, went to the Inn and asked to be seated. After the host shook his head and pointed to the sign, the brothers went directly to the federal courthouse and filed, as provided for in the 1875 Act, "an action at debt" against Davis for the statutorily prescribed penalty of $500 each. They filed in the United States District Court knowing that their old friend and former United States Attorney Marcus Clay had been appointed by President Hayes to be the sole federal district judge in Louisville, and upon Davis's admission that his restaurant would not serve Black patrons, not even any longer at the picnic tables out back, Clay entered judgment for $1000 plus $220 in court costs in favor of John and Cyrus Adams.

As soon as the case against Davis had been filed, plans were made to bring it to the Supreme Court to assert, once again, that neither the Thirteenth nor the Fourteenth Amendments grant Congress the power to prohibit private racial discrimination. Their goal was to persuade the Court to reconsider its 1876 decision upholding the Act. On appeal, with the financial support of Southern business and political figures far and wide, Davis was represented by Louisiana Attorney Robert Marr. Marr was a leading White supremacist who had won the Decuir case in the Supreme Court and had gained notoriety for the fervor of his political and legal arguments in favor of racial segregation. His job briefing the case was made easy by the existence of Justice Bradley's Circuit Court opinion striking down the Act and by the briefs that had been filed in the Hartfield case by Reverdy Johnson, who Davis probably would have hired had Johnson not died in a fall shortly after arguing for Rogers.

In addition to reiterating the legal arguments made previously by Bradley and Johnson, Marr added his own flair. Where Johnson's brief had masterfully made the case that Congress lacked the power under either the Thirteenth or Fourteenth Amendment to regulate private racial segregation and exclusions from businesses, Marr evoked what he termed "the natural proclivity of the two races to remain separate," proclaiming that "all the repulsion, all that keeps the colored and the white races apart in the United States, is the effect, the consequence of that natural instinct, that pride of race, without which no people can ever become truly great. The law cannot, and should not require the master of an establishment of any kind to put together persons who would be disagreeable to each other or to seat, at the same table, in the same railway coach or in the same theater, those who would be repulsive, the one to the other."

Adams's lawyer, local Louisville attorney Aaron Tyler, who had incidentally studied law at Justice Harlan's alma mater Transylvania Law School, responded just as one would expect when the other side is trying to persuade the Court to overrule its prior decision, arguing that nothing has changed that would invalidate Chief Justice Lincoln's reasoning in favor of upholding the Act. In fact, he stated, "if anything, the need for enforcement of the Act is now greater than ever before, as we may observe many places revert to the lawless and discriminatory treatment of our colored citizens that prevailed in the years leading up to Congress's decision to adopt the Act." Tyler quoted at length from Lincoln's Rogers opinion and the brief filed in that case on behalf of the Grant administration by Solicitor General Samuel Phillips. Tyler concluded his brief with the following: "It may be true that nothing that happens in the chambers of Congress or in the halls of justice will open the hearts of our fellow citizens to view our Black brethren as worthy of entry into their social, economic, or political lives. But the Constitution demands that the law treat them as such, and the refusal to provide service in places of public accommodation, amusement and transportation would be a revocation of the citizenship for which so much blood was spilled and on which so many hopes and dreams are pinned. Our plea to this Court is simple, and can be stated in one majestic word: justice."

When the Justices retired to their conference room to discuss the case, the Chief Justice said, "Gentlemen, we expressed our views on this matter just a few short years ago, and I propose that we affirm the judgment without opinion. There is nothing more to say." Justice Bradley, whose views on the matter were also clear from his opinions in the Hartfield case, broke protocol by speaking before his more senior colleagues. He exclaimed, "There is certainly much more to say! We need to hear from those of us who were not present for that earlier decision. I, for one, adhere to the views I expressed in Rogers, and I believe that the Harris case is more consistent with my views than the Chief Justice's. As much as we may abhor the discrimination at issue here, Congress usurps the power of the States when it attempts to regulate private business practices." Seeing that his colleagues were not on board with his proposal, the Chief Justice then initiated the traditional process of allowing each Justice, in order of seniority, to express their views on the case. One by one, Justices Miller, Field and, of course Bradley, expressed the view that the Court's expansion of federal power in Rogers was erroneous and had not withstood the test of time, with Harris seriously undercutting its premise. Only when Lincoln turned to Harlan, now the fifth most senior Justice, did Lincoln's view receive support. Harlan made three arguments: that rights of citizenship were at stake, that the particular businesses covered by the 1875 Act were affected by the public interest and thus more like an arm of the State than a purely private business, and that the activities of these businesses had an impact on interstate commerce and thus fell squarely within Congress's domain as recognized in the Decuir case. Among the remaining Justices, only Matthews agreed with the Chief Justice and Justice Harlan, and so when the round of voting was complete, the Court had decided to declare the Civil

Rights Act of 1875 unconstitutional. As the Chief Justice said when confirming the tally, "If he ever was, Senator Sumner is most certainly no longer resting in peace."

It took Justice Bradley very little time to draft his opinion for the Court overruling United States v. Rogers and holding the Civil Rights Act unconstitutional. Most of the opinion was a rehash of his earlier opinion for the Circuit Court and his prior dissent at the Supreme Court. The only significant additions were a refutation of Justice Harlan's Commerce Clause argument and a statement that the Court's current disposition of the case is consistent the Harris decision. Bradley said, *"It is now suggested that power to pass the Act was contained in the Constitution before the adoption of the last three amendments, principally that the Act is a regulation of 'commerce among the several states'. In some of its applications, this may be so, especially with regard to modes of transportation between one and another of the States. But the Congress made no such claim of power when it passed the Act. It relied exclusively on its powers to enforce the Thirteenth and Fourteenth Amendments to the Constitution, and unless and until Congress tells us that it is exercising another of its powers, we are bound to take the Act as we find it, as a bare assertion of power over the rights recognized in the Amendments, not as being derived from the Constitution of 1789."*

Upon his request, Chief Justice Lincoln allowed Justice Harlan to draft an opinion for the three dissenters. Harlan spelled out his theory that businesses covered by the Act were different than ordinary private businesses because they had traditionally been required by State law to accept any customers willing to pay the prescribed fare and because *"many operate only under State-granted licenses, which places them perfectly within the purview of the Fourteenth Amendment."* He also developed the Commerce Clause argument in light of the Decuir decision: *"the Court has created a damned if you do, damned if you don't scenario. In the Decuir case, it was held that only the federal government may prohibit racial discrimination in transportation. At the time, the Decuir decision was understood to have little import since the Act under consideration today was already on the books, ready to provide the rule of decision on the next journey in which African-Americans were not recognized fully in their citizenship. Now we are told we must wait yet again, this time for Congress to check the correct box. This stingy attitude toward Congress's power degrades us as a Court and recalls an earlier age when the choice of the wrong form of action doomed even the most valid legal complaint. Whether such devices are ever appropriate, they are, I submit, certainly not so when hearing the precious plea against the stains of race and servitude."*

More fundamentally, Harlan expressed the view that the Court had become entangled in the law's trees to the exclusion of a view of the forest in a manner that constitutes a perversion of justice: *"Constitutional provisions, adopted in the interest of liberty and for the purpose of securing, through national legislation, the rights of national citizenship, have been so construed as to defeat the ends the people desired to accomplish and which they supposed they had accomplished by changes in their fundamental law. The court has departed from the familiar rule requiring, in the interpretation of constitutional provisions, that full effect be given to the intent with which they were adopted. And there can be no doubt that these provisions were designed to secure freedom from race discrimination to colored citizens and to all who come within the jurisdiction of the United States. Discrimination against our colored fellow citizens is undoubtedly a badge and incident of slavery and a denial of full and equal citizenship which Congress has been granted ample authority to prohibit."*

32

WILLIE CULPEPER

The decision in Davis v. Adams was announced on October 16, 1883. Chief Justice Lincoln was so distressed and embarrassed by it that he could barely bring himself to attend the session of the Court at which the opinions were read. As Justice Bradley read excerpts from his opinion for the majority, the Chief Justice could be seen fiddling with the papers on his table and occasionally scratching out marginal notes on some of them. He was apparently editing a draft opinion in another case. Justice Harlan's face reddened as Bradley uttered the phrase "it would be running the slavery argument into the ground" in reference to the lack of support in the Thirteenth Amendment for Congress's prohibition of race discrimination in businesses open to the public.

When it came time for Harlan to read his dissent, he set out to read it in its entirety, all 14,000 words of it. Perhaps he thought if he went on long enough his colleagues in the majority would see the light; perhaps he was channeling the spirit of Charles Sumner, who never thought there were too many words to express his views on civil rights. Harlan might have gone on forever had he not lost his place after some of his papers slid off of his desk onto the floor behind him as he emphatically turned to the next page. After the session concluded, as the Justices shuffled out of the courtroom to remove their robes, the Chief Justice took his fellow Kentucky native by the arm and said simply, "We've lost it John, and I fear it's not coming back."

The decision, which became known as "the Civil Rights Case" was celebrated wildly by some and mourned incredulously by others across the Southern United States. Black families in cities where Whites and Black Americans lived in close proximity could hear the hollering and celebratory gunfire as they struggled to understand how Chief Justice Lincoln's Court could abandon them. While some White-owned restaurants and theaters were happy to continue taking money from their Black customers, many others shut their doors to people of color almost immediately, and others segregated their Black customers into separate rooms or to the least desirable locations. On the rails, where due to the expense and inconvenience the railroad companies had no desire to segregate their passengers, White men took offense to Black Americans riding in the first-class cars together with White "ladies." Credible threats of violence sent many Black Americans scurrying to the smoking cars, even if it meant exposing them and their young children to vulgar talk and a dangerous environment.

Violence occasionally occurred when Black passengers with first-class train tickets were forcibly moved into second-class cars by White passengers, often with the assistance of conductors. One such incident occurred near Conway, South Carolina, in December, 1883, as members of the Culpeper family began travel on the Atlantic Coast Line from their home to visit relatives near Petersburg, Virginia. In accord with their tickets, Virginia and her twenty-year-old daughter Rosemary took seats in the Ladies' parlor while Randolph and eighteen-year-old son Willie, on leave from the United States Army, took their places in the first class cabin. The Culpepers knew that they might be pushed toward the second-class car regardless of the tickets they held, but they had resolved to resist.

When the White Dobson family from Petersburg boarded the train for their return journey home, the father, Raymond Dobson, was surprised to encounter Mrs. Culpeper and her daughter in the Ladies' parlor where his wife and two daughters intended to ride for the nearly 300-mile journey. Dobson found the conductor in the first-class car where the Culpeper men were seated and demanded that all of the Culpepers, male and female, be moved to the second-class car. Second class on the Atlantic Line was one of the least desirable rail cars in the country. Smoking, spitting, swearing, drinking, and gambling were common pastimes among the White male passengers. It was at the front of the train where opening windows to fight the stench would welcome billowing smoke and glowing embers from the engine.

Randolph and Willie were chatting in the first-class car when they overheard Mr. Dobson and the conductor agree to remove Mrs. Culpeper and Rosemary to the smoking car. Randolph told his son to stay put and followed the conductor and Dobson into the parlor, and when they approached Virginia and Rosemary, he positioned himself in front of the Culpeper women and said, "No one is sending my wife and daughter to that filthy place. They have tickets for this car and they are going to stay in this car." Raymond Dobson grabbed Randolph and began to shove him out of the way. Culpeper began fighting back, and the conductor and several more White travelers joined in and grabbed Randolph, aiming to throw him off of the train. Two of the men held Virginia by the arms to prevent her from coming to Randolph's aid. Sensing the commotion, Willie came into the parlor to see men holding his mother's arms. As he rushed toward them, one of the men drew his six shooter and fired once, hitting Willie in the chest. He collapsed on the spot, and died in his U.S. Army private's dress uniform, Virginia wailing as she cradled his head and Rosemary slumped over sobbing in her seat. The conductor allowed Randolph back onto the train to retrieve his son's body. The porter put the family's luggage on the platform, and the train left on its journey to Virginia.

The killing of Private Abraham William Lincoln Culpeper was big news across the country. Northern papers equated Willie's killing with a lynching, and chalked it up to the Southern desire to return to the pre-War denial of the rights of Black citizens. The Chicago Tribune, a staunchly Republican paper, called for reenactment of the Civil Rights Act under the Commerce Clause coupled with energetic federal enforcement "even if it requires the redeployment of federal troops to quell the racial insurrection that has gripped the former Confederacy." The Black press across the country decried the mistreatment of people of color, although only in the North could editors safely call for resistance to oppressive treatment at the hands of White supremacists.

In the South, the reaction of the White press was more muted, with many papers expressing regret over the loss of life, especially of a member of the armed forces. The Memphis Daily Appeal opined that the root cause of the killing was the lack of clarity concerning segregation, which encouraged Black Americans to "step over the line into the domain of social equality." This widely shared thought inspired Southern states to enact what they called "Separate Car Acts," which required that rail passengers be assigned to "equal, but separate" cars according to their race. The first Separate Car Acts were passed in Louisiana, Mississippi, Tennessee, and South Carolina, with the remaining former Confederate states quickly falling in line. Even West Virginia, which was birthed out of the rejection of pre-War secession, adopted a Separate Car Act.

Six days after he was killed, Willie Culpeper was laid to rest in the "colored" cemetery in Conway, next to the grave of his younger brother Floyd who had died in infancy. Randolph had telegraphed Frederick Douglass, and, recalling his two encounters with Willie, Douglass got on the (segregated) train to Conway to attend the funeral. At Randolph's insistence, Douglass spoke at the funeral, the last to do so before the preacher's closing prayer for a peaceful rest for Willie and a better world for those he left behind. Douglass began quietly, recounting his meetings with Willie and the family, and lamenting that even a hardworking, patriotic family like theirs was not safe in America. Over and over he returned to the refrain that "here was a man, a citizen and soldier, protecting his mother from the mob." Douglass, who always found inspiration in the founding documents of the United States, concluded, "We love America, we love America despite what it does to us, what it doesn't stop doing to us, we love America, we are proud to wear a badge proclaiming that we are 'citizens of the United States,' but for too many of our fellow citizens, that badge is overshadowed by the color of our skin, we love America, our beloved Willie dedicated himself to defending all of our freedoms, we fight for the dignity of citizenship, the dignity of simply living a productive life of peace and security, we keep loving America and it does not love us back. Willie, God rest your soul and God bless your family with the strength to carry on without you."

No one was charged with a crime for Willie's death, and the Black community understood that any unrest over it would likely be met with merciless violence.

EPILOGUE

In early 1885, after it became clear that the requirement of separation would be enforced much more effectively than equality, a group in New Orleans calling itself the "Citizens Committee" was organized to oppose enforcement of the Separate Car Act. Much of their funding came from railroad companies hoping to sell their Black passengers first-class tickets without having to bear the expense of two separate cars. Ultimately, they would launch an unsuccessful test case to challenge the Separate Car Act as violating the Equal Protection Clause of the Fourteenth Amendment. As strongly as they believed they had the law and justice behind their efforts, they knew deep down that it was hopeless, that the Supreme Court was composed of segregationists who would rule against them to preserve national peace and unity.

Meanwhile, as the Court's term progressed, Chief Justice Lincoln found himself more and more in the Court minority, alienated from his newer colleagues and frustrated with his inability to protect, much less advance, the civil rights agenda that he had so firmly embraced early in his tenure at the Court. On March 4, Chief Justice Lincoln had sworn in Grover Cleveland as President, the first Democrat elected President since before the Civil War. Cleveland had criticized Reconstruction as a "failed experiment" and did not, to say the least, view civil rights enforcement as an important federal priority. Lincoln felt every single one of his seventy-five years of age, and was ready to return to Springfield and rest.

On Thursday, March 12, 1885, the Justices met at 10 am to discuss cases that had been argued that week. In the afternoon, the Chief Justice hosted a luncheon to celebrate his seventy-sixth birthday, and after receiving his colleagues' congratulations, Lincoln informed them that this term of the Court would be his last, that he would retire to Springfield as of June 1. He also said that his greatest regret as Chief Justice was that he had not succeeded in persuading Congress to appropriate the funds to erect a building for the Court, "for we have sometimes found it difficult to persuade our Congressmen that we are an equal branch of government as we reside as sub-tenants in the least desirable apartments of their building." Later that day, he transmitted his official resignation message to President Cleveland and congressional leaders. Cleveland's response was to thank Lincoln for his service and to suggest he would proclaim a national day of thankfulness and celebration for Lincoln's service as President and Chief Justice. Lincoln declined, but at Cleveland's insistence, he agreed to a parade in his honor on June 1, after which he would travel quietly to Springfield, rejecting suggestions from many quarters that he take a whistle stop tour across the eastern half of the United States during which his career could be celebrated.

The parade was way beyond Lincoln's expectations. From a reviewing stand symbolically erected halfway between the White House and the Supreme Court's chambers in the U.S. Capitol Building, Lincoln, Cleveland, the entire Supreme Court, and dozens of political figures reviewed forty-one horse-drawn floats, one for each State of the Union and one representing each of the three branches of government, and a massive assemblage of active and retired members of the military, in a parade that rivaled the Grand Review of the Troops conducted at the conclusion of the Civil War. The procession lasted more than eight hours, and the heat and humidity left those in attendance exhausted. Lincoln spent much of the day chatting with those around him, cracking jokes about the threadbare Civil War era uniforms worn by many of the older veterans, while wishing he was already sitting on his porch in Springfield.

Most of Lincoln's personal effects had already been sent to Springfield, and on June 2, the former President and retired Chief Justice boarded a special train from Union Station in Washington in a private car and set out for home. The 800-mile trip took Lincoln through Maryland, Pennsylvania, Ohio, Indiana, and into Illinois, where to Lincoln the sun seemed a little brighter, the breeze a little cooler and the water a bit more refreshing than what he had become accustomed to in Washington. By and large he was left alone during the trip except when, on a few occasions, the train made an extended station stop and news got out that President Lincoln's train was in the station. More than once, Lincoln found it necessary to come out on the rear platform of the train and wave to the cheering crowd. Although people virtually begged him to say even a few words, Lincoln never spoke except to say thank you. Many onlookers were surprised by his appearance—a bit stooped over with a fully grey beard, and little hair left atop his head when he took off his hat to wipe the sweat away, and a cane that left his hand only when he gripped the platform's railing for balance.

In Springfield, almost before his trunks were unpacked, Lincoln resumed seeing visitors on his porch, mostly local friends and associates, with an occasional tourist and the odd visiting dignitary mixed in. Late that summer, a young man with dark skin approached the ever-present police detail that guarded the walkway in front of Lincoln's house. The visitor, smartly dressed with a faint moustache and hair pressed down and sharply parted on the left side, was on his way from his home in Massachusetts to begin studying that fall at Fisk College in Nashville, Tennessee. He handed the officers a letter of introduction from Frederick Douglass "of Washington, D.C.," and his calling card which read "William Edward Burghardt Du Bois, Great Barrington, Massachusetts." The young man had traveled to Washington to pay a call on Douglass, who he greatly admired, and Douglass insisted that he make the detour to Springfield before his journey to Nashville. Douglass saw something special in this intelligent, well-spoken young man, and he thought a visit with Lincoln would strengthen his resolve to work toward justice for their fellow African Americans. Du Bois could see Lincoln on the porch behind the guards, rocking slowly with his distinctive light grey beard and his trademark stove pipe hat. The guards let him pass, and as he approached, he saw that the elderly man's facial features were outlined by wrinkles best described as deep crevices into which one could nearly insert a quill pen.

As the young Du Bois walked up the steps, Lincoln motioned for him to take the seat to the immediate left of his rocking chair. On the opposite side of the former President stood a pitcher of ice water and a pair of empty glasses. Lincoln offered, and Du Bois poured two glasses, one for each of them. The first words out of Lincoln's mouth were, "Enjoy it young man—ice gets to be a precious commodity around here this time of year." After introducing himself and handing Lincoln his calling card, Du Bois read Douglass's letter of introduction, which included a statement that "this young man is certain to be among the leaders of the next generation of warriors for justice. I pray, Mr. President, that you will provide him with wise counsel and words of inspiration as he embarks on his educational journey, a journey that has been and still is denied to too many members of my race." He then tried to hand the letter to Lincoln, but Lincoln refused, stating that he ought to keep it as a memento of his meeting with Douglass.

Du Bois sat in the chair to Lincoln's left, looked over at Lincoln, waiting for him to speak. Lincoln seemed to be staring off into the distance, searching for the words of advice he might render. First, he suggested to Du Bois that he should extend greetings "to my old friend Fred, and tell him to come for a visit one of these days."

Then, after a long contemplative pause, he said, "Frederick's letter, and the reason for your visit remind me of one of the most puzzling stories in the Bible, the Egyptian pharaoh's refusal in the midst of the plagues to free his Hebrew slaves and let them travel to the promised land. Pharaoh does not refuse of his own free will. Rather, the book tells us that God hardened pharaoh's heart, and this hardening of the ruler's heart led to two great calamities, the death of each and every first-born son in the land of Egypt and then the drowning of Pharaoh's army in the Red Sea. I cannot believe that the benevolent God that granted us this great land and all of its innumerable bounties would at the same time harden our hearts so that we cannot make a more perfect union. Our slaves are free and yet even after the Southern chariots were drowned in the Red Sea of bloodshed, the hearts of our Southern brethren stay hardened, preventing our nation from achieving the new birth of freedom we have so long sought. I have tried all these long years, in the White House and on the bench, and off, to persuade my brethren, North and South, to open their hearts to the true will of the Almighty. We are answered, it seems, with deceitful words and malignant hearts. I am convinced that only through persuasion will we move beyond the spiritual civil war we have been fighting since the moment we laid our weapons down in the spring of '65 and move beyond this more imperfect union we seem to have created since. Young man, it is the task of your people of your generation, and the open-hearted of my people of your generation, to fight this war. Your weapons are your faith, your determination, and our nation's collective devotion to the ideals our fathers instilled in us at the founding of this experiment in republican government, ideals that have until now remain unattained. It is to that end that I hope you will devote yourself, and for which I hope your education will prepare you. If not, I fear another generation and yet another will be lost."

Lincoln spoke these words in a clear quiet voice, looking not directly at Du Bois but straight ahead, as if his audience was the entire country or only himself or nobody at all. Du Bois mumbled, "Thank you Mr. President," and then when he got his voice back, he added: "One thing I know, Mr. President, is that to have any hope to succeed, me and my people will have to do it ourselves."

***

Abraham Lincoln's life in Springfield remained quiet, rejecting every request from Republican politicians, friends, and former colleagues to become involved in politics or even to speak at events marking important occasions. His single exception was a yearly appearance at Springfield's Independence Day celebration, but even then he would speak only briefly and only to thank his fellow Springfield residents for their friendship and support and to urge everyone to "have a good time while remembering what we celebrate and those who sacrificed themselves to preserve it." He wrote few letters except for a consistent and lively correspondence with Frederick Douglass, whom he considered to be his closest friend in the world after the 1882 death of Joshua Speed.

Lincoln continued to receive visitors at his Springfield home, and there were many, including Douglass who came every February to celebrate the President's birthday, Lincoln's former private secretaries John Nicolay and John Hay and journalist Noah Brooks, who could never convince Lincoln to agree to be interviewed for a biography he wanted to write. His most frequent visitor was his son Robert who had returned to Illinois in 1885 after serving as Secretary of War under Presidents James Garfield and Chester Arthur. He also saw his former law partner William Herndon on occasion. Only one former President called on him—Chester Arthur accompanied Robert Lincoln from Chicago to Springfield for a visit in the fall of 1885. By then, Arthur was the only living former President, as Grant, Hayes, and Garfield were all dead, and Lincoln outlived even Arthur who died in November of 1886 after a brief illness.

At the dawn of 1889, as Lincoln's eightieth birthday approached, his friends and associates marveled at his quick wit and his apparent physical health. He seemed to shed some of his characteristic melancholy, and he allowed the City of Springfield to hold a large celebration of the occasion, on two conditions—that he not be expected to make a speech, and that Frederick Douglass be given the honor of making the final toast of the evening. That September, he made a visit to Chicago to check up on Robert, who was practicing law while also helping support a school for neglected boys on the northwestern edge of the city. Lincoln was in such good spirits that he spent several days alternating between his son's stately home on Lake Shore Drive and the school, where he met the boys, read to some of the younger ones, and told tales of the Civil War and his experiences in Washington. City residents were thrilled to see the former President and Chief Justice strolling along the lakefront with his grandchildren Mamie, Little Abe, and Jessie in tow. Lincoln even thought about politics, thinking he might be of use to newly inaugurated Republican President Benjamin Harrison who had defeated Democrat Grover Cleveland, returning the presidency to Republican hands.

Lincoln returned to Springfield in early October, refreshed but fatigued from his weeks in Chicago. His life returned to normal, mainly staying at home reading and greeting visitors on the porch, or inside as the weather got colder. On the morning of December 8, he awoke with a determination to become involved in politics once again. He dispatched a telegram to President Harrison offering his services "if you can find a suitable role for me in your administration." That afternoon, he dined at home with his one-time law partner William Herndon, who brought along one of his niece's pies for dessert. After dinner, the men adjourned to the porch, Lincoln in his favored rocking chair and Herndon in the seat that had once been occupied by the young Du Bois, and often by Frederick Douglass. In the midst of their conversation,

Lincoln stood, telling Herndon he felt a headache coming on and might go lie down. Lincoln then collapsed back into the chair and died almost instantly, apparently from a brain aneurysm that had burst with little warning.

Abraham Lincoln was 80 years and eight months old when he died, having lived longer than any American President. His legacy of public service was matched only by that of George Washington, commanding general in the Revolutionary War and the first President under the Constitution of 1789. It would be nearly six decades more until a new generation of activists, led by a Methodist preacher from Atlanta, would have success in advancing the cause of civil rights. They drew great inspiration from Lincoln, but they also knew that their success was on their own shoulders, not on the words of the Constitution or the actions of their White friends and allies, however well-intentioned they might be. The defeat of the pernicious doctrine of separate but (un)equal was aided by the most liberal Supreme Court in the nation's history, likely out of a mixture of commitment to justice and fear of the consequences for the country if the Court allowed the White establishment to continue to deny Black citizens their legal, civil, and human rights.

Douglass returned to Springfield for Lincoln's funeral, and he was given the honor of delivering the final eulogy at a packed ceremony at the new state capitol building. Douglass had a well-earned reputation for being brutally honest, regardless of the occasion, and in this nearly two-hour address, he stayed true to form, offering an honest portrayal of his friend from Illinois, excerpts from which follow:

Truth compels me to admit, as a colored man, even while smitten a heavy grief, and as we treasure his name, that Abraham Lincoln was not, in his early days, in the fullest sense of the word, either our man or our model. In his interests, in his associations, in his habits of thought, and in his prejudices, he was a white man. He was pre-eminently the white man's President, entirely devoted to the welfare of white men. He was ready and willing at any time during the first years of his administration to deny, postpone, and sacrifice the rights of humanity in the colored people to promote the welfare of the white people of this country. In all his education and feeling he was an American of the Americans. He came into the Presidential chair upon one principle alone, namely, opposition to the extension of slavery. His arguments in furtherance of this policy had their motive and mainspring in his patriotic devotion to the interests of his own race. To protect, defend, and perpetuate slavery in the States where it existed Abraham Lincoln was not less ready than any other President to draw the sword of the nation. Or so it appeared.

When, therefore, it shall be asked what we have to do with the memory of Abraham Lincoln, or what Abraham Lincoln had to do with us, the answer is ready, full, and complete. Though the Union was more to him than our freedom or our future, under his wise and beneficent rule, and by measures approved and vigorously pressed by him, we saw that the handwriting of ages, in the form of prejudice and proscription, was rapidly fading away from the face of our whole country; under his rule, and in due time, about as soon after all as the country could tolerate the strange spectacle, we saw our brave sons and brothers laying off the rages of bondage, and being clothed all over in the blue uniforms of the soldiers of the United States; under his rule we saw two hundred thousand of our dark and dusky people responding to the call of Abraham Lincoln, and with muskets on their shoulders, and eagles on their buttons, timing their high footsteps to liberty and union under the national flag; under his rule we saw the independence of the black republic of Hayti, the special object of slaveholding aversion and horror, fully recognized, and her minister, a colored gentleman, duly received here in the city of Washington; under his rule we saw the internal slave-trade, which so long disgraced the nation, abolished, and slavery abolished in the District of Columbia; under his rule we saw for the first time the law enforced against the foreign slave-trade, and the first slave-trader hanged like any other pirate or murderer; under his rule, assisted by the greatest captain of our age, and his inspiration, we saw the Confederate States, based upon the idea that our race must be slaves, and slaves forever, battered to pieces and scattered to the four winds; under his rule, and in the fullness of time, we saw Abraham Lincoln, after giving the slaveholders three months' grace in which to save their hateful slave system, penning the immortal paper, which, though special in its language, was general in its principles and effect, making slavery forever impossible in the United States. Though we waited long, we saw all this and more.

Can any colored man, or any white man friendly to the freedom of all men, ever forget the night which followed the first day of January, 1863, when the world was to see if Abraham Lincoln would prove to be as good as his word? I shall never forget that memorable night, when in a distant city I waited and watched at a public meeting, with three thousand others not less anxious than myself, for the word of deliverance. Nor shall I ever forget the outburst of joy and thanks-giving that rent the air when the lightning brought to us the emancipation proclamation. In that happy hour we forgot all delay, and forgot all tardiness; and we were thenceforward willing to allow the President all the latitude of time, phraseology, and every honorable device that statesmanship might require for the achievement of a great and beneficent measure of liberty and progress.

And since that time we witnessed the change. We found in the elder Lincoln a true friend, an advocate for us and our rightful place as citizens of this great country, whose constitution aspires to freedom and security for all. And though he did not fully succeed, and though the forces of evil have regained their footing in those formerly rebellious places, on this occasion, we can only do honor to the memory of our friend and liberator, the man who more than any other lived up to the ideals captured in that sacred document that was so wisely bestowed upon all of us, white and colored alike, reconceived after that bloody war with liberty and justice for all.

AFTERWORD: AUTHOR'S NOTE

We can only imagine how history might have changed had Abraham Lincoln survived the Good Friday plot, and what life would have had in store for him and for Black Americans in the succeeding decades. My limited study of Lincoln and of the history of racism in the nineteenth century left me optimistic on one score and pessimistic on another. My optimism involves my sense that Lincoln's position on race might have evolved in a progressive direction. While he lived, his views on race were closer to those of his Vice President Andrew Johnson's than those of the Radicals in Congress and his Cabinet, like Sumner and Stanton. But when confronted with the reality of post-Civil War oppression of the freedmen and people of color throughout the South, I would like to believe that Lincoln would have embraced measures like the Civil Rights Acts of 1866, 1870, 1871, and 1875, and that he would have appointed like-minded Republicans as Supreme Court Justices, potentially avoiding legal abominations like The Civil Rights Cases and Plessy v. Ferguson.

My pessimism is over American society's reaction to what might have occurred in law and society had Lincoln survived. Try as I might, I could not write a history in which racial equality (social and legal) prevailed across the country and in which we all lived happily ever after as one big American family. Again based on my limited study of American history, Liberty and Racism appear to me to be the evil twins that serve as a sort of yin and yang of American society. The most vehement American advocates for freedom from government oversight seem to always be among those most eager to prevent their fellow citizens with darker skin from enjoying those precious liberties so central to the story of America. Perhaps there is a happy ending lurking somewhere in the story of America. If so, I hope it reveals itself soon.

Although this book is a work of fiction, and many of the events and conversations are fictional, a significant number of the events depicted actually occurred, some as described and others with my alterations and embellishments. Most of the people mentioned in the book lived and were involved in the events depicted. Some of their statements, oral and written, are either quoted from or based on statements made by the actual person, while others are completely fabricated. A few were made by a person other than the one to whom the words are attributed in the book. To avoid the necessity of fabricating citations, I have not included footnotes or endnotes even though many of the words in this book are copied or paraphrased from other sources.

Of course, since I witnessed none of the events depicted, I relied upon numerous sources to construct the historical outline that contains my narrative.

What follows is a brief and general chapter-by-chapter specification of fact/fiction/embellishment followed by a bibliography of sources I consulted during the writing process:

The episode described in the prologue is fictional. Some of the people involved, including most obviously the young lawyer Abraham Lincoln, lived in the time and place, while others I created out of whole cloth. The places are all real places and the Underground Railroad route to Canada was real, although I do not know if any escaped slave took the precise route described.

Chapter one describes actual events based on eyewitness accounts of varying reliability, including a claim that Oliver Wendell Holmes Jr. was at City Point with Lincoln and cried out "get down you idiot" as Confederate bullets whizzed around the President's head. The events at Appomattox Court House occurred except that the business about the sword exchange, the pledge to work toward national unity, and Lee's visit to his family estate did not occur. The order to Sherman to limit destruction on his march to the sea was also my creation.

Chapter two begins with an embellished account of actual events except that some of the details of the April 12 plotting are fabricated. The chapter veers off into fiction when Lincoln survives the assassination attempt and the bullet meant for him strikes an unlucky fellow from Indiana. Walt Whitman did volunteer as a nurse in military hospitals and he was fired when the Secretary of the Treasury read a draft of Leaves of Grass. Many of the details of other events on April 14 are true but embellished.

Chapter three is a fictional account of the investigation and trial built around some accurate details. Of course, John Wilkes Booth was never interrogated. His recitations are from plays by William Shakespeare including The Tragedy of Julius Caesar and Hamlet. All details in this and succeeding chapters that depend on Abraham Lincoln surviving the attempt are, of course, fabrications. The controversy over military commissions did occur. John Surratt did not return to face justice. In truth, he was captured in Egypt after hiding with the aid of Catholic priests everywhere he traveled, lending support to the characterization of the Lincoln assassination as a Catholic plot.

Chapter four is fiction although the story bears some similarity to actions taken in real life by Andrew Johnson. The accounts of efforts of Southern states to oppress their citizens of color are based on reality. Frederick Douglass was not involved in the Freedmen's Bureau but accounts of its activities are based on fact. The conflict between Lincoln's Reconstruction policies and those of the Radical Republicans reflects reality.

Chapter five is a fictionalized account of real events.

Chapter six is a fictionalized account of similar real events. The Culpeper family did not exist.

Chapter seven is a fictionalized account of real events. The accounts of the actions of Members of Congress are generally accurate.

Chapter eight is built around real race riots in Memphis and New Orleans, but Grant and Lee's unity tour is complete fiction. The attack on the Black church in Memphis was part of the riot there.

Chapter nine is a fictionalized account of the development and passage of the voting provisions of the Enforcement Act. The slaughter of Black delegates to the convention in New Orleans is not fiction. Land grant colleges are real but the details about them in this chapter are fabricated. Andrew Johnson did embark on a politically disastrous speaking tour known as the "Swing around the Circle."

Chapter ten is a fictionalized account of the move toward more radical reconstruction policies including the Fourteenth Amendment and civil rights bills. Many of the details of political events in Southern states are drawn from actual developments.

Chapter eleven is fictional insofar as Grant has to convince Lincoln not to run for the third term and Lincoln and Grant conspire to enable Lincoln to become Chief Justice of the Supreme Court. Mark Twain's appearance is based on his relationship with Grant. Chase's presidential aspirations are based on the historical record.

Chapter twelve's account of the nomination process for the election of 1868 is largely accurate except for the references to Chief Justice Chase stepping down from the Supreme Court and the maneuvering surrounding that non-occurrence. Chase did float the idea of running as a Democrat but it didn't go anywhere. The discussion of the origins of the Fifteenth Amendment is based on historical accounts.

Chapter thirteen tells a fictional story of the end of Abraham Lincoln's second term, but includes reported historical details on Grant's inauguration.

Chapter fourteen is fiction insofar as Lincoln is at the Supreme Court. The Supreme Court decisions described are real but of course in reality, Lincoln had no involvement in them.

Chapter fifteen is based largely on historical accounts of the political environment surrounding Reconstruction efforts and the difficulties that impeded efforts to protect Black citizens. In particular, the elements of the story involving Senator Hiram Revels are based on historical accounts and official documents. The discussion of enforcement cases and further legislation is based on historical accounts and official records about the Enforcement Act, the 1870 elections, Ku Klux Klan violence, and the debate over segregation in the schools in the District of Columbia.

Chapter sixteen is based on historical accounts of the establishment of the Department of Justice and the actions of early heads of the department. The account of the drafting and passage of the 1871 Ku Klux Klan Act is based on historical accounts and official records.

Chapter seventeen accurately describes important Supreme Court decisions that were made without Lincoln's involvement.

Chapter eighteen is a largely accurate account of Grant's reelection and second inauguration except of course for Lincoln's involvement.

Chapter nineteen begins with an accurate historical account of Colfax but then veers off into fiction when the Supreme Court reviews the convictions in the Cruikshank case. In reality, the Supreme Court exonerated all of the defendants, and no one was held accountable for the slaughter.

Chapter twenty is mainly a largely accurate account of the Bradwell and Slaughterhouse decisions except that Lincoln's opinion in the latter case differs substantially from the actual opinion in the case, which has been criticized for its narrow reading of the Privileges and Immunities Clause. The vignette about baseball is built on actual facts but in reality, the White Field remained off limits to non-White players and teams.

Chapter twenty-one's episode in the Rough Squirrel and the resulting litigation is complete fiction. In reality, the entire Civil Rights Act of 1875 was struck down for the reasons suggested in Justice Bradley's opinion for the Circuit Court, although it happened later than the book's depiction.

Chapter twenty-two is fiction, including the episode at the Blue Boar Inn and the resulting "Davis plan." This is my sense of what might have happened if energetic enforcement of the 1875 Act had continued.

Chapter twenty-three is built on the fictional foundation of the previous chapter but its depiction of resistance to the Act is based on reality. The Yazoo County episode is fictional as is the journey north of two Black residents of the area.

Chapter twenty-four is built on historical depictions of the controversy surrounding the 1876 presidential election.

Chapter twenty-five is a fictionalized version of the Electoral Commission's proceedings that draws, in large part, on official records, but of course without involvement of Abraham Lincoln. The Wormley's conference took place but my account includes substantial embellishments.

Chapter twenty-six is a somewhat accurate account of the Commission's decision and the proceedings in Congress, but nothing that Lincoln said about it is based on historical fact.

Chapter twenty-seven's account of the Hayes inauguration, his early moves as President and Grant's post-presidential activities is based largely on fact, including the fact that Hayes took the oath a day early in case Tilden took the oath the next day.

Chapter twenty-eight is based on historical accounts of the situation under Hayes and the educational opportunities for Black citizens.

Chapter twenty-nine contains an accurate account of the Decuir case, of course without Lincoln's involvement.

Chapter thirty is fiction about Abraham Lincoln and his family built around some historical details concerning Mary Todd Lincoln and their son Robert. The case descriptions are largely accurate.

Chapter thirty-one is a fictional account of the Court's reconsideration of the earlier decision upholding the 1875 Act and returns the law to where it actually landed.

Chapter thirty-two is fiction.

The Epilogue is fiction with Frederick Douglass's eulogy adapted from a speech Douglass delivered on April 14, 1876, at the unveiling of the Freedman's monument in memory of Abraham Lincoln in Lincoln Park, Washington, D.C. This monument depicts a freedman kneeling before Lincoln who holds a copy of the Emancipation Proclamation. A June 2020 article in Smithsonian Magazine details how Douglass criticized the monument in a recently-discovered letter as not telling the "whole truth of any subject which it might be designed to illustrate. . . . What I want to see before I die is a monument representing the negro, not couchant on his knees like a four-footed animal, but erect on his feet like a man. There is room in Lincoln park for another monument, and I throw out this suggestion to the end that it may be taken up and acted upon." Criticism of the monument along these lines was renewed in 2020 with calls to remove it as demeaning to Black people. A version was removed from Boston's Park Square in 2020 for that reason. Proposals to remove the version in Washington are ongoing.

BIBLIOGRAPHY

In researching and writing this book, I relied on numerous sources, including original documents and secondary sources. Because the book is fiction, I decided against including footnotes or endnotes, opting instead to list the sources I relied upon, sometimes with brief annotations. In addition to the sources listed here, I consulted numerous judicial decisions, many of which are mentioned in the book.

For the outline and details of the period covered in the book, I relied most heavily on Foner, Eric. *Reconstruction: America's Unfinished Revolution, 1863-1877* (New York; HarperCollins 1988). Everyone interested in this fascinating and frustrating period of American history owes Professor Foner an enormous debt of gratitude.

Other sources I consulted include:

Foner, Eric. *The Second Founding: How the Civil War and Reconstruction Remade the Constitution.* New York: W.W. Norton & Co., 2019.

The Electoral Count of 1877: Proceedings of the Electoral Commission and of the Two Houses of Congress in Joint Meeting Relative to the Count of Electoral Votes Cast December 6, 1876 for the Presidential Term Commencing March 4, 1877, Washington Government Printing Office 1877, which is largely a transcription of the proceedings of the Electoral Commission of 1877 which was created by an Act of Congress to determine which electoral votes should be counted from the disputed states, Florida, Louisiana, Oregon and South Carolina. I accessed this volume online, including a copy that resides in the Harvard Law Library that was digitized by Google Books. *Electoral Count of 1877: Proceedings of the Electoral Commission and of the Two Houses of Congress in Joint Meeting Relative to the Count of Electoral Votes Cast December 6, 1876, for the Presidential Term Commencing March 4, 1877.* Washington, DC: Government Printing Office, 1877. An inscription indicates that Harvard's copy was donated to the library by Supreme Court Justice Nathan Clifford, who presided over the actual commission.

Dray, Philip. *Capitol Men: The Epic Story of Reconstruction Through the Lives of the First Black Congressmen.* Boston: Houghton Mifflin Company, 2008.

For details on the life of Ulysses S. Grant, including his relationship with Mark Twain: Chernow, Ron. *Grant.* New York: Penguin Books, 2017.

Shofner, Jerrell H. "Fraud and Intimidation in the Florida Election of 1876." *The Florida Historical Quarterly* 42, no. 4 (April 1964): 321-30. Accessed October 31, 2020.

Stearns, Marcellus L. "The Election of 1876 in Florida." *The Florida Historical Quarterly* 32, no. 2 (1953): 81-91.

Swanson, Ryan A. *When Baseball Went White: Reconstruction, Reconciliation & Dreams of a National Pastime.* Lincoln, NE: University of Nebraska Press, 2014.

Donald, David Herbert. *Charles Sumner.* New York: Da Capo Press, 1996.

Scharfstein, Daniel J. *The Invisible Line: A Secret History of Race in America.* New York: Penguin Press, 2011.

McPherson, James M. *Battle Cry of Freedom: The Civil War Era.* New York: Oxford University Press, 1988.

Douglass, Frederick. *Narrative of the Life of Frederick Douglass.,* New York: Oxford University Press, 1999.

Puleo, Stephen. *The Caning. The Assault That Drove America to Civil War.* Yardley, PA: Westholme Publishing, 2012.

Schweninger, L. "Black Owned Businesses in the South, 1790-1880." *Business History Review* 63 (Spring 1989): 22-60.

Wilkerson, Isabel. *Caste: The Origins of Our Discontents.* New

York: Random House, 2020.

Trefousse, Hans L. *Rutherford B. Hayes*. New York: Times Books, 2002.

Van Alstyne, William W. "A Critical Guide to Ex Parte McCardle." Arizona Law Review 15, (1973): 229-269.

Blight, David W. *Frederick Douglass: Prophet of Freedom*. New York: Simon & Schuster, 2018.

Dalton, Tom. *Frederick Douglass: The Lynn Years, 1841-1848*. (2017).

Flood, Charles Bracelen. *1864: Lincoln at the Gates of History*. New York: Simon & Schuster, 2009.

Fryer, Tony Allan. *The Passenger Cases and the Commerce Clause: Immigrants, Black Americans, and States' Rights in Antebellum America*. Lawrence, KS: University Press of Kansas, 2014.

Du Bois, W.E.B. *The Souls of Black Folk*. Cambridge, MA: Harvard University Press, 1903.

Bell, Derrick. *Silent Covenants; Brown v. Board of Education and the Unfulfilled Hopes for Racial Reform*. Oxford: Oxford University Press, 2004.

Dirck, Brian R. *Abraham Lincoln and White America*. Lawrence, KS: University Press of Kansas, 2012.

Equal Justice Initiative. *Lynching in America: Confronting the Legacy of Racial Terror*. (3rd ed., 2017). https://lynchinginamerica.eji.org/report/

Shugerman, Jed Handelsman. "The Creation of the Department of Justice: Professionalization without Civil Rights or Civil Service." *Stanford Law Review* 66, (2014): 121-172.

Foner, Eric. "Rights and the Constitution in Black Life during the

Civil War and Reconstruction." *The Journal of American History* 74, no. 3 (December 1987): 863-883.

Kendrick, Benjamin B. *The Journal of the Joint Committee of Fifteen on Reconstruction, 39th Congress, 1865-1867.* New York: Columbia University Press, 1914.

Maltz, Earl. *Civil Rights, the Constitution and Congress, 1863-1869.* Lawrence, KS: University Press of Kansas, 1990.

McKitrick, Eric L. *Andrew Johnson and Reconstruction.* New York: Oxford University Press, 1988.

Mitgang, Herbert. *Abraham Lincoln: A Press Portrait (The North's Civil War).* 2nd ed. New York: Fordham University Press, 2000.

Donald, David Herbert. *Lincoln.* New York: Simon & Schuster, 1996.

Carter, Steven. *The Impeachment of Abraham Lincoln.* New York: Vintage Press, 2013.

Belz, Herman. "Salmon P. Chase and the Politics of Racial Reform." *Journal of the Abraham Lincoln Association* 17, no. 2 (Summer 1996): 22-40.

Zinn, Howard. *A People's History of the United States.* New York: Harper & Row, 1980.

April 24, 1867: Richmond Streetcar Protest," Zinn Education Project, https://www.zinnedproject.org/news/tdih/richmond-streetcar-protest/

Hardy, William Edward. "'Fare well to all Radicals': Redeeming Tennessee, 1869-1870." PhD diss., University of Tennessee (2013), available at https://trace.tennessee.edu/utk_graddiss/2432/.

Wang, Xiaomen. *The Trial of Democracy: Black Suffrage and Northern Republicans, 1860-1910.* Athens, GA: University of Georgia Press, 1997.

Kelley, Blair L.M. *Right to Ride: Streetcar Boycotts and African American Citizenship in the Era of Plessy V. Ferguson.* Chapel Hill, NC: University of North Carolina Press, 2010.

Winters, Ben. *Underground Airlines.* New York: Mulholland Books, 2017.

Barnett, Randy E. "From Antislavery Lawyer to Chief Justice: The Remarkable but Forgotten Career of Salmon P. Chase." *Case Western Reserve Law Review* 63, (2013): 653-702.

Cresswell, Stephen. "Enforcing the Enforcement Acts: The Department of Justice in Northern Mississippi, 1870-1890." *The Journal of Southern History* 53, no. 3 (1987): 421-440.

I also consulted the following internet-only resources:

Maranzani, Barbara. "The Unlikely Friendship of Mark Twain and Ulysses S. Grant." Biography. com. Updated May 1, 2020. https://www. biography.com/news/mark-twain-ulysses-s-grant-friendship.

Graves, Donet D. "Wormley Hotel." The White House Historical Association. Published January 22, 2016. https://www.whitehousehistory.org/wormley-hotel-1.

The White House Historical Association. "Frederick Douglass, 1818-1895." Accessed March 16, 2021, https://www.whitehousehistory.org/frederick-douglass.

Knipprath, Joerg. "Ex Parte McCardle (1869)." Constituting America (essay). *The Liberty Lab, Inc.*, 2017. https://constitutingamerica.org/ex-parte-mccardle-1869-guest-essayist-joerg-knipprath/.

Bullock Texas State History Museum. "African Americans." Accessed March 16, 2021, https://www.thestoryoftexas.com/discover/campfire-stories/african-americans.

Snyder, Anna. "Photos From the Archives: The Old Capitol Prison and the Lincoln Assassination." Ford's Theatre. Accessed March 16, 2021, https://www.fords.org/blog/post/photos-from-the-archives-the-old-capitol-prison-and-the-lincoln-assassination/.

Made in United States
North Haven, CT
23 July 2025

70957396R00176